ACADEMY OF OUTCASTS

ALSO BY LARRY CORREIA

Monster Hunter International

Monster Hunter International
Monster Hunter Vendetta
Monster Hunter Alpha
Monster Hunter Legion
Monster Hunter Nemesis
Monster Hunter Siege
Monster Hunter Guardian
Monster Hunter Bloodlines

Saga of the Forgotten Warrior

Son of the Black Sword
House of Assassins
Destroyer of Worlds
Tower of Silence
Graveyard of Demons
Heart of the Mountain

The Grimnoir Chronicles

Hard Magic
Spellbound
Warbound

LARRY CORREIA

ACADEMY OF OUTCASTS
Published by Vault
In association with Aethon Books

ISBN 978-1-63849-303-7 (paperback)

First Aethon & Vault Edition: August 2025

Printed in the United States of America.
1st Printing.

Aethon Books
www.aethonbooks.com

Vault Storyworks
www.vaultstoryworks.com

Cover art by Matt Sellers. Cover typography by Steve Beaulieu.
Print formatting by Kevin G. Summers, Adam Cahoon, and Rikki Midnight.

ACADEMY OF OUTCASTS

1

I was fourteen when I decided I was going to be a wizard when I grew up.

It was just another day, working down in a hole, chipping Red, when our tunnel boss gave us an urgently whispered command.

"Don't move. Don't nobody move."

My crew froze in place at Ned's words, because there were a whole lot of things in a lava tube that could kill a humble crawler like us, real quick.

It gets really dark inside a tube, so we were used to getting around by feel. The cadre had issued Corm and Ned light charms, but they kept those off while we worked. The magical white light blotted out the gentle glow that told us when there were flakes of precious Red embedded in the walls, and that glow told us where to dig. The elemental deposits here were giving off just enough light that I could barely make out the form of Boss Ned crouched a few yards below me, holding perfectly still, one hand raised in warning.

I was on my knees, sweat stinging my eyes, with my chipping hammer clutched in one glove and a steel scrapper in my other. Neither would be a very effective weapon if we'd accidentally blundered into some creature's den. Not that there was room enough to fight anyway, since the sloping chute we currently occupied wasn't much wider than my shoulders.

From the sound of his nervous breathing, Corm was a couple feet above me, and ready to flee back toward the surface. Corm had always been the skittish one.

"What is it, boss?"

"Shut up, Oz," Ned snapped at me. "I'm trying to listen."

There was a sound coming up the tube, like a wet mop being dragged across a sandy deck. Ned's ears must have been going bad from decades of hammering, because I recognized what the noise was long before he did, and it made my guts turn to water.

"That's a gurgler!"

"Calm down, kid. We're not deep enough for gurglers." Ned checked the metal band on his wrist. "It's barely a hundred and fifty in here. Gurglers don't break through walls where it's this cool."

But I knew what I'd heard, and it scared me to death. "We've got to go."

We didn't know if gurglers had thoughts like a regular animal, or if they were even alive at all. They might have been a natural phenomena of this realm, or some wizard's lost construct, but in the end, it didn't really matter, because they'd kill you all the same.

That sickening, sloppy noise came again, much louder this time.

A faint orange light appeared far below.

"Turn back." Too late, Ned grasped that I'd been right. "Get to the surface!"

Corm was the youngest and smallest, so he was able to roll over and start climbing. It took me a little more effort, then I was clambering up right behind him. Our thick gloves and protective clothing kept us from slicing ourselves to pieces against the sharp rocks, but I still managed to bash my head hard enough it would leave a bruise through my padded leather helm. I risked a glance back toward Ned, who was desperately scrambling, and saw that the orange light was gaining on us.

"Faster, Ned! It's right behind you!"

Heat rose up the tube from the gurgler, washing over us so brutally I nearly swooned. I'd been suffering before, but that had been the constant, low-level suffering I was used to. This heat was *so much* worse. This was so nasty hot, it hit me in the lungs like a hammer. I'm talking the kind of heat that would render the hardiest crawler unconscious in seconds and cooked in a minute.

The band around my wrist began to glow blue as the sudden increase in temperature set the protective enchantment off. The air around me dropped from deadly to miserable. The magic charm enabled me to breathe and think again, but my only thought was *escape.*

Ned started screaming, because the near heat of the gurgler was greater than what his charm could protect him from. Smoke rose past me as Ned's leather armor blackened and caught fire.

I looked back to see the gurgler filling the tunnel, a blob of half molten rock, churning and hungry. Because gurglers were things of the depths, where the plane of fire was nothing but burning energy, it was slowing down and solidifying as it neared the surface. In the deeper tunnels they moved so fast that by the time crawlers knew a gurgler was upon them it was already too late.

Above shone the crimson light of our sky. We were almost there. I tried to shout for Ned to hurry, only to inhale nothing but pain.

The gurgler's breath was an invisible toxic gas. It must have been extremely poisonous because it caused the activation of another of the protective charms I'd been issued. The air around my face turned from stinking sulfur to bland and breathable. The only reason I was still alive was water and air magic, but the shoddy charms us crawlers were issued wouldn't last for long.

I was stronger and a better climber than Corm, which made a big difference even on this gentle slope, so I quickly caught up to him. "Keep moving! Get out of the way!"

Except Corm was stopped at the entrance and shrieked. "I can't!" He pointed outside. "There's an Elemental!"

The tunnel was too narrow to push past him to see for myself, but Corm wasn't stupid. There was no mistaking one of those deadly predators for anything else. When us crawlers came across a roaming Fire Elemental, our only options were to run and hide, or fight and most likely die. Normally we'd be safe in a lava tube until the monster passed by, but not with a gurgler roasting us from below.

Encountering one fire beast was unfortunate, but they could be avoided. Ending up stuck between two meant certain doom.

I caught a glimpse of the deadly creature as it stalked past. Bipedal, the thing was gigantic, its flesh made of iron and fire, and so heavy, it's footfalls shook the ground. In the distance I could hear the rest of our crew panicking as they ran for their lives, for Elementals always attacked people on sight. The second Corm stuck his head out, that thing would rip us to bits.

Death below, death above, we were trapped.

The gurgler got its hooks into Ned and dragged him into it. In seconds, our tunnel boss was just *gone.*

Corm panicked in witnessing Ned get dissolved and leapt out of the tube, running as fast as he could.

The Elemental flashed by the opening. There was a terrible roar as it struck. A burst of fire rolled over the tube entrance as it pounced on its prey.

I remained there, breathing my rapidly dwindling magic air, in a lava tube hotter than an oven, the gurgler slowly closing in below, and the angry beast screaming its fury above. I felt helpless, terrified, and angry all at once. When I threw my scraper at the gurgler, it hit with a hiss and stuck there, steel glowing and softening, but the thing kept coming.

All I could do was hope the Fire Elemental would move on. They were notorious for their impatience.

An awful minute passed as death inched nearer. The blue glow from the protective band began flickering, as was the white light of the air charm. When either of those went out, the gurgler would overwhelm me before it even reached me. I had no choice but risk the surface.

Whispering a quick prayer to my family's patron, Ketekunan—the Saint of Perseverance—I took up my pathetic little chipping hammer and climbed out of the hole.

The surface workers had fled back to the safety of the barge. There was no sign of little Corm except for his crawler pack lying there on the black rocks, with smoking claw marks through it. This one was twelve feet tall, so it had probably eaten poor Corm in one bite.

The monster's great horned head swiveled my way and it snorted fire when it saw me standing there, pathetic. Unable to outrun it, I lifted my hammer and screamed an incoherent challenge.

As soon as two tons of fiery doom began stomping toward me, I forgot my challenge and ran!

The Elemental caught up in an instant. Didn't even need to hit me to knock me off my feet; its mass shook the ground enough to do so. I skidded across the black rock, then desperately crawled over the steaming surface. Huge claws descended to spear me.

There was a blinding crack of light, and the creature lurched to the side. Sparks flew from its burning hide as magma blood spilled from the hole. Rolling out of the way, I barely managed to avoid getting stomped, even as droplets of blood struck me and sizzled holes through my protective leathers. There was another flash, green this time, and it bellowed in agony as it stumbled away.

There was a lone man walking directly, fearlessly, toward the beast. He held a glowing wand in each hand.

When the Fire Elemental spotted him, it spread its arms, lowered its shoulders, and roared. It was so loud, I desperately covered my ears.

"You are not fit to challenge me, brute. Begone."

A bolt of lightning leapt between the man and the monster. Flaming blood sprayed as the molten giant was hurled across the rocks. The crackling energy scalded my eyes.

The monster got up, took one last angry look at the man who bested it, and then fled, limping, across the lava field.

"Where's the rest of your crew?" the mage—for surely that's what he was—asked me.

Half blinded, half deafened, I was shaking too much to talk, but pointed toward the hole I'd climbed out of. The wizard, who wore the colors of the Argents—the family which owned my family—went over to the entrance and scowled down at the gurgler there.

"They're all dead?"

I managed to find my voice, "Two crawlers are dead." I was still too shocked to really comprehend what that meant. "I think the surface crew ran back to our barge." Which was the smart thing for them to do when an Elemental appeared. Normally we'd have been fine waiting it out, if it hadn't been for bad luck and worse timing. "That gurgler chased us out of the hole. It ate Ned."

"An unfortunate waste of valuable laborers." He talked like a foreigner, having to consider his words before speaking them, but his uniform was similar to the standard armor worn by the Argent family's enforcers. Only, those men were armed with steel, while this one was armed with magic. He plucked a different device from his belt, pointed it down the shaft, and I flinched at the violent *snap*. The gurgler let out a high-pitched squeal as it died.

"That thing will trouble you no more."

Having defeated two deadly beasts as if it was nothing, he went to where Corm's pack had fallen, picked it up, stuck one hand inside, rummaged around, and came out with a handful of Red flakes. He nodded at Corm's last harvest, before dropping the Red back into the pack, and slinging it over his shoulder. "Tell your bargemaster your life was saved by Gaul Haddar, and I have claimed this magical element as my payment."

The wizard walked away.

The rest of my cadre came back to rescue me a short while later. Corm and Ned's families wailed for vengeance while our trappers went after the wounded Elemental, tracking it by the residual heat of its spilled blood. I'd been burned, though not too bad. I was more shaken than anything. I'd used up two enchantments to survive, the cost of which would be added to my family's contract to be worked off. I lived while my friends had died. It wasn't the first time that would happen, nor would it be the last.

Most importantly, that was the day I vowed that I would never be helpless again.

2

My whole life, I'd heard stories of other worlds. Nice places. Places that weren't made out of fire.

The handful of outsiders I'd met over the years were all amazed that anyone could survive here. To them, Fogo was a very frightening place. With the sky being blotted out by endless storms, while the land beneath was in constant flux, melting and reforming, mountains growing, bleeding rivers of lava, which exploded into steam as it reached our temporary, constantly boiling, seas. One time a trader visiting from the Core had even referred to Fogo as *a nightmare hellscape.* His terror had given all us locals a good laugh.

Silly merchant. Hell is where pirates, murderers, and oath breakers go when they die. This is just *home.*

Yet the trader wasn't entirely wrong because we were all very familiar with nightmares. Everyone on Fogo had those, because there was no shortage of gruesome ways to die here, and it was a challenge to go to sleep without thinking about any of them. No matter how alert your bargemen were, all it took was one unexpected volcanic eruption and whole families would get roasted to death in seconds. Viscious Elementals were constantly on the prowl. I still wore the scars from where I'd been mauled by a lava dog when I was twelve.

It was hard to imagine other realms where life was easier, where the ground didn't burn your feet, the air was free of smoke, and it rained water instead of ash, but the encyclopedias insisted this was so. A century ago, one of our kinder masters had bought a full set of all twenty volumes of the *Encyclopedia Ettymus* to be shared across our barges so our cadre could be better educated.

As a boy, I'd managed to get my hands on most of those books and would read each of them cover to cover, devouring every single article about all the many kingdoms of the Seven Realms, their traditions, histories, and everything in between. Sadly, I couldn't read them all. Too many volumes had been lost, because paper did not react well to fire, and fire was the one thing we never lacked.

At the time, I considered myself an expert, alphabetically speaking, on all topics from A through the first part of C, G, and a little bit of H, N through P, though a big chunk of O had gotten torn out at some point before I got it, probably to be used as a bargemaster's butt paper, and volume Z, or at least the top half of the last book, because the bottom half of every page had gotten too charred to read during an Elemental attack. The surviving part was water-damaged and hard to read from the smudging, but I think I got the gist of it.

All that studying taught me there were other, kinder worlds, but also a few places even harsher than Fogo, just in different ways. Except, whenever I talked about those distant places to other members of my cadre, I was warned they were not for us. Our place was to mine the Red, to harvest magic from the plumes and from the molten flesh of the Fire Realm creatures we managed to kill. We were taught to take pride in this, for without us, the Core would freeze, the Great Machine would stop turning, and all would be lost. In exchange for our Red, the Core sent us food shipments, water magic so we could drink and fight the fires, air magic to be able to levitate our barges out of the path of the constantly shifting lava flows, and life magic to heal our burns and repair our smoke scarred lungs.

Thus it was, thus it would always be. Or at least that's what the elders said, though even at that age I already suspected that was all trogshit and lies.

"State your name."

"Carnavon."

"Your full name."

"Ozwald Carnavon. My friends call my Oz."

"I didn't come to this horrid realm to be your friend, boy." The mage tester's eyes flicked across the list of all the youth who lived on this barge, and she frowned as she found my entry. "This says you are fifteen years old?"

"That's correct, Tester. I turned fifteen last week."

"Then you're already too old. Even if you had sufficient magical abilities to be recruited into an academy, your training should have started years ago."

"I still get the chance to test though, right?"

"It would just be a waste of my time." She waved one hand dismissively. "Send in the next child on your way out."

I was used to crushing disappointment, but her dismissive attitude was too much. "That's unfair."

"Which is true for most things. Begone."

Luckily for me, there was one other person in the room to appeal to, so I looked toward Bargemaster Gax. The wizard from the Core was a very important lady, but this was Davis Gax's barge to command, and my family had worked with his for generations.

"I didn't get to test when I was the right age because the tester back then said our barges were too far to travel to from where he was. Please tell her, Bargemaster."

Luckily for me, since having an auditor visit was an important thing, big fat Gax—who was usually drunk by noon—hadn't yet hit the bottle today and remained sober enough to come to my defense. "The boy speaks the truth, Tester Ewing. Last time one of you came through, our cadre had been sent off to the far end of the Great Steam Rift to mine the plumes, and the Core folk wouldn't stray that far from the safety of the gate. It's been years since this cadre has had a proper testing."

The woman from the Core struck me as snooty and aloof, cold as her magic city was supposed to be. "An understandable decision on the last tester's part. We are few in number, exceedingly busy, already have more qualified applicants than the academies have openings, and the odds of finding a suitable candidate among slaves is virtually nil."

Gax grew indignant. "We're not slaves."

"Oh, that's right. Slavery is illegal in this realm. You're *indentured servants.*" She sneered. "That's *so* very different."

Just the magic trinkets this wizard wore were probably worth more money than our entire barge, but Gax had been a proud man once, and it seemed some of that pride still lingered. "We both got our orders, Tester. Just that I get my orders from the Argent family, and that's who asked you to come out here to check their workers for potential. If you don't feel like doing so, then I'll be sure to put that in my report, and you can explain to the baron why you didn't want to do your job."

I'd never even seen Baron Argent myself, but my dad had warned me it was best to stay beneath his family's notice, because he was a stern and impatient ruler, quick to outrage. Though none of us were important enough to meet the baron, we'd all met some of his guard force, and they were notorious for how little mercy they possessed for thieves or anyone who got hooked on the Red. If their master was anywhere near as cruel as his enforcers, I really wouldn't want to make him mad.

Apparently, neither did the mage tester, because she thought it over, then sighed. "Fine. We shall continue."

I couldn't help but grin at my good fortune, for though I couldn't admit it in front of the tester, I'd been practicing on my own for the last year, and I'd even managed to wring a bit of magic out of leftover Red dust enough to bind it to an object. So far, I'd been able to make a nail warm up slightly on its own, meaning I could do *something*. Just needed someone to teach me how to do magic right.

Gax and the tester sat behind a table, while I stood on the other side, in the room the Bargemaster used for important meetings with his crew. Which seemed appropriate to me, since this was the most important day of my life. I was going to demonstrate my worth and get sent to an academy to be trained as a mighty wizard. This was my chance to get out of this realm. There'd be no more miserable labor in the dark and hot. My future was going to be one of wealth and fame. Wizards were so valuable, I'd not just be able to earn myself a better life, but I'd be able to buy my entire family's freedom too and take them someplace better than here.

"Are both your parents alive, Mr. Carnavon?"

"Yes, Tester."

"Do you have siblings? I only ask because in the exceedingly small chance that should you rate well enough, they will all need to be tested as well. Potential tends to run in the family."

"There are six of us."

"Are you literate?"

"Yes."

That seemed to surprise her. She made a note. "Your occupation?"

"Crawler."

She looked to Gax, for the sheltered Core dweller didn't understand what that title meant.

"We use the thin ones to climb through the lava tubes searching for loose Red and he's not hit his growth yet… Just put down miner."

"Very well." Another note was scribbled. "Any criminal offenses?"

I was insulted she'd even ask, for we Carnavons were too proud to steal. Well, except for the dust I'd managed to sweep into my pockets for experimentation, but that was going to a higher cause than making the Argents slightly richer. "None, ma'am."

"His family is honest, hard workers, who never complain nor cause trouble. Not a brawler or restless one among them." Gax must have owed my dad a favor to lie so brazenly, because all Carnavons loved to fight. Bare knuckle boxing and wrestling matches were how we cadre folk passed the time whenever we couldn't afford to get drunk. As for not spreading discontent, the only reason my father hadn't organized a labor strike was because he knew the Argent enforcers wouldn't hesitate to kill us all. "The Carnavons are the best family I've got."

"Physical ailments or mental instability? Addictions, poor character, or unsavory proclivities?"

"None, Tester."

Mage Tester Ewing checked all the right boxes for me, then she put her pen down and removed a large copper bracelet from her wrist. She wore at least a dozen magically infused charms, each one of different color and construction. She held the bracelet out toward me. "Take hold of this, Mr. Carnavon."

Reaching across the table, I did as I was told, as she kept two of her fingers wrapped around her end of the bracelet and gave it a small tug to make sure I wasn't going to let go.

"I will now attempt to measure your innate magical abilities. Do not move. If you wiggle or fidget it may break my connection." She closed her eyes.

I hadn't even realized she'd used her spell until the charm stung my hand. It took me a moment to understand what I was experiencing, because I'd never felt anything truly *cold* before. I understood the concept, but ice was an unknown thing on Fogo.

The test was surprisingly short.

"That will be all, Mr. Carnavon."

I let go of the charm, and immediately went about rubbing my hands together for the friction. "How'd I do?"

She didn't bother to answer, but next to my name she wrote *zero.*

"I'm guessing that's not good?" I asked, but the way Gax cringed told me the answer.

"Correct."

"But I can use magic!"

"Most everyone can use it somewhat. True Nulls—someone latently immune to magic—are actually very rare and valuable in their own peculiar way. The overwhelming majority of most sentient races are of zero rank, which means magic affects them, and they can utilize someone else's prepared enchantments, but they possess little innate natural ability to work magical elements themselves. Since it takes an unrealistic amount of effort and expense for them to progress in talent, no further energy is to be wasted on them."

"What does that mean?" I asked, already dreading the answer.

"It means you are nothing, Mr. Carnavon. The Core has no use for you, and you may return to your hole… Next."

3

The life of a Fogo cadre is harsh. When I was little, I didn't even really grasp just how difficult we had it, as I had no other life to compare it to. We worked ourselves stupid in places that no sane man would willingly go, gathering magic we couldn't even understand, to trade for the things we needed just to survive. Life was short and cheap. Most of us died young, and all of us died tired.

Fogo is a realm in constant flux, and whenever it ripped itself apart, upon those healing scabs was where we'd earn our living. On floating barges constructed from greywood imported from the Core and imbued with protective magic to keep from combusting, we traveled from place to place. Landing and settling for a time to mine the Red from the scars of the Realm of Fire, until the world inevitably turned on us and chased us away, and then we'd repeat the process again somewhere else.

There is a weariness that comes from this kind of labor that's hard to explain to someone who hasn't experienced it for themselves. With pick and shovel, we'd break and turn the smoldering ground searching for the precious Red. You just work and work and work, until your muscles can't go anymore, and then you work more anyway. Your mind detaches and goes to some other place so your body can keep moving. You get so tired you can sleep hanging from a harness or even standing up.

All the human laborers—and human was what most of us in the cadres were, though there were a handful of other races—wore the enchanted charms to protect us from the heat. These were our most prized possessions, because to lose one while working on the surface meant almost certain death. Even then, magic could protect us from sustained temperatures, and even short bursts of fire, but if there was a magma burst through your tunnel wall, your charm was only good for giving you enough time for death to hurt more.

Such was life on Fogo.

"It was a stupid idea anyway," my sister told me, because she was always supportive like that. "Thinking the likes of you would ever go to the Core City. You were born on a barge for heaven's sake!"

"Then I guess if I'm really lucky, I'll die on a barge, old, like Grandpa did after he broke his back working for the thankless Argents his whole life. If I'm unlucky, I'll get cooked in a tube or ripped apart by an Elemental while I'm still healthy."

"But still, a wizard?" She snorted at my hubris. "Of all the things, you actually thought you were going to be a *wizard*?"

"Shut up and shuck your snails."

The two of us were working at the railing, with a basket of volcano snails between us. Our job was to pry them out of their black iron shells and toss their red fleshy bodies into the cooking pot for dinner.

"The Argents own our family's contract, there's no getting out of that, but you're smart, Oz. You can read. You know some math. Go to their city. Work their docks. Maybe go to work for one of their traders."

"So I abandon the family, but stay on Fogo, working to make someone else rich, while the rest of you rot on this barge. No thanks."

I was only a year younger than Gilda, but that never stopped her from being bossy and opinionated at me. "You dream about being a wizard because you read all those books, with the stories about magic and heroes, and their contests with thousands of people watching in their giant stadiums in their cities in the sky, and all the other magical miracles of the Nexus." She grabbed a snail from the basket that was big as my fist, jabbed her knife into the squirming thing, and started levering it back and forth. "But that's all bunk."

"No, it's not."

"Yes, it is." The meaty snail popped out with a sucking noise. "Listen, Oz, we're only who we are. Thinking we're better than what we are just gets people like us in trouble. Remember cousin Daniel?

He got uppity, decided he'd do anything to get off his barge, couldn't take one more day of it, and look what happened to him."

"He got caught stealing a crate of Red and was executed for it. That's not the same thing at all."

"Hardly. Daniel decided he wanted more. He was never content with what he had. So he made Gaul Haddar's enforcers mad, and then they were out to get him. You're never going to be content either and you know it."

I didn't have anything to say to that, because Gilda was right. Yeah, I wanted more. So what?

I just sat there angrily stabbing snails and evicting them from their iron homes. The meat went in the pot. The empty shells went into a bucket. We'd melt most of those down for the ore, while the prettier ones could often be sold to the traders. Apparently, people in the other realms would buy them as decorations, which sounded ridiculous to me.

"Look, I'm not trying to be mean, little brother, I'm just saying it doesn't do any good to get your hopes up. Be realistic, like me."

"Last I heard your big plan was to wait until all the cadres gather at next year's moot, ask for a husband, and then hope for a suitor who isn't a bum, so you can get onto a nicer barge before having lots of babies."

"Exactly. That's a realistic and achievable plan. And I'm pretty enough I could probably land me a bargemaster's son."

"Such lofty goals."

The ten barges of our cadre were currently parked on a flat black plain. Weeks had passed since this new ground formed, so it had cooled enough that our people could debark and walk on the surface for several minutes at a time even without protective magic. It was odd to stay this long in one place without having to move, but a new ridge was growing a few miles away, and leaking grey smoke, so we'd probably need to leave soon before it blew.

I'd been climbing and crawling through tunnels all day. Every muscle hurt. My back ached, my hands were so sore I was having a hard time holding my knife. There were a hundred tiny burns on my arm and shoulder from when I'd gotten hit with a shower of sparks earlier. I could barely keep my eyes open. Even my face was too tired to put on a fake smile for my sister.

"You know why I really want to be a wizard, Gilda?"

"Tell me."

"There's nothing worse than feeling helpless. Wizards are powerful. They can do things, change things, bend the world to their will. Nobody pushes wizards around."

"You don't know that. There's a city full of them on the other side of the gate. You've met two wizards in your entire life. One was a snob who everyone sucks up to in the hopes she'll send their children off to a fancy academy, and the other is an enforcer who breaks the knees of anyone who owes the baron money and sends the ones who can't pay off to the debtor's prison."

She hadn't seen Gaul Haddar effortlessly defeat a terrifying Elemental. "Their lives matter."

"So do ours."

"Do they?" I shook my weary head. "To us they do. To everybody else, we're nobodies. We've been doing the same thing for generations and nobody even knows who we are. If I get burned to death tomorrow you guys are the only ones who will notice. When a great mage dies, people write songs and stories about their lives."

"So that's it? You need an entry about you in one of those fancy books? Someday under the letter C there will be Carnavon, the greatest mage to ever live in the Core and Seven Realms, and amazing were his deeds. Who cares what outsiders think? As if your own family caring isn't good enough, but the notice of some scholar in a flying castle is?"

Gilda didn't get it, which was fine. She was the sort to always be happy, no matter how rotten the circumstances. If that future husband she was planning on got killed mining the Red, she'd just find a new one and carry on. If her kids died working off our family contract, she'd have some more. Our people were resilient like that.

As the family dreamer, this was a conversation I was sick of having. "That's all the snails, sister. You'd better get to cooking them if you want dinner ready by the time Dad's crew gets back."

"You're just trying to avoid the continuation of this awkward talk about how you need to face facts you're never going to be a wizard."

I got up and left, because you can love your family, but still want to toss them over the side of your barge.

All of us Carnavons shared a cabin on the main deck. It wasn't much, but it was better than the poor bastards assigned quarters below decks. At least we had windows to open. The thermometer on this deck said it was a comfortable ninety degrees right now. But having an entire family shoved into two small rooms and the patch of decking in front of them didn't leave much in the way of privacy, when I needed to practice my spell craft, I had to go below.

Two hundred people lived on Barge 519. Most of us had been born here. Few ever left, and if they did, it was just to fill a hole on a different barge just like ours. Almost nobody ever lived long enough to buy back their contract and earn their freedom, and even if they did, where would they go? All they knew was travelling in their caravans across Fogo, gathering Red to sell to the Argents for money they'd then spend at the Argent company store on enchantments they needed to survive while gathering more Red.

It was an endless cycle of frustration, which was why the people of the Fogo cadres tended to be bitter and cynical. There was something to be said in favor of accepting that your life was going to be awful, and everything was forever rigged against you, and that was all there was to it. People like Gilda took pride in accepting their misery. They could even brag about it. It was suckers like me who kept getting our hopes up, thinking there might be something else better.

I guess I just wasn't the accepting kind.

My secret chamber of wizardly experimentation was the stern side rope storage room, and I arrived there, angry and motivated. To hell with Tester Ewing. She was an idiot, calling me a *zero* with such disdain. She'd pronounced I was average like that was some kind of insult. Except, she'd also said that someone like me learning magic would be difficult and expensive. She'd never said it was impossible.

I kept my bag of Red dust well hidden behind a greywood beam. Technically, my having this was a crime, as anything I gathered belonged to the cadre first to sell, and then the profits would be distributed to our families. Which was another raw deal, since us Carnavons outworked everyone here. I worked harder than anyone else my age, and still managed to spend half the hours I should be resting practicing magic. Don't know what their excuses were, the bums.

I'd only read a handful of books in my life, and none had been about spell craft. Everything I knew about how magic worked was extrapolated from articles in the *Encyclopedia Ettymus*. Each of the seven realms produced a unique magical element, which powered various effects. Those seven elements could be combined in different formulas to create different spells. They could also be bound to various items, usually made of metal, to be stored for later use. Different host metals could also change the effect. And all that got bound together by the will of the mage and his ability to manipulate unseen forces with his mind.

My problem—beyond a lack of knowledge, proper education, and natural inclination—was that I had a very limited number of materials to experiment with. I had Red dust. That was it. That was the only magical element available to me, and from what I'd read, and what the traders paid, this particular Red was of the lowest quality. The good stuff came from deeper within the plane or harvested directly from an Elemental's heart.

There was also air, water, and life elements aboard this barge, but those were all bound to valuable items which I didn't dare risk, because we needed them to survive. The magic which lifted our barges, and the tank that produced all our water, were so complex and expensive that they belonged to the Argents, and our cadre just leased them. Experimenting on one of those would surely get me executed by the enforcers, of that I had no doubt. And the smaller items, like our protective charms, were still incredibly valuable, and we were perpetually short on them as it was.

The only variety in my experiments was what material I tried to bind the Red dust to. I'd worked with bits of bronze, copper, iron, steel, and one time even got brave enough to borrow one of Mom's precious golden earrings which she kept in a box and almost never wore, and I'd managed to return it to her only slightly deformed from the heat of the experiment. She took them out so seldom she still hadn't noticed.

For tonight's practice, I decided to try something different, and pulled an iron snail's shell out of my pocket. I didn't know how pure the metal was, as I'd never worked in the barge's foundry, and I didn't know if it having been grown by a living thing instead of dug from the ground would make any difference, as the encyclopedia never mentioned anything about that. But it was worth a shot.

As always, I was careful to cover my mouth and nose with a scarf before working with the Red dust. Breathing some in would give you a feeling of euphoria—every crawler had experienced that on accident at some point. Actually ingesting it was supposed to make you feel amazing. I'd never tried that myself, as my parents always warned me how addicting Red was, and everyone in the cadre knew of someone who'd consumed too much of the element, and the resulting mutations were always awful. I'd seen a couple which had scared the piss out of me, with miners losing their minds, going homicidal, breathing fire, or trying to go swimming in the lava, that sort of thing. Thankfully the enforcers usually found and took away the Red addicts before they got that bad though.

Not having any idea about the proper ratio, I gave the snail shell a sprinkle of Red, then thought better of it and coated the whole thing. After Tester Ewing insulted me, I figured I might as well go for it. I'd prove her wrong or die trying. Then I sat on the rope pile, took the shell in both hands, and concentrated on the element.

I'd learned this part by trial and error. Red had a feeling to it. I'd spent so much time digging for it in the dark that I felt like I could sense its presence. All the luckiest miners said the same thing after a big score. *I just felt like it was there and I started digging.* So I'd used that feeling, focused in on it, and found that when I did so, I could visualize the particles in my mind. And once I did that, then I could nudge them about. Sometimes I was able to push the Red into the metal and it would fuse there, filling the item with capable magic.

So far, every spell I'd created had been basically the same. I could make an item warm up, though one time I'd gotten a nail red hot fast enough to burn a welt on my hand. For what they paid for the material we mined, I was certain real wizards must have been able to wring all sorts of different effects out of it. All I could currently do was gradually make things hotter, which was a fairly useless skill to have when you lived on the ragged edge of the Elemental Plane of Fire.

I sensed the magic and gently nudged it against the snail shell with my mind. I was rewarded with a glowing light, pale, but bright enough to briefly illuminate the rope room. *I'd done it.* The shell had been successfully infused with fire magic.

Suck it, Tester Ewing.

I was going to practice and learn and get better, and then the next time a tester came to Fogo, I was going to rank higher and they'd have no choice but to recognize my achievement. I was going to earn a spot in one of the prestigious magical academies in the Core, become a master wizard, then come back here, pay off my family's contract, and blast Elementals to pieces for fun and profit.

Now I just needed to activate the magic to see what the effect of my formula of a generous dusting of Red on a two-inch volcano snail shell would be. Real wizards could program their spells to activate automatically when the circumstances were right, like the charms we used to breathe when surrounded by poison gas, or to resist sudden surges of heat in the depths. I'd read that Core duelists and gladiators even wore enchantments that could turn into magical shields just in time to stop a bullet or blade. Putting that kind of criteria on my spells was far beyond me for now, so I'd just have to will it to start and see what happened.

Having learned my lesson and earned a scar from the burning nail, I activated the snail shell, then set it down on the floor in front of me and began counting. After one second, it began to glow. At three seconds, the shell was bright as a cooking fire, but wasn't burning the boards beneath. The heat was contained, and it was only releasing light! I'd created a lantern! That was a truly useful spell!

At five seconds, the snail shell exploded.

4

"Where am I?"

"You are on a cot, Mr. Carnavon. In the shoddy cabin your bargemaster declared to be a sickbay, so you could be attended to by what I believe to be a butcher, masquerading as a surgeon. When he was done stitching up your wounds—ugly work that—I sent him away… though I suppose you do not have butchers here. You can't grow animals big enough to require such tradesmen."

Everything was blurry, I was dizzy, wanted to throw up, and my head *really* hurt. "What happened?"

"That is what you will explain to me now, so that I may know what punishment you deserve."

I lifted my head just enough to see a man standing at the foot of my bed. I gasped, recognizing him as the Argent's wizard enforcer, Gaul Haddar. The gasp was a mistake, because that's when I realized there was a hole in my chest.

"Lie still, stupid, or you will pop a seam and ruin your butcher's sewing job."

If Haddar was here, I was in deep trouble. As the mercenary mage the leaders of the Core assigned to our baron to protect his interests in Fogo, Haddar took care of the problems the regular enforcers couldn't handle. He'd only arrived in this realm just over a year ago, and rumor among all the cadres was that if things got bad enough for Haddar to get involved, someone was about to get tossed in the lava. It was openly said he had the patience of a Fire Elemental, the mercy of an ash storm, and the blessings of the baron who owned our lives to do whatever he wanted to us. The most subversive among us thought Haddar had been brought here to serve as the baron's assassin, removing anyone who got in the Argent family's way.

We were all scared of Haddar accordingly.

"That Red wasn't stolen," I managed to wheeze. "I'm no thief."

"You think the theft of a handful of decayed element would drag me all the way out to the ass end of hell's fiery nowhere? I'm here because you blew a two-foot hole in the side of an Argent barge, idiot."

Haddar's features were sharp and unforgiving. His hair and beard were black streaked with grey, and his skin was brown, like the encyclopedia said was common in realms that actually got lots of sunlight, which was the opposite of us, who were all pale because our sky was made out of haze and smoke. He carried two swords and at least four wands on his belt and could probably kill me with any of them.

"Did anybody else get hurt?"

"Fortunately for you, no. If they had, then you would bear the responsibility of fulfilling the remainder of their contracts."

"It was an accident."

"It was an example of why fools shouldn't play with magic. I have already recreated your spell so do not waste my time with lies. Why were you attempting to make weapons? Are you plotting an uprising? Are you conspiring to sell these weapons to pirates?"

"What? No. Of course not!"

"You made a grenade out of some creature's shell. I found a bucket full of these shells in your family's cabin. Why would a mere crawler mass produce explosive magic, unless he is up to no good?"

"I only enchanted one. They're just leftover volcano snails… We eat them."

"You *eat* those things?" Haddar sounded disgusted by that.

"They're flavorless and you have to chew them until your jaw hurts before you swallow, but it's still meat." And it was one of the only things the Argent's couldn't charge us an arm and a leg for, like they did everything else they imported. "Ask anyone aboard, they'll tell you the same. I was experimenting on one because it was metal, and it was handy. I didn't know it would blow up."

"So you've attempted spell craft like this before?"

"A few times," I lied, unless you could consider hundreds of attempts *a few.*

"Then you're lucky you haven't killed yourself and everyone else on this barge. I should slay you, just for this insolence alone." Haddar shook his head, annoyed. "Only a rank four mage or above should attempt new combinations, and even they should be closely supervised in case things spiral out of control. Many wizards, better men than you, far smarter than you, have died horribly toying with that sort of thing, and they've taken a great many innocent lives with them."

"I swear, I didn't mean any harm."

"The ignorant rarely do." Haddar sneered. "Your good intentions did not save you from the chunks of high velocity iron which pierced your body, or the concussive force that smashed into your head. It was only through using up a very expensive healing charm that your surgeon-butcher saved your life."

I'd been lucky. The last thing I remembered was my snail grenade glowing brighter and brighter, and then everything went black. "When you say *expensive*..."

"*Very* expensive. You are lucky your bargemaster has a merciful disposition to expend such a valuable resource on the likes of you. Now your family must pay for your foolishness."

Even our weakest charms were extremely pricy. "I'm really sorry."

"I came here searching for pirates. A rather dangerous gang of them have been raiding cadres along the borders of the Argent family's territory. I thought this explosion might be an act of sabotage, but it appears it is just the act of a dumb boy playing with fire. I was contracted to kill pirates. I *enjoy* killing pirates. You're a delusional imbecile, but you are no pirate."

Haddar sounded genuinely disappointed that he wasn't getting to murder anyone right this minute. "I promise I'm not a pirate, sir."

"I have already questioned the rest of your barge mates and have examined the scene. Your enchantment was rather crude, yet I must admit, it was innovative. Do you not understand how unpredictable magic is? There is a reason my kind receive so much training. Why would you attempt this on your own?"

I thought about lying again, but since this was the effortlessly terrifying man was who'd first inspired me to try my hand at magic, I told him the truth. "I intend to be a wizard someday."

"But you are not a wizard now nor will you ever be. Your bargemaster told me of your recent testing and failure. Your mother told me of your great disappointment. When I first saw the smoking hole in the room of ropes, I'd thought maybe your blowing yourself up with magic had been a suicide attempt."

My people followed Saint Persistence. Suicide was anathema to us. "Why would I do that?"

"It would have made for an ironic and amusing form of protest. When denied magic, to shake your fist at your betters, defiant, while declaring, I'll show you who can do magic! Then *boom*! *Ha!*" Haddar's laugh was genuinely frightening. He frowned when I clearly didn't get his meaning. "My tribe would have found such a death poetic… However, since you are alive, it remains my duty to punish you on behalf of my employer."

I knew it. My life was over.

"This barge is property of Baron Sagard Argent, entrusted to Bargemaster Gax, who will also surely punish you for violating the rules of your cadre and endangering your people. To pay for the damages to the baron's property, five more years have been added to your family's contract. An entire healing charm was used up saving your miserable life, which will cost another five years of labor. That is ten years of one man's labor. You, or the members of your family, will work off this debt or face the consequences. Do you understand?"

I gave him a sullen nod. Even if I'd blown the entire stern off the barge, our engineers would be able to fix it in a few days. The real costs were the materials needed, because pretty much everything we used had to come by way of the traders, as Fogo produced nothing but ore, Red, and sadness.

"Do you wish to protest this reckoning, Mr. Carnavon?"

"Would it do any good?"

"No. It would not."

I hadn't thought so.

Just for the privilege of existing here, with the food I'd eaten and the magic I'd used to live, I already needed to work until I was thirty years old to buy out my contract. This would take me to forty, and it was rare for a miner to survive that long without getting crippled or killed. Other members of my family could donate their hours toward mine, but that would just delay their own freedom that much longer, and it always seemed like the harder we tried, the more debt we accrued. Even with bonuses to close the gaps quicker, my grandpa had died still working off his father's debts. Maybe Gilda had been right, and I should just accept we were damned no matter what.

Except I wasn't that easily deterred, and with nothing to lose, I asked, "Then I've got a request for you, Mage Haddar. Let me work off those years I owe the baron in your service. I can help you fight pirates."

"Your brain has swollen from the blow to your head. You are too young to be an enforcer."

"Maybe not an enforcer, but I can be your guide. You're not from this realm. This is a treacherous place."

"I have noticed."

"I know Fogo. I know the Red trade and the cadres' traditions. I can help you."

He saw right through my sad attempt at making myself useful. "The baron has already given me trackers and soldiers. I came here to judge and sentence you, not reward you. Yet you think if you serve the fearsome Gaul Haddar, you would be able to learn magic from me? That is not how it works. Only master mages—those who have achieved the tenth rank—are allowed to take on students of their own. Masters may grant permission for one of their students to take on apprentices outside of their academy, but mine has not done so. My school's techniques are secret. I am sworn to keep them safe. It is not my place to share them."

"If you are not a master mage, then what rank are you?"

Haddar grew annoyed by my questions. "I am of the eighth rank."

If an eight could destroy Fire Elementals as I'd seen him do, I couldn't even begin to imagine what a ten was capable of. "That's pretty close."

"It is not. Even if it was, I still wouldn't teach you. My magic is meant for war. There is currently no war worthy of my attention, so I was sent here to give my oath to Baron Argent that I would protect his family, enforce his will, and kill those who wrong him. This is not where I would choose to be, but I too must obey my orders." Haddar held out one hand to show me he was wearing several rings, one of which glowed a faint green. "I come from a desert land, so I thought I understood what hot was, but in this place, I am forced to use magic continually to not be overcome by your miserable soul sucking heat. It is like living in a baker's oven. I will not suffer this indignity just to share the glory of my victory over the baron's enemies with someone else. I do not want your help, and I cannot teach you."

That crushed me worse than the ten-year sentence had. Or at least it did in that instant, while I was concussed, before the horrible realization that I still had tens of thousands more back-breaking hours digging in the dark and hot ahead of me.

5

Our caravan of barges moved slowly above the black surface. With our cargo bay heavy with Red, our maximum speed was only about ten knots. The ash storm was closing on us a whole lot faster than that.

Bargemaster Gax stuck his head out of the bridge door and shouted, "Are we clear for set down?"

A bunch of us were waiting along the edges in expectation of that question. I leaned over the railing to look directly below, but could already tell from the smoking orange lines that the ground beneath wasn't solid enough. It seemed inviting, but that was a lie. Those black rocks were floating on top of a soup of molten death. Our weight would be sure to flip them, our barge would slide in, and then hundreds of us would die in a matter of minutes, because even enchanted greywood couldn't withstand that much heat for long.

There was a chorus of *nos.*

"Damn it." Gax went back into the bridge, probably to see if he could coax any more speed out of our ancient mobile home. "Spot me a place to land, Carnavon!"

The bargemaster wasn't talking to me. He meant my dad, who stood at the prow with a magical far seer raised to his eyes. Myles Carnavon was a Red mining legend, who could understand the whims of Fogo easy as breathing, which was important because there were no maps for a land that was in constant flux. Finding a safe place to land here was a matter of instinct and reading the terrain, and my dad could tell the temperature and solidity of a rock just by looking at it.

My older brother, Robbie, was at the railing between me and Dad. "The other barges are going to have to find their own places to land."

It was just like Robbie to be concerned about the rest of our cadre, as he was the kind hearted one of our bunch, who genuinely worried about the welfare of everyone else all the time. Though good as he was, the truth of it was the girl he was engaged to marry was on one of those other barges, and Robbie was pretty sweet on her.

"We can't help them. It's every barge for itself right now," Dad cautioned. "Their bargemasters are skilled. They know what they're about... Wait..." He twisted the wheels on the back of the viewing device to focus the magical eyes it sent ranging ahead of us. The Argents would surely bill us for the magic being used up so we're able to see better, but it beat dying. An ash storm was dangerous to even a landed and tied-down barge. If it hit while we were suspended fifty feet in the air, getting buffeted by those wind gusts was a surefire way for us to crash and die. "There!"

"You got something?"

"Fifteen degrees to port," my dad shouted toward the bridge. "Four miles ahead. Stable and flat ground, one hundred yards across, one fifty wide."

"On it." I could barely hear Gax's response over the wind. "Fifteen degrees to port."

I glanced back to see the storm chasing us now filled half the sky. The color was a menacing white, which meant the ash was burning extra hot today. Fire tornados, big as our barge, spun circular patterns through the ash storm's center, while lightning struck continually all along the periphery.

"That's barely big enough for us to land on, and we'll still be hanging over the sides," Robbie said. "If you're off..."

"Your old man is never off. Now run back to the cabin and warn Mom and the others to suit up. I want everybody in all their protective clothing, masks, hoods and all, and wearing all their charms. Tell Reece and Jaydee to go below to help with the landing poles. Then you come back and help me."

"Yes, Dad." Robbie hurried off.

I waited until the gentler soul was away. "Is it bad?"

"Yeah, it's real bad." An experienced hand, Dad had already done the math in his head. "That's the only sorta solid ground we can reach before that monster is on top of us, but it's not a good spot. I'm guessing that island is just under a thousand degrees, so the silicates should be solid, but we still might throw up some vent plumes when we drop weight on it."

Nothing was quite as exciting as lava spraying over the sides of your home. "You want me to go turn the globe on and start producing water?" That should have been the bargemaster's call, but everybody knew in times of crisis, Myles Carnavon was the one in charge, especially if it was late enough in the day for Gax to have gotten his drink on, and it was four in the afternoon.

"Yeah. Do that. The extra weight will slow us down, but we'll need full tanks to fight the fires if we catch a plume." He tossed me his ring of keys. "I'll go break the news to Gax. And, Son…"

I'd already started toward the ladder. "Yeah, Dad?"

"Do not play with the giant expensive magic water globe."

Blast a hole in the barge with magic *one time* and you never live it down. "That accident was over a year ago."

"You're still tempted to mess with it though."

He had me there, and he also knew I'd continued trying to teach myself magic in secret, but I was already sliding down the ladder. I ran for the globe as soon as my boots hit the lower deck floor.

The main cargo bay was the biggest space on our barge, and it was currently stuffed with Red. We'd gathered several tons of it, dust, flakes, and even quality nuggets. This had been a good expedition, probably one of the best our cadre ever had—the over quota bonuses would knock years off all of our contracts—and we'd been on our way back to sell it to the Argent's refiners when the ash storm appeared on the horizon.

Ash storms were fast. Our barges were slow. A few of our cadre argued to dump the weight of our treasure so we could go faster, but the rest of us had shouted them down. No risk, no reward, and we'd worked too damned hard for this load. So we'd run and hoped for the best. Except the storm hadn't relented. The blasted thing had grown bigger and angrier, and was nipping at our heels. Fogo was malicious like that.

Some of the other barges in our caravan had decided to dump their Red, and as a result, they had quickly outrun us. We'd watched their treasure be subsumed into the lava. They might live, or they might still die, but either way they'd be poor. Other barges had already picked out whatever temporarily solid ground they could, and hunkered down to weather the storm. We'd lost sight of them in the ash behind us. We'd tried to split the difference, hoping the storm would change course, but now it was too late, and it was time to land or die.

I reached our five-thousand-gallon water tank and checked the gauge, which showed it was nearly empty, and then checked the thick glass window to make sure the gauge wasn't stuck. Sure enough, there was only a few hundred gallons sloshing about below me. The tank was so big it extended through the bay, into the lift deck below, and its dome stuck out the main deck above. We tried to keep it as empty as possible while on the move because water's heavy, but if a rough landing happened, we were going to need as much on hand as possible to fight the inevitable fires.

The hatch was locked—as you really didn't want just anyone screwing with your most precious resource—but I had Dad's keys. He was Gax's second in command and had access to everything. If the rest of the cadre knew he'd given his wannabe wizard son they keys to the second most powerful magic on our barge, they'd be furious. They were still mad about last year's accidental destruction of the rope room by snail grenade, but we really didn't have time for that right now. Dad trusted me, and that's all that mattered.

Floating atop the water was a cerulean sphere, about the size of my head. The enchantment was designed to be idiot proof, so all I had to do was tap it twice with two fingers. It immediately began to glow a pale blue and clear water started to leak out. We were going to need more than that, so I tapped it again. The light got brighter. The water flowed faster. Two more taps set it to maximum yield, and now the water level in the tank was visibly rising. I hurried and closed the hatch and spun the wheel to seal the gasket tight before any of the valuable liquid sloshed out.

I knew nothing about the Elemental Plane of Water. I didn't even know what their element was actually called. We called ours Red. I assumed they called theirs Blue. That was just logical. Instead of crawlers, did they have swimmers? That wasn't the kind of detail the encyclopedia went into, so I had no clue. It was difficult for me to imagine any realm that wasn't perpetually on fire. Since all the elemental planes constantly crossed and invaded each other, Fogo had bits of earth—where else would we land? And air—how else would we breathe? And even occasionally water, though those new seas always boiled away, which was why we had to import magic or else no one made of mortal flesh and bone would be able to live here at all.

Once I was certain the tank was secure, I ran back to the ladder. In the short time I'd been below, the storm had gained on us. The white wall loomed imposingly overhead. Hot flakes were already swirling through the air. I pulled on my goggles and flipped up my protective hood, because I knew from experience those ashen bits hurt like crazy and fused right to your skin.

Most of our able-bodied men were either on the lowest deck preparing the landing poles, or up top prepping the lines to secure us to the rock. Normally my dad would be here supervising the work, but I found him one level up, at the bridge, arguing with Davis Gax.

"There's no way, Myles. Nobody could be travelling through that thing."

My dad held up the far seer. "I know what I saw back there. It was a barge, but not like any of ours, sleek and black as the rock beneath it. When we changed course, they matched us. They were tailing us until I lost sight of them in the ash."

That sounded crazy, but my dad wasn't the imaginative sort. I was the only one in the family with that particular curse. "Pirates?"

"I think so," Dad answered. "And they're either madmen or highly skilled to risk staying aloft in a storm like this."

Pirates were why we always travelled in caravans. There was safety in numbers. One barge was easy pickings, ten barges were a force to be reckoned with. Only right now, the rest of our barges were scattered across several miles, with some already locked down, and others still on the run.

"If it's like Myles says, it might even be the *Inferno*," muttered one of the deck crew.

"That thing is a myth," Gax snapped. "We don't have time for foolish superstitions. Any barge would have to be running light and have air magic with power and stability far beyond ours to even think about following us through this."

I butted in, "Our barge's lifter was already a hundred years old when the Argents bought it. And if the pirates got a real mage aboard who can finesse more power out of it—"

"We don't need a crawler's opinion right now, Oz."

That stung, because at the end of this expedition, I was getting promoted up from crawler. Mostly because I'd grown too tall, and my shoulders had gotten too broad to work the lava tubes anymore, but a promotion was a promotion. I still shut up though, because Gax was the bargemaster and he had enough things to worry about already.

My dad was good at persuading Gax, because Dad was usually right; should have been the one in charge if it hadn't been for his combative ways, and everybody knew it. "Listen, Davis, if I'm wrong, I'm wrong, and we opened the armory for no reason. But if I'm right…"

"Fine. Here's to hoping you're wrong." Gax went to his bargemaster's chair, picked up the clay bottle there and took a big swig of something potent to calm his nerves. "Open the armory and put your boy, Robert, on lookout. He's a trapper. He's got good eyes. But I need you overseeing the landing. We won't have to worry about pirates if we crash and burn." Then Gax looked around at the members of his bridge crew and barked, "And don't any of you dare say a word about imaginary pirates chasing us or everyone will be too worried about getting murdered to concentrate on their duties of getting us set down safely. You got that?"

"We won't be safe for long if pirates board us right after we land. Visibility is gonna be bad. Robbie will need help."

Gax relented, "Alright, Myles, he can have both our other trappers. But I can spare no more men than that for now! If he sees anything, he can sound the alarm and we'll prepare to repel boarders."

"Excellent decision, Bargemaster." Then Dad hurried out of the bridge, and I followed him. Once we were outside in the howling wind, he snarled, "Gax has lost his edge. His instincts are cold. He can only handle one problem at a time, but problems aren't polite enough to wait their turn."

"I turned on the water globe like you said. The tank's filling."

"Good lad." When I went to hand Dad's keyring back to him, he shook his head. "Keep those and go unlock the armory. Then you'll help Robbie on topside watch. Got it?"

"Me?" It was an honor to be so trusted.

"Yeah. You're more reliable than most of these bums." Dad pulled up his mask as the hot ash started to pepper his face. "Just don't screw it up and embarrass the Carnavon name."

"I swear I won't." My people were counting on me, so I'd do whatever I had to do. "Do you think it really might be the *Inferno*?"

"All I know is I saw an odd-looking craft, and we're still a long ways from the trade lanes so shouldn't have company. But it's doubtful the *Inferno* exists. A powerful wizard who preys on miners? Sounds to me like a story made up to scare cadres into never straying too far out of our lanes. Think about it, if there was a gang of robbers so brutal they never left survivors, then how would anyone know the name of their barge?"

Our old barge didn't even rate a name, just a number, 519, but the way Dad said that made me wonder if he was just trying to make us both feel better. "That makes sense."

"It could still be regular bandits too greedy for their own good. If any of them saw how fat and heavy with ore our barge looked, and they thought they could catch us unawares and alone, their hunger might make them stupid. The storm will probably take care of these fools for us, and if not, a few bullets will scare them off. Now get out of here."

I ran to the armory, trusting that Dad was right, but a troubling idea gnawed at the back of my mind. A year ago when I'd been interrogated by Gaul Haddar, he mentioned being hired to come to Fogo because a particularly dangerous pirate gang had begun operating here. What kind of pirates would be so dangerous that it would require paying a killer wizard to come from an entirely different realm to hunt for them?

That thought bothered me enough that I took a detour on my way to the armory. Since I'd blown up the rope room, my new secret chamber of wizardly experimentation was in one of the little supply rooms. I removed the loose board in the back of the narrow space and got out the few items I had successfully enchanted which might be useful in case of an attack. If Gax found out I'd once again endangered our home by creating these, he'd be furious enough to kick me out of the cadre. Getting exiled would ruin my name and no other cadre would want me. With still owing the Argents decades of labor, they'd surely stick me in doing something awful for them or I'd end up in debtor's prison.

So I was extra careful to make sure my magical items were secure and concealed. These were only to be used in an emergency, where the consequences of not having them would be worse than the consequences of getting caught with them.

Having gotten his orders too, Robbie met me in the armory, and he was accompanied by the only other two trappers who lived on our barge. It took tough men to chase Elementals for a living, and Joey Gowan and Harrison Kilroy looked the part; all muscle, scars, and devil-may-care attitudes which I'd always envied as a humble crawler. Their protective leather clothing had extra plates sewn on, in the hopes of keeping an Elemental's claws and fangs from burning through, and each of them wore a few extra magic charms to maybe keep them alive a bit longer in a fight. They had a lot of experience tracking and shooting the smaller Elementals, but the big ones, like the one that almost ate me once, were beyond their capability to kill unless they were already sick or wounded.

My oldest brother was the newest and youngest trapper in our cadre, but we Carnavons had a reputation for annoying levels of competence and bravado to uphold, so of course one of us had taken the job. "You brought the keys, Oz?"

It seemed stupid to me that our cadre had to keep our best weapons locked away, but those were the Argent company rules, and we were just blessed to live beneath them. I hurried and unlocked the padlock on the big metal chest.

Robbie threw the heavy lid open. "Alright, boys. Let's guard us a barge."

Inside were four rifles, dangerous as could be, made of steel, brass, and wood that had been enchanted to resist catching on fire. Each of the rifles was engraved with the crest of the Argent family, along with a number so their auditors could track them. Weapons like this were rare, very expensive, built by dwarven craftsmen in the Core, imported through the gate by the Argents, and then leased to our cadre. We mined the Red for them, sold the Red to them, and yet the Argents still charged us for every single bullet we fired defending their Red. It was quite the scam our nobility had going on.

Robbie handed a rifle to each of his friends, then took one for himself, the fourth remaining unused. A month ago, our fourth trapper, John Broder, had unwittingly stepped on a thin crust of rock that had looked far more solid than it was, broken through, and melted one of his feet in a lava puddle. He worked on our float crew now, hobbling around the lowest deck on a peg leg, which was a sad change for a proud man who'd once roamed the surface hunting Elementals.

I pointed toward the last rifle. "Dad said I can stay and help you. I might as well do it armed."

"They're complicated devices, wasted on the untrained," Killroy said.

"Robbie showed me how his worked."

"That I have," my brother admitted, before looking to his companions. "He's cocky, but Oz is a scrapper."

Killroy looked to Gowan, and they both shrugged. At worst, I'd be one more set of eyes.

Robbie took up the last weapon and held it out to me, but when I went to grab it, he pulled it back. "You remember what I taught you, right?"

"Don't point it at anything I don't want to kill. Don't touch the trigger until I want to kill something."

"And?"

"Uh…" While I tried to remember Robbie's lessons from the couple of times I'd been allowed to handle one of the things, Kilroy pulled the lever to open the action of his weapon to check if it was empty. "Never assume it's not loaded!"

"Close enough." Robbie gave me the rifle.

"I forgot how heavy these are."

"That's not just the steel, kid, that's the weight of *responsibility*," Gowan growled at me. "Shoot any of us on accident and I'm tossing you over the side. You lose that, and the Argent's will stick us with another year on our contracts… What've we got left for ammo, Rob?"

My brother was rummaging through the chest. "One box of twenty."

I was surprised. Those waxed paper shells were pricy, but I thought for sure we'd have more than that on hand. "That's it? Five shots each?"

"Who says the new guy gets five?" Killroy asked.

Fair point. The trappers actually knew how to hit things.

"The Argents only issued us a couple hundred rounds when we set out. We've been out for a long time without resupply and had to shoot a whole pack of lava dogs to keep the last site safe," Robbie explained to me. "That's what happens when Gax finds a rich spot and doesn't want to leave."

Gowan snort-laughed. "It's a good thing the bay got filled up, because one more day landed there and us three would've been reduced to throwing rocks at the Elementals."

"This is what's left." Robbie held out two shells to me. "So don't miss."

I'd never actually shot a real bullet at anything, even in practice, but Robbie had drilled me on the fundamentals and I'd paid attention because I found the process fascinating. Everyone knew guns were far weaker than magic, but they were more useful than strong language. "I'll try."

"Keep those inside your clothes until you need to load them because the paper will catch fire if hot ash gets on them," Killroy warned. "And keep the muzzle down. If you keep it up, ash will float into the barrel and start to stick. If your barrel gets plugged, it'll blow to pieces when you go to shoot it."

That was good to know.

There was one other gun on our barge, but that was the bargemaster's traditional hand weapon, issued by our noble family as a badge of authority and a tool to put down mutineers. Though in my entire life, I'd never seen Gax wear the thing. He'd probably gotten too fat for the holster belt to fit around him. For all I knew, he'd sold that gun in port and used the proceeds to buy more liquor.

Beyond our handful of guns there were a whole lot of picks and shovels on this barge, and a bunch of angry people who'd be happy to swing them at a pirate's head. Our job was to keep our eyes peeled and let everybody else know if they needed to start swinging.

We put on more protective clothing, buttoned up, and checked each other's gear to make sure everything was sealed tight and that our water bags were full, and then we went back out into the storm.

6

The ash was flying fast. The grey bits sizzled when they hit leather and left orange embers burning there. Visibility was down to ten yards, tops, and everything beyond that was a swirling haze. The thermometer on my enchanted band said it was a hundred and fifty degrees. This was just the leading edge of the storm. It was going to get a whole lot worse.

Just from the feel, I could tell we were descending toward the solid ground Dad had spied, but the winds were so strong they were pushing tons of greywood about like we weighed nothing. The barge was shaking like the old girl was about to fall apart. Whoever had the helm—Dad most likely—must have been working hard to keep us from getting slammed off course. Steering took great skill and a steady hand, because we were basically balanced atop a cushion of magically generated lift. If the air magic device which powered that invisible pillow so much as stuttered, we'd drop like a stone. It was a good thing the enchanters of the Core were so good at their trade.

Robbie had given me the port side watch. As I moved along the main deck, I checked every door to make sure the latches were sealed. The enchanted greywood would shield the interior enough for the inhabitants to not bake, but if a door blew open, the hot air would rush in and all that cooling magic would get wasted. While us four idiots were out here trying not to die, most of our cadre would be enjoying a relatively comfortable hundred degrees inside, as they readied the gear and heavy poles necessary for us to land on.

I'd helped with that job many times. It was hard labor, moving giant beams with pulleys and levers, and then adjusting how much each leg stuck out until the barge was level and secure—because flat was a relative term on Fogo—before the air magic could be shut off. Then it was settle and hope. During this process, everyone else would be manning their stations, ready to fight fires. The only folks who didn't have a duty station were the children who were too young, and the few moms left to watch after them. Only a handful of our cadre were full time dedicated barge crew—the rest of us were laborers of one kind or another—but when our barge was on the move, we all served as crew in some capacity.

Our descent was gradually slowing. There was a *thud* that made the whole barge shake. That would be the guide pole hitting rock. A pillar of fire shot up from below, but no lava rained down. That was good. Fire usually passed by. Lava sticks to you.

I wiped the ash from my goggles with my glove and looked toward the crow's nest. That's what we called the little lookout tower over the bridge. I knew that crows were a kind of bird, though I'd never in my life actually gotten to see a real bird. Regardless, by tradition that was what we called the narrow little perch that Robbie was holding onto right now.

My brother was courageous, because even though the wind was trying to hurl him down, he was going to remain up there with the far seer pressed against his face searching for pirate danger as long as he could. We Carnavons weren't the biggest or strongest family on this barge, but nobody had grips like ours, because wielding a chipping hammer all day will give you a handshake that can crush bones, and Robbie wasn't about to let some little fifty knot wind gusts break his hold on the iron bars of our crow's nest.

There was a mighty flicker of lightning, close enough that I could feel all the hairs on my arms stand up. I didn't know if the charms protecting us from fire would do anything against lightning. By my meager understanding, the forces were elementally related. Since I'd been chastised by Gaul Haddar and Bargemaster Gax, I'd not given up on my goals teaching myself spell craft, I'd just been more careful and discreet in my practice. So though I was curious to see what would happen, I really didn't want Robbie to get electrocuted. That was a magical experiment best left to another day!

"Get out of there, dummy," I shouted.

He probably couldn't hear me, but luckily, Robbie's bravery didn't outweigh his sense for once. As the blue light crackled through the air, he hurried and climbed down before tempting fate any more than he already had.

There were more thumps and thuds as the rest of the barge legs were lowered. Bursts of fire and intense heat rose over the sides as the poles found gas pockets, but it was nothing the greywood couldn't absorb. I kept moving, constantly scanning, which was getting more difficult as the ash thickened and sweat dripped into my eyes. The thermometer said it was a hundred and seventy outside my suit, but my magic charm was keeping the interior at a level where I could continue to function just fine. Gax had sent his trappers to be our eyes, but we'd not talked about having anyone come relieve us on watch, which we'd need sooner rather than later if the temperature kept climbing.

I'd been told the reason the Argents had brought humans to Fogo to use as laborers centuries ago was because our internal temperature mostly stayed the same despite the outside temps. The first Red miners had been scaly lacertians. Their armored skin didn't keep their insides from overheating, so they hadn't lasted. Then they'd tried dwarves, because dwarves were supposed to be good at mining. They'd done better, just not as well as my ancestors.

Turns out that with a little magical assistance, humans could adapt to damn near any environment. Shield us from burns, replace our water, and we could work for shockingly long periods in intense heat. That didn't mean we enjoyed it, and we'd certainly complain the whole time.

The wind was so bad I had to lean into it to walk at all. Finally, I had to give up and grab hold of the railing. After a minute, even holding on was too fatiguing, so I unfurled my safety rope and clipped it onto the steel bar.

The barge lurched as the air magic was cut.

Foom.

Our set down caused globs of lava to splash up over the side, but thankfully none of that lethal spall landed on the deck… On my part of the barge at least. I could only seen about five yards now, so beyond that, who knew?

I checked my thermometer. One ninety. Without enchantments, a man would only last a short time in that kind of heat before heat stroke and organ death. Even then, I had to keep sipping water from the straw in my mask to replace the sweat running out of me. If it hadn't been for my leathers, my skin would've already been eaten by the ash. As it was, I probably looked like an Elemental, lumpy and covered in glowing embers.

Despite my distress, I kept searching for threats. My people were counting on me. I would not let my family down. Even when you own nothing, you still own your reputation. No matter how much it sucked, I told myself that I was Ozwald Carnavon, and I'd rather be damned than known as a shirker.

As it got hotter, the ash thicker, and my charms had to keep working harder to keep me in one piece, I began questioning myself. This was futile and stupid. I needed to get out of here before I got hurt. I was using up good magic for nothing. There was no way any pirates would have the skill or capability of reaching us in this. *If* they were real, they'd probably already crashed and we'd never even know, because by the time the storm passed, their craft would've burned and the wreckage would just look like another pile of ash. And if they hadn't crashed or run off, I could only see a couple of yards now anyway, so I'd not be able to give much warning at all.

Discomfort makes even the toughest miners into whiners.

It was hard to hear anything over the howling, but thought that might be the fire bell in the distance. That meant some part of the barge had caught fire. My friends and family would be fighting it. They'd need help. I should go help them with the pumps or hoses.

The thermometer was now reading over two hundred degrees. How much over, I didn't know, because that's where my thermometer stopped. It had to be better inside.

But I stayed at my post, because that was what was expected of me.

A few minutes later, the black pirate barge came out of the swirling grey ash directly overhead.

7

The pirate barge was closing fast, and they must have been insane to try and board in this wind. We'd be lucky if they didn't ram us.

I rushed for the bridge, and almost yanked myself off my feet when my forgotten safety line snapped tight. Despite my clumsy gloves, I got it unhooked, and ran.

A moment later, I was pounding my fist against the bridge glass to get the crew's attention. Gax and his crewman looked my way. Knowing they wouldn't hear me over the wind, I pointed upward and gave the hand sign for *danger*. Our cadre's silent signal language wasn't very precise with the descriptions, so I couldn't tell them what kind of danger, but they'd figure it out.

To his credit, Gax immediately lumbered over to the big metal tube that extended through all the decks, picked up the hammer chained to it, and began beating it like a drum. I couldn't even hear the alarm through the thick glass, but that rhythmic banging would travel through all the decks below to alert the rest of our cadre.

That drum only got banged for pirates or monsters. Anybody who wasn't on a hose or a pump fighting fires would be grabbing something useful for bludgeoning or stabbing and heading for the nearest chokepoint. Our cadres didn't get raided often, but it was a common enough occurrence that we always had a plan in place.

Frightened and excited, I turned back into the wind and pushed toward where I'd seen the pirate barge, to find that their craft were almost level with us now. My warning would only buy us a minute or two. I sure hoped that would make a difference.

There were shadows moving atop the enemy barge.

The action of the Argent rifle was difficult to operate with my thick gloves, but I pushed the lever on the side until it clicked and hinged open to reveal the chamber. I unbuttoned my chest pocket, careful to palm the paper shell to protect it from the flying ash, and got out one of my two precious cartridges. I shoved it into the chamber and quickly pushed the lever back into place. Robbie had shown me how it would close with a metal-on-metal *snap* telling me it was all the way closed, but all I could hear right then was my own rapid breathing.

Another of our trappers must have seen the pirates too, because there was a muted *bang*, and one of the shadows fell over.

I'd never been in a battle before, but in that moment, I didn't have the space in my head to really think about it. I was scared and they were here to rob my home and kill me and my entire family. That's all there was to it. So I put the rifle to my shoulder, cocked the hammer back with my thumb, and tried to align the metal sights at my target—just as Robbie had shown me—only to discover there was so much ash stuck to the rifle that I couldn't even see the sights at all. I brought it back down and started brushing hot ash away as fast as I could.

The pirates began hurling things over their side. I couldn't tell what those were until a grappling hook landed near me. The rope it was attached too was pulled tight, and the hooks caught onto our railing.

There were more shots, barely audible in the storm, and then the pirates started shooting *back*. Chunks of greywood were torn from the wall next to me, yet I stood there like a fool, an ember coated statue, as lead flew past my face and splinters hit my back. I was too busy concentrating on what Robbie had taught me and trying not to mess up the order of operations to do the sensible thing and flee.

Sights brushed clear, I raised the rifle again, looked down the top, found the metal post on the end, and let it hover over a vague shape I thought was a pirate swinging a rope. I angled the rifle so the post was centered in the rear notch, and placed my finger on the trigger. Which promptly caused the rifle to go off before I meant it too because my heavy gloves were so thick I hadn't even felt the trigger give. The last time I'd played with one of these my hands had been bare.

The rifle kicked me in the shoulder and bruised my cheek.

By some miracle, the pirate I'd been aiming at toppled over the side and fell toward the hot ground below.

That was the first time I'd ever killed a man, and I was so surprised at actually hitting him at all, that the fact someone had just died didn't even really register.

More bullets landed around me. More grapples pulled tight. The enemy barge was getting closer. In a few more seconds they'd be jumping across. I wrestled with the action, trying to pry it open. Robbie had warned me the pressure of firing often made the metal seize up. My fear made me extra strong, and I cracked the action open hard enough that I was lucky I didn't snap the hinges.

One of the trappers appeared next to me, so covered in embers I couldn't even tell who it was. He thumped me on the shoulder then shoved me toward the bridge. That was smart. If I kept standing here while I reloaded I'd end up shot.

The unknown trapper fired. Another pirate went down.

I got behind one of the hoists we used to pull buckets of ore up from the surface. Made of thick wooden beams and iron bands, I figured it might even stop the bullets meant for me, so I hid behind it to reload. The ash was so thick on the deck now that my knees left dents in it. It was a struggle to get the charred remains of the last cartridge out of the chamber with my clumsy gloves, but the wax coating helped it to not stick. I retrieved my last cartridge, absolutely terrified it was going to get hit by a spark and detonate in my hands, but I managed to get it into the action and closed without blowing any of my fingers off.

The other trapper started after me, and then lurched against the wall. He slid down, leaving a streak of blood, then fell on his face.

The man who'd shot our trapper pumped a triumphant fist in the air.

I shot that pirate in the chest.

I'd not even thought about Robbie's checklist that time. I'd not even realized what I was doing until I'd done it.

I ran out from around the hoist, grabbed hold of the straps on my fallen comrade's suit, and started dragging him farther down the deck toward cover. He was a big heavy bastard, so it was probably Gowan, but I had Red miner strength and desperation, and he managed to help me by flailing and kicking himself along through the ash.

I got him around a corner and to a hatch, which of course was locked—as it properly should have been—so I began pounding on it desperately. With the intruder drum sounding, our cadre would be locked down, waiting for a breakthrough. They weren't going to open a hatch just because someone was knocking. I switched to the cadence us crawlers used to signal each other while working in the tunnels.

Whoever was on the other side must have recognized it, because the wheel began to spin.

I laid Gowan there—at least I assumed it was him—next to the door. He grabbed hold of my coat and shouted something, but I couldn't make out the words. Then he thumped the pouch on his chest, and I realized he was showing me where the rest of his ammunition was stored. Careful, I opened the pouch, found three more shells, and hurried to shove them into my pocket before the ash could get them. By the time I'd done that, the clenched fist on my coat had relaxed, as he'd either passed out or died.

The hatch opened, and the masked cadre on the other side grabbed Gowan and pulled him through. "He's been shot!" I bellowed, though they probably wouldn't hear me, and then Gowan and his rescuer were back inside. For just a second, I was tempted to go with them, but it wasn't my job to hide. I shut the hatch and returned to the fight.

Once reloaded, by the time I made it back around the corner, the barge was a few feet away and a yard above. Pirates were leaping across the gap onto our deck.

If this wasn't a crisis sufficient to reveal my magic, I didn't know what was!

Except there wasn't time to dig out one of my enchantments before a pirate was on me.

The one who landed the closest had to be seven feet tall and so broad he'd have to turn sideways to fit through a hatch. He was as bundled up against the storm as I was, obscuring his face, but he was so damned huge this had to be an orc. Most of the weapons on our barge were tools first, killing implements second, and this pirate was armed with a wickedly curved sword in one hand and an axe with a hook on the back in the other. Those were *not* for mining.

The orc's helmet visor swiveled my way. I was spotted. Without hesitation, he started my direction.

I didn't even have time to aim. All I could do was thumb back the rifle's hammer and fire from the hip.

There was a puff of dust and ash as the bullet hit the orc low in the side. The impact spun him a bit, but only slowed him for a moment, then he began running straight for me. There was no way I'd be able to reload in time, so I reflexively started backing away. I barely managed to get behind the hoist as the orc reached me. I ducked as the sword got planted deep into the wood just beyond where my head had been, severing the safety ropes. Then I stumbled back, narrowly avoiding the axe which got stuck into the deck, and slipped on the hot ash, falling on my ass.

Kicking out with my boot, I hit the orc in the arm before he could tug the axe free, but I might as well have been kicking rocks for all the good that did. My only option was to scramble backwards as he lifted his axe to chop me to bits.

Suddenly, the orc's leather helmet jerked back. When his head came back around, a fresh hole had appeared in the mask.

As the orc stumbled, spitting teeth, I grabbed the lever which worked the hoist, and pulled as hard as I could. The beam swung around, smacked the off-balance pirate, and sent him over the railing to his doom.

I looked back to see who's shot saved me, and from the round shape, it could only be Bargemaster Gax standing there, his symbolic pistol of office extended in one shaking hand. Apparently, he'd not sold it for liquor after all!

Pirates were swarming across our deck, nothing more than threatening shapes in the grey. They were trying to batter and chop their way through the hatches to get to the valuable Red and vulnerable people below. Gax was desperately gesturing for me to head his way, probably to lock ourselves in the bridge, but this was my *home*. It made me furious that these bastards thought they could just steal all that we'd bled and sweated and some of us had died for. My anger outweighed my fear so much that I was able to stand up on shaking legs and start toward the pirate barge, reloading as I went.

With rifle ready, I fished an iron snail shell from my pocket. I had a good arm for throwing rocks—we all did, because it helped to scare the smallest Elementals away—but the wind was gusting so strong that I needed to get close to be sure. Luckily, the ash made visibility so bad that I was able to get within ten feet of my target before getting spotted.

The figure standing atop the enemy barge was tall and lean, with a cloak whipping madly about his shoulders in the wind. Oddly enough, this pirate wasn't wearing a mask or goggles, so must have been protected by a spell powerful enough to keep the hot ash from sticking to him.

When he saw me approaching, he gave a cruel smile, as if amused by my futile efforts to stop his raiders. He leaned on a staff made of gnarled wood, and had long white hair blowing in the wind. From the pointed sweep of his ears and the unnatural thinness of his limbs, I realized this was an elf. I'd never seen an elf before, hadn't even known there were elves on Fogo.

Regardless of how he'd gotten here, in five seconds there'd be one more elf in hell, as I concentrated on the shell and activated the Red magic I'd previously embedded into the iron. Then I threw it as hard as I could against the wind.

My snail grenade hit the pirate's deck and bounced, beginning to glow as it rolled between the feet of the raiders who were waiting their turn to come plunder my home. I'd already pulled out my second shell and activated it before the first one turned lantern bright.

I was blinded by a blue flash, and the next thing I knew, I was flying backwards. Even as my body was sliding through the ash, I was thinking *that had been fast.* Only then did I realize the elf was pointing his staff at me. He'd struck the railing in front of me with some kind of magic. The iron bars had been left twisted and smoking. My snail spell hadn't gone off yet.

Then it did.

The explosion hurled pirates and pirate chunks in every direction. There was a flicker of sparks around the elf as iron snail fragments struck an invisible magic shield.

Then I recalled that I'd just activated another shell, which was *still cooking in my hand*, already glowing orange as I hurried and chucked it as far as I could. Since I was lying on my back, it was more of an awkward lob, up and into the wind. *Too close!* I scrambled up and ran from the elf's magic and my own.

I risked looking back as the second snail grenade went off over the pirate's black barge, peppering them with more iron fragments. As several pirates dropped, there were more flickers around the elf as his enchantments absorbed the hits. Now that was a neat trick!

The elf wizard demonstrated another trick as the hoist I was standing next to got smashed into kindling.

Even though his attack spell missed me, it was as if the strongest gust of wind I'd ever felt picked me up and slammed me against the nearest cabin. I lost the rifle as well as all the air in my lungs.

My head was spinning. There was a wetness all over my back that at first I thought must be my own blood pumping out, but it was the water bladder I wore that had broken open, not me.

That bolt of power had been meant to obliterate me, except the once nimble pirate barge had twisted in the wind, throwing off the wizard's aim. My snail grenades must have wounded or distracted their helmsman.

As their barge was shoved away by the wind, all the grapple ropes snapped tight. I couldn't hear the elf's commands, but he was obviously infuriated and bellowing commands at his crew.

Denied a quick victory and easy treasure, the pirates were retreating. The grapple ropes were released, and the barge began floating away from us, abandoning some of their own. I quickly lost sight of them through the ash.

They'd already lost, so they shot us with their cannon just out of spite.

8

"State your name."

"Carnavon. Ozwald Carnavon."

The mage tester had to go back many pages in his ledger before he found my entry. I already knew what it said.

"Carnavon? Formerly of the Barge 519?"

"Yeah, that's me."

"It says here you already tested when you were fifteen years old."

"That's correct, sir."

The two of us were in a room at the traders' guild house in Fort Silver. I sat on one side of the table, the tester on the other, with a few lit candles and his records between us. The last tester from the Core had been a mean lady named Ewing, sneering and bossy. In comparison, Mage Tester Pivorotto seemed like a kindly grandfather. Regardless, I went into this interview expecting just as little mercy from him as his predecessor. My place would not be earned through pity or charity, but by effort.

"That would make you almost nineteen years old now."

"Yes, sir."

"When my colleague tested you previously, she declared you to be a zero. Is that correct?"

"It is."

He absently scratched the wild grey tufts of hair above his ears. The rest of his head was bald. "Then why are you here? There's no formal magic instruction anywhere on Fogo, so you've had no chance to improve in rank."

"I've been self-taught."

He chuckled at that. "Sure you have."

"What's so funny? I am."

"Did the traders put you up to this? You can't be self-taught because you've got both eyes, all ten fingers, and from the way you walked in, neither of your legs are made of wood. No terrible disfigurements. No extra limbs, or ears or noses growing from your head. It's a rare wizard who teaches himself without self-destruction or wild curses and out of control mutations. Magic is serious business, so please don't waste my time. There are hundreds of candidates in this realm waiting to be tested and—"

"Magic is serious business." I dropped my coin pouch on the table. "Which is why I will pay you a serious wage for your time."

He looked at the pouch, incredulous. "You can't *bribe* a mage tester, son. If any of us sent some talentless dope to the Core, their fraud would be discovered immediately, and we'd be shamed into exile for lying."

"It's not a bribe. Merely a respectful thank you for taking the time to perform an unscheduled test. I'm only looking for honest results, Tester."

Curious, because normally it was the nobles who determined who among their subjects was to be tested rather than the uppity subjects themselves, Pivorotto picked up the pouch and opened it. "These aren't coins."

"That's six ounces of solid Red, plucked directly from an Elemental's heart, and never logged into any Argent books. Do with it what you will."

"That's very generous of you." Mage testers were all practicing wizards themselves in constant need of magical elements to fuel their spells, so Pivorotto quickly closed the pouch and hid it in his pocket. "Very well then. I believe I can make time for this unscheduled test."

He readied his pencil and prepared to make updates in the ledger.

"Are both your parents alive, Mr. Carnavon?"

"No. They're not."

"Oh." He put a line through the previous entry. "My condolences. Do you have siblings?"

"Four living."

He crossed out that part too. "My, what a sad difference a few years can make."

I wasn't about to tell him the story of how I'd failed to protect my family barge from the cannon fire of wrathful pirates, so I just said, "Fogo's an unforgiving realm, Tester."

"From what I've seen, that is true. You remain literate?"

"Reading material is sparse here, but I didn't get dumber since the last tester came through."

"Fair enough. We don't normally test anyone twice though. Occupation?"

"Trapper."

"Chasing down Elementals? Very dangerous work, that." A new note was written. "Any criminal offenses?"

"Several."

Curious, Pivorotto looked at me, waiting. "And those offenses would be?"

"Practicing magic without permission. Endangering my cadre through magical experimentation. Destruction of Argent property. Hunting on Argent lands without permission. Brawling in public. Several of those, actually. Disturbing the peace a few times." I had to pause and try to remember if there were any others. "Loitering."

It took the tester time to write all those down, and he was forced to abbreviate because the page didn't leave that much room. "It seems you are quite the ruffian, Mr. Carnavon."

I was sure I looked the part to someone from the Core. I'd thought about lying to him, but the Argents kept meticulous records and never forgot a transgression against their rules, no matter how far out on the frontier the offense had taken place. "Not particularly, sir. I'm fairly civilized by local standards."

"They do say a land of fire breeds fiery temperaments."

"Who says that?"

Pivorotto partially leaned back. "Well, come to think of it, I don't know if I could name the particular philosopher it originated with, but it's something which is commonly said in the Core and accepted as a basic truth about your people. Not that we get many of you Fogo folk there… Do you have any physical ailments, mental instabilities, or addictions?"

"I'm squared away there, Tester..." An unfit trapper was a soon to be dead trapper. "Aren't you going to ask about my character or, I believe it was unsavory proclivities?"

"So you remember that part?"

I nodded.

He laughed. "I was afraid to ask after you listed off all that criminality, as I've nearly run out of space to make notes. But is there anything you believe the magical academies should know about you?"

"Put down that I'm no quitter."

"An odd request, but I shall respect it." He began writing. "Let the record show Mr. Carnavon is not a quitter. There you go. That will be forever recorded in our sacred halls."

"Thank you."

He took one of the charms off his wrist. Unlike the previous tester, whose charm had been made of copper, this one was white and carved with intricate designs. "Since you remember the process I shall—"

"Wait."

"What?"

I had a lot riding on this moment. I'd worked my ass off, used up piles of Red experimenting, and studied everything I could get my hands on—and I was pretty sure most of those how-to-do-magic guides were nonsense written by deluded fools and charlatans rather than actual wizards—and all my future plans hung on what this test was about to tell me... So I was scared to find out if I was still pathetically normal, and years of effort had been wasted on a dumb dream, or did I actually have *some* ability to improve and make something of myself.

"I just need a moment to prepare is all."

"Alright." Pivorotto appeared confused by that as he set the bracelet on top of his ledger. "My time is important, but that much high-quality magical element will purchase a remarkable amount of my patience. Frankly, I could use the break, having spent my entire day simmering in this heat, only to disappoint children and their hopeful parents."

I remarked on his testing charm, "That's not metal."

"It's not. It's ivory."

"What's ivory?"

"It is an organic substance, like bones or teeth, produced by certain animals. It bonds with magic rather well. This particular charm was fashioned from the tusks of a doom whale from the Morbid Sea of the Elemental Plane of Water. And yet I expect a fascination with the science of zoology is not why you're stalling, is it, Mr. Carnavon?"

I sighed. "Are you originally from the Core, Tester?"

"I am. Born and raised."

I'd assumed so, since he was so red faced and sweaty. Core dwellers were always uncomfortable even in the gentlest parts of Fogo with magic working to cool them. "Then you can't possibly imagine what it's like to want to be from somewhere else."

He nodded at that. "Though I've travelled to six of the seven realms, the Core will always be my beloved home."

"Is the Core really as grand as they say it is?"

"Eh… The city is vast. I suppose *grand* would depend entirely upon which part you find yourself in. The Pallentine is beautiful beyond your imagination. It's sections float above the city like clouds, each palace a majestic jewel connected by bridges of gold. And the Collegium…" Pivorotto sighed wistfully at the memory. "Oh, the Collegium, it is the home of the academies and the center of magical research, a place of scholars and knowledge, incredible inventions, and works of living art, where things that are considered miracles in the other realms are commonplace."

I'd read about all that in the encyclopedia. "The Core City is where the legendary wizard, Primopolus, built his tower, the tallest building that's ever stood on any world."

"It was. Tragic what happened to it."

"Was?"

"The tower… It fell over, Mr. Carnavon."

That hadn't been in the book. "When?"

"Fifty years ago!"

Well, that explained things. It wasn't like our handful of half burned books were up to date. "That's unfortunate. I really wanted to see it someday."

"I was only a boy when it toppled, crushing whole neighborhoods beneath! The hubris of Primopolus shook the entire Core! But the city moved on, as it always does. It has to, since millions of people live there."

That number was so big I couldn't really comprehend it. I'd grown up with a couple hundred people crammed onto one barge and that had been suffocating. "How do they all fit?"

"Rudely. Though manners go a long way toward retaining civility between the various factions. Sleights that would result in an immediate duel in the Pallentine are common among the rougher common folk of the Aventines. Then there are several lower levels, where poverty and crime are rampant, and beneath all that lies the ruins of the empire which existed long before the Nexus Council was formed and the Great Machine was built.

"Down there is where dark things lurk. I've never gone myself, but have heard there are caverns full of ancient structures which go on for miles. Each district of the city is as different as any two kingdoms of the realms. There are hundreds of languages spoken there, as every nation and race has an enclave or two, but most of the masses know the trade tongue enough to converse with each other."

"That's what we speak here."

"It is. A bastard strain descendent of it at least. The human workers of Fogo were brought from the Core hundreds of years ago, yet I can understand your people easily enough."

That was good to confirm, because being able to actually communicate with the denizens of the Core was a vital part of my plan. I didn't have the time to try and learn another language.

Pivorotto had continued speaking wistfully about his home, "And speaking of the gates which brought your people here long ago, and me so recently, one cannot talk about the wonders of the Core without recognizing the importance of the Great Machine which stands at the center of it all, constantly turning as it has for thousands of years. It is the marvelous Nexus which connects us all together across the worlds. Each day it rotates to connect to another realm. Seven realms, seven days of the week, a perfect schedule which never deviates."

"Well, it did once," I pointed out.

"Yes, but it is impolite to talk about the lost realm." He shuddered at the terrible thought. "On the seventh day, the Core stands alone, as that gate remains forever barred. Despite that loss, the Great Machine continues to turn. It is amazing to watch in action, and it's an incredible feeling to walk across the threshold and actually step between worlds. I've done this dozens of times, and yet it still takes my breath away. It is a wonder that a mere week is all that separates any traveler from reaching any other realm."

"I've always wanted to go there."

Pivorotto gave me a sad smile. "Then you'd best try to become a servant of your nobles so you can take their Red to the Core's markets to sell, because I hate to break it to you, son, the odds of you testing well enough to gain admittance to a Core academy, especially at your age, are slim indeed."

"I'm aware of the odds."

"Are you though? You just gave me a bunch of valuable element so I can most likely dash your dreams against the floor. The academies are in such demand that they're turning away natural rank twos unless they're still young enough to be properly trained before they become a danger to themselves and everyone around them. At your age, you'd have to be a savant to be accepted, born a natural three at least, and we already know you're not. If you possessed such an exceptional aptitude for magic, the last tester to come through here would have caught it."

"Unless she made a mistake."

"The difference between a three and a zero would be like mistaking a dragon for a piglet, Mr. Carnavon."

The carvings on the ivory reminded me of something, and since I had bought a Core man's attention, I had one question he might be able to help me with. "Look at this." I took a charm from my pocket—an iron band enchanted with a protection from fire—and gave it to him. "Do you recognize this makers mark?"

"I can tell just by the feel this magic has got some depth to it. Ah yes. Whoever made this is rather capable. A quick, simple, but solid enchantment." Pivorotto held the band close to the candle and squinted, trying to see the carving better. "This is elf script. That's not something I'm able to read. I didn't know there were any elves in Fogo."

"I've only ever met the one," I said truthfully. "Do you know who made this?"

"I don't. But from the style of the spell, I'd wager that the maker studied at the Wynlyn Academy." He gave the protective band back to me. "It's one of the most prestigious schools within the Collegium, which accepts only the most gifted of candidates. For every hundred viable applicants I have found in my career, Wynlyn will only take the top one or two. If that was enchanted by one of their graduates then it's worth quite a bit."

I'd taken that band off a pirate's corpse. All the raiders who'd died on my home barge had been wearing charms from that same maker. I filed away the tester's words for my future vengeful needs. "Good to know."

He picked up the ivory and held it out for me to take the other side. "Shall we continue?"

Before taking the test, I had one last thing I needed to be sure of. "I read once that when it comes to practicing magic, sufficient dedication and concentration can overcome a lack of natural aptitude enough to still achieve mastery of the subject. Do you think that's still true, Tester?"

"I would imagine that's true for any endeavor a man could set his mind to with sufficient passion, not just magic… but there's also a reason there aren't any gnome gladiatorial champions in a city that has an abundance of musclebound orcs and lobs."

"You went to an academy. You surely know many wizards. Could a lowly rank zero work his way into becoming a master. Yes or no?"

He thought it over, which was an indicator of a man who actually cared about giving a completely honest answer. "Theoretically. Though if you speak of true mastery and not just utilizing someone else's charms, then yes, *but* it would be rarer than a master painter who happens to be blind or a musician born deaf yet capable of performing in the best symphonies. There's a vast gap between the imagined and the plausible."

"That's good enough." I took hold of the charm. "I'm ready."

The spell was simple. The test was quick. The ivory turned so cold in my hand that it had to be what ice felt like.

The tester stared at the charm, as if baffled by what it had shown him. "Well… huh…"

Taking that to mean he was done, I snatched my hand away and curled it into a fist, desperate for warmth. "What does *huh* mean?"

Except Pivorotto was too busy thinking to answer me, and he quickly scribbled another note, which I could still read though it was upside down.

Rank One.

I began to laugh. *I knew it!*

"Well, that is most unusual!" The tester was flabbergasted. "Perhaps my predecessor did make a mistake after all."

"I really don't think she did." I wasn't about to let thousands of hours of effort and practice be stolen away from me by some cheap excuse. Ewing had been cruel, not incompetent. This was *my* victory. I'd earned that first rank. "I told you I'm self-taught. That's how much better I am than last time."

"Huh…" he said again, genuinely surprised. "That is truly rare."

"Rare as a blind painter or deaf musician?"

"There abouts." He spread his hands apologetically. "Alas, impressive as this achievement may be, especially done on your own—"

"Using only one element," I added, though I felt like I knew Red like the back of my hand now, I looked forward to seeing what I could do with the opportunity to combine it with the others.

"Indeed! But sadly, a rank one is still insufficient to gain the notice of one of the Core academies. I'm terribly sorry."

I was still grinning. "No worries, Tester."

"However, I would happily put in a good word for you with your nobles. I'm sure the Argents would be delighted to have someone of even the first rank already under contract. They'll probably offer you some position with more opportunity to pay off your remaining time faster, which has to be far safer than trapping Fire Elementals for a living!"

That was awfully kind of him, but the attention of my rulers was the last thing I needed. The test confirmed my efforts hadn't been in vain, my plan might actually work, and I wasn't about to get sentenced to doing maintenance on barge floaters and water globes for a thankless baron for the next couple decades instead.

"Thank you, but I'd prefer for you to not tell the Argents anything."

"I'll refrain from speaking about this if you wish, but I must present them a full report when all this year's testings are over. Honor demands I can't hide a positive result any more than I can lie about a negative one."

"I'd not ask you to do otherwise, but this report of yours won't be done right away, will it?"

Pivorotto wiped the sweat off his brow with a handkerchief. "I've still got to travel to several different cadres along the rim. I'm afraid I must suffer in this infernal heat for several more months at least."

"Perfect. Not your suffering. I mean the timing."

"I really don't understand." This must have been terribly confusing for him, to have someone come so far, yet fall short of obtaining glory and riches, and still be so happy about it. "You seem oddly content with this disappointment, Mr. Carnavon."

"It's no disappointment, Tester. No disappointment at all." I stood up to leave. "Now if you'll excuse me, this blind man needs to gather his paints."

9

Fort Silver was where Fogo connected to the Nexus. This was one of the four places along the edge of the Elemental Plane of Fire that had been tamed enough to turn into a real permanent settlement. Because regular living things couldn't survive deeper inside the plane, the Fort was situated on the outer rim of where the realms of earth, air, and water often trespassed. Over the centuries, wizards had captured those other elemental strands and bound them eternally to this one spot with time magic. This was the one patch of rock for hundreds of miles which wouldn't melt, the air wouldn't escape, and the lake would never boil away.

A few hundred years ago, the Argent family had finally made enough money selling Red to bring a significant amount of life magic to their home. It was said the Green could make anything bloom, and sure enough, they'd even managed to grow a small forest around Silver Lake. The first time I'd seen a tree, I stared at it for an hour. It was a plant, taller than me, green with soft puffy leaves, and that had been simply inconceivable. Yet some of the beams on our barge had been fifty feet long, so I understood logically that there must be trees in other realms which grew that big. It's just, when you come from a land made out of fire, it was difficult to imagine such things.

I'd never been to any of the other three permanent settlements on the Plane of Fire. Each of those had their own gate. I assumed they also had fleets of barge-based miners, a different bunch of nobles to boss them around, and their own particular problems. To reach any of those would take weeks by lumbering barge, crossing treacherous, constantly shifting terrain the whole way… Or one could simply wait here in Fort Silver until the Great Machine aligned with our gate, cross over to the Core, spend however many days it took for the Great Machine to connect to your desired destination, and walk through in an instant. All a traveler needed to do was abide by the rigid schedule of the Great Machine. Seven days a week for seven different realms, four weeks in a month, twenty-eight different gates.

That was the theory at least. I'd never left Fogo, so my knowledge of how to travel across the realms was based entirely on what I'd been told and had read. Tomorrow was Fireday, when the Great Machine would be pointed once again at this plane, and more specifically, our crossing at Fort Silver.

On the one day a month the connection was made, the Fort was incredibly busy. Today was the relative calm before the storm. All month long, barges came and went, unloading Red and loading supplies. Every month the Fort Silver warehouses slowly filled with Red and any other material valuable for export. Once the gate opened and trading began, the wealthier merchants would move their wares through on pallets levitated by air magic. The less successful merchants would use wheeled carts pulled by domesticated trogs.

As the Fogo traders entered the Core to sell their wares, Core merchants would cross to our side to deliver vital supplies. As our warehouses were emptied of Red, they'd be refilled with food from the other realms. Mostly rice, grains, dried fruit, and some cured meat, to get distributed to the barge cadres. There were fancier delicacies traded too, and rumor was that the Argents had a special room in their castle that kept food fresh and delicious forever. Such things were supposedly common in the other realms, but even as excited as I was by magic, I found such outlandish tales hard to believe.

As I walked through the narrow streets of Fort Silver, I was amazed at how loud and crowded this place was. There were a hundred times as many people living here as there had been in my entire cadre, even before the destruction of Barge 519. And then I tried to imagine what it must be like in the Core City, which was supposedly so vast, all of Fort Silver could fit in one tiny corner, unnoticed. So the stories went… Though if everything went according to plan, I'd see for myself soon enough.

All the buildings in Fort Silver were made of fitted black stones. Despite the permanent air magic, it remained difficult to breathe. Everyone in Fort Silver always had a cough. That's just how it was. The locals took it for granted. The air was usually better out on the fiery rim, probably because we didn't have to share it with various industries and so many other lungs.

My destination was a tavern between where the barges docked and the warehouse district. That location told you exactly the types who'd frequent such an establishment. When I entered the main room a whole bunch of surly laborers, bargemen, and miners glanced my way. The few who recognized me nodded in greeting, then everybody went back to their drink and pipes. With their cargo delivered and staged, the hard part for them was done. Now it was drink, smoke, and wait to see how much the traders would earn them for their efforts.

After Fireday, the Great Machine would have moved onto the next elemental plane in line—water—our merchants would be back from the Core, and this place would either be celebrating, with bargemasters happily buying drinks for everyone, or it would be filled with miserable bitter cusses, angry drinking, and itching for a fight against some stranger so they could get their frustrations out with their fists.

The men I was looking for were at a table in the back corner. One of them was a poor excuse for a miner, kicked off his barge long ago, who now made his living by doing unsavory odd jobs here in the Fort. "Hey, Jemmy." Then I nodded at the stranger next to him. "And you must be the trader."

"Bart," the trader said by way of introduction. He was round faced, soft around the middle, and about my age, so probably new to such an important position.

"Have a seat, Oz." We all called our local hoodlum Smiling Jemmy, because he liked to show off the two gold teeth he had in front. "How'd your fancy wizard testing go?"

So Jemmy had heard about that. Not a surprise, since he probably kept up on most of the goings on in Fort Silver, just to insert himself into everyone else's business for his own advantage. I don't know how a crook like him managed to avoid the enforcer's wrath... Probably a whole lot of bribes.

"It went good enough." I sat down.

"So you're a mage now?"

If only it were that easy. "Naw. When it comes to magic, I'm barely qualified to clean the Argent's toilets."

"The baron's got a magical privy?"

"Sure. Why not?"

"Still sounds nicer than being a trapper. You lot are absolutely mad," Bart said, but with respect. "I'm from here on solid ground. I can't imagine marching over fresh crust, searching for fiery things that want to eat me, armed with nothing but a gun and some charms!"

I didn't mind having the city folk of the Fort think of me as a little crazy. That rep helped keep me safe here. Who'd want to cross someone who tracked Fire Elementals by choice? "The rifle's handy, and we don't set foot on the wastes without our charms, but a trapper's best weapon is his wits."

"Respect to you then, Trapper." With the polite introductions out of the way, the trader got down to business. "So… Did you bring the money?"

"Calm down, Bart. The Carnavons are known as men of their word. Oz wouldn't have us go through such efforts without having our rightful payment with him as promised. Right, Oz?"

"Of course I've got it. Thanks for arranging this, Jemmy." I took out three small coins and set them on the table. They were there just long enough for Bart's eyes to get wide with greed, before Jemmy swept them away and out of sight. Which was probably wise, because those coins were from the Core, far more valuable than our Argent company scrip, and men had gotten stabbed to death for things of far less value in places far nicer than this. "Enjoy."

"Oh, we shall," Jemmy crowed. "Now onto business."

"Alrighty then." Bart cleared his throat, as if he'd practiced delivering his criminal instructions in the mirror and wanted to sound confident. "There's a blue painted crate in the alley behind this place. Hidden inside you'll find an armband that marks you as a trader associate, approved to cross the gate. Take that and wear it tomorrow. Be at the associate's board twenty minutes before sunrise. A couple of my men are going to come down with a fever and be too sick to haul cargo. I'll call for last minute replacements. Raise your hand, 'cause you're gonna get picked. Then follow me and do exactly what you're told. Got it?"

"Got it."

"Any questions?" Jemmy asked.

"Yeah," I addressed this to Bart. "You've been to the Core?"

"I have. Twice." He seemed very proud of that. "This will be my third trip to the market. Someday I hope they'll let me stay to work for our buyers. They cross and then stay a whole month at a time, negotiating deals for the next passage. Can you imagine a whole month in the Core City? I hear even their poor live better than our nobles."

So Bart had only been to the market, which was the area immediately outside the Great Machine. Of course, some low-level trader wasn't going to know much about the rest of the city, which consisted of dozens of different districts, built on top of the ancient civilization that had existed before the creation of the Great Machine. "What can you tell me about blending in there?"

"Oh, don't worry about that. There's more going on than you've ever seen. Mobs of people in every direction, all dressed funny, talking funny. They say there's a thousand kingdoms, and there's folks from all of them in the market. There's traders from every realm, moving all sorts of goods. It's overwhelming to the senses. You're gonna see dwarves, lizards, gnomes, weird critters from every plane, and sometimes there's even elves!"

My glower at that last one must have been obvious.

"Oz don't care for elves," Jemmy warned. "Bit of a sore spot, that."

"Oh..." Bart clearly didn't know what to make of that information, so he continued, "They don't talk much to anyone else. They're kinda stuck up like that, comes from living for hundreds and hundreds of years I suppose. Only other thing I can say to be prepared for, it's *cold*, like this deep chill that goes to the bones, but to the Core folk it's normal, and you'll hear them complaining about all the heat coming out the gate on Firedays. I guess the other days of the week it gets even colder, which is hard to believe. Its bright too, on account of they can see the sun clear with no smoke in between. Even their clouds are white! Not like ash storm white, but cool and soft. So you're gonna be half blind and all cold. You'll want to be ready for that."

"Noted. Do the Argent enforcers go into the market with you?"

"Yeah. A few walk with us, but nobody dares rob anyone else in the market. The Core has a city watch who make our enforcers look like babies. They're basically an army, complete with their own wizards. They take no guff off nobody. The Argent enforcers are there to make sure none of us traders try to skip out of our contracts early by running away."

"That's going to be an issue for me then."

Jemmy spread his hands apologetically. "I'd need quite a few more coins to arrange the complicity of an enforcer for something big as aiding a skip out. Especially since Haddar got here. Their fear of displeasing that wrathful bastard far outweighs their traditional greed."

Since I'd arrived in Fort Silver, I'd heard many more tales of the frightening foreign wizard annihilating anyone who crossed the baron. I suspected just as the laborers in this tavern would take their frustrations out on each other, Gaul Haddar's frustration at not being able to catch the *Inferno* was causing him to be extra cruel to the oath breakers he could catch. 519 hadn't been the last barge of ours to be destroyed by those pirate bastards.

"If the enforcers bust you trying to run, they'll stick years on your contract. And if they do, I don't know you. You say otherwise, I'll deny it. You're just some worker I hired that morning. On the bright side, if you do manage to slip away on the other side, there's no way the Argents will ever find you… Though they'll stick those extra years of punishment on your family's heads instead, as well as the entire rest of what you already owe."

"Yeah… I know."

For once, Jemmy wasn't smiling. "I will say, knowing your family's reputation, I was a little surprised by this turn of events, Oz."

Being branded a run-away would condemn my brothers and sisters with decades of extra labor to work off between them, and that would surely get passed onto their children, and their children's children, because the game was rigged against us, the numbers we were supposed to work off just grew bigger and bigger, and hardly anyone ever earned their way out. It was out of loyalty to our families that more of us didn't break our contracts, because it took a selfish bastard to profit from the suffering of his kin.

"That's all part of my plan, Jemmy."

10

"So you want me to help you *fake* your death?" Davis Gax stared at me as if I'd gone mental. "Are you daft? Have you been snorting Red dust and turned your brains to mush?"

With 519 destroyed, Gax was a bargemaster no more, but with years still on his contract, the Argents weren't about to let all that valuable experience go to waste. Gax now lived in Fort Silver, inspecting other barges for problems while they were landed and waiting to take on supplies. I'd found him wandering between the gigantic legs of Barge 836, checking the greywood beams for cracks.

"My brains are fine. I know what I'm doing, Gax. I've got a plan."

"Does that plan include Robert drowning you in lava when he finds out you're shirking and putting your family in danger?"

My brother was the eldest surviving Carnavon, which made him head of our branch of the family. He was also an honest, hard-working, Gods and Saints fearing man, so of course I wasn't going to tell him what I had in mind. Robbie had enough to worry about. He was responsible for my younger brother, and now had a wife and a daughter of his own. He'd try to talk me out of it, and when that inevitably didn't work, he'd try to punch me out of it. He'd probably win that fight too. My elder brother was tough as trog hide.

"Robbie can't ever know. He's too honorable."

"Oh, so he's too honorable to lie for you, so you come to *me*? How am I supposed to take that Oz?"

"The opposite of honorable isn't dishonorable. It's pragmatic."

Gax just shook his head and went back to checking the enchanted iron bands wrapped around the base of the landing legs for the excess scorching indicative of magic about to give out. From how much trouble his joints seemed to be giving him, the last few years hadn't been kind to the man. He'd lost so much weight that his once full jowls now hung like sad empty bags on his face.

"Robert would kill you. Gilda would *extra* kill you."

Elder sister Gilda had been married off to another barge, but she'd taken in our little sister after Mom and Dad had been killed on 519. Even with a new last name, Gilda was still part of the Carnavon family contract, so the Argents would likely punish her for my insolence too.

"That she would."

"She'd say you're being selfish."

He was right that Gilda would probably say that, but she'd have guessed wrong about my motivations. "I'm not running away for me, Gax. I'm running away for *them*. We're never going to earn out, no matter how hard we work. You know it. I know it. Deep down, they all know it, but they're too stubborn and proud to admit it."

"Carnavons having too much stubborn pride? I must gasp at this shocking concept I've never considered before."

"I'm serious. If I can get real training in the Core and become a proper mage—"

Gax snorted at that.

"Then I can earn enough to buy out all their contracts once and for all. A year of a real wizard's labor has to be worth a century of trapping. I can free my whole family. I'm not going to the Core to escape Fogo, but so I can eventually return strong enough to beat this place."

"You can't *beat* Fogo, kid. It is what it is and always will be. Sweltering miserable suck and disappointment where you work your fingers to the bone and nobody cares a trogshit what you do, and they'll knife you in the back anyway, and you'll put up with it every single day until you die."

Gax was extra grumpy when he wasn't drinking, and from what I'd seen, he'd pretty much given that habit up since the day we'd crossed paths with the *Inferno*. He probably blamed himself the same way I did. Surely Gax wondered if he'd been sober, would he have done something differently that might have changed our fate that day? While I always wondered if my magic had been stronger, instead of just wounding the *Inferno*, could I have destroyed it before it turned its cannons on us?

Neither of us would ever know.

"Accept your fate, Oz. Find a new barge. Get a wife. Hell, half the girls in Fort Silver are in love with the brooding trapper boy who talks good, reads books, still has all his teeth, and hunts deadly Elementals for fun, so that shouldn't be hard. Have some kids, so that way after you die, somebody will remember your name."

"And curse that name for leaving them a life of indentured servitude. My family has always had your back, Gax. You've been like an uncle to me. If you won't do this for me, then do it for my dad."

"Oh, that's low down and manipulative right there, Oz. Coming at me like that, invoking family. You really think Myles Carnavon would want his brightest son abandoning his family to chase after dreams of wizardly glory?"

"Yeah, I do. After I got caught the first time, who do you think kept sneaking me extra Red dust so I could continue practicing? Who do you think suggested the best parts of the barge where I could work on enchantments without attention?" What I didn't add, was that after the infamous rope room explosion, my dad had also helpfully pointed me towards places where, if I'd accidentally blown myself to pieces, the collateral damage would be low. "Risk versus reward governs every other part of a Red miner's life. Why would learning magic be any different?"

Gax stopped his inspections to really look at me. His eyes were watery. "Myles was my best friend, but he always was a cunning bastard who was good at getting what he wanted out of others. I'm thinking you inherited that trait."

It was time to be completely honest. I owed Gax that much, at least. "There's one other reason I need to go."

"I suspect I know what it is."

"Yeah, you probably do." I took out the iron band that had been worn by one of the pirates who'd boarded us on that fateful day. "Someday, I'm going to find these bastards."

Gax knew exactly what the band represented, because all the bodies from the *Inferno* had worn charms with the same makers mark. "You want revenge."

"Damn right I do. So do you."

"Of course I do! But the Argent's pet wizard has been searching the rim for that elf for *years* now and found *nothing*. The *Inferno* is a ghost. Word is, it's raided barges from all four forts on the plane. They kill all the miners and crew, steal that hard earned Red, then vanish without a trace. Haddar's a realm-walking, head-collecting, cold-blooded killer who takes every day those pirates live as a personal insult. You think you'll succeed where someone like that has failed?"

"I don't know. I have to try."

"I respect that." He gave me a grim nod, for if there was anyone who wished death on that elf more than me, it was Gax. We'd both lost loved ones and our home, but Gax lost his entire purpose in life too. He'd never be entrusted with another barge, and he'd live out the rest of his life here, doing maintenance on other bargemasters' crafts. It was a sad end to hard life. "How do you intend to find him?"

"I don't know yet. I'll figure it out. But I can't do it here with what I've got now. Only if I can get rich enough to buy my family's freedom, when I return to Fogo I'll be a man of resources. Real resources. I'll find a way."

"Well then, Oz." Gax picked up his kit. "Since you seem committed to this lunatic stunt. Follow me."

I didn't know if I'd persuaded him or not, but Gax led me toward a tiny shack in the shadow of the landed barge.

"I need someone of good repute to corroborate the circumstances of my death. If I get killed in the Argent's service, then my contract is void, and my remaining years get struck from the ledger. Robbie and Gilda will be in the clear."

I'd thought this was a tool shed, but when he opened the door, there was a cot in the corner. This was where Gax lived.

"Yeah, this is my place. How the mighty have fallen, right?" He gestured around the dreary little space, which had very little inside of it, except for some empty food tins and dirty clothing. "When do you need to go missing and when do you need to be confirmed dead?"

"I can go missing tonight. Dead, ideally sometime tomorrow."

"The cause of death seems obvious enough. Big Elementals, at least one large enough to devour a man whole, are rare this close to the Fort, though not unheard of. I can tell the enforcers I saw sign of one roaming near the barges, and that when I ran into a trapper friend of mine, I asked him to go take a look to make sure. This landing ground being my duty station, that would make my asking you for aid an official request on behalf of an Argent agent. Alas, brave young Ozwald Carnavon, who was always happy to serve the interests of his baron, was never seen again."

"That works. Fireday morning you can send one of your workers to the lava flats just out past the last barge. There he'll find my rifle, some of my clothing, partially burned of course, and one of my issued charms. All of which are valuable things no trapper would ever willingly leave behind."

"A fine plan. Very tragic, but a not-at-all-suspicious way for a trapper to meet his end. You're sure you want to do this? There's no coming back from this kind of fraud."

"Sure as I've ever been of anything in my entire life."

"Alright then." Gax bent down with a tired grunt and pulled a small box out from beneath his cot, which he then offered to me. "I want you to have this. It might be useful on your journey. I hear the Core ain't all sunshine and kindness."

I took the box and opened it. Inside was a single shot weapon made of steel, brass, and wood, with the number 519 engraved on its side plate.

"This is your bargemaster's handgun. I can't take this."

"Why not? I've got no use for something that was mostly for symbolic tradition anyway. Our barge is gone, and officially, that gun was lost with it… so should you get caught with it, I'm just going to tell the enforcers you must have stole it while our barge burned." Gax chuckled at his wit, but then slowly grew somber. "The reason I give you this, should you ever find that wicked elf, this is how you'll repay the favor I do by lying for you now. When you kill him, use my gun to do it."

11

The official motto of Fogo was engraved into the black rock over the entrance to the Argent's keep.

Weeds. Not flowers.

The enforcers at the gate saw the associates' armband I was wearing and let me right through. With thousands of traders and laborers coming and going through these walls every Fireday, nobody got more than a cursory glance. The place was just too busy for anything more than that.

Shuffling along with the rest of the predawn mob, I looked like every other worker who served the various merchant companies. The regular clothing of us Fogo folk who came from the barge cadres was usually thick and protective. The sheltered people of Fort Silver didn't have to worry about sudden spark showers or getting molten slag on them, so they usually wore lighter clothing to try and stay comfortable. Those whose jobs required them to go into the Core all owned some cold weather gear, which got worn but one day a month. All the workers trudging along beside me were carrying bundles of coats, cloaks, sweaters, hats, scarves, and gloves they could put on before entering the notorious chill of the Core market.

I'd bought a pack and some laborer clothing from the company store. Inside the pack, I'd hidden Gax's pistol, it's belt and holster, and the one box of ammunition he'd had for it. There was nine rounds left in the box, with an empty space that once held the bullet he'd put through an orc pirate's face to save my life. My few enchanted items were also hidden in the pack, because regular workers who lived in the safety of Fort Silver didn't need bands to protect them from fire or scrub their air. My arms felt light but naked without the usual metal bands.

I'd left one of my charms and my issued rifle for Gax's employees to find. The serial number on the weapon would be matched to my name on the ledger. That find would be in line with Gax's testimony, so the Argents would hopefully assume one of their many trappers had gotten himself killed and eaten by an Elemental, which was a common enough occurrence.

By the time the Argents updated their records and stamped dead and void on my contract, I'd be in the greatest city in all the realms, convincing one of the magical academies to accept me. That part of my plan was rather vague because I knew so little about the ways of the Core, so I would have to play it by ear.

The outer keep consisted of a huge open area, entirely surrounded by high walls. The Argent family castle—the inner keep—was on a ridge ahead of us. It was a vast and imposing structure. From high atop those mighty towers, our noble family surely looked down at the rest of us with scorn and contempt. I'd seen the castle from town before, but up close it was even more intimidating. As the workers continued to march along, I lost count of how many enforcers patrolled the walls above us. They all looked comfortable and well-fed, which kept them loyal enough to break the occasional cadre strike.

We walked around a corner and I gasped as I saw the Fogo Gate for the very first time.

The grizzled laborer standing in line next to me heard my reaction and laughed. "You must be new on this detail."

"Yeah. I just got this job."

"I made that same noise my first time. The gate sure is something, ain't it?"

It was *something* all right.

Made of the same black rock as everything else in Fort Silver, the gate was an arch that had to be nearly fifty feet tall and well over a hundred wide. Only, unlike all the buildings, this wasn't a bunch of carved and stacked blocks, because the gate had obviously been *grown*.

The legends claimed that long ago, a mighty wizard—the first Argent—had journeyed to this part of the Elemental Plane of Fire from the Core. He called up a gigantic plume of lava, used his incredible power to twist it into this shape, and then frozen it in place to harden. He'd then bonded the inside of the arch to the Nexus, and that connection had lasted for thousands of years since.

I'd seen enough arcing lava plumes shooting across the surface up close to be convinced that this particular legend had to be true. This one would have been big enough to cut an unlucky barge in half. Even having seen them in action, it was still difficult to comprehend how much destructive force such a thing was. How mighty would a wizard have to be to seize control of such a thing, bend it to his will, and tame it?

To someone who could barely do a few spells, it was frankly awe inspiring.

"Well, if you're lucky, they'll need more hands and you'll get picked for a work crew today and actually get to go through to the other side. Though if it comes down to you or me, seniority wins, and I need the extra pay. Sorry, kid. That's how it is."

I said nothing in response, because the coins I'd paid Jemmy and Bart surely outranked his seniority.

The outer keep was a gigantic field, and on trading days the whole place was packed. Our sky wouldn't brighten for another hour, but the merchants were already patiently lined up before the massive gate, waiting their turn. Dozens of air carts, which were basically miniature barges in principle, were landed, waiting and saving their magic. Then there were rows of wheeled carts and wagons. All of which were loaded heavy.

Each of those merchant outfits had workers attached to move cargo, and assistants to help sell their wares. There were even individual traders whose company consisted of nothing more than themselves and a dolly or handcart with a few things loaded on it. Those traders were most likely just striking out on their own, or they were the unlucky and impoverished who'd previously earned their way into the merchant ranks, but who must have lost their air carts or trog wagons in some deal gone wrong, now forced to start over again. I'd been told trading was a very competitive, cut-throat business, and from the desperate look in their poorer traders' eyes, I believed it.

Once I found the associates board, I waited nearby. There was already a great and anxious crowd formed around it. There were many notices posted on the board, though it appeared hardly any of the laborers could read them. The literate few held the advantage, as they could read which merchant companies were actively hiring more help, and then run off to find them. But there were a few who could read among the workers, who read the notices aloud for the others' benefit. Those made a good profit for doing so, as those they helped find work promised them a cut of their day's earnings. I could probably have earned a bit of money reading to the rest of them, but I certainly wasn't going to draw any attention to myself at the hour of my escape.

When Trader Bart walked up to the board, he looked around until he spotted me, before shouting, "I need two strong backs for Fendral Company. Twenty scrip for a full day's labor." A bunch of hands went up, mine included. He pointed at me and the senior man next to me. "You two will do."

It was lucky Bart picked the only one who knew I was new here. Last thing I needed was someone whining about a new guy cutting ahead in line, drawing the others' attention to what I looked like. Not that it was likely anyone would remember my face enough to match it to the description of some dead trapper. The paths of us cadre folk and the Fort Silver residents rarely crossed. It was doubtful my death on the outskirts of town would be newsworthy enough for the comfortable people of the Fort to even hear about it. To them, only fools went outside the protective barriers of their permanent magic.

Grabbing my pack, I ran after Bart. The junior trader was playing it calm and did a good job pretending to not know me. "Alright, Mister Fendral needs you two on one of our wagons. Do either of you know how to drive a team of trogs?"

"I do, trader." And it was fortunate for me the senior man did, because we had no space for beasts of burden on a barge, so I'd never worked with any animals.

"Good. You'll unload our Red on the other side once we find a buyer, then you'll be loading a shipment of tools to bring back, which you will deliver to the Fendral warehouse on Walcher Street. Understood?"

"Yes, trader," we both said at the same time.

Bart led us to a big, six-wheeled wagon, which had two trogs hitched in front. Squat and toad-like, the trogs thick skin was constantly slick with a mucus they secreted, which helped regulate their temperature. The gigantic creatures were not native to Fogo but were one of the only animals which were able to survive here. In my limited experience, trogs were foul smelling and foul tempered, but they were strong and available.

"Check the cargo. Make sure everything's secure. And if there's so much as a scratch on a Fendral crate, it's coming out of your scrip." Bart waited for the other worker to get started on the ropes, before catching my eye and giving me a nervous wink, as if we were grand conspirators in some sweeping plot. I nodded respectfully in return, because I just needed him to get me through the gate and then keep his mouth shut.

Fendral Company must have been of middling importance, because there were dozens of other carts and wagons waiting in line ahead of us.

"Looks like we'll be working together. I'm Cole. What's your name, kid?"

I said the first name that came to mind, "Tom."

"It's your lucky day, getting a job your first time at the board."

The other laborer kept on trying to make casual conversation, but I mostly ignored him. I wasn't being rude, just too nervous to talk. He probably thought my anxious state was due to crossing the gate for the first time. Sure, stepping into an entirely new world was part of it, but I was busy counting Argent enforcers and trying to guess which wagons they'd be sticking closer to. If I got caught trying to run, they'd probably stick another fifty years on my contract, send me straight to debtor's prison, or maybe even kill me on the spot. Stealing was a serious crime, and skipping out on your contract was a theft of the Argent's time.

"You're gonna want to watch this," Cole warned me. "There ain't nothing else like it."

As dawn approached, the gate awoke.

With our skies perpetually choked with smoke, it was rare for anyone in Fogo to actually see the sun. We could tell it was there by the beams that snuck through. As the first light crept over the walls of Castle Argent and touched the base of the arch, something changed. I couldn't see anything yet, but could sense it building in the air. There was an energy that made the hairs on my neck stand up, like when I was about to bind Red to metal, only a hundred times stronger.

"You feel that?" I asked.

"Feel what?"

"Never mind." It went unsaid, but my sensing the gate's magic was probably a result of having achieved the first rank of wizardry. If I'd not learned to enchant objects, I wouldn't know what I was feeling. This was like that, but ten thousand times stronger.

Cole pointed at the right bottom of the arch. "See there? Right now we can see through to the other side, and it's nothing but the Argent's field, but there's a little bit of the other side appearing on the edge now."

Sure enough, visible through the arch was nothing but dark, flat ground, then gradually, a white line began to move. Behind that line was a sliver of *somewhere* else. That had to be the Core.

It was like our world was painted on a curtain, and that curtain was being pulled back. As the glowing border slowly moved, the view into the next world increased. As the Argent field shrank, the other side was so bright, I had to squint. Our world was mostly black and red. The Core appeared to be white and illuminated in golden yellow light.

There was someone waiting on the other side. He was dressed in a fancy uniform that screamed ceremony. His clothing was as militant as that worn by our enforcers, just less practical, and in different, much brighter colors, and with far more decorations. When he looked through and saw Fogo and all the waiting merchants, he shouted some greeting which I could barely hear, but the way he pronounced it sounded memorized and formal. Then he lifted a curled horn to his lips and blew. The instrument produced a noise so loud it had to be augmented by magic.

"Who's that?"

"The Core warden. I think his job is to be the first one to look through the Great Machine's connection each morning, and we're not allowed to cross until he gives permission."

From reading about the closing and barring of the seventh gate in the Encyclopedia Ettymus, I knew how that tradition had gotten started. "He's checking to make sure there's not a terrible evil waiting on the other side to invade the Core."

"Huh… that happen often?"

"Just once before, a long time ago."

"Oh. Didn't know that. Anyways, I know the warden looks silly in that outfit, with all the golden ropes and jewelry and whatnot, but we've all been warned that office is always held by a deadly wizard, so we're never to mess with him. If he says jump, you jump. My grandpa told me that he once saw a merchant lip off to a warden, and the warden turned the merchant into a snake! Poof. Right there on the spot."

As soon as the gap between worlds was wide enough, the first of our merchants walked through. Even though I'd known that was inevitable, my mouth still fell open at the sight.

"The Great Machine turns the same speed all day. See that line? It'll just keep moving left, inch by inch. By lunchtime, it's all the way full, the whole gate is open to traffic, and there'll be wagons passing through nonstop. From then on, the opening starts to shrink, and on the right, it'll be Fogo again. At sunset, the gate's all the way closed and will stay that way for a month. I've seen this a hundred times and it never gets old."

Ropes creaked as all the trogs began to stir and grunt. They'd been doing this once a month for their entire lives. This wasn't magical to them. It was just what they were expected to do. The carts which were powered by air magic slowly rose as their merchants activated them. Those would be carrying tons of Red, yet could be pushed about by one man's hand.

More merchants walked through the widening gap. And then the gate was big enough for the first cart to glide through.

Standing alongside our wagon, I tried to hide my hands, so nobody would notice them shaking.

The line began to move.

12

We were getting closer to the gate.

As soon as the connection was wide enough for multiple people to get through simultaneously, merchants from the Core started coming out our side. It was one thing to read about other kingdoms, but it was something else entirely to see their people in the flesh. The first cart to float through was manned by humans—like most of us Fogo folk were—but their skin was dark, even darker than Gaul Haddar's, and their clothing was wildly different than what I was used to, with pants of shiny silk and flamboyant capes made out of the skin of some spotted animal. Their cart flew a yellow flag and was filled with vegetables I didn't even recognize.

The next company through was made up of dwarves, short, thick, and hairy, who bellowed hearty greetings at the merchants they recognized on our side. Their wagon was being pulled by horned animals I'd seen poor drawings of but didn't know what they were actually called. Gilda had insisted they were unicorns. Robbie had called them rhinoceros. And then the two had argued over the supposed differences. These were thickset as the dwarves, so probably rhinoceros.

The laborers waiting around the associates board cheered when they saw the contents of the dwarf wagon consisted of kegs of beer. That would surely be a quick sale to one of the local traders.

There were Fogo merchants returning home after spending a month in the Core procuring special goods. Their carts were filled with rare and specific items which we needed from the other planes. Priests of the various Core churches made their way, probably coming here to do missionary work. Various functionaries and officials did whatever it was governments actually did. I had no idea what use they served.

Company after company crossed over, each one wildly different from the last. They flew many different flags, representing their home kingdoms. As the wagons went through, some found a spot and set up shop in the Argent's field, so our Fogo traders could buy their wares. Others, their deals had already been arranged in advance, so they headed straight to their destination warehouse in Fort Silver to make their deliveries. Those who needed laborers or guides hired from the men waiting at the associates board. It was risky to hold out for a job from an outsider employer, as there might not be work to be had at all, but the Core folk paid in real coins far more valuable than Argent company scrip.

It was a remarkably efficient system, and the inner keep was rapidly filling with sellers.

A group of adventurers sauntered through the gate like they owned the place. I knew their type well, because as a trapper, I'd earned some extra money guiding people like this to their destinations. There weren't very many fixed points of geography in Fogo, but some of those ruins were believed to hold great treasures. Unfortunately, they also held incredible dangers. Adventuring struck me as an incredibly stupid way to make your living, because I'd guided a couple parties to their destinations, but never had to guide any out!

There were only a few wagons left ahead of us. Beyond them was an incredible view of a vibrant market that stretched for *miles*, filled with more people than all of Fogo's barge cadres and the population of Fort Silver put together. The sky over their heads was *blue*. Actual blue. And there were *clouds*, fluffy and white.

I'd been so enraptured by the view I'd not heard the enforcer walk up to me. "Stop your wagon." I flinched when I saw who was speaking, but he didn't seem to care. Men who got paid to inflict violence upon others probably got that sort of reaction a lot.

"Pardon me, enforcer?" I tried to play dumb while I decided if I needed to make a break for it or not. My first panicked thought had been that Jemmy ratted me out for a reward, but the enforcer looked too bored for it to be that. "What was that?"

"Are you deaf? I said stop the wagon. Leave a space."

"What for?" Cole asked as he pulled on the trogs' reigns. "Who's cutting in line?"

"Make way for the ambassador. Diplomatic mission takes priority over merchants." He jerked his thumb back toward a small group of people walking toward us. "Argent business."

One of our trogs hissed at the enforcer, upset that its routine had been interrupted because it took a lot more effort to get a wagon started than it did to keep it slowly rolling. Cole thumped that trog over the head with a rope and it stopped.

The diplomatic mission turned out to be several loud young men wearing Argent colors and their handful of obvious bodyguards. The one in the lead was a big, handsome, swaggering fellow, and he was telling his friends a boisterous story involving lusty elf girls, which was so obviously exaggerated—if not entirely fabricated—that even I could tell it was trogshit, and I only caught about thirty seconds of the tale as they wandered by. The nobles were followed by a few servants carrying luggage. They weren't going to a negotiation. They were going on a holiday.

I kept my head down while they were close, because while the nobles were paying us no mind, their bodyguards appeared keen, like the sorts who might remember a suspicious face. Junior Trader Bart walked by to check on why we'd been stopped. When we made eye contact, he looked very nervous. I just shook my head, as if to say it was no big deal. Thankfully, Bart kept walking.

"That's our ambassador?" Cole asked the enforcer once they were past.

"That's the baron's middle son, Dardick, and ambassador is his title, so best watch your tone. He's got important business to attend to in the Core every month." The way the enforcer said that made it obvious how little he believed it himself.

"Aye. Pretty girls and fine liquor is serious business," Cole agreed.

The enforcer laughed. "Carry on."

Cole thumped the trogs, and they grudgingly began to pull. I climbed aboard our wagon. The back was filled with casks of refined Red, representing thousands of hours worth of some miners' efforts. In a few minutes, we'd be in the Core, and our trader would try to sell this for as much as they could. The more they got for it, the bigger some barge's reward would be, and theoretically at least, their cadre would be that much closer to buying their freedom.

"This is important work you do," I told Cole with sincerity.

"You say so, Tom." He started putting a sweater on. "Best bundle up."

The gate was so close now, the chill coming off it prickled my skin. I hurried and got my new coat out of the pack, careful not to dump Gax's handgun on the ground, because that would certainly draw an enforcer's attention. The new clothing was so thick, I immediately began to sweat and found myself wishing I was wearing my charms.

The diplomats went over. We were next.

You'd think there'd be something more to it, crossing from one realm into another in the blink of an eye, but this was more like walking into a cold, bright tunnel than anything else. I didn't know how far the Core was from Fogo. Thousands of miles? Millions? But to the Great Machine such distances simply didn't exist. For one day a month we were practically neighbors.

The cold was like walking into a wall. "Fuck me!"

"Welcome to the Core City. I hear you get used to it, and those who stay for business between trading days claim they do at least, but I've never been here long enough myself for it to stop feeling bloody awful!"

It was so cold my teeth hurt, but the market was *stunning*. The sun was so bright that I couldn't see where it actually ended, it all just turned into an endless colorful blur. I spun around to look back the way we'd come, and sure enough, there was good old Fogo. Then I looked up, to see that on this side, the gate wasn't an arc of lava frozen in place, but a grey stone structure, every inch of which was carved with beautiful images.

I looked up even farther to realize the grey stone gate was being held aloft by two gigantic statues, probably a hundred feet tall each, of a powerfully built man and beautiful woman, both in what I thought must be wizards' robes, only they had wings of carved fire sprouting from their backs, and their hair had been carved to appear as if it was on fire. It was difficult to tell, since it was so high above me. Even farther up, past the statue's heads, was the Great Machine.

"Sweet merciful Saints. That's..."

"Impressive, ain't it?"

It was the biggest thing I'd ever seen. Far taller than the Argent's castle, it was a mountain of metal, complicated as the inside of a clock, with pipes, and girders, and I could even make out tiny figures of people up there working on it.

Even more impressive, that entire mountain was slowly rotating.

The encyclopedia had told me of how at the base of the eternally moving pyramid was the Nexus, which was the magical effect we'd just crossed through. It took exactly seven days and nights for the Great Machine to make a complete circle. During the daylight hours, it was aligned with one of the seven realm gates. I looked excitedly in both directions to get a glimpse of the other gates, but from this angle, they weren't visible. The metal mountain was simply too big to see around.

Then I looked past the pointed top of the Great Machine, and realized that reading about floating cities does them no justice, because actually seeing one in real life takes your breath away. There were buildings up there, palaces perched atop islands of jagged stone like impossible islands in the sky.

My home had moved about on air magic, and each of those islands were easily a hundred times bigger than any barge, and we barely got fifty feet above the ground. The closest of the sky islands was a couple hundred yards away, the others suspended so high above that I couldn't make out any of their details. The islands were connected by bridges, grey or golden arcs—just as Tester Pivorotto had said—and some of the bridges even turned in lazy spirals going all the way to the ground, past the horizon of the marketplace.

I was suddenly very dizzy and feeling rather insignificant.

"Don't forget to breathe, Tom. I ain't unloading all this by myself."

I had to hold onto the side of the wagon to keep from toppling off, as my poor mind tried to comprehend the miraculous nature of a city where all seven magical elements—and the knowledge of how to use them—were so abundant. How was I going to impress people who built things like *this* enough for them to let me join their number?

This wasn't the time to lose focus. My family needed me to succeed. I had brothers and sisters to free and ghosts to avenge. So I said a silent prayer to Saint Persistence, and forced my attention away from the most powerful magical device in history and the sky castles of its rulers, back toward the market—which though incredible in its own right—was downright humble in comparison to the magical wonders above.

We were descending a gentle ramp toward the market, which was like unto the Argent's field and its gathering of wagons, only incomprehensibly greater. From what I could see, the Core market was atop some manner of raised disc at the base of the Great Machine, which had to stretch for over a mile in every direction, and beyond that edge was more gleaming city. There were untold thousands of people. There were hundreds and hundreds of stalls, each one flying a different banner, and filling every row between them were barking traders and curious shoppers.

I'd been told that, like the Great Machine itself, the Core market around it never stopped moving. Seeing this endless churn, I believed that.

Today was Fireday, but tomorrow this place would be flooded with traders from the Elemental Plane of Water and all their corresponding goods. The next day would be air, and so on. The cycle would repeat, as it had for centuries, each world getting from the others everything they needed to survive, while the Core which made that trade possible prospered and thrived.

The farther we got from the gate, the cooler it became. I began to shiver, so I put up the hood of my coat. This was the coldest I'd ever been, but many of the foreign merchants and workers were going about their business wearing hardly any clothing at all, as if somehow this place was comfortable to them. I wondered if this was what outsiders like Haddar or Pivorotto felt in Fogo, only in the opposite direction. No wonder they were constantly using enchantments. I'd been here for all of two minutes, and it felt like my ears were going to snap off.

I took note of where the guards were, both Argent and Core. Our enforcers looked dirty and slovenly in comparison to the Core City Watch. They wore dark blue uniforms with copper buttons, and were armed with a variety of weapons. Various guns, swords, and clubs completed their attire, even wands, which meant some among them were probably actual wizards. All of them wore various enchantments, rings, amulets, and buckles, which were surely capable of different effects. To a man, they looked hard as nails, though most seemed good natured enough as they interacted with the crowds. Still, I had no doubt that good nature would turn cruel quickly if I got called out as an oath breaking thief.

It would be stupid to run now. Just like trapping Elementals, patience was vital. Making your move before you understood the terrain was how trappers died young. I needed to take my time and understand the lay of the land first. It would probably take a while for Bart's employer to sell all this Red, and then for me and Cole to unload it. I'd use that time to observe things and look for opportunities to disappear.

As we reached the bottom of the ramp, Bart pointed us in the correct direction, having to shout to be heard over all the noise, "Mister Fendral's reserved us a spot on the next row over. Come on."

This section must have been meant to cater to the wizards, as most of the tables we rolled past were covered in various magical elements. We were restocking the merchant's Red, but among that was impossibly blue liquids, corked bottles containing a perpetually swirling mist, and powders brown, green, and black. It appeared that last one was always kept in glass case under key, so customers could look, but not touch. From the prices noted on the signs, the ingredients varied wildly in quality. Money and magic were rapidly changing hands. I wished that I could get close enough to inspect those wares, because I'd never even seen any of the other elements in their raw form before, but to do so would attract suspicion.

Everyone around us was speaking the trade tongue in dozens of different accents. I could barely understand half of them. There were so many voices all at once, my ears began to ring like I'd just fired a rifle.

The Fendral Company wagons set up shop halfway between the edge of the disc and the fire gate. Fendral was a small man, full of fast talk and jittery movements, and he sang the praises of our particular strain of Fogo Red for anyone who walked by.

My job was to hobble the trogs in case they tried to wander, but the beasts were happy to lie down and take a nap as soon as they were unhitched. Then there was nothing for Cole and I to do but pass the time and wait for our employer to make a sale. Argent enforcers watched the ends of our row for thieves or runaways, quick to turn back any curious workers who tried to wander out of our area. Sightseeing might lead to a temptation to just keep on walking and never look back.

So, I sat and observed the customers. They were mostly merchants from other realms, but from their manner, I was able to pick out people who must have been wizards who were here shopping for elements. Traders, regardless of where they were born, all wanted to haggle, and Fendral was happy to engage. The normal people, when told a price they didn't like, kept walking. I noted that though they were of different races, kingdoms, and manner of dress, the magic users could be picked out by the extra charms they wore. Enchantments were placed on metal, bone, and even wood, worn or carried in various ways, everything from nose rings to decorative spikes to hold up a lady's hair.

Most of those wizards had symbols embroidered on their clothing, usually on the chest or sleeve, which I assumed signified their particular school. I really wanted to speak with those, but couldn't think of a way to do that without having Fendrel yell at me about pestering the customers. Harassment was his job.

Instead, I observed the wizards, how they conducted themselves, how they spoke with each other, and most importantly, which direction they went after finishing their purchases. Most went the same way. Tester Pivorotto had told me the Collegium district was where most of the magical academies were located. I assumed that was where most of these mages were headed, so that was the direction I would run.

All I needed now was the opportunity. The enforcers must have been growing tired standing there all morning with so much excitement going on around them. I thought about untying one of the trogs and setting it free to rampage about, but I didn't want one of those nasty things to step on some poor innocent Core dweller.

I got my needed distraction when somebody tried to assassinate the Argent ambassador.

13

As the day went on, Mister Fendral only managed to make a few small sales, none of which required strong men to carry casks. Cole's wife had packed him a lunch. There were a few days of survival rations in my pack, but I was too nervous to eat, so instead watched the wizards buy elements, when I spotted the elf lady.

It was the white hair that caught my eye first. It wasn't like the white hair of a normal human who'd gotten old and frail, but was rather lustrous and bright. She was tall as I was, which was very tall for a woman, and then I realized she was also shockingly beautiful, perfect as the statues carved around the gate. It took me a moment to grasp the fact that her face was a bit *too* pretty, and then I saw those damned pointy ears and understood what I was looking at.

The second elf I'd ever seen was far better looking than the first one, and although she wasn't trying to rob and murder my family, I couldn't help but reflexively dislike her anyway.

When she stopped to talk to a vendor across our aisle, Cole took my staring at her the wrong way. "Ah, yes. Lovely, ain't she? There ain't no elves on the Plane of Fire."

"There's at least one," I muttered.

He must not have heard me. "Hard to believe she's probably old enough to be your great-great grandmother. Elves live forever, you know."

I started to tell him that the encyclopedia had taught me that wasn't correct, but I suppose to a miner who'd be lucky to live long enough to see his contract filled, four or five hundred years might as well be forever.

Like the other wizards, she wore the symbol of her school of magic. It was the same Elvish style writing as the pirate's makers mark, with obviously different letters and shapes. Tester Pivorotto couldn't read Elvish, but I was absolutely certain she could. As much as I didn't want to deal with an elf, I couldn't let this opportunity pass.

"I'm gonna go to talk to her."

"I admire the confidence, boy, but that woman is a *bit* above your station."

"I only want to ask her a question."

"Are you daft?"

"Maybe a little." I glanced over, Fendral was busy haggling with some stout little men who barely came up to his waist—those had to be gnomes—so I had a moment. "I'll be right back."

I left the trogs to their snoring and walked across the aisle, careful to not bump any of the shoppers. Somehow, even with her looking the opposite direction, the elf sensed my approach, and turned to give me a haughty look. "What do you want, hotlander?"

Hotlander? I didn't know if that was an insult, a compliment, or just a statement of fact. Nor did I have any idea how to speak to a high and mighty elf mage, so I dipped my head as we'd been taught to do when an Argent was around, and addressed her as politely as possible.

"If I may bother you for a moment, I have a question."

It turned out elven facial expressions were similar to those of us humans, just a bit classier, and my presence obviously annoyed her. "I already have a sufficient stock of *naur* and require no more, merchant. Do not waste my time with your offers of *special deals.*"

Naur must be what elves called Red. Before she could walk away I held up the pirate band. "I just want to know whose name is on this. It's written in Elvish and nobody where I'm from reads your language." I didn't know if that was true or not, but if there was anyone who did, they weren't talking to the likes of me. "Please."

She scowled at my impertinence but ultimately relented. I'd always been told I had an earnest face, and I must have looked extra pathetic standing there shivering in the cold.

"Fine. Let me see it." She took the band and turned it over in her remarkably delicate hands. "The spell craft upon this is potent, but hastily done."

"I think the enchanter was in a rush and making a bunch of them."

"A graduate of the Wynlyn Academy should be ashamed to produce such shoddy work."

This was the second wizard who'd applied that name to this particular charm. "Wynlyn?"

"I know this formula well, for it comes from my school." Her eyes narrowed when she found the mark. "Is this intended as some manner of insult?"

I had no idea what she was talking about. "No. I just want the name of who made that."

"It is a name, but not of a person. Rather, a place. A place most offensive to be reminded of." She tossed the band back to me, as if disgusted to have ever touched it.

I caught it. "But what's it say?"

"*Aarhobad.*"

Luckily for me, alphabetically that had been one of the first entries in the first volume of the *Encyclopedia Ettymus*. "That's the elf name for the lost realm, isn't it?"

"It is, and I do not know why anyone would invoke that foul memory to mark their craft. Good day, hotlander." With a sniff, the elf spun and walked away.

Shoving the band back in my pocket, I watched her go, confused by what this meant. Why would a murderous wizard stamp the elf name for the Realm of Time on the charms he was supplying to pirates? That made no sense.

"What are you doing, dummy, chasing off customers? Tom. *Tom!*"

It took me a moment to remember that was the alias Fendral knew me by, so I hurried back to our wagon. "Apologies, Mister Fendral."

"Get back here. These gnomish gentlemen are buying two fifty-pound casks of Red and you're going to carry those to their stall for them."

"Yes, sirs. Happy to do so." Especially since their spot was likely farther away from the eyes of the Argent enforcers so I might be able to drop the casks off and keep on walking. The gnomes were squat, strange looking little creatures, but I'd been told gnomes were extremely intelligent and hardworking—both attributes worthy of respect—so I was unfailingly polite. "I will fetch your Red, sirs."

"Hop to it, Tom," Fendral snapped at me, then he noticed something down the aisle. "Look industrious, everyone. Here comes the baron's son."

Sure enough, Fogo's supposed ambassador was strolling down our row, accompanied by his buddies and bodyguards. It was too far away to hear, but it seemed he was once again telling a story in a loud and animated way as they wandered. This man may have represented the greedy family which had kept its boot on my family's neck for generations, and his father was a right cruel bastard, but every time I'd seen Dardick thus far, he'd been jovial as could be. When he passed the elf wizard, he paused his story long enough to tip his hat at her while flashing a flirtatious smile. Her reaction to that display was even colder than the one she'd given me. Today was not her day when it came to meeting annoying *hotlanders.*

Not seeming to care in the least that he'd just been shunned by the beautiful elf, Dardick went back to his story and continued our way. "So anyways, as I was saying, after my hunting companions had gotten snatched and carried away in the other griffons' talons, the last of the beasts was perched on a ledge right over where I was hiding, hungry and searching for me!"

This story sounded slightly more plausible than the lewd tale Dardick spun through the gate, but I needed to go get the gnomes their Red. After whipping his junior traders into shape, Fendrel was standing there, trying to look successful, probably hoping to impress our nobles as they walked by.

I was picking up a cask when a spell went off, flattening everything on our aisle.

The impact flung me down. The lid popped off the cask and Red spilled everywhere as it went bouncing away. Dust and debris fell from the sky. I rolled over to see that a circle of stalls had been swept over and some merchant's air carts had been flipped. Flags whipped violently in a newly formed wind that had come seemingly out of nowhere. A great many customers had been knocked down, and those who remained standing had shimmers or glows about them, as they'd only stayed on their feet because of the automatic activation of the protective charms they wore.

From the way the wind was picking up colorful element from all the damaged stalls and spinning them into the air, this spell was in the shape of a cyclone. Our trogs croaked loudly in fear and tugged at their ropes when a sick green light formed in the middle of the cyclone. Something about the color of that light screamed *poisonous* to me.

Mind still reeling, I at least had the sense to scramble to where I'd left my pack, rip it open, find my crawler's air purifying chain, and put that around my neck. Except the green light immediately began to *dissolve* the wood and metal of the broken stalls around it. I really didn't think my little charm was going to do anything about *that*!

"It's a caustic curse," someone shouted as glowing tendrils of doom began to extend from the sickening light. "Run for your lives!"

Most people did, but a few of the wizards stood their ground, as if they were going to attempt to combat the growing menace somehow. That level of magic was far beyond my meager understanding.

Dardick Argent must have been right next to the spell when it'd gone off, because he was lying on the stones, unconscious. Even though his body was surrounded by visible rippling effects from the kind of powerful protective enchantments only nobles could afford, he'd still gotten the stuffing knocked out of him by the initial burst. Two of his bodyguards grabbed hold of his arms and began dragging him away, while the curse ate the ground right behind them.

One of the other knocked down Argent retainers wasn't so lucky. I winced when I saw what caustic magic capable of crumbling rock did when exposed to skin and the muscle beneath. That looked like a painful way to die.

Gnomes may have been small, but they were dense and low to the ground, so the two little merchants bowled me right over as they pushed past to escape. My coworker, Cole, was untying the hobbled trogs, too kind hearted to let the poor dumb beasts get killed by some nightmarish curse.

Now was my chance to run. I'd needed a distraction. An evil spell burning a hole through the great market certainly qualified! I threw my pack on and started moving with the crowd.

Except then I saw the elf woman who'd translated for me. She had been struck by one of the flipping air carts and was trapped beneath it. A glowing tendril of death was heading straight for her kicking legs.

The smart thing to do was to keep running and gain my freedom. The dumb thing to do was to rush back into the swirling maelstrom of caustic destruction to risk my life trying to help a stranger.

I didn't even hesitate.

Running back into the wind, my air enchantment automatically came on like I was back in a lava tube filling with toxic gas. The light would dissolve your flesh, but everything around the light was poisonous too. This was one nasty spell!

The remaining wizards were launching counter attacks to stymie the curse. Some shouted words that made the world shake. Others utilized wands or staves to focus their energy, or made motions with their hands, almost like our cadre's silent sign speech. There were flashes of light, cracks of thunder, even a winged serpent made of fire that flew into the cyclone before it came apart in a shower of sparks.

All I knew was that I was confused and very afraid.

"Help me!"

I ran around the green tendril of doom and found that the elf had been pinned between the cart's edge and a very solid wooden stall. Whatever protective enchantments she was wearing, they'd kept her from getting crushed on impact, but she must not have had any magic handy to grant her the extra strength sufficient to lift a few hundred pounds of cart off of her. The cart's lifter appeared to have gone out, so I squatted and grabbed hold of the iron handles on the side.

"Ready?"

"Hurry!" The spell was only a foot away from her leg now.

Fast as I could, I rose and lifted with all my might. The cart weighed *a lot*, but luckily, I'd gotten to spend my entire life moving rocks, and desperation makes you stronger. The cart barely moved a few inches, and I wasn't going to hold even that much for long. With muscles already quivering I shouted, "Go!"

She wiggled free, and the instant she was clear, I dropped the cart, and this time it slammed flat against the stone with a *bang*. Her enchantments had spared her from many broken bones, but we were still in danger.

"We need to get out of here."

Except the elf didn't run. She reached into the folds of her dress and pulled out a wand. Then she went to join the other mages trying to contain the evil spell. When she pointed the wand at the nearest tendril, it was frozen in place by a ghostly fog. That bit of the caustic curse solidified into a green slime, which then crumbled into ash and blew away on the poison cyclone.

She faced the wind and shouted, "Flee, hotlander."

That was the best idea I'd heard all day.

14

I made my way through the panicking crowd. As traders and customers tried to get away from the danger, blue uniformed watchmen ran toward it. Behind me came a terrible commotion as several more wizards joined in battling the curse.

Some of the Core folk were clearly terrified, while others stood there, dumb and disbelieving. Danger must have been a rare enough occurrence here in the market that it was easier to deny something bad was happening than it was to react to it. Everyone responded differently to danger. Some wanted to linger and gawk at the display of magic. Others turned into blubbering, crying animals the second they felt fear and became desperate to escape, even if they did it in a stupid self-defeating manner, like the one woman who ran face first into a stall.

During all this commotion, I could pick out of the crowd those who were like me, who probably came from more dangerous kingdoms. They stayed calm, moving away because they sure weren't going to stick around something that might kill them just to see the pretty lights.

"Move along. Proceed in an orderly fashion toward the bridges." A blue uniformed Core enforcer walked calmly among the mob, using some sort of magic to magnify his voice to be heard over the racket. "No shoving. There's nothing to see here."

The Core City Watch's standards were very different than mine, because I'd just seen magic melt a nobleman's face off, but I was happy to continue in an orderly fashion toward freedom and whatnot.

The market was so huge, that only a couple hundred yards away from the magic battle, the crowds here didn't even know what was going on. People were shouting questions at those of us who were obviously rushing away from something. I spotted opportunistic thieves taking advantage of the chaos to grab items off of tables while the merchants were looking the other way. I suppose in my own way, I was no different than those dishonorable trash, except instead of trinkets I was stealing back my life.

I just kept on walking.

The noise of the wind and magical attacks died off. It sounded like the wizards and watch had gotten the curse under control. With the danger seeming to have passed, the flow of the crowd slowed, and now they began to mill about, confused. There were calls for healers. Parents who'd gotten separated from their children climbed atop tables and shouted to find them, while children cried for their parents. Angry merchants demanded answers, and all the City Watch could do was try to placate the traders because they didn't know what was happening either.

"I can't believe this. Who would dare unleash dangerous magic in the market?"

"This never happens!"

"Was it an accident? It had to be an accident."

"What's the meaning of this? It's been years since anyone violated the pact."

"It's Fireday. I bet it was one of those angry hotlander savages!"

When I heard that last one, I put my hood up, kept my head down, and hurried along my way. I had no idea what was going on, and I certainly didn't want to get blamed for it. I headed in the direction I thought the Collegium would be, for that was where I intended to make my future.

After ten minutes, I still hadn't reached the edge of the market. This place was inconceivably vast. Everything my entire cadre owned would fit on a single row, and probably not sell because it was considered too shoddy. Treasures, clothing, furniture, tools, and weapons were in abundance, and the part I was walking through now was filled with so much food, all of Fogo could feast for a year straight and not make a dent in the supply.

When I looked back toward the Great Machine, distance gave me a much clearer picture of it. From here I could see a couple of the other gates. To the right of the fire gate was the water gate, which was also held aloft by two great statues, only they were not of men, but of creatures I didn't recognize. Where our gate's artistic style was fire and volcanoes, theirs was waves and fish. I'd never actually seen a real-life fish, but I'd come across drawings in the encyclopedia, so that's what I assumed those carvings were supposed to be. While the fire gate had a ramp, the water gate had an empty channel, which would surely fill tomorrow.

To the left of the fire gate was the gate which had once connected to the seventh realm, which was now barred forever. It also had a pair of massive statues holding it up, but they were both missing their heads, so I didn't know what they once represented before the fall.

From how excited or afraid the people around me were, it had been a long time since anything like this had happened in the market. This was supposed to be a place of essential commerce, where differences were put aside. The idea of violence in the market was abhorrent to them. From the conversations I overheard, there was the occasional brawl, or even a sword or gun fight between various factions and warring kingdoms who ran into each other here, but unleashing a powerful curse which would endanger so many bystanders was unheard of. It was just my dumb luck that history had been made the day I'd gotten here.

When I finally reached the edge of the market, I had to pause to take it all in. My initial guess about the shape of the market being a circular plateau around the Great Machine had been partially right, for far below me was an entire city cloaked in shadow. That shadow was cast by another floating city situated directly above it. High over that were even more neighborhoods, with huge stairways and ramps connecting those islands all the way up into the clouds.

The market's plateau was in the middle of a valley, surrounded by mountains even taller than the artificial mountain of the Great Machine in the middle. As far as I could see in every direction were buildings. Buildings were cloistered up every slope and mountainside, regardless of how steep they were, with towers reaching so high, and precariously balanced, that I didn't know how they managed to cling there. I'd been told Fort Silver would fit in one corner. That had been an understatement.

It was so overwhelming I had to look back toward the nearby dark lower city. Through it flowed many mighty rivers, not of lava, but of *water*. The closest we got to a river made of water in Fogo was the little streams that flowed from the Argent's artificial lake down into Fort Silver. Except then I realized that rather than meandering their paths because of terrain and gravity, these were straight lines. Those weren't rivers at all, but man-made canals, each with enough water in them it would take my old barge's water globe a century at maximum output to raise one of them an inch.

There were more elevated roadways connecting to this edge of the market's plateau than there were spokes on a wagon wheel, and each of those bridges was wider than the biggest avenue in Fort Silver. Some went up. Some went down. I'd seen a lot of people I'd assumed to be mages going this direction but didn't know which bridge they'd taken. When everything was so incomprehensibly fancy by my standards, I had no way of guessing which of these distant districts might be the Collegium. I'd not thought to ask Pivorotto if it was one of the flying ones.

There were hundreds of people on foot alongside wagons, air carts, and people riding various types of animals, all of which seemed nicer and cleaner than our mucus coated trogs. There were even wheeled carriages powered by magic that had no drivers, but seemed to move about on some predetermined schedule, picking up passengers. From here, the many tons of goods which had been purchased in the market today were now being dispersed out into the rest of the city.

As much as I wanted to flee the market, I stopped for a while to watch. Even as big as the market's plateau was, it still overspilled its boundaries, and there were stalls and vendor wagons set up on all the bridges too. There didn't appear to be any Argent agents nearby, so I should be safe. In a place so crowded, quiet was a relative thing, but I found the most secluded spot I could, at the end of a row near a bridge, and leaned against a rail overlooking the shadowed neighborhood below. The nearest stall was selling books, and it took all my willpower to restrain myself from browsing. I only had a handful of Core money that I'd been able to scrounge up over the last year in Fogo, and I'd be a fool to spend any of that yet.

Excitement and walking had kept me warm. Now that I was being still, the cold set back in, chilling me to the bone. I couldn't imagine how the Core folk lived like this. Most of them were walking around with bare arms as if this weather was pleasant. Thankfully, my heavy clothing didn't stand out that much, as there were some who proved equally as uncomfortable as me, or perhaps they just wore robes, gloves, and masks which hid their entire form out of some sense of modesty. There were even a few tall, grey-skinned people who wore devices over their faces that enabled them to breathe. I wondered what realm they came from.

An hour after the cursing, the place returned to what was probably considered normal around here. It was amazing that someone had died nearby not too long ago, and the people were still gossiping and guessing about what happened, but already most had gone back to conducting their business.

The section Fendral Company had gotten put in must have catered to a more magical clientele, because obvious mages were fewer here, and a lot of the Core's wealthier citizens—at least I assumed they were because of the niceness and cleanliness of their clothing—wore various enchantments. I may have been inexperienced in this realm, but I noted they still had rich and poor here, just like home, and the rich tended to come and go from the upper bridges, while the poor tended toward the ones sloping downhill.

Wizards were wealthy, so logically reaching the Collegium meant going up. I picked the most likely bridge and set out on my quest for glory.

There was a city enforcer standing near the entrance to that particular bridge, and though I'd done nothing that I thought to be suspicious, he took note of me and began walking my way.

I immediately stuck my hands in my pockets, kept my eyes down, and tried to look innocent.

"Hold up."

"Me?"

"Yeah, you. I'm talking to you, hotlander."

I thought about running, but figured enforcers would be like Elementals, where if you run, they'd be compelled by instinct to chase you. If I looked guilty of something he'd assume I was guilty of something. So I tried to stay calm and put on a friendly face as I smiled and asked, "What can I do for you, enforcer?"

"The title's Watchman." He had the face of a man who'd stopped a great many fists with his nose, and he looked me over as if he suspected me of all manner of heinous crimes. "There was a ruckus back on row twenty earlier involving some Fogo folk. Were you among them?"

The nature of my clothing and paleness of my skin must have marked me for what I was. There was no use pretending I was from somewhere else. "I'm here from Fogo, but I wasn't there for that. What happened?"

"Word is someone attempted to assassinate your ambassador with some foul magic. Luckily, it got contained before it could spread and cause too much damage. You wouldn't know who'd be inclined to try something like that here, would you?"

"I don't." But since I doubted he believed me, in my pocket I found the small bag of Red I'd brought with me and pinched a bit of it between my thumb and forefinger. "Terribly sorry."

"Uh huh… Regardless, how about you come with me back to the scene so my inspector can ask you a few questions."

"I'd love to, but I can't." I pulled my hands out of my pockets and held them out apologetically, hoping he wouldn't notice one of them had just gotten dusted in Red. "I'm supposed to pick up a delivery around here. If I'm late, my boss will get angry."

"Your merchant can wait." The watchman was done messing around and placed one hand on his truncheon. "Let's go."

I concentrated on the dust. I'd only managed to teach myself a handful of spells, but I'd gotten this one down to where it worked most of the time. If it fizzled I'd get a club to the head and then probably a trip back through the gate in chains. If it worked, I was going to run like hell.

It worked.

The Red dust became agitated, floated off my skin, and ignited in a flash. I wasn't using enough of it to stick and burn anything, but it was really hot and bright. I called my creation *Carnavon's Shroud of Fire* and was rather proud of it.

I'd not intended to hurt anyone, but forgot that a little burst of fire energy someone from Fogo would consider mildly disorienting might be downright terrifying to a Core dweller. The watchman was probably a tough guy in a fight, but the heat clearly scared the hell out of him because he leapt back, crashing into a few shoppers, and all of them went down in a flailing mess of limbs, as he screamed, "I'm blind! I'm blind!" over and over.

"It's only temporarily!" I shouted. "Sorry!"

I ran for the upper bridge I thought might take me to the Collegium, but there were more blue uniforms farther down it, and they were looking this direction to see what all the yelling was about. So, I turned to the left and went to the next road bridge. This one went downward and had less traffic. I figured I could run downhill faster than up, so I took it.

The last couple of years I'd spent running after or from angry Elementals, across surfaces far more treacherous than gently sloping stone, so I was very quick. I bolted between the people carrying their purchases, ran past carts pulled by domesticated animals or human muscle. There didn't seem to be any magical transportation on this path.

There was shouting above. I assumed the City Watch were chasing me, but didn't dare look back. To do so meant slowing down. I tried really hard to not crash into anyone and was mostly successful. Those I wasn't, yelled at me and shook their fists.

A few hundred feet down the plateaus side was another platform with an intersection of roads. I stopped there, breathing hard, turning in a circle, trying to decide which way to go. There were permeant buildings here, similar to the worker barracks in Fort Silver. The people on this platform looked a whole lot rougher than those I'd seen in the market, and some of them even seemed bemused by my predicament.

"Oi!" There was a little old lady sitting on a stool there, trying to sell a basket of wilted vegetables. "You running from the blue and coppers, newcomer?"

Was I that obvious? "Yes, ma'am."

"Lucky for you I hate those bossy bastards. Don't go that way." She shook her head at the level path. "Best head down there." She pointed at the lower road. "Watchmen might go into the Slump sometimes, but they don't ever go into the Under Slump, 'cause that's Latrocinium territory."

I didn't know what any of those things were, but it seemed like sound advice. "Thank you."

I ran another half a mile downhill, and there was no sign of any pursuit. The road got worse, with pot hole puddles and cracks big enough for real plants to grow out of. There were no more merchant stalls here, replaced by tents and beggars. People were looking at me funny, so I slowed to a quick walk. It grew steadily darker, not because of the lateness of the day, but because I was heading into the shadow of the floating city directly above us.

A metal sign had been set next to the road, with a message engraved upon it in several different languages. The sign had been here long enough to be almost completely rusted over to the point of illegibility. I could barely read the version in the trade tongue which announced that this district had been officially condemned by the Council, all residents needed to vacate immediately, if you entered you did so at your own risk, and they bore no responsibility for your safety. The date of this proclamation was nearly fifty years ago.

There was a big stone arch over the road, and engraved upon it was *Lower Aventine.*

Someone had roughly painted over the old name *Welcome to the Under Slump.*

15

The difference was so stark, I might as well have walked through another gate into an entirely different realm. If that was the case, then the Under Slump was the elemental plane of poverty. From the little bit I'd taken in, it made the nastiest parts of Fort Silver sound pleasant. It was wreckage, trash, graffiti, and bums far as I could see. How the hell was I only a few miles from the splendor of the Great Machine?

We had slums on Fogo, but I understood the nature of the people who ended up there. Those hopeless places were for oath breakers, or those too dumb, lazy, or violent to maintain a membership in a cadre or mining company. They wound up living together, with the dregs scratching out a mean existence however they could, which often involved a brick to your head before helping themselves to your scrip.

The Under Slump had that same kind of despair about it, just a hundred times bigger, and I was an alien here. The ways of these people were foreign. While I knew how to keep from getting robbed or murdered in Fort Silver, this place was a mystery. I'd have to be stupid to go in there.

Only I'd just thrown magical fire in a watchman's face, so I certainly wasn't going to turn back. It was venture into this destitute warren or risk getting caught and sent back to Fogo in chains.

So into the Under Slump I went.

Everything was dim here in the shade. The district that floated above was appallingly close and blocked most of the sunlight. Looking up at untold millions of tons of rock, held aloft only by gravity defying magic, filled me with a sense of impeding dread. It felt as if the whole thing might fall and crush me at any time without warning. *Splat.*

What would it be like to live beneath that weight? I'd barely arrived, and having a whole town threatening to smash me was already fraying my nerves. I felt pity for the people who called this place home, and I'd spent most of my life on top of barely crusted over lava.

And it appeared *thousands* of people lived here. I couldn't believe how crowded the Under Slump was. Most of the residents appeared human, though they must have hailed from a hundred different kingdoms from how different they looked. There were also gnomes, dwarves, and a few other things I wasn't sure what they were, like the very large blacksmith with four arms, which was apparently quite handy for using a pair of tongs and two hammers simultaneously.

The big buildings here must have been rather nice once, as most were carved from a pale white stone and featured graceful pillars and arches. Except they hadn't been maintained for a long time. Everything was crumbling or decaying away. Vines grew up the walls. There were plinths where there had clearly been statues once, but those were missing now. I guessed all the decorations had probably gotten stolen and sold in the market above.

Between the ancient buildings of stone were hundreds of smaller structures of wood, thrown together in the most haphazard manner possible. Between those homes and shops, ran dirty children and skinny dogs. I knew what dogs were, because there were a few of them in Fort Silver. Wood and wire pens made several appearances, holding flocks of feathered animals with twitching heads. Those had to be birds, and since these looked plump and good for eating, they were probably chickens or pigeons or turkeys or something. I'd never seen a bird in real life, but my barge had gotten shipments of their dried meat, and it'd been pretty good.

With plans interrupted, I needed to figure out how to make my way through this dismal place and find the Collegium. Walking without a plan would only get me more lost. There was some trash burning in a pit, so I stopped there to warm my hands while I oriented myself.

Looking straight up made me nauseous. This was how a bug must have felt before a boot smashed it flat. The underbelly of the floating neighborhood was clearly visible, down to the pipes that must have served as its sewer. Some of those leaked. I turned my view back to the street level, which though threatening, was far more calming than the sole of that epic boot.

There were clotheslines strung between the various buildings, and a matronly woman came out of a shack to hang up some shirts to dry.

"Excuse me, ma'am."

"What you want?" she snapped at me, but I was just glad she still spoke the trade tongue down here. "I got nothin' for the likes of you."

"I'm just asking for directions. Do you know how to get to the Collegium?"

"Why? That's wizard town. You want to see the big time mage fights? Nobody here can afford tickets to those. Them's for the entertainments of fancy folk. We got our own gladiators down here, only they ain't snobs."

"I just need to know how to get there."

"Back that way, up the road, up the ramp, take a left. Up to the market, next road on the right."

Which was as I'd feared, because that was how I'd gotten here, and it would probably be crawling with watchmen ready to roust anyone who looked like they were from Fogo. "Is there another route?"

"I suppose. That a ways." She gestured deeper into the Under Slump. "Other side of the neighborhood, when you get out of the shade, go up the back slope to the Slump, then cross over from there. But you go that way you got to pay the Latros a toll."

"Who are the Latros?"

"The Latrocinium. Carcalla's boys." She looked at me like I was stupid. "Carcalla runs both Slumps. Best to stay on his good side, newcomer. You cross the Latros they'll feed you to the hogs."

That sounded rather ominous. "Thanks for the directions."

I went around the corner, found a spot I thought was away from prying eyes, and got out Gax's handgun. The holster and belt would stay hidden beneath my coat easy enough, so I buckled on the rig, loaded the gun, then holstered it. I had no idea who Carcalla or his Latrocinium was, but I knew the best way to avoid trouble in Fort Silver had been to not look like easy prey. It was better to look like it would take effort to hurt you, and best to look like you didn't have anything to make that effort worth it. I assumed this place would be similar.

Little had I realized, the woman followed me around the corner, and she laughed when she saw me putting the gun away. "You aiming to get yourself killed, boy?"

"No, ma'am. I'm not. Hence the gun." I also had my knife, some Red, and a couple snail grenades, but I'd brought those to try and impress magical academies with my spell craft, not win a gang fight.

"You pull that little thing on a Latro, they're gonna eat you whole and shit out your bones. Just go the easy way or pay your taxes." She wandered back to her clothes hanging. "Damned salty tempered hotlanders. You people are always looking to fight everybody at the drop of a hat, I swear."

"Hang on. Wait." That sounded personal and way too on point. "You know someone else from Fogo?"

"I don't know what part of fire they hail from, but the Roches and Skerrets live over on Rellotis Street in the crumpled house."

I didn't know those family names, but there were a lot of barge cadres in Fogo. "Which way is that?"

She pointed. "Go six blocks. You'll know it when you see it."

Feeling a bit more confident now that I was armed, I went the direction she'd indicated. The whole way was just more squalor and ruin. The air was filled with smoke, not from volcanos, but from cooking fires and workshops, and the city overhead blocked any clearing breeze. It was so difficult to breathe, I was tempted to use my air charm again, but noticed hardly anybody in the Under Slump wore anything enchanted, so flashing a charm would probably just make me a target for robbery.

Even without a show of magic, I was still a target. I was an obvious outsider in a savage and apparently lawless place, carrying a pack which could potentially have something of value in it. I tried to move with confidence, as if I was supposed to be here and knew right where I was going. Idle young men watched me pass by, but they must have been feeling too lethargic to harass a stranger.

Cadre tradition demanded that when you came across a traveler from another barge, you offered them your hospitality, and then helped them on their way, no matter what. I could only hope that those old ways were still practiced among the Fogo folk here, because I could really use some help.

Rellotis Street must have been a mighty thoroughfare once, for it was wide and straight, with gigantic buildings on both sides, though a few had fallen down. People still lived in the rubble anyway, and wooden shacks sprung up between the great stones. Most of those didn't even have roofs, but they probably didn't get much rain, on account of being stuck beneath another neighborhood that felt like it was about to fall and smash us at any moment.

I *really* didn't like it here.

The crumbled house was as obvious as the lady had suggested. It must have been really tall once, but the bottom of the Slump had sunk down enough to crush the upper floors. Logically I understood magic was keeping it afloat, but seeing all that rock resting on one damaged mansion created the illusion that this one spot was holding the whole thing up.

Not knowing what else to do, I went up the steps to where several bums were loafing aimlessly, and announced, "I'm looking for the Roches or the Skerrets."

Most of them ignored me, but one dwarf with a filthy grey beard looked up from his stupor. "Who's asking?"

"You can tell them it's a Carnavon of Barge 519, come to pay his respects to other Fogo folk."

"Ah, fresh out the gate, are you?" He got up. "Well come on then. I'll introduce you."

Inside the crumpled house, many of the walls were missing. Dozens of people lived in here, with whole families in each room, separated by nothing more than hanging blankets. The rough and crowded nature of the place reminded me a bit of a barge. No wonder Fogo folk had settled here.

Except a cadre took pride in their barges and kept them clean, unlike this place where every corner was piled trash. And we trusted each other, like an extended family, and only the most dishonorable among us would ever dare steal from someone else on their barge. Here, it looked like everyone kept their valuables close. Those sleeping laid on top of their purses. We had mice and rats in Fort Silver, for vermin always found a way to sneak through the gates, but I'd never seen so many as I did scurrying about here, and these animals were big and defiant compared to ours.

The mansion must have been decorated with statues and paintings once, but everything of value had been stripped, and that art replaced with crude drawings on every available surface. A few were pictures, usually of a vulgar nature, but mostly it seemed to be just people writing their names, as if desperate to leave some proof they'd ever existed at all.

The dwarf led me through what must have once been a grand ballroom, now filled with tents, and a wooden table where a man was chopping meat with a cleaver. There were flies buzzing all over his wares.

"What happened to this place?"

"Eh? Same as it ever was," the dwarf said.

"No, I mean this whole part of the Hub City, the Under Slump. The Core is supposed to be a place of glory and wealth, where magic is everywhere, and up above it looks that way, but this…" I gestured at the bleak mess. "Why?"

"I suppose they only tell you realmers about the good parts they're proud of. They don't tell you what happens when all that mighty magic starts breaking down. This place used to be real nice, until the Upper Aventine started to slump. Decent folks moved away. It's been getting a bit closer every year. One day, the last of that magic will let go and we'll be flat." The dwarf giggled at the thought.

"Why don't they fix it?"

"Oh, newcomer, you've got a lot to learn about the real world. I hope you live long enough to learn it." He stopped at a doorway and held out his open palm.

I thought he was trying to shake hands, which the encyclopedia said was a custom of greeting or farewell demonstrating mutual respect in many realms, except he reacted oddly when I grabbed his hand and squeezed it. Which was when I realized he'd been asking for money for guiding me here.

"Sorry. I can't afford to give you anything." Which was true enough, as I only had a few Core coins to my name, and no idea how to earn any more in this place.

"Figures." He shook his head in disgust as he plucked his hand away and wiped it on his trousers, like I was the dirty one in this transaction. "Anyways, Skerrets own this part. Good luck."

I went inside. The windowless hall was dark but there was a light at the end. Broken glass crunched under my boots. It smelled bad in here, and I thought about saying to hell with this and turning back, but voices sounded ahead, and unlike all the strange accents I'd been hearing all day, these sounded closer to home.

I entered the light to find several men sitting around a table, drinking and playing cards. Their skin no longer had the paleness of a sunless existence, but they retained the general look of my people. They all scowled at me and moved as if reaching for weapons, but I was quick to raise my open hands in the cadre sign for friendship.

"Easy, friends. I'm just passing through. It's good to see someone from home."

"Who the hell are you supposed to be?" one of them at the table asked suspiciously.

"I'm just a traveler. I came through the fire gate today."

"Barge and family?" Another demanded.

I noted there was a big 373 painted on the wall behind them. These weren't Fort dwellers. They were from a barge cadre like me. There would be no fake names used here, because they'd surely see right through my lies.

"519, crashed and burned, may Saint Persistence guide their souls. Family Carnavon. I'm Ozwald, son of Myles."

"A Carnavon, you say?" the man at the head of the table slowly mused. He was the oldest present, bald, with a big black beard, and the way everyone paid attention as he spoke, that told me this was the head of the family. "Is that so?"

"Yes, sir. Mr. Skerret, I'm assuming?"

As he nodded, I saw there were more men coming in from a side door I'd not noticed before. Then I heard the crunch of broken glass as somebody walked up the hall behind me. One picked up a hefty stick from a pile of firewood. They were downright hostile for some reason, as if this cold place had smothered the hospitality right out of them. This sure wasn't the warm welcome I'd been expecting from Fogo folk.

"I was just hoping to find someone who'd give me some advice about navigating this city, as I'm unfamiliar with its ways, but if I'm intruding, I'll happily leave you to your business."

"Oh, it's no intrusion, Mr. Carnavon," said the headman. "It must feel good to have finally bought out your contract… unless of course, you skipped out?"

Well, maybe I would lie a *little*, as it wouldn't surprise me if the crafty Argents paid rewards for the return of runaways… and the logical place for a runaway to seek shelter would be among their countrymen. I sure wished I'd thought of that before walking in here.

It would be supremely dishonorable for cadremen to turn on their own in such a treacherous way, but so far, the Skerrets weren't striking me as a kindly bunch.

"My contract was satisfied as of last Deathday. I'm a free man now."

"Good for you, lad. You must be a hard worker to accomplish that so young." Skerret's smile didn't make it to his eyes. "Though I must say, I find it an odd coincidence that only a few hours after someone tried to murder the big dumb Argent boy in the market, a stranger shows up out of nowhere to ask us some innocent questions."

"A stranger with some magic upon him, at that," one of the men off to my side said. Which meant he was probably of the first rank or above to be able to sense my hidden charms.

They were tensing up for violence. "I may have pocketed a few souvenirs from my time in the Argent's service before I left, but I assure you, gentlemen, that I've got nothing to do with that attempted murder."

"Of course you didn't, *watchman*," said the magic one. "That's why you're here checking on us, who've agitated against the Argents."

"You can't be serious? See this face? Does this look like the face of a man who basks in the glorious sunlight to you?"

"An Argent enforcer then. One of the devil Gaul Haddar's men, searching for whoever tried to kill his boss's heir."

It didn't surprise me that Haddar's reputation for brutal thoroughness made it through both sides of the gate. "I swear I've got nothing to do with them."

There was a bad energy in the air, that kind of feeling you get right before things go horribly wrong, as if I'd just stepped on what I'd thought was solid crust, but could now hear the hissing lava beneath.

"I'll level with you, Mr. Skerret. I didn't earn out my contract. I'm a runaway looking for sanctuary. I was working for a merchant. When that curse went off in the market, I bolted."

Except he must have given a hand signal I'd not caught, because they looked ready to beat me down.

"He came alone," said the unseen man in the hall behind me.

At that confirmation, the boss nodded for his boys to proceed.

And everybody started hitting me.

16

The one with the big stick swung for my knees, but I managed to jump aside. Unfortunately, the one coming from behind kidney punched me, and while I stumbled, the low-level wizard slugged me in the cheek. Sweet Saint Olga, that hurt. The punches came in fast after that, from too many directions, and though I blocked a few, that damnable stick caught me over the head and left me seeing stars. I went to my knees.

The magic one grabbed a handful of my hair and pulled back hard. "Who sent you?"

"Nobody."

He looked to his boss, who clearly wasn't buying it. "Beat him 'til he talks."

Except when they went to do so, I grabbed the wizard's hand and twisted his thumb back until he squealed and let go. I punched the next one in the balls, stood up, shoved him away, then turned and popped the hallway guy right in the snout.

They'd probably expected me to lay there and cower, but we Carnavons were no strangers to brawling. Our family heritage consisted of spiteful determination, thick skulls, and fists of stone.

The stick nailed me again, this time in the back, but I caught the next incoming swing. Despite how the wood stung my palm, I locked on with a miner's grip and wouldn't let go when he tugged. Stick boy was surprised by that, and even more surprised when my fist knocked his front teeth out. Magic man grabbed my coat. I threw an elbow, finding his nose with it. He landed on the table, which collapsed, throwing drinks, cards, and coins in every direction.

Three more of the Skerret boys who'd been sitting there sprang up to join in, while their family boss watched, seemingly annoyed by the show. There were a bunch of them, and one of me, so I ran like I had an Elemental trying to eat me.

The one in the hallway attempted to block my way, but he was dizzy from getting his nose flattened, so I rolled right over him. Sadly, I landed on some of that damnable glass I'd been stepping on earlier, which cut into my knees as I slid across the floor. That was the least of my problems right then, so I bounded back up and kept going, mob of Skerrets right behind me.

So much for our traditions of hospitality.

Once out of the dark, I ran through the crumpled house. On the bright side, despite being the Skerret's neighbors, the other residents of the giant hovel didn't intercept me, and nobody was inclined to get involved to help them. On the downside, none were going to help me either.

I was heading for the front door when I spotted a couple men coming up the stairs from the street. A Skerret chasing me shouted, "Yo, Roche, grab that fool!"

These two also had the look of Fogo folk, and they'd certainly help their kin beat the hell out of me, so I didn't even give them the chance to think about the sudden request and crashed right through them. I had elevation and momentum on my side, so they went tumbling down the stairs. I tripped, rolled the last few painful steps, and popped right back up, sprinting down Rellotis Street.

The dwarf who'd guided me to the Skerrets was lying at the bottom of the steps again, and he shouted after me, "You should'a tipped me a coin. I would'a warned you they were a gang of cut throat scum!"

The Skerrets caught sight of me, and the race was on. I had to push my way between the humble crowds. My pursuers didn't have that problem, because from the bloody noses, split lips, and anger in their voices the locals knew to get out of their way or else.

We kept running for a couple blocks. My heart was pounding and they were gaining on me. My only hope was to get out of view. I wasn't going to do that on the main street, so I took a left at the next alley. It was filled with trash and rats. Thrashing my way to the end, I hid around the corner of a pile of bricks. The instant I stopped, my lungs rebelled against the putrid air and I started coughing. I had to activate my air charm just to keep breathing.

One of them must have seen me dip into the alley, or one of the local witnesses pointed out where I'd gone, because they came in after me, leaving me no choice but to run again. I went down the alley and turned onto the next street. Then the next. Then I had to double back and take a different alley when I noticed one of the Skerrets had gotten ahead of me somehow. This place was a maze. And they knew it well, while I didn't.

I spied stairs leading downward to an even lower, darker level. Taking those, slipping and sliding, I nearly broke my ankles because the stones were slick with green slimy mold, which wasn't something we had to deal with back home.

The people of this lower level of the Under Slump were even poorer and sadder than those above; an impossible achievement if ever there was one. There were also fewer humans. A couple of skinny orcs bought bowls of stew served up from a big pot by a hunched over frog-faced creature dressed in rags. There were strange, extremely hairy, gnome sized things, and they immediately retreated into their shacks as I ran past. I took cover behind a mound of garbage to catch my breath.

I didn't know how to get out of here, but there were more stairs to the side, even narrower and slicker than the last set, going down to an even deeper, darker level. I *really* didn't want to have to go farther down. From what I'd read, beneath the Core City lay the ruins of the ancient civilization that predated the Nexus, and nowadays, those dark caverns were a lost underworld of old magical experiments and degenerate monsters.

Cut throats or not, Skerrets and Roches must be nearly as stubborn as Carnavons, because they came down the stairs after me. When the orcs saw the first of them arrive, they made threatening gestures and shouted unintelligible slurs. More humans kept coming until the orcs were severely outnumbered, so they wisely took their supper bowls and walked away.

The boss, Skerret, yelled a question at the frog-thing, who croaked in fear and promptly pointed right at where I was hiding.

Well… down it was.

I didn't even make it twenty steps before I lost my footing and ended up bumping and sliding all the way to the bottom on my ass. Getting up, it was so dark down here, that if I tried to keep running, I'd surely break my neck. Slowing to a stumbling walk, I kept my hands extended in front of me. A crawler's light charm was in my pack, but there was no time to find it, and turning on a light down here would only serve as a beacon telling the Skerrets exactly where to go to beat me to death.

And murder me they certainly would, because I'd bloodied some of them and led them on a chase in front of many witnesses. The Under Slump was a whole lot bigger and worse than the nastiest parts of Fort Silver, but I reasoned there were some universal truths when it came to gangs, and one of them was that they couldn't abide losing face. They'd worked too hard not to kill me right now. I didn't know what kind of criminals they were, but surely they were up to something nefarious to be that worried about secret watchmen or enforcers spying on them.

Sure enough, a light source was moving down the stairs. From the white color, it was magic, so at least one of them had a charm that would enable them to spot me. The treacherous steps slowed them down a bit, but they'd be on my trail again soon.

There was some light ahead, so I stumbled along in that direction. It turned out to be coming from a metal grate in the ceiling. Above came the noise of people walking, having normal conversations, and going about their business. That little bit of extra light coming from the upper level didn't make me feel any better, because it revealed an unnerving scene all around me. There were animal bones everywhere. A gigantic rat was gnawing one of the bones, and when it saw me, it stood up on its hind legs and ran away, still holding the bone in its hands.

Yes. *Hands*. I'd not known there were rats with hands. The Core was full of surprises.

I kept going. The predominate sound here was water dripping. A cold drop hit my neck and rolled down inside my shirt, which was so uncomfortable that I'd rather have gotten showered by sparks. My feet splashed into a puddle, and with each step, the water kept getting deeper and deeper. It rose over the tops of my boots and instantly soaked my feet. When the water was up to my knees I had no choice but to stop. From the sound of all the water moving, this must have been an underground part of that giant canal system I'd seen from above. If I tried to cross it, I'd surely drown.

The magical light was getting closer. "Give it up, Carnavon," someone shouted. "Unless you can hold your breath a real long time and swim real good, which we know you can't because there ain't no swimming in Fogo, you're trapped."

I was scared, blind, and freezing, but that threat made me angry. This wasn't a *trap*. I'd spent the last few years trapping deadly Fire Elementals. Trapping was a test of skill, courage, and wits. They were just a bunch of bullies who'd gotten lucky I didn't know the terrain, and their only threat came from their sheer numbers. Calling that a trap was an insult to my profession.

If it was a fight they wanted, then it was a fight they'd have. So I waded back onto dry land and clumsily moved to the side until I found a low stone wall I could crouch behind. That would be my fortress. I knelt there, took my pack off, and began groping about in the dark for my enchantments.

One of the Skerret's shouted in surprise, and there was a rattle of bones. "Damned ratlets! Scram."

So that's what the little rat-men must be called, which was some useless trivia to file away before my murder, but I just focused on getting my enchantments ready. Some of them were Argent issue, like the light charm or the necklace which purified the air in front of my face. Others were of my own invention, like the shroud of fire, my handful of steel screws, or the snail grenades.

"I tried to be nice," I shouted toward the approaching light. "I didn't want any trouble, but you had to go and break cadre traditions. I don't know what trogshit barge you come from, but that's not how it's done where I'm from."

"Don't get all high and mighty with us about traditions, kid. The bargemaster who got my family exiled from our cadre was a Carnavon."

We had cousins all over the place, and a bad tendency to end up in positions of responsibility, so that wasn't too much of a surprise. "Did you deserve it?"

"Well, yeah, but that's besides the point."

The fact I'd challenged them made them slow down a bit. Now that their magical light was nearer, I could see it was a wide tunnel I'd been wandering down, about ten yards across, probably built for drainage. When I glanced behind me, there was nothing but dark water and a tunnel roof that gradually came down to meet it. I wasn't getting out that way. Mr. Skerret hadn't been lying about that. My air charm could filter poison, but I really doubted it would be able to keep my lungs from filling with water. A tunnel seemed a fitting place for me to fight to the death, because I'd spent most of my life expecting to die in a tunnel. I'd just always thought I'd die surrounded by lava, not water. Probably roasted by a gurgler, not mangled by the hands of my countrymen.

"We don't have to do this. I'm no watchman. I ran from them today. That's how I ended up here. I'm not an enforcer either. I despise the Argents. I skipped out on my contract. I'm not spying for them."

"Even if you're telling the truth, we're a bit past that now, kid."

I drew Gax's pistol. Hopefully the wax coating on the paper shells had protected the cartridges from getting wet. When I cocked the hammer, the metal-on-metal noise was very loud inside the tunnel.

"He's got a gun," one of them warned.

"Damned right I do!"

"So do we," Mr. Skerret responded. And there were at least three or four *clacks* as their weapons were readied. "And we got more."

That development wasn't surprising in the least. "You all can surely kill me, but I swear to Ketekunan, Saint of Persistence, that I will take some of you with me."

"If we're invoking powerful figures now, even the dreaded Carcalla respects our hold on the crumpled house. We run that part of the Under Slump. You think any of my boys are scared of getting shot by some lowly bargeman?"

"Go to hell. I'm a trapper."

"Ah, we got us a lava walking man of danger here. So you probably know how to shoot pretty good then, Mr. Carnavon?"

"I killed a few pirates the first day I fired a rifle, Mr. Skerret, and that was a long time back. Fucking try me."

With gun in one hand and snail shell in the other, I risked a glance over the top of my little fort. My foes were just shadows in front of the white light. I'd been hoping they were clumped together enough I could hit them all with a snail grenade, but they'd wisely spread out from one end of the tunnel to the other, so that was unlikely.

I ducked back down to reevaluate my plan, but they'd spotted me.

"No use hiding. Come out and take your beating like a man."

"I'm not hiding. This is what we call a *defensive position.*"

He laughed. "I like you, kid. But you're either lying to us, so you're a threat and somebody means to try and pin that assassination attempt on us. Or you're telling the truth, and I can turn you over to the Argent's for a sizable bounty. We get this over with fast I can even get you back to the market before the gate closes… Dean?"

"Yeah, boss?" I recognized that voice as being the one who knew some magic.

"Fry his ass."

The wall in front of me exploded.

The wave of force threw me back into the water. Gravel that had been pulverized from the rocks splashed down around me. All I could see was a blue streak from the flash that had accompanied his spell.

Saints, this wasn't even a real wizard! This was some scrub gangster trash nobody, and that was still one of the most powerful spells I'd ever seen. I'd been deluded to think I could come here and make it as a mage.

Except in that moment, the only future I could afford to think about was measured in seconds, not years. Still underwater, I concentrated on the snail shell clutched in my fist, activated the embedded Red, and thrashed my way back upright. I came out spitting nasty water and incoherent curses.

Half blind, all I could make out was shapes moving my way, laughing at my misfortune.

I hurled the snail shell out between them. It hit the ground and bounced. It must have begun glowing because one of them shouted, "Scatter!"

I pointed Gax's handgun at the moving shape I thought was their wizard. Even if I could see the sights, which I couldn't on account of the bad light and the flash that scalded my eyes, I'd never fired Gax's pistol before, so I had no idea how accurate it was. By faith and instinct I pulled the trigger. The *boom* was incredibly loud in the enclosed space. I was rewarded with a yelp, but if it was from an actual impact, or just the surprise of a near miss, I didn't know.

With my snail grenade about to cook off, I lay back beneath the water, broke open the pistol's action, and pulled out the ruined case. When I got another paper cartridge from the loops on Gax's belt it felt softened by the water. I could only hold my breath and pray the wax seal kept the powder dry.

The snail grenade was even louder than the gunshot, and even beneath the water, I still felt the *whump* against my ears.

Pistol reloaded, I came up gasping to find the Skerret's light charm had been dropped in a puddle. Between the rippling water and fresh smoke, crazy flickering lights were being cast on the walls. Some of my foes had thrown themselves down to try and avoid the grenade and probably made it in time, but one man began screaming, "Me thumbs gone! He blew me thumb off!"

"Shut up and shoot him!"

I cocked the hammer and pointed the pistol at the blurry shape who bellowed that order.

Click.

So much for the quality waterproofing of a plane that had almost no water.

I dropped back down. There were a series of *bangs* as I crawled through the water back behind the remains of the wall. There were splashes as bullets hit. Then one bounced off the rock next to my head and the deformed projectile sped off with a whine.

The barrage stopped. I risked a peek. While some of them were reloading, the others were approaching, probably with knives to carve me up. They were spread out, so I might only hit only one or two with my remaining grenade, and it was useless against the closer ones without blowing myself up with them.

"You're a dead man, Carnavon!"

Sad part was, Mr. Skerret was most certainly right about that. I pulled a handful of Red infused screws from my pocket and concentrated on activating their magic. They immediately began to warm, and within a second were hot enough to burn my skin. Thank goodness Red was waterproof! Then I tossed the screws over the wall.

I called this particular creation, *Carnavon's Screws of Chaos.* When I'd first discovered this combination, I'd set fire to our trapper's camp and nearly scared poor Harrison Killroy to death. My brother, Robert, had not been pleased. I'd gotten most of the kinks worked out since.

The screws hit, bounced, and began emitting a whistling noise, before they started to careen about wildly under their own energy. They weren't nearly as fast as bullets, but they were red hot, furious, and flying about out of control. When they hit water they hissed and died in a puff of steam—which was not something I'd ever been able to test before—but the ones that hit clothing or skin tended to stick and burn.

Skerrets and Roches cried out as they were bitten by the angry chunks of metal. The ones who'd been closest threw themselves into the water to try and quench the flames. There was a lot of splashing and yelling.

I was feeling pretty cocky about the effectiveness of my spell craft, until their wizard hit me with that blue spell again. The rest of my shelter disintegrated and I was flung back hard against the tunnel wall. He must have only known one spell, but he was certainly good at it!

With everything bruised, I hit the water in a deeper spot and panicked, flailing, when I didn't immediately touch the bottom. I couldn't breathe! My feet touched something solid, and it took everything I had to struggle back toward solid ground. I got my head above water and briefly gasped for air.

A Skerret threw a rock and hit me in the side of the head. Reeling, I went back under. I was blacking out. I was going to drown.

Except something bumped me underwater, sliding smoothly past. Whatever it was, it was big, and it was *fast.* It also must have noticed my pathetic kicking, because a very strong hand grabbed hold of my arm and dragged me to where I could touch the ground, before letting go.

As I crawled onto the ground, coughing and gagging, head spinning, barely holding on to consciousness, I slowly realized there were angry, wounded Skerrets all around me, pointing guns and brandishing knives.

It was over.

"To hell with the Argent's reward. We're gonna take this pain in the ass, saw his head off, and take it back to the crumpled house to hang on the wall as a trophy."

"My pleasure, boss." One of them knelt next to me with a fat blade in hand, but then he stopped, steel inches from my neck, as he noticed something moving in the water. "Oh shit."

A grey fin was slowly rising above the surface.

"It's that squalo!" one of them cried.

"Nobody make any sudden moves. Back away from the water, real slow."

The thug who'd been about to cut my throat stepped back gingerly, with a look of utter terror on his face. He cringed when his boots made a splash. The fin just stayed there, unmoving.

Some were pointing their guns at the fin, or more likely, the creature it was attached to, hidden beneath the surface.

"Don't shoot it, idiots," the family headman ordered. "Their skin's too thick. You'll just make it angry."

Not knowing what a squalo was to strike such fear into a band of murderers, I lay there, mostly submerged and perfectly still, as the Skerrets carefully backed away.

"Should we put a bullet into Carnavon at least?"

"Are you stupid?" the boss hissed. "It must have smelled his blood in the water and been hungry enough to come looking. You spill more blood you're likely to drive it into a feeding frenzy and it'll kill half the neighborhood. Leave him to get eaten and keep walking."

One of them picked up their light charm from out of the puddle.

The fin rose a bit more, and in front of it, the top of a triangular grey head broke the surface. Two small black eyes stared after the light, unblinking.

"It's looking right at us. *Run!*"

It was like my vision was a tunnel, and that tunnel was closing in. The last thing I saw was the two black eyes studying me, and beneath those were a whole lot of sharp white teeth.

17

It was the cold that brought me back.

I was freezing, soaking wet, and shivering. I'd never experienced cold like this before. Hell, I'd never *imagined* this kind of cold before. My head really hurt. Well, everything hurt, but mostly the spot where I'd gotten brained by a rock. My splitting headache got a whole lot worse when someone bellowed—

"*GREETINGS, HUMAN.*"

I flinched and put my hands over my ears, though that did no good because the sound hadn't come from outside my head, but in it.

"*A sudden pain reaction. This mammal is receptive to communication! Forgive me. Distance is near. I will project with less force.*"

I didn't know where the voice was coming from. It was pitch-black, I was still lying in the water, so if I'd been moved it hadn't been far. I'd also not gotten devoured, considering the last thing I remembered was rows of teeth. I still had the pistol in my hand, but it was useless with soaked ammo. I managed to crawl out of the water, and made it a few feet before flopping over, dizzy.

"*Are you ill? If you are going to die anyway I should eat you, so you do not go to waste.*"

That wasn't even threatening, more a statement of efficiency. It wasn't a voice, so much as letters unfolding in my mind, making sentences that I then *heard* by thinking them.

"I'm not dying," I managed to gasp between the chattering of my teeth. "I'm just cold."

Something big got out of the water and padded over next to me. It grabbed hold of my neck and squeezed, as if it was about to choke the life out of me. I struck it repeatedly in the arms, which were hard as iron bars, so it didn't seem to notice the blows.

Then the unseen creature let go. In my head appeared a strange image, almost like some of the creature anatomy pictures in the encyclopedia, except the letters next to the drawing of a flayed open human body were indecipherable to me.

"*Pulse slow. Temperature low for a human. You are hypothermic.*"

That wasn't a word I was familiar with, but as the letters appeared behind my eyes I got the general idea from context. I started to say that I needed my pack, but before I could get the words out of my now very sore throat, the creature somehow knew what I was about to ask for.

"*Your bag made of animal skin and filled with food and magic is here.*"

There were some heavy footsteps and splashing as it went to where I'd been when I'd gotten blasted by the last arcane bolt. Then there was a thump as my pack landed on the ground next to me. It was a struggle to get inside of it, not just from the darkness, but because my hands were so damned cold my fingers were numb. I was shaking so bad that even when I found the little copper bowl it was a struggle to hold onto it.

This bowl had been one of my earliest successful experiments with infusing various metals with Red. As soon as I concentrated on it, the embedded magic began to heat up the copper. I could get the bowl hot enough to boil water, but for right now, I just needed it warm enough to restore some feeling to my hands.

Once that was accomplished, I told the terrifying, yet oddly helpful creature, "I need to get someplace warm and dry."

"*That sounds unpleasant. I know of such a place. Follow.*"

"I can't go upstairs. The Skerrets might still be waiting for me."

"*Not above. I found hostility above. Humans set me on fire. So I ate some of them. It was a misunderstanding.*"

It was extremely weird to converse this way. The creature didn't make any sounds, so from the letters pushed together in my head, it'd been assigned a voice by my imagination which sounded like an oblivious and emotionally stunted man yelling in my ear. With a bit of concentration, I got that down to normal tones.

"*This way please.*"

"Hang on." I couldn't follow him because I couldn't see a damned thing, so I found my light charm and activated it.

A horrific monster was looming over me.

It was over six and a half feet tall, built as broad shouldered and barrel chested as a dwarf. With thick arms and huge hands, it stood on two legs, but there the resemblance to anything I'd seen before ended, for its head was a smooth wedge, featureless except for two piercing black eyes and a gigantic mouth, which fortunately remained closed. When I'd seen it open previously, the sight of all those teeth had scared the piss out of me. The monster had grey skin, which looked to be of an odd texture in the poor light, and it wore nothing but a bandoleer of pouches over one shoulder and a rough loin cloth.

"*Yes. I have fashioned what the land dwellers call* pants. *I have found humans seem more comfortable around me when I wear pants.*"

"I imagine so… Are you reading my mind?"

"*Only the top part which is about to be formed into spoken language and projected aloud by your vocal cords. I cannot see beyond that.*"

"How? Is that some kind of spell?"

"*This is how all squalo communicate. Squalos do not have vocal cords. Those are a common development from races of the other planes, but rare in my realm.*"

"What's a squalo?"

"*I am squalo. You are human. Most humans cannot receive squalo projections well. Their brains are too soft. Your brain is only a little soft. This is a rare mutation. I have not gotten to speak with many here. If you die, I would still eat you, but it would make me sad. Come along.*" The monster began walking down the tunnel. On its back was the fin that'd poked out of the water. I noticed webbing between its stubby fingers and toes, and hanging from the back of the bandoleer was an odd short sword, constructed from a strange material I'd never seen before.

"*That is coral,*" it explained without looking back.

I didn't know what that was, but the squalo could have easily killed me while I'd been passed out and hadn't, so I felt inclined to trust it. Certainly, a sad state of affairs when a carnivorous underwater monster was friendlier than my own countrymen.

I clutched the bowl to my chest and let the heat warm my core. The squalo walked and I stumbled along after. The splitting headache and nasty chill was making it really hard to keep my balance. Plus, everything here was just so damned slick. I tripped and fell a few times, and each time I did, I was sure the monster considered eating me and getting it over with for my own good.

It led me to a narrow side tunnel I'd missed on my blind passage through here earlier. Inside seemed to be only us and scurrying ratlets, who eyed me hungrily from the edge of my light, but squealed in fright and ran as soon as they saw the squalo.

"*That reaction is because I have eaten many of their kind. They are diseased, but edible. They are also very rude.*"

"Oh… You been down here feasting on ratlets for very long?"

The squalo paused, as if looking for the right human letters to string together to send to my mind. Apparently, time was not a concept which translated easily for it. "*The Great Machine has rotated past my gate three times since my arrival.*"

So that was either three weeks, or three months, depending on if it meant the plane he came from, or the particular location on the other side, assuming water had four locations like fire. "So you're from the Elemental Plane of Water?"

"*That is what the mammals of the Nexus name it.*" And then my mind was bombarded with a bunch of brief, flashing images. It was hard to explain. Like being submerged in the canal again, only a thousand times worse, more confusing, and incomprehensibly vast. "*That is our name for it.*"

Overwhelmed by visions of cave cities made of coral inhabited by an empire of silent predators on the edge of an endless ocean, I stumbled and fell over again.

The squalo stopped to wait for me.

"Go on. I'm fine." In truth, I found this whole thing fascinating, and this odd communication distracted me from the bruises, cuts, scratches, head injury, and cold induced stupidity. I staggered back to my feet and we set out again. "From those pictures, the whole thing's underwater, and except for the parts where the other realms intrude, just like mine."

As an experiment, I tried to picture Fogo, with the endless churning fire beneath a brittle shell of land and trespassing air, just to see if the squalo would get it.

The creature's head tilted to the side. "*That is rather clear. Your brain is even less soft than I thought. What were you called in the fire realm?*"

"My name? Carnavon. Oz Carnavon."

It turned back to stare at me with its beady little eyes. It's features were so blank and it's method of communication so stunted, I had no idea what it was feeling.

"What?"

"*That is a powerful name.*"

"Not where I'm from, it's not."

It's head twisted to the other side, which I took to indicate curiosity, but that was just a guess with this inscrutable emotionless thing. "*In preparation for my mission, I learned the letters of several Nexus languages in order to project them into soft brains. In the lost Elemental Plane of Time, Carnavon was the word for an eater of meat.*"

I could see why this toothy fellow would appreciate that. "And what do they call you?"

That question brought about another bombardment of a whole bunch of different images, rapidly unfurling, half of which I couldn't understand at all. I managed to not fall over at least. There were visions of stalking prey, a feeling of unrelenting single-minded dedication, and then a whole lot of bloody violent thrashing when that prey got caught in the squalo's jaws.

I think the only reason I caught that the first part was about hunting, was due to my background as a trapper. The methods were wildly different, but the feeling was the same. I also caught on that this was a young adult male squalo, and by the standards of his people, he wasn't a very noteworthy one… yet.

"Wow. Alright then."

"*The rough translation of my name into your trade language is Tracks the Blood Trail Regardless of Extreme Temperatures or Crushing Pressures.*"

That was a mouthful. "How about I just call you Trax Bloodtrail for short?"

"*I find this acceptable, Carnavon.*"

18

The warmer, drier place Trax led me to turned out to be a large brick room. From the red light coming through the grating above and all the pipes that were hot to the touch, we were beneath some manner of Red powered furnace, which probably provided heat to some of the buildings in the Under Slump.

Some other creatures were already here, but I was the only human. There were more of the frog-faced things, clustered around a small cooking fire, and a couple of gigantic bipedal lizard creatures with scaly blue skin huddled in a different corner. Those must have been lacertians, as I'd read about them in the encyclopedia. Every head and weird bulgy eye protuberance in the room turned our way as Trax and I entered.

One of the lizard men hissed at the squalo. The other reached for a hatchet lying on the ground by its side. Trax stared back at them for a long moment, and then the lacertians slowly, grudgingly, turned away.

"What did you tell them?"

"*That our empires have made war before, but that war is not here. Then I showed them how if they were rude I would bite their necks until all their blood came out.*"

"That's rather diplomatic of you." I waved at the frog things. They croaked at me a few times, necks puffing, before returning to their supper of what appeared to a cauldron of bubbling slime. I found an unoccupied corner next to a scalding hot pipe and took my coat off, wincing as I discovered several new bumps and bruises. The Skerret's mage had done a number on me. I was lucky my spells had worked as well as they did, and I'd given worse than I'd gotten.

"*You are a mage?*"

"Sorta. I'm a self-taught amateur rank one. That's why I came here, to get into an academy, and get some proper training, so I can become a real wizard someday. And you? With all the eating people I assume you're not any kind of emissary."

"*The devouring of their flesh was not my intent. I am a monk.*"

"Huh..." That was certainly unexpected considering how terrifying he looked. Where I was from, monks were devotees of various saints, taking care of shrines, and trying to live by their patron's principles. "I didn't see that coming."

"*Monk is the nearest word you have. squalo have no saints. I seek enlightenment through understanding. I have come to the Nexus to observe, study, and document the culture of the various land species. On occasion, we trade with you, but your ways are puzzling to the squalo.*"

I got my soaking wet boots off and turned them upside down to let the water drizzle out. "So we're both here to learn."

"*There were some in the market whose brains were not soft. We were cordial. They welcomed me. Then I explored. I came down here. A few humans were very rude. They set me on fire. So I ate them. This has proven to be a setback to my mission.*"

Trax sent me another image, this time of a ghastly murder scene, with severed limbs and big puddles of blood on some street of the Under Slump. No wonder the Skerrets had been so afraid of him. "Yeah, I can see how that might have gotten you off on the wrong foot with the locals."

"*I have hidden in the canals ever since.*"

I dumped the contents of my pack and spread them out so they would dry. Then I carefully pulled the rest of Gax's cartridges off my belt and put them next to the hot pipe in the hopes some of them hadn't gotten ruined. The steel of the gun might rust, but I didn't have any oil to clean it with. My equipment cared for, I started checking my injuries. Everything hurt. They'd beaten the ever-living hell out of me. At least none of the cuts were deep enough to need stitches, and I hoped there'd been nothing in the water that would cause an infection. Dying of some weird rotting disease in an underground frog hole would make for an ignominious end to my quest.

Groaning, I leaned back on the bricks and got out one of the sticks of dried meat I'd brought. I was still freezing and in a lot of pain, but I was also starving, and eating made for a good distraction from the suck. I went to take a bite, except Trax was still standing there, staring through me with those beady little eyes. My countrymen here might have forgotten our traditions of hospitality, but I was better than that and would share what I had.

I held out the stick. "Want some?"

With incredible swiftness, Trax swiped the whole thing from my hand. There was a flash of sharp white teeth, and a day worth of my rations was gone. He didn't even chew before swallowing it.

"*So this is the concept humans call* sharing. *I have heard of this.*"

"Yeah. Kind of. It's just helping someone else with what you have, when they don't have that themselves."

Trax got up and disappeared back into the tunnel. He moved so quick and silent on land that I couldn't even imagine what he was like in his home realm. While he was gone, I ate another greasy meat stick. With my killer aquatic friend gone, the lacertians started glancing my way, probably deciding if they could get away with killing me or not. There was a surprised *squeak* from out in the dark, a *crunch*, and then Trax came back carrying something hairy and smelly. He sat down across from me, cross-legged, then held out the dead rat creature.

"*Want to…* share?"

I looked at the raw dead ratlet and shook my head. "Naw, I'm good for now. Thanks for offering."

"*A polite refusal. Fascinating.*"

"Don't worry. If I wanted some I'd say so. Good job."

Trax's cold black eyes looked at me, then the ratlet, then back at me. Then he tossed the whole critter in his terrifying mouth, and this time it was big enough he had to chew. That sight would haunt my nightmares. A few sickening, bone crunching seconds later, Trax was done, and projected, "*I must document this discovery.*"

From one of the pouches on his bandoleer, he removed a crystal sphere and pressed it against the side of his head. The obviously enchanted thing was probably recording his strange thought pictures. Of course, it wasn't like a creature from the Elemental Plane of Water would use ink and paper.

After Trax put the crystal away, I asked, "So what customs of the Core dwellers have you learned about so far here?"

"*Pants and sharing.*"

"Sounds like your mission is off to a splendid start." But if being able to understand his odd mode of undersea communication was so rare, his lack of success was understandable. "I'm new here too, but maybe I can help you."

"*Most humans can receive only the simplest images. An intermediary would be useful in my search for understanding. You would help me. I would help you. Is this* sharing?"

"Close enough." Excitement and trauma makes a man very sleepy, but I worried that if I closed my eyes for long, one of the denizens of this subterranean lair would certainly murder me, or at minimum, steal my belongings.

"*You may rest, Carnavon. I will remain on the lookout for predators. Squalo seldom sleep. If I become hungry, I promise to only eat more ratlets and not you. You are too useful for me to eat.*"

"Great. Night, Trax."

And that was how I made my first friend in the Core.

19

In the morning, my things were still right where I left them, and mostly dry. It turns out having over three hundred pounds of muscle and teeth sitting next to you crunching ratlets all night is a real deterrent against thieves. The frog things were still there, but the lacertians were gone. I thought Trax might have eaten them while I was asleep, but there was no blood, so they'd probably just left. It looked like the powder of four of my cartridges had survived getting wet, so I loaded Gax's pistol, put on my still soggy coat and boots, and we set out.

Trax was full of questions.

"*What is this* Collegium *you seek?*"

"That's the part of the city where the wizards congregate. All the magical academies are there. I'll get one of them to accept me. As for you, there's bound to be more people smart enough to understand squalo speak, as well as all sorts of interesting things for you to learn about. Come to think of it, are there any others of your kind already in the Core?" Finding some of my countrymen hadn't worked out very well for me, but it might for him.

"*There are a few squalo here, but I cannot involve them in my quest.*" Trax didn't elaborate further, so I left it at that.

"So here's my plan. We're going up into the light, and we're going to walk right across the Under Slump. Nobody is going to hassle me because they're scared of you, and anybody who tries to hassle you, I'll talk them down and explain you're friendly."

"*If that does not work, then I eat them?*"

I was beginning to suspect that *friendly* was one of those human concepts Trax was going to struggle with. "We're going to try real hard to avoid that."

"*Very well.*" His word pictures didn't convey emotion very well, but I think he might have been a little disappointed at that.

We had to stop at the water where we'd met so Trax could take a swim. He explained to me that squalos needed to submerge themselves in water at least once a day or they would gradually sicken and eventually die. Which meant he'd have a hell of a time on Fogo, though I suppose he could live in the Argent's lake in Fort Silver if he was ever really determined to visit.

Then we went up the steps to the Under Slump's lower level. On my brief trip through yesterday, this had seemed a dim and dismal place. Today it was a bit more hopeful. Or perhaps that was just my mood, because it was still dark, dirty, and rather seedy. That said, there were a great many creatures here from the various kingdoms and realms, and they were going about their business just like every other settlement I'd ever seen. There were shops and industries, vendors hawking their wares, and families raising their children. There were more of the frog creatures here, selling ratlets roasted on spits.

Nobody even seemed to notice me, but all of them grew afraid when Trax appeared. Some took cover. Others ran away. Hairy or webbed hands were placed on the hilts of weapons. Mothers shooed their curious children toward safety.

"Trax, how many of them did you eat when you got here?"

"*Only three. And they had all been very rude to me first.*"

If this was the reaction he got at the stranger level, and it seemed civilization degraded the farther one went down in the Under Slump, there was no way we were making it out the top part without getting accosted. "Change of plans. We need disguises."

"*I am familiar with this concept.*" Trax sent me the mental image of some terrible sea creature with far too many arms changing the color of its skin until it perfectly matched the terrain around it. "*But squalos cannot do that.*"

"You go back down and wait for me. I'll see what I can come up with."

One of the nearby vendors was selling clothing. The merchant was small, green, and hideous, with huge eyes meant for seeing in the dark, and gigantic ears like a bat. He peeked over his table and asked in a high-pitched voice, "Is that squalo gone?"

"He's gone, though I don't think he's dangerous unless you provoke him."

"That's what the shark men always claim, until the blood frenzy comes upon them!"

It pained me to spend any of the Core coins I'd earned guiding adventurers across Fogo, but I didn't see much choice. "What do you have in really large sizes?"

An hour later, Trax and I made our way across the Under Slump. I had traded my almost new Fogo coat for a worn and battered heavy cloak from a local tailor. It wasn't near as warm but hopefully I wouldn't stick out as much. I kept my hood up and my head down. My squalo companion was wide as a fat Orc, so all I'd found that worked for him was a big blanket that I'd cut a hole from the middle for his head to stick through, and then I'd bought a big basket to place as a hat over his oddly shaped head to hide it.

As ludicrous as Trax looked, it still managed to mostly work, because the farther we got from the canals the less any of the locals assumed the hulking figure by my side was the infamous squalo which had recently been terrorizing the lower levels. All manner of strange creatures made their home beneath the sinking Aventine, so Trax wasn't the only mysterious thing lumbering about.

Luckily, I didn't spot any Skerrets, Roches, or anyone else who was obviously from Fogo. I did see a bunch of other rough sorts who must have belonged to a different gang, because they all wore a black band with the same complex yellow symbol on their arm.

"*I am unfamiliar with that sign, however, I recognize their confidence. These are the apex predators of this sea.*"

Trax could communicate silently to me, but I had to whisper back because I wasn't very good with making mind pictures. "The guys you ate, they weren't wearing that black band, were they?"

"*No.*"

Thank the saints, that would make getting out of here a bit easier. Everyone of that gang I'd seen had been armed, many of them openly carrying enchantments, and all of them looked hard as nails. I could only assume these were the Latros I'd been warned about, who controlled both the Slumps enough to scare off the real city watch. We were probably going to have to pay them some kind of poll to pass, and these were not the sorts I could risk angering. So much for my coin.

"*I do not understand...* coin."

"You don't have money underwater, Trax? Huh..." I wasn't even sure how to start explaining that concept. "Don't worry about that for now. We just need to find our way up and out." I was excited to be out from beneath the shadow of the Slump—which still unnerved me every time I glanced upward—and on to riches and adventure in the glorious Collegium.

The back road out of the Slump was very busy. Apparently, many poor folks lived down here but worked up above. We joined the throngs and shuffled along. People were carrying baskets and bushels, and those squawking birds I thought must be chickens, and one lady was pulling an animal I assumed was a goat by a leash. I caught Trax staring at the goat.

"*That looks flavorful.*"

"No."

The fine stone bridge curled gently upward, held up by intricate supports of steel beams. Except we reached a spot where the stone had snapped off, probably when the upper Aventine started to sink, and we continued along on a newer path made of shaking wooden beams and creaking ropes. After several minutes climb, we were even with the floating Slump. Its bottom was stone with pipes sticking through it. More leg muscle burning climbing, and I could see that atop the Slump were many great buildings, similar to those in the Under Slump, also decaying, but not nearly as badly as below.

At the top was a plaque which read *Upper Aventine*. Just as below, somebody had defaced it with paint, so now it was just *Slump*. One of the men wearing the black band approached us. He wore a pistol on one side of his belt and a wand on the other.

"These other travelers are known, but I don't recognize you, strangers."

"No, sir." I put on my most charming smile and was as deferential as if I'd been talking to an Argent enforcer. "We're just passing through on the way to the Collegium."

"That so." He grew suspicious of the bruises and scratches on my face, then looked over at Trax, looming there in his blanket and basket. "What's that thing?"

"A monk from the Elemental Plane of Water," I said with absolute honesty. "I'm showing him around."

With blanket and basket, Trax was a rather ponderous sight, though probably wasn't the weirdest thing the thug had seen here today. "The Mage's Road is over that way, but by order of Carcalla, it's gonna be one Tetar to come and go between the Slumps freely."

"Of course, my good fellow." It physically hurt to hand over another of my precious coins to pay for the simple act of walking, but at least that was one of the smallest ones. There were ten Tetars to an Obol. Of those, I had but one.

Trax must have sensed my anxiety. "*This one looks flavorful as well. If I ate him, you would not have to give him your small round metal.*"

"It's all good," I said to the toll taker, but my words were mostly to placate the squalo.

The thug took the coin, bit it to test the hardness, and satisfied it was real, waved at the other black banded man guarding the high road to let us pass. "You two are good for the week. That's the pathway to the mage's town there."

The wooden bridge that rose from the Slump was somehow even more rickety than the one we'd just walked up. It sloped raggedly upward for hundreds of feet, before it finally linked up with more of the original ancient stone road above. That must have been where the Aventine had been anchored when it first began to sink. At least it looked like the locals had adapted an efficient system, as each time it sank a bit lower they could steal a board from the shrinking bridge below to add to the growing bridge above.

At the far end of that stone corkscrew was another neighborhood, not floating, but built atop a plateau on a mountainside, which its mighty palaces had overgrown until they precariously balanced over the edge. From the center of that plateau, a great tree grew, taller than anything I'd ever imagined.

I started up toward the Collegium and my destiny. Trax tested his massive weight on a board, and when it didn't immediately shatter and send him plummeting to his doom, followed.

It was a long climb, enough to make the muscles of my legs hurt, but at least the exertion kept me warm.

Rickety wood connected with magically shaped stone and my journey toward becoming a wizard got that much more real. I was less than half a mile from all the magical academies and my glorious future with one of them. Which one would accept me? There were seven specialties. Would I become an enchanter? An invoker? A conjurer? And once I graduated, would I become a fearsome war wizard, or an engineer creating floating cities and incredible machines? There were so many possibilities I could barely contain my excitement. However it shook out, I'd work hard as I'd always done, strike it rich, set my family free, and take my revenge on the pirate who'd wronged me, so help me Saint Persistence.

From up here, the view was so breathtaking that everything seemed possible. The Core City stretched for what could have been forever beneath and above me. From here I could see the slow turn of the Great Machine. Beyond the city were distant mountains, green fields, and endless forest, all lit by a glorious sun that was so bright, it stung my eyes. I pretended the tears that formed were from the glare, rather than being moved by the beauty.

At the first intersection of ancient, suspended roads, there was a platform. In the middle was a wooden board with many messages, advertisements, and official pronouncements posted on it. While I paused to catch my breath I looked over the notices. One of them caught my eye, because stamped on it was the Argent's silver mark.

Baron Sagard Argent offers a reward of fifty Obols to anyone who provides information leading to the arrest of oath breaker, Ozwald Carnavon. He is wanted for the attempted murder of Ambassador Dardick Argent, the theft of over two hundred pounds of pure Fogo Red, and other general lawless behavior. If you have information on his whereabouts, contact the Argent embassy in the Market District. Posted 2nd Waterday of the Tenth Month, 4581 AN.

"Oh shit fucking hell."

Trax's basket hat turned side to side. "*I smell no feces, procreation, or devils here.*"

My mind was reeling. There were no witnesses, so I tore the notice off the board before anyone else could see it, crumpled the paper into a ball, and shoved that in my pocket.

This was slander. I'd had nothing to do with the caustic curse in the market. I'd not stolen anything from the Argents except the remaining years of my own life, and certainly not a small fortune in Red. Worst of all, how did they know my real name?

Realizing there was only one possible explanation, I muttered, "Bart, you son of a whore."

"*I do not know this Bart. Why is his mother a prostitute?*"

"Bart's the dishonest trader scum who surely gave up my name the minute the Argent's asked." Only, if that much Red went missing, two hundred pounds was far too much for someone to have just walked off with it during the chaos unnoticed… "That crooked bastard Jemmy set me up."

"*I am very confused.*"

I doubted two Fort Silver losers knew anything about an assassination attempt against a nobleman, but after they'd agreed to help me run away, they probably decided to steal a bunch of Red for themselves, knowing the enforcers would conveniently blame it on the guy who'd gone missing during the same market trip.

"I've been betrayed. I bet Bart moved that Red from one of the other wagons sometime before that caustic curse went off. There's no way he would've robbed anything after all the watchmen were paying attention. Oh no… My family… He gave them my name, Trax. That means the Argents are gonna stick a thousand years on my brothers and sisters' contracts."

The basket hat tilted to the side. I'd lost the poor squalo entirely. "*I do not know what is happening, but I will gladly eat those who have wronged you with this terrible rudeness.*"

I had to think fast. I was a fugitive now. But this was an Argent proclamation. I hurried and checked the board, finding nothing about me from the Core City Watch. Fogo was just one small settlement, and not a very rich or important one from what I understood. The Argents were probably nobodies here. What were the odds anyone in the Collegium would even hear about this reward at all? And what was fifty Obols to a wealthy mage? I'd earned the equivalent to one Obol just by guiding adventurers to their destinations over the last few years. Surely fifty would be beneath the notice of anyone from the legendary Collegium.

But how many other boards were there like this? How many notices had the Argents posted across this gigantic city?

There was so much I didn't know, but there was no going back now. I had to stick to the plan.

Except instead of buying out decades worth of contracts to free my family, it was going to take *centuries.*

20

The Collegium was every bit as grand as I'd been told, with feats of magic being so common, the locals seemed to take them for granted. Shops advertised their wares with moving illusions that floated in the air above the entrances. People rode about in magical conveyances, like a merchant's air cart, just far more luxurious. There was even a chariot pulled by animals that had been cast from bronze and animated by magic.

Sadly, the Collegium was as unwelcoming as it was stunning.

"State your business," one of the guards ordered.

This was the tenth academy I'd tried to gain entrance to today, so I put on my friendliest smile, and did my best to not let my desperation show. "I'm seeking an audience with one of your instructors."

"What for?"

"Potential admittance."

The two guards shared a knowing glance, then they both snickered.

I tried sophistry at the last academy and failed miserably, so this time I tried being completely honest. "I know your mages must get unqualified applicants bugging them all the time, but hear me out. I've tested. I'm capable."

"What official rank are you then?"

"Only the first, but—"

"Rank one?" He laughed at my foolishness. "I'm a two, and I was lucky to get a job watching this delivery door."

This wasn't the main gate along the walls of the prestigious Miswar Academy, but I hadn't even made it close to the front one because there had been a massive steel golem with glowing eyes posted on their drawbridge, and it had told me "*Begone*" when I'd admitted I didn't have an appointment.

"This is the Collegium, boy. A rank one is nothing here."

"I only need a moment of their time to demonstrate—"

"The only thing you're getting a moment of is my boot kicking your ass. Master Miswar's given strict orders he's never to be bothered by the petitions of random Slump trash. Move along."

I raised my hands apologetically and backed away.

Trax was waiting for me at the end of the alley. "*Did that go well?*"

"Not particularly."

"*Should I eat them?*"

Tempting as that was, I told him, "Naw, they're just doing their jobs."

I stopped next to my squalo companion and looked down the street at all the magnificent palaces, towers, pyramids, and hanging gardens. It was like each of the wizards was compelled to show off the architecture of their home kingdom, so no two holdings were of the same style. Then there was the great golden tree in the middle, grown hundreds of feet tall, with homes built onto the branches. I supposed that meant once I became a master mage, my academy would need to be built on a barge which I'd tie to the edge of the Collegium's plateau.

"*I think it is good you do not let your continual failure make you feel like the failure you clearly are.*"

"Thanks, Trax…" I wasn't going to let his innocent honesty get me down. "Alright, we'll try that one next." I nodded toward a towering edifice with white stone pillars out front. "How about this time I try to use you to gain entrance again?"

"*That resulted in terrible rudeness last time.*"

"How was I supposed to know the squalo Empire conquered and enslaved that wizard's ancestors five hundred years ago?"

"*That was not a reason for him to throw rocks at me. I should have eaten him.*"

Luckily, I'd apologized profusely and gotten everyone calmed down at the Dragomir School of Invoking before anyone had gotten anything more than their feelings hurt. We'd still gotten tossed out and told to never come back. It was turning out that squalo weren't exactly loved in most of the kingdoms of the Nexus. "I'm thinking all that eating people over the years might be what soured them against your kind, Trax."

"*Curious. I had not considered that.*"

From what I'd gathered about Trax's people so far, that was likely true. To them, you were either food or you weren't, and it didn't take a whole lot to move someone between those two categories. "Just let me do the talking."

"*I cannot talk.*"

"It's just a figure of speech. Come on."

The campuses of the various academies were all walled off. They all came across very secretive, competitive, and standoffish, cold as the weather here. And while thinking about the weather, apparently, this was the season they called autumn. Which was why all the leaves were turning from green to yellow or red. I wasn't used to trees at all, let alone colorful ones. Winter was supposed to get even *worse*. Since Fogo didn't have seasons, I struggled to imagine such a thing.

The sign on the white pillars declared this one to be the *Academy Frunza Tarlev*. There were a lot of people coming and going, many around my age or younger, and all wearing the same stripped shirts, which must have been their student uniform. I assumed it was the end of the day for them, because the students were heading to the various shops and pubs on the block. I'd not tried to befriend any students yet, as they'd likely have no power to get me accepted anywhere, but if I kept getting denied, that would likely be my next avenue of attack.

The academy's giant wooden doors were open for the students to come and go, and there was only a single person who remained there, sitting on a stool, observing everyone who passed by. From the metal breast plate he was wearing and halberd leaning next to him, this must be their doorman. He was of an unknown-to-me race, large, muscular, with orange skin that had bumpy black rock formations growing out of it, pointed ears, and narrow angry features.

"*That is a lob,*" Trax projected helpfully. "*They are a warrior tribe from the Plane of Earth.*"

"Your ancestors ever mass murder any of his ancestors?"

"*Not that I am aware of.*"

That would have to do. I walked up the steps and approached the doors. The departing students didn't even notice me, but they instinctively made room for my large companion.

"Hello, good sir. May I have a moment of your time?"

The lob looked me over dismissively, then grunted.

"I am accompanying this monk on his scholarly journey from the Elemental Plane of Water. He would like an audience with one of your instructors."

"No."

Well that was abrupt. Not quite as daunting as the metal golem, but close. "Master Bloodtrail here has journeyed a great distance to study the ways of—"

The lob stood up, which revealed he was a few inches taller than Trax. Which meant he towered over me. "We're closed."

"If we come back tomorrow could we—"

"No." He leaned over and picked up his halberd.

My foreign emissary scheme wasn't working, so I switched tactics, "Well in that case, I myself am looking for the chance to speak with—"

The lob swung the haft of his weapon at me.

At that casual speed, the round shaft probably wouldn't have injured me too badly, but it would have really hurt. Except instead of hitting me in the arm and teaching me a lesson as intended, the wood landed with a *smack* against Trax's big grey palm.

I was stunned by how fast the squalo moved. He'd been standing to my right and the attack came from the left, and Trax had still gotten there first. *Damn.*

The lob frowned and pulled on his weapon, but Trax wouldn't let go. The basket hat tilted a bit, and I didn't even have to wait for the squalo's question to get projected into my mind.

"Nobody's getting eaten."

One of the students had seen the commotion and asked, "Do I need to summon a watchman, Uzun?"

The lob grunted in the affirmative and his already squinty eyes narrowed dangerously. I didn't know anything about his people or his plane, but Trax's casual interception of his attack had clearly been taken as an insult.

"No need. We'll be going now. Sorry to trouble you." I grabbed Trax's blanket and tugged. "Time to go, Master Bloodtrail."

Trax let go of the halberd, and for a second I thought the lob might take a shot at him out of spite. Luckily sense prevailed, and he held off long enough for us to retreat.

We kept walking for a while just in case they called the City Watch anyway. I'd seen a few of those blue uniforms and copper badges on the street, but so far we'd managed to avoid them. If they accosted us, they'd be sure to realize where I was from, and that would lead to some really uncomfortable questions that would probably end up with me in chains.

The sun was going down, signaling an entire day wasted, being shunned and turned away, often in the most demeaning way possible. "I'm sorry for the lack of success."

"*I am having a fine time.*"

"Really?"

"*I am discovering much about the ways of the surface dwellers. I have learned that many land mammals are exceedingly rude.*"

"They're not all assholes."

"*Clearly not. A creature made entirely of anuses would be very impractical. They must possess many different internal organs to function.*"

I sighed. "That's… never mind." Then I noticed some of the striped shirt Frunza Tarlev students had been following us. "We might have a problem."

There were four in total, and though this was the wealthiest place I'd ever seen, their haughty attitude didn't seem that different than the gangs of Fort Silver, or the Latrocinium of the Under Slump. I suppose that's just the way things were with bullies. Always present, regardless of the niceness of your location. Our altercation with their surly doorman must have caught their attention and amused them for some reason.

Since this was a place of peace and order crawling with watchmen, I wasn't expecting violence. The worst these would probably do was mock or harass us, but even that might be educational. All four of them appeared to be human, which was by far the most common race in the Core from I'd noted, but I had no idea from which of the many kingdoms they'd come from.

"Let's stop for a second and see if we can make new friends."

"*You do not seem very good at that, Carnavon.*"

"I'm not, but I try." I waited for the student mages to approach, and though they were all probably a little younger than me, I reminded myself that each of them had to be ranked far higher than myself. I was a nobody in the Collegium, a fact everyone here seemed intent on reminding me of.

They obviously weren't prepared for me to greet them with a big smile. "Hello, friends. What a fine day this has been in the glorious Collegium."

"It is glorious. We keep it that way by reminding the Under Slump dregs to stay down in the shade where they belong." Clearly, this was the leader, because in addition to setting the tone, he was just a bit taller, a bit better looking, and wealthy enough that each of the many rings on his fingers was clearly enchanted.

"You don't belong here," one of the enthusiastic sidekicks added, in case I was too dumb to catch the first one's meaning.

"Yeah, I gathered you think that," I told the kids. Which was strange that I thought of them as kids, since I wasn't that much older, but it was probably because while they'd been learning magic in the center of the realms, I'd been on the ass edge of nowhere risking my life crawling through lava tubes or hunting molten monsters. "However, we've got business here in the Collegium."

"Oh really?" the leader sneered. "What's that business then? Begging for scraps?"

"I'm seeking admittance to a magical academy to continue my studies, and…" I gestured at my squalo companion, "this is Master Trax Bloodtrail, a monk and scholar of some renown, from an ancient empire deep within the Elemental Plane of Water."

"*Hello.*"

When Trax projected that greeting, one of the four winced and put his fingers to his temple as if he'd develop a sudden headache, but the others must not have gotten it at all.

"That's a dumb grey ogre with a basket on his head, and you're dressed like a beggar and smell like you slept in a sewer, slumper."

He wasn't far off about where I'd spent the night, but he was exaggerating the smell. I'd even taken a bit of an unwilling bath yesterday. But if they thought I was from the underbelly of the Core City instead of Fogo, at least my attempt at a disguise was working.

"I'll have you know that's a mighty squalo, and I'm a self-taught mage of the first rank."

They all had a good laugh at that. I kept smiling like I was in on the joke, even as I imagined breaking their noses and blackening their eyes.

"No wonder Gladiator Uzun told you two to beat it. What's your scam?"

"There's no scam, my friends. I'm a humble student of magic, hoping to learn more, just like you."

The leader laughed heartily at that. "You're nothing like us. You're deluded thinking any academy would give the likes of you the time of day. There're fifty applicants on a waiting list for any given spot in the worst of the academies, and most of those waiting still come from families of note, which you obviously don't."

I'd not realized there was that much demand. "I suppose that means I need to demonstrate that I'm more capable than the rest of them then. What's the best way to go about that?"

"I can't tell if you're pretending to be stupid on purpose, or you're just genuinely that stupid."

Turns out I'd been spoiled by being raised in a barge cadre, because we were so quick to throw fists over perceived offenses it kept everyone far more polite than in this gilded city. It was one thing to eat trogshit in the presence of the nobles who held your family's contract, it was something else entirely to take it off of some haughty stranger who meant nothing to me. I was done being nice.

"Where I'm from, talk like that gets a man stabbed. Lucky for you we're not there. But anyways, the stupidity is feigned but the curiosity is real… So, how would I go about proving that I'm more worthy of an academy slot than a fop bitch like you?"

Since I'd said all that in the friendliest possible manner, it took them a moment to realize those were fighting words. This was someone used to dishing it out, but not taking it. "How dare you?"

"If you thought that was daring, you should imagine what I would've done in response to your words if there weren't some watchmen standing at the corner." I nodded that direction for all of our benefit, just in case one of these was feeling feisty enough to try something. From what I'd seen, unruly behavior was frowned upon in the streets of the Collegium. The four of them noted the watch too, and from their reaction, it appeared I'd guessed right, and there'd be no hands thrown for now.

"It's your lucky day, stranger."

"Oh, you've got no idea how wrong you are about that. But as I was saying, how would someone like me go about proving I'd be a more valuable student than you?"

"Challenge him to a mage fight, Charlu!"

"Yeah, Charlu, challenge him."

The leader clearly didn't mind that suggestion. "I don't think this slumper's got the stones for that, boys."

I'd read about how some kingdoms had elaborate systems of dueling, and they also had sanctioned mage fights here to settle disputes and for the entertainment of the masses, but I didn't know the specifics of how to conduct one. I'd barely met this idiot, and didn't particularly want to kill him, but after the frustrating time I'd had here so far, I couldn't say I minded the idea that much.

I rubbed my hands together in anticipation. "So how's that work? Do we fight to the death? Or do I just need to maim you?"

It must have been how I asked in such a nonchalant way, for their leader to take an unconscious step away from me. I didn't know what realm he hailed from, but Charlu might have just realized I came from somewhere where life was very cheap. He was obviously having second thoughts about provoking me, but was too invested now and couldn't look like a coward in front of his crew. "Sanctioned mage fights last until one yields or can't fight anymore. Deaths are rare."

"But if you die, do I get your spot?"

All four of them stared at me for a long moment, unsure how to take that.

"*If he dies, may I eat his corpse? Meat should not go to waste.*"

The one who seemed capable of receiving squalo projections grew pale and wide-eyed at that, so he'd at least caught some of Trax's meaning. "We should go, guys. These two aren't worth it."

"Hold on. You all started this, and now I'm curious. If I kill a student in one of these mage fights, do I take his place in the academy or not?"

"Of course not!"

"Well that's bloody pointless then."

Charlu sneered, but he also must have had the sense sufficient to realize I'd probably been the wrong man to pick a fight with. "You're no slumper. You're from some barbarian realm. Here, we battle for honor and to bring glory to our schools. Something a peasant like you would never understand. You're beneath contempt and unworthy of my time. Let's go."

Surly and now kind of itching for a fight, I let them walk off while successfully resisting the urge to hurl insults after them.

"*Was your attempt at friendship successful, Carnavon?*"

"Sadly, Trax, I think my efforts might have fallen a bit short."

"*Unfortunate. It seemed to be going so well… I am hungry now.*"

As was I, but I had little in the way of supplies left, only a meager amount of money, and I doubted we'd be able to afford food or lodging in this district. I'd seen no vagrants in the Collegium. Trying to find a quiet corner to sleep here would surely attract watchmen to roust us. As wonderous as it was to observe a sunset not covered in smoke, I doubted lingering in this district after dark would be conducive to my staying free.

"I suppose it's back down to the Slump then, and we'll try some more academies tomorrow." It was difficult to keep the disappointment out of my voice, but as I'd told Tester Pivorotto, I was no quitter. Just like mining Red, nobody expected to make a big score right away. You just kept chipping.

As we walked back toward the corkscrew bridge, all the high and mighty wizards didn't even notice us. Trax was obviously a physical force to be reckoned with, but that wasn't special here. The wizards' heads were in the clouds, surely thinking about their next spell craft invention, wild adventure, or monumental accomplishment. What was I, an inconsequential runaway, to the men who built floating cities or brought statues to life? I couldn't even make it past the lowliest members of their staff to gain an audience.

I was going to have to get creative, I just didn't know how yet. *Help me, Saint Persistence.*

There was a fellow lounging near the bridge, and I noticed him because he was looking right at us. He was short, thin, carrying a stout cane, wearing a fine long coat, and one of those popular triangular hats. Despite being human, he had a face that was rodent looking enough that I hoped Trax didn't mistake him for a ratlet snack.

"Greetings, hotlander. Got a moment?"

So my new cloak only went so far for disguising my origins. "Can I help you?"

"Yes, I think you can. Your knocking upon the doors of the various academies drew the attention of some of my associates, who told me about you, and then I overheard your conversation with the entitled lads from the Frunza Tarlev school. Ah, the rambunctiousness of youth. How I miss it."

I looked back and confirmed that we were a good half a block from where I'd run into them. So if he'd been listening in, it was through magical means. "I didn't catch your name, sir?"

"I didn't give it, but you may call me Borg. I'm assuming yours is Carnavon?"

He had me there, but I'd rather not commit in case there were a bunch of Argent enforcers lurking just out of sight. "You know what they say about assumptions, Mr. Borg."

"Indeed I do. And it's not Mr. Borg." He opened his long coat to show me the copper badge on his belt. "It's *Inspector* Borg, of the Core City Watch."

Well… shit.

21

"Don't fret, Mr. Carnavon. If I wanted to arrest you, you'd already be in shackles." Inspector Borg smiled like a merchant in the grand market trying to sell me something. "I will make this an easy choice for you. Come with me peacefully, answer my questions, and then be on your way. Or attempt to run—or even more foolishly throw Red in my face to try and singe one of eyebrows off like you did to a watchman in the market—and I'll boil your blood and explode your guts where you stand."

When Borg tapped his cane on the ground for emphasis, the illusion that made it appear to be a mundane hunk of wood dissipated, and now I could sense the powerful enchantment on it. The cane's handle had been carved to look like a dragon's head, and its tiny eyes glowed an unnatural blue. I had no doubt his kindly delivered threat was a valid one.

"*Are we making friends again, Carnavon?*"

"Not now, Trax."

Borg politely tipped his hat toward the squalo. "This does not concern you, distant traveler. squalo are a rare sight here, but I heard rumors about your reception in the Under Slump. Only that district is a lawless place, all the buildings are condemned, and it's forsaken by the city fathers, so your actions there, justified or not, don't interest me. I'm here to speak with Mr. Carnavon. You may go."

Something was telling me that Borg was a rather capable mage, and with one shout he could bring a whole lot of help running, so I'd best cooperate for now. "I'd prefer not to have my guts exploded, sir."

"A wise choice. And considering your people have earned such a terrible reputation for irrational fiery tempers, a pleasant and unexpected one. Come along."

Seeing no other way out, I followed him. When Trax followed me, Borg looked back and frowned. "I said you are free to leave, squalo." He made a motion with his free hand. "Shoo."

"I believe Trax is my travelling companion now, Inspector."

"Is that so? Very well. My observers told me he's only eaten a few pigeons since you two arrived in this district, so we'd best feed him then. Squalos become rather irritable when they're hungry, dangerous when they're irritable, and insane with a desire to kill when overcome with their blood lust frenzy."

I looked to Trax, but the basket was hiding his guilty little black eyes, except Trax probably understood the concept of guilt as poorly as he understood everything else. "I'm assuming that eating the street birds is frowned upon here, but I swear I didn't see him snatch any of your birds, sir."

"Unsurprising. Squalo are notorious for their speed."

"*This human compliments my hunting ability. I like him. He is not to be eaten.*"

"Trax says he likes you."

"I shall take your word for it. The underwater picture thought speech eludes me. If you can understand him clearly, you have a rare gift, Mr. Carnavon."

Borg led us to a tavern at the end of the street. He must have been what he said he was, because the watchmen we passed saluted him. Despite having me and a squalo in tow, he didn't ask them to help keep an eye on us, nor did he ever ask me to disarm, and he surely sensed I had some magic on me—not to mention my gun and knife—so he had enough confidence in his abilities to think we weren't much of a threat.

The place was busy, but the proprietor recognized Borg and sent us to a nice table in the back. The fireplace wasn't lit, which was unfortunate. I'd been freezing since I'd gotten here. No stranger to larger clients, the staff dragged out a reinforced chair for Trax.

We sat down and Borg immediately ordered, "A bowl of stew and an ale for the two of us, and a bucket full of whatever you've got with lots of raw meat and fat in it for the big fellow. Put it on my tab."

Once the server left, Borg got right to the point, "Here's the deal, Mr. Carnavon. I know you were there when someone set off that curse. You're new here, but there are certain rules that everyone who trades in the Core must abide by, and one of those is that the Grand Market remains sacrosanct. Whatever wars or contention is going on between the various factions across the realms, those things are left on the other side of the gate. The market must have peace or else. Trade must go on. Every kingdom depends on the goods and magic which flow through the Nexus. Do you understand?"

"I believe so, sir."

"I've also got you dead to rights for assaulting a uniformed member of the City Watch with a minor fire cantrip and can run you in on that charge if I so choose. Do you understand that as well?"

"Well… I was under a bit of duress at the time and—"

He held up one hand and gave me that huckster's smile again. "I'll stop you there. In normal circumstances I'd have you publicly flogged before being locked into the stocks for a couple days for a transgression like that. Watchman Wirth looks like a fool without his eyebrow, and he'd gladly beat your skull in if given the chance, but I've got more important things to deal with first. Like finding out who violated the rules of the market by trying to murder a visiting noble."

"It wasn't me."

He snorted derisively. "Of course it wasn't you."

It was good to hear he didn't consider me a suspect, but I was a little insulted by the dismissive attitude. "Why couldn't it be?"

"Don't get your dander up, hotlander. That wasn't some mere preprepared enchantment any zero could set off on a whim. That spell was the work of a powerful wizard with an affinity for air magic. It was only contained by the combined efforts of several capable practitioners who happened to be nearby, and only at considerable danger to themselves. If they'd not been there to chain it early, it might still be eating a hole through the market, and merchants hate that sort of thing. A spell like that would require at least a seventh or eighth rank mage to use. You're what, a two?"

"One," I admitted.

"Exactly. It takes decades of dedicated training to unleash something capable of that much ongoing destruction, and unless you've got the best illusion magic I've ever heard of, you're not a century old mage trying to deceive me. The Fogo ambassador only survived by luck and virtue of the *many* protective charms he was wearing, half a dozen of which got used up on impact and he still almost got killed anyway."

Our food was brought out. The stew smelled delicious. A large wooden bucket full of raw meat, blood, and viscera from various animals was placed in front of Trax. He swept the basket off his head, picked up the bucket in both hands, opened his jaws wide, and began to chug it down. I'm not a delicate individual by any means, but that was still deeply unsettling to witness.

"I give you my word that I had nothing to do with that curse. I've got no love for the Argents—none of us in Fogo do—but I wish Dardick no specific harm."

"Sure, you don't. From what I've been told about life in Fogo, I'd hate them too." It was difficult to hear the inspector over the noise of Trax's chewing and slurping. Borg watched the spectacle for a moment, then turned away, cringing. "My theory is that you simply took advantage of the chaos in the market to flee from your poor situation back home, trying to escape into the city of opportunity."

I said nothing in response to that, because I was undeniably guilty of breaching my contract, and surely Borg had been told about that.

"Listen, Carnavon, I enforce the Code of the Core here. I don't give a damn about whatever rules your nobles made up for lava land. Slavery is illegal here. I know they call it by some other gentler name where you're from, but I'm not some slave catcher. You ran, that's between you and them. Personally, I find the institution of slavery abhorrent, but the Core needs its elements."

I didn't know if Borg was actually that understanding, or if he was just being conciliatory to gain my trust, so I remained guarded. "I saw one of the Argent's reward notices. I didn't steal any Red either."

"I didn't think you had. That's the oldest trick in the book. Whenever someone like you runs away from his old life in the market, a bunch of valuable goods inevitably walk away with some junior merchant, while the runner gets blamed for it. Again, as far as the watch is concerned, that's between you and your nobles."

"That's kind of you." It was hard to hide the suspicion from my voice.

"It's not kindness. It's the Code of the Core that we must offer sanctuary to anyone from any realm who seeks it in good faith, but we offer nothing more than that. Expect no handouts here. All are welcome in the Nexus, and while here, you will live or die based upon your own industry. Some of the churches might offer charity, but the city never does. You will adapt to our ways or perish."

"*Just like the ocean,*" Trax projected as he slurped up an intestine as if it was a giant noodle.

"If nothing's free, then in exchange for not arresting me for scorching that watchman, I suppose you want my help to find out who tried to murder Dardick Argent in your precious market."

"You're a fast learner." He leaned way back in his chair. "I'm not very familiar with your realm. So who do you think did it? Who had something to gain by killing Dardick Argent?"

"Honestly, I've got no idea."

Borg just shook his head in extra animated disappointment. "That's not good enough. Maybe a night in the stocks will jog your memory after all."

I honestly didn't know what else to tell him. "You want me to make something up? Because I swear before all the Gods and Saints that I don't know. The first time I ever saw him was that morning. I've got nothing to do with Fort Silver politics. Up until yesterday, my job was trapping Fire Elementals. Trappers don't exactly run in the same circles as barons' sons."

Borg spent the next half an hour grilling me about what I'd seen. He asked about who else came through from Fogo, and about everything on both sides of the gate. He wanted to know about specific customers, and anyone I'd seen hanging around who looked odd or out of place. Problem was, with that being my first time through the gate, everything had been odd or out of place to me. He asked about the reactions of the people when the curse had gone off, and then if I'd seen anyone acting strange in the aftermath. Again, how were you supposed to act while an acid cyclone was trying to melt you?

Essentially, I was pretty much useless to him, but at least the stew was good. And by good, I mean *incredible*. It was by far the most different spices I'd ever tasted, and the ingredients were actually fresh. I gobbled it down so fast I gave the squalo a run for his money. The food in the Core was so much better than I was used to that even if he decided to arrest me, I'd go to the stocks fat and content.

"That's all the questions I've got for now, Mr. Carnavon."

"Can I go? Because I've been as forthcoming as possible, Inspector."

"I believe you have, and all that earnestness inclines me to like you, which is why I'm going to level with you now. We've been observing you all day. This little quest of yours to get into an academy? It's not going to work. Mages run this city. They're our ruling class. They determine who gets a chance and who never can. They keep the number of academies small for a reason. It's a prestigious club, and you're not in it."

"You're a mage."

"I'm a public servant. Accent on servant. The city fathers recruit academy graduates and then advance them to wherever they're most useful. Rank determines access. I worked all the way up to five because I've got a knack for keeping the peace. You can get all the way to six through demonstrating your power to a tester, seven or eight maybe if you're undeniably talented. But to advance beyond that requires approval of a majority of the Nexus Council. Which gets real political, more who you know than what you know."

That was a strange idea to me, while sitting in this unnatural city that only existed because some wizards willed the Great Machine into being and connected it to all the realms forty-five hundred years ago. "Why wouldn't they want more capable wizards? With more, stronger wizards, they could accomplish greater things."

"Don't be gullible. Why do you think every noble family out there pays testers to comb through their subjects? Because the more of their people they've got naturally talented enough to get into an academy, the more power their kingdom might gain in the Core. If it was open to everybody, it's not special anymore. That's why the Code says only rank tens can take on students or approve apprenticeships out in the realms. Only tens can start academies, and only the Council can promote someone to rank ten. Well, there's the old ways of advancement, but that's rare nowadays. And beyond rank ten, for those few powerful enough to attain the higher ranks of wizardry, those can demand a seat on the Council. The Council sure isn't going to give that opportunity to anyone who disagrees with how they run things."

I got the feeling the inspector was being a little too open. This was a subject he was obviously bitter about on a deep and personal level. "Why're you telling me all this?"

"I'm saying, ones, twos, from poor kingdoms, guys like you—or me back in the day—at best we end up as gears in the Great Machine. You can use some elements, make some enchantments, learn a handful of spells, that's still valuable. My advice is get out of this city, pick a new realm, or go to the countryside, find a job, pay your taxes to your new kingdom, live a long and happy life. Or if that's too safe for you—saints know I was young once myself—hire on with some company as an adventurer. Travel the realms selling your skills. Whatever. But at your level? The Collegium is *not* for you."

Even Trax sensed my defiant anger rising at those words enough to look up from licking his slop bucket.

"I've got bigger plans than that. I've got people, alive and dead, counting on me."

Borg sucked on his teeth. "Well, that's unfortunate, because here's more bad news for you. The Argents are conducting their own investigation into the assassination attempt, and I'm not just talking about the lazy functionaries they've got managing their holdings here in the Hub, but somebody legitimately dangerous. Yesterday I was told your baron's right-hand wizard will be rushing across the Plane of Fire to get to the next open gate to come here and personally oversee the search as soon as possible."

"Gaul Haddar," I muttered.

"From that tone, you know of him too." Borg gave me a knowing chuckle. "Then you know how damned you are. Because that same Code of the Core which says this city will welcome you also declares its none of our business if anyone from your old realm shows up to take you back. The City Watch doesn't meddle in internal faction affairs unless they violate the Code somehow. Haddar will be here next Fireday, and from what I've heard about Gaul the Mutilator Haddar, he won't be nearly as understanding as I've been."

"The mutilator?"

"I was in the audience for some of his fights in the arena here years ago. That title was well earned." Borg shuddered at a memory. "I keep the peace, but some wizards are built for war. He's one who clawed his way to his current rank through spilling blood. The Council sent him away because there's no place for men like that here in civilized times."

Things just kept getting worse, so I took a deep breath before asking, "So that's why you're telling me to get out of town?"

"I'm not telling you anything. That would be an official act. I'm just dispensing helpful yet nonbinding advice. If you stay, Haddar will find you, and as long as you're unaffiliated and no other faction or kingdom will protest the Argent's claims to your life, Haddar will do as his mad desert honor demands and send you back to your baron as a thief and possible collaborator with whoever tried to murder his son. Good luck with that."

The next Fireday gate connection would be to Fort Oro. It took our ponderous barges a long time to move between the four permanent settlements on the Plane of Fire, but surely a wizard of Haddar's skill had a faster method of travel available to him. Haddar was so menacing, I almost pitied whoever tried to assassinate Dardick Argent, because he'd kill the hell out of them. Then again, my poor dumb self would certainly get caught up in all that retribution. Which meant I needed to give up my dreams and run or perish. Worst of all, that meant abandoning my family after shafting them with the massive debt of my broken contract.

Unless...

"What would I need to do to get affiliated, so someone other than the Argent's could claim me?"

"That's what you've been trying to do all day. Academies count as factions, same as any principality or large enough company. If a master wizard took you on as a student, that would satisfy the Code, but like I already explained, that's about as likely as a snowstorm in your home realm."

It was Waterday evening. That left me five days to find my place.

22

Airday morning, I woke up in the dirt next to a murky drainage ditch with a price and a lump on my head, the label of thief, and a very limited amount of time to accomplish the impossible.

We'd spent the night on the outer edge of the Slump, in an area used by the locals to pitch their trash over the side. Trax had spent the night in a drainage ditch, and I'd only known where he was because his back fin had been sticking out of the water when I'd gone to sleep. I'd used his disguise blanket to try and stay warm, but it still made for a night of miserable cold. Between the discomfort and nerves, I'd barely gotten any sleep at all.

When I rose, Trax was already awake and recording his thoughts onto his crystal sphere. I got out my warming bowl in an attempt to return some feeling to my hands. "I guess it's time to get back to work."

Trax returned his memory crystal to its pouch. "*Do you think there will be more buckets of flesh to consume? That was pleasant.*"

"Don't set your expectations too high. You'll just get disappointed."

"*Unrealistic expectations seem to define your quest though.*"

"You really know how to dampen the old enthusiasm, Trax."

Our camp site hadn't been too awful. The murky ditch turned into a waterfall at Slump edge, and that would be rain by the time it hit the Under Slump. However, I looked like a vagrant, and there was no place to bathe or even clean up. My shoddy appearance wasn't going to help me impress my way into the mighty halls of wizardry. I needed to figure out how to either improve my status here or earn enough coin to fake it.

I combed my hair with my fingers, and thought about washing my face with ditch water, but that would probably just make things worse. I said a brief prayer to Ketekunan asking for help, but working was more honorable than begging, and Saint Persistence rewarded effort. So effort was what I'd show him. Once Trax was back in his not so clever blanket and basket hat disguise, we set out for the Collegium.

When I saw the other bridges, I considered taking Borg's advice and walking away. Leave the city and start a new life. Or I could go back to the market and offer my meager rank one services to an adventuring company. Today the Great Machine was pointed at the Realm of Air, tomorrow would be Earth, then Life, then Death. Then the gate would be closed for a day as the Nexus aligned with the lost Realm of Time, and one day later, Gaul Haddar would arrive to collect my head. If I was still here and not associated with some powerful Core entity by next Fireday, I was dead meat.

Trax perked up at that thought. "*Meat? Where?*"

"Sorry, Trax, it's a figure of speech. Though I suppose if Gaul Haddar kills me outright, you should probably just eat my corpse afterward. I'll have died a failure, so what does it matter?"

"*Thank you, Carnavon. That is the kindest thing any land dweller has ever told me.*"

Trax was as oblivious as I was bitter. Leaving now meant abandoning my family to be punished for my crimes, and that I would not allow. I'd either earn a place of status here sufficient enough to force the clearing of my name, or I'd return to Fogo to spend the rest of my life breaking rocks in debtor's prison. Better for me to pay for my mistakes than my brothers and sisters and their kids and grandkids working off my sentence. My parents would go unavenged, and their killer would remain free. The whole situation left a sour taste in my mouth.

We spent the morning approaching other academies. As Inspector Borg predicted, I was shunned at each and every one. Some were coldly polite. Others were downright cruel. Not one of them would give me the chance to show off the few spells I'd created. Desperate would-be mages like me were so common that some of them set up on the streets outside of the various academies and performed shows of their magic in the hopes of attracting a real mage's notice. That wasn't an option for me, because the only spell I had which wouldn't get me arrested for endangering the public was to heat up a copper bowl, and I doubted gradually bringing water to a boil would be a crowd pleaser.

Adding to my annoyance, the other aspirants' displays were actually really good. Since today was Airday, most of the visitors were from that realm. When I found myself at the park around the great tree of the Wynlyn Academy, I stopped to watch several illusionists putting on incredible shows. There were moving images of monsters and heroes from myth and legend, and of different Saints undergoing the trials that had caused the Gods to make their paragons of a specific virtue. Some of the illusions looked so real, it felt like I could reach out and touch them. Some weren't just illusions of sight, they also made sound, with the roar of battle and the crash of steel against steel.

It was a display the likes of which I'd never seen before, and these were the amateurs!

And yet the real mages barely even seemed to notice as they walked past. Occasionally, a wizard would be amused enough to drop a few small coins at the feet of an illusionist. I'd paid more for Trax's moth-eaten blanket than they gave to a would-be student who just created a work of breathtaking beauty.

That was certainly a blow to my confidence.

I'd not tried my luck at the Wynlyn Academy yet because this was where my nameless pirate enemy had most likely studied, so I sat on a bench in the shadow of their vast tree to gather my courage. From the traffic coming and going, it appeared most of the Wynlyn students and instructors were elves, and they struck me as a haughty bunch. Like all the other academies, Wynlyn's campus was protected by a wall, only this one wasn't made of stone, metal, or brick, but of some thorn bush which had been magically reinforced and twisted into shape. The thorns on those branches looked sharp as needles. Anyone who tried to climb over it would be in a world of hurt.

The only opening in that living wall was protected by a pair of human guards wearing steel breastplates shined to a mirror finish. There was a fountain in the park, so Trax went to splash in it. I believe the odd birds swimming in the fountain were called ducks, and I assumed Trax probably ate a few of them while I wasn't looking.

The leaves of the giant tree had been falling off and piling up everywhere, which I'd been told was normal for this thing they called autumn. The park must have been a popular place for the Collegium's residents, as it was very crowded. I went unnoticed in my humble hood, quietly observing visitors arriving at the Wynlyn Academy. Those with appointments, the vines of the gate untwisted and moved aside to let them in. Then there were other arrivals, where the gate stayed closed, and the haggling with the guards began.

It appeared that unless they were confirmed by a tester to have an outstanding natural aptitude, there was no talking their way through those vines without offering up a *donation*, and from the size of the purses changing hands between the academy staff and ambitious parents buying interviews for their children, getting in that way required wealth far beyond my destitute means. Once the guards were properly bribed, then the gate would open, allowing the families inside.

I'd always been told elves were nearly immortal, so they were above petty human concerns, but the elves who ran the Wynlyn Academy sure seemed to appreciate money as much as the rest of us.

After I'd been sitting there for a while, a human girl approached the gate. She caught my eye because she was around my age, and rather pretty in a very striking way. Fogo girls tended to be dark haired and pale skinned. This one was blonde and tanned. Fogo girls didn't grow their hair out nearly as long as this one had either, because really long hair was just one more thing to catch on fire. Her clothing was similar to the baggy silks and flashy cloaks the other visitors from the air realm had been wearing, just patched and a bit shabbier. From the looks of her clothing she might be as broke as I was, though she was groomed well enough she'd certainly not slept in the dirt next to a ditch. Even the way she moved was exotic. Fogo girls walked with purpose. This one's walk was so graceful and airy she might as well have been dancing.

The girl stopped in front of the two guards and declared loud enough for the whole park to hear, "I am Azarin Garzade, wizard of the first rank, daughter of Mazdak Garzade, champion Haatari storm chaser, and I demand an audience with your master."

From getting rejected for two days straight, I figured I knew how that was going to shake out for her, and sure enough, the guards began to laugh. It looked like she took that personally and began to argue with them. I couldn't hear the rest of the exchange, but as the girl got angrier and more animated, the guards obviously didn't care. She must not have had sufficient money for a bribe, or any parents or guardian with her to make up that difference. It wasn't until she got back to yelling volumes that I could make out what she was saying.

"I'll have you know I've mastered *three* spells. Now I will demonstrate my skill!" She threw open her cloak with a flourish, revealing that she wore some kind of enchanted glove on her left hand. "Behold as I harness the power of the wind."

If this stunt actually worked and got her through that gate, I'd risk throwing my last snail grenade in the park for their amusement, but I doubted it would, since these same guards had been dozing through the most impressive illusions I'd ever seen.

From where I sat, the girl appeared nervous but determined as she lifted her arm high, closed the glove as if she was grabbing hold of something, and shouted, "*Ascend!*"

Immediately, she was pulled straight into the air like she was clinging to an invisible rope that had just gotten tugged on by an invisible giant. Having dealt with barge lifters and air carts, I was familiar with levitation magic, but this was a lot more rapid and violent. Several people in the park went *oooh* and *ahhh* as she rapidly rose forty feet before opening her hand. That must have broken the spell, since she hung there for a heartbeat, then began to drop. The *oohs* turn to *oh nos.*

Except she aimed the glove at the ground, spread her fingers wide, and shouted, "*Descend!*"

Her plummet instantly turned into a much softer, slower fall, not too different from how the golden leaves were drifting down from the Wynlyn's tree. Swaying back and forth, she was still going pretty fast, but had probably slowed down enough she wouldn't break her ankles on landing if she was graceful, and she looked *very* graceful. Her cloak and golden hair were whipping in the wind around her, which added to the theatrics. I had to admit, I was impressed. That would be an incredibly useful pair of spells for getting on and off a barge in a hurry.

The girl had a huge smile on her face, as everything seemed to be going perfectly for her. Except that expression turned to terror as she realized that rather than continuing straight down to the grass, the breeze was diverting her toward the wall of thorns. She adjusted where her glove was pointed, but it was too late. "No, no, no, no, *no!*"

She *almost* made it. Everyone in the park cringed as she crashed directly into the wall of thorny doom and disappeared into the vines.

A second later, *a lot* of profanity and screaming came out of the thrashing shrubbery.

The guards abandoned their post as they rushed to the crash site to yell at her, "Get out of there!"

"I'm trying to, you fucking knob! Ouch!" The poor girl shouted as she tried to extricate herself, which just resulted in her getting stabbed more. "I didn't—fuck! Damn it!"

I went over to see if I could help. It was a sad statement about the nature of the Collegium that none of the other witnesses bothered. Trax appeared out of nowhere next to me, still wet from the fountain, and there were feathers stuck to his blanket. Which surely meant some poor duck had met its end at his terrifying jaws.

"Quit damaging our wall or we'll call for the City Watch," one of the guards declared.

"I swear on Naanwaala's tits, do you think I'm doing this for fun?" She was hanging a couple feet off the ground, and all her fighting had only gotten her half unstuck. She still had one arm and one leg hopelessly entangled, her cloak was shredded, and she was bleeding from a bunch of tiny lacerations. "Don't just stand there, dolt, give me a hand!"

The guards weren't inclined to risk getting poked, but me being a helpful sort, I rummaged through my pack and found my work gloves. They'd protected me from sharp rocks, they'd surely be able to handle some thorns. "Hang on, air realmer. I'll help you."

"This must be the trash collector," one of the guards sneered.

"Do your job," the other told me, as they returned to their gate, laughing at her misfortune.

"You can both fuck right off then!" she shouted after them. "I'll find a better academy!"

"Quit wiggling," I warned her. "You're just making it worse."

"That's easy for you to say, stranger who isn't being stabbed a million times."

"True, but that doesn't make me any less right. So hold still before you slice open an artery."

That shut her up.

It took me an awkward, painful couple of minutes to get her extricated—those thorns were bastards. I got stabbed in the arms a good twenty times as I tried to not make everything worse. It wasn't until Trax finally figured out what we were doing and actually helped that we got her lifted free. Turns out squalo skin is tough enough Trax didn't even notice the thorns.

Trax set her down, and the three of us stood there, with me bleeding a little, and her bleeding enough I was impressed that she'd not passed out yet. Half her clothing hung in tatters. There were sticks stuck in her hair and scratches on her face. Despite all that, she was still rather cute, even if it was in a loud, profane, and angry sort of way.

"Thank you, kind sir, and..." she looked at Trax, whose basket hat had gotten stuck to the wall, revealing his toothy face, "your fish-man thing." Then she shook one bloody fist toward the guards. "Whatever he is, he's more noble than you useless fucks!"

I didn't know much about the Realm of Air, but she had a mouth on her befitting a Red miner, and that I could respect. "Do you need a healer?"

"You got one handy?" She cringed as she plucked a particularly obnoxious thorn out of her hip, held it up, and saw that it was a quarter inch long. "Fucker!"

I'd seen a church of Olga the Merciful one street over. "I know where one might be. Can you walk? It's not far."

"Give me directions. I'll limp there eventually."

"That's dumb. Lean on me. Come on." I gently took her by the less injured side and placed her arm over my shoulder. She was nearly as tall as I was, though all the air realm people I'd seen today had been tall and slender. Which made sense. They probably had lots of room to stretch out there. As soon as we started walking, she got blood on my new cloak, which caused me to have a very troubling thought.

"Hey, Trax, this blood isn't going to drive you into a feeding frenzy like Inspector Borg said, is it?"

"*No. That is a common misconception. Squalo blood frenzies are only for battle or festive occasions.*"

"A what now?" the girl asked. Apparently, like most people, she was unable to receive my companion's words clearly. Then she grimaced as Trax sent us both a picture of what he considered a *festive occasion.* "Naanwaala's ass! Why'd I just have a vision of eating hordes of ratlets?"

"That's how Trax communicates. He means well. Who's Naanwaala?"

"She's the Saint of bad decisions and painful embarrassing fuckups."

I wasn't sure if that one was canonical, but there were a whole bunch of Saints. Who could keep track of them all? "I'm Oz Carnavon."

"Azarin."

The people on the street were getting out of our way, not out of concern, but because they didn't want to get blood on them. Mages sitting at little tables outside of their restaurants looked up from their tea, askance at our sad state. I'd not been here long, but had a suspicion the block immediately around the Wynlyn Academy had to be the most aloof part of the already snooty Collegium.

"That was some impressive spell craft."

"The first one went off perfect. The second, I didn't exactly stick the landing. The density of the air is off here. I knew I should've practiced a few times after crossing the gate." Azarin looked down at her ruined pants. "Damn it. I wore my best outfit to impress the wizards."

"You're trying to get into an academy?"

"I am. That's why I started with Wynlyn. They're supposed to be the best of the best. I should've known better. Fucking elves. Sorry. I don't normally curse this much, but this really hurts."

The audacity of that made me laugh.

She scowled at me.

"That's not at your discomfort. You went straight to the top. I respect that. I'm looking for an academy too."

"You're a wizard?" she asked incredulously.

Why was that so damned hard to believe? "I am. Thank you very much."

"No offense, you just look like a ruffian."

Sure, I was dirty, unshaven, and wearing a cloak fit for a derelict, but I was no common thug. And to think by Fogo standards I'd been considered the handsome gentleman. "I'm the same rank as you, trying to earn a spot myself."

"How's that working out for you?"

"I got here the day before yesterday. I almost got eaten by a caustic spell, assaulted a watchman, got assaulted by a gang, and every academy I've tried has spit on me. Other than that, it's been great."

"I was warned it would be tough to get into an academy." Azarin snarled as she found another thorn stuck in her back, pulled it out, and tossed it down in disgust. "But I've got nothing to go back to in my realm."

"All or nothing," I agreed, thinking it was nice to have someone to relate to in this unforgiving city. "I get it."

It was like she was talking, not to make conversation, but to think about something other than hundreds of tiny puncture wounds. "So, you're rank one. How many spells do you know?"

"Four."

"Not too bad. I've got three."

"I caught that when you shouted it to everyone in the park and the guards."

"Those fuckers… But three's a lot for a rank one. Four's impressive. What kingdom are you from?"

"Fogo, in the Realm of Fire."

"So that's why you've got the pallor of a cave dweller and dressed for winter on a pleasant day. I'm from Stormwolk." She announced that like it would impress me or something, but I'd never heard of the place. "Not all of us air realmers are prissy illusionists. I'm a storm mage, all the way. Move like the wind, strike like lightning."

It was pleasant having a reckless girl leaning against me, even if that lean was mostly due to the dizziness which accompanied blood loss. "I'm good at setting things on fire or blowing them up."

"Nice. I've always wanted to try Red. I've only been able to experiment with Clear."

I'd not even known that was what the air realm called their element. "Maybe later we could get together and compare notes."

We reached the small church I'd seen, and I'd known which Saint was served here because of the statue of a very plump lady outside. Though the people of the Collegium were too good for the likes of us, thankfully, the Olgaites here turned out to be just as tender hearted as the ones back home, as they rushed out to offer Azarin aid the moment they saw someone in pain. It was a sin for the followers of Saint Olga the Kind to not help someone in need. Luckily that tenet of their faith held even in a place as cold as this.

"Thanks again, Oz." While the nuns helped Azarin away to tend her many wounds, she looked back and flashed me a mischievous smile. "I'd wish you luck in your quest, but you're my competition now!"

"I'll see you around, Azarin."

After they'd taken her into the church, Trax projected, "*You find that female appealing.*"

The thought had crossed my mind, and apparently I'd been thinking it loud enough for the squalo to pick up on it. "Well, sure I do. I've known lots of pretty girls, Trax, but she's interesting. Kind of different than I'm used to, you know?"

"*So that is why you were thinking about what would be the best strategy to successfully mate with her?*"

That made me blush. "No. And you need to calm down."

"*The best way to impress a squalo female is to establish dominance by killing large prey for her. I would recommend giving her a whale. Females love whale.*"

"Mind your own business, Trax."

23

Airday had turned out to be another frustrating failure. I'd finally been able to talk to some real instructors, but they'd snubbed me too. Some were more polite than others, but the message was always the same. They had no openings, and a long list of superior applicants waiting for when they did.

Inspector Borg had been right. It was an exclusive bunch, and I wasn't welcome. It was either be so brilliant they couldn't live without you, or rich enough they couldn't afford to ignore you. I'd wasted one of my last coins buying a drink for a senior student in a tavern, only to be told his master was turning away everyone whose parents couldn't afford to gift the academy hundreds of pounds of magical elements, or the equivalent amount of money.

I was no thief, but hearing that made me wish I really had stolen all that Red like I was accused of. If I'd had those casks, I could buy my way into an academy. Instead, the proceeds were surely lining Bart and Jemmy's pockets now.

Long after sundown, Trax and I took the low road back to our humble drainage ditch campsite on the edge of the Slump. My squalo companion was eager to record his thoughts, and I looked forward to curling up around my warming bowl to try not to freeze through another night. Hopefully, I'd dream up some ideas about how to make a whole lot of money, fast.

There were gladiatorial arenas in some parts of the city, and I'd seen advertisements for mage fights in the Collegium. One was coming up soon between two of the academies, and I'd overheard a lot of conversations about how people were placing their bets, and some had been wagering significant coin. Those fights were trained wizards though, a few ranks above me. Which made me wonder, surely there had to be some kind of organized event for us lowly rank ones? Though there were probably rules in place so I couldn't just huck a snail grenade at my opponent and shoot them, because from the way people talked, mage fights usually weren't lethal.

If there *were* lower matches which might be settled by fists, I'd seen hardly anyone in the Collegium who looked like they were tough enough to go bare knuckle against a Red miner. There wasn't much else to do in Fogo but drink and scrap, so even the weakest of us knew how to fight, and there was no such thing as a weak Carnavon.

"*You would inflict violence on other members of your species for this* money *thing?*"

"It's not ideal. I'm just pondering on the possibilities is all. It wouldn't be enough to bribe my way into an academy, but it might be enough to improve my station here so I've got a better chance."

"*And this potential conflict troubles you? If you are victorious, obviously you should eat the defeated.*"

My companion had a rather direct sense of morality. "I'll have to check what their rules are on that."

When Trax was done recording his thoughts about the day onto his crystal sphere, he flopped into the water with a splash. "*Good night, Carnavon.*"

"Night, Trax."

I watched the moons and stars as I tried to figure out my next move. It was a rare occasion we got to see the stars in Fogo due to the endless haze. Here, there were millions of them visible out past the floating palaces. As cruel as the Core had been to me so far, it really was a wonderous place.

Out of ideas, I drifted off to sleep.

An unknown amount of time later, I woke up with a boot on my neck.

A dark shape loomed over me, pointing something shiny and metal at my face. There was a *clack* as a gun's hammer was cocked. "Move and I'll scatter your brains."

Startled and confused, I could barely breathe with all the weight resting on my throat, and trying to get away was out of the question. There was just enough moonlight to see that several shadows had crept into our camp. Someone activated a light charm, blinding me.

"The squalo's in the ditch," someone whispered. "I see its fin sticking out."

"Good. Freeze the water, Dean," ordered the man standing on me. "No need to tangle with that beast."

I was awake enough to recognize the voice now. It was Mr. Skerrett, once of Fogo, now a gangster of the Under Slump, and he'd come to have his revenge. I slowly reached for Gax's pistol holstered at my side.

"Naw, I wouldn't try that, young Carnavon."

There was a *crack* and a flash of blue. I flinched, and for a second thought he'd shot me, but that had come from their mage using a magic wand on the ditch. Trax's fin dropped beneath the surface as the water rapidly hardened into ice around him.

"Don't worry. For now you're worth more to me alive than dead." Skerrett took his foot off my neck as two of his boys rushed up and hauled me to my feet. One pulled open my cloak, and the other took Gax's pistol. Then he slugged me hard in the stomach.

"That's for blowing me thumb off!"

He'd hit me so hard it would've dropped me wheezing if someone hadn't been holding onto my arm. As it was, I staggered and gagged, bent over around the blow. Then for good measure he whipped me over the head with what had to be the barrel of my own gun, which split open my scalp and left me reeling.

"What about the squalo, boss?"

Mr. Skerrett went over to execute my trapped friend.

"No! Leave him alone," I managed to gasp as he aimed his gun. "Trax has done nothing to you."

BANG!

The bullet hit the magic ice and chips flew.

"You son of a bitch! I'll kill you, Skerrett!"

Mr. Skerrett frowned when he saw the bullet failed to penetrate enough to hit Trax. "Unfortunate… Leave it. There's no reward for the shark thing. Hopefully, the cold will kill it, and if not, by the time it gets free we'll be in the market getting paid."

They were turning me over for the reward. "You two-faced trash. You talked like you hated the Argents."

"I do hate them, but fifty Obols is fifty Obols. Let's go, boys."

24

I was shoved roughly to my knees, and then the bag was pulled off my head.

It was so bright, I was forced to squint to see anything at all. A light charm had been set to levitate right in front of my face. There was someone on each side of me, and at least one more on the other side of the light. That one asked, "So this is Carnavon?"

"In the flesh." That was Mr. Skerrett. "Everything he had on him is in the pack." There was a thump as something got dropped on the floor. I heard the jingle of charms and the *clunk* of something metal inside. "We'll be taking our reward now."

"Enforcer Tulio has your money. He'll pay you on the way out. You can leave now."

"It was a pleasure doing business with you, Ambassador." Skerrett slapped me hard across the bloody back of my head. That stung, but since my hands were tied behind my back there wasn't anything I could do about it. "Nice knowing you, Carnavon."

The Skerretts walked out and the door closed behind them, leaving me with the representatives of a noble house which wasn't known for their mercy. In fact, they were kind of the opposite.

"That whole Skerrett family is nothing but robber trash," someone else said from an unseen corner. "They got kicked off their barge because they were accused of selling stolen equipment. Their behavior in this city has been a stain on our reputation ever since. If the Skerretts weren't allied with Carcalla I'd gladly have had them all killed just to save Fogo the embarrassment of being the place that spawned them."

"But they got me what I wanted right now, Norbert, which is all that currently matters." The light spell lifted until it came to rest against the low ceiling. "How are you doing tonight, Mr. Carnavon?"

"I've been better," I answered truthfully. I blinked until I could sort of see Baron Argent's son sitting on a stool in front of me. The necessity of him being seated became obvious when I realized one of his legs was wrapped in bandages and there was a crutch leaning next to him.

He saw me staring at the wounded limb. "I got clipped by a chunk of your caustic spell. It still hurts like a bastard, even with the aid of magical healing. Took a chunk right out of my calf, it did." He held up his thumb and forefinger about an inch apart. "That big! If I'd not been wearing so many protective charms, you pricks would've killed me dead. Good effort though."

"I had nothing to do with that, I swear."

Dardick Argent gave me a big fake smile. "Well, that sure convinces me of your innocence. What about you, Norbert?"

The fat man standing in the corner snorted.

"Pay no attention to Cousin Norbert. He's our local trade representative and keeps an eye on things here in the Core for us, but all that consorting with city folk has rendered him a suspicious sort. Now let me introduce you to Paulo and Rufino." Dardick nodded toward the back of the room, and when I swiveled my head to look, I saw two very belligerent-looking bodyguards standing there. "They don't talk much, but they're masters at making other people talk, if you get my meaning."

So those were the guys who were going to torture me. *Lovely.* One of them was sharpening a great big knife, while the other was holding a hammer meant for chipping Red, but would probably work equally as well against my bones. When I looked down, I realized I was kneeling on a tarp, so as to keep the embassy's nice wooden floor free of blood stains.

"There's no need for those tools, Ambassador, because I'm already feeling really talkative, and am happy to help clear up any misconceptions."

"You're well spoken for a laborer."

"Barge cadre, sir. 519 took pride in us growing up well cultured. We even had a few books. I already talked to the City Watch about what happened in the market, and they let me go because they knew

I had nothing to do with that foul and reprehensible attempt on your noble life."

"That was nice of them to catch you and not notify me."

"Which watchman did you speak with?" Norbert asked.

"Inspector Borg. Little fellow, big mustache."

Dardick looked to his cousin at that name. "Is Borg one of them who cooperates with us?"

"No. Borg's a true believer in the Code and nothing else. He's unbribable. Believe me, Dardick, we've tried. Word is his family fled to the Core because of some tyrant, so Borg's got a soft spot for runaways."

"I suppose that explains why I had to get you delivered to me by the local hooliganry instead of the local authorities, Mr. Carnavon. Unfortunately for you, we Argents are a bit less trusting than Core folk. Which I'm sure you'll find understandable, seeing as how I'm the one you people have been trying to murder."

"Borg's clever and he'd rather die than let his beloved Great Market be scandalized," Norbert explained. "If he thought this boy had anything to do with the assassins, he would've surely taken him into custody."

"I agree," I quickly added.

"I bet you do," Dardick said. "Regardless, I need to be certain. Hey, Paulo, when you're interrogating people for my father, how many fingers do you usually need to break on someone before you're absolutely sure they're telling you the truth?"

"Three, maybe four. Depends. We talking multiple breaks per finger, how much I grind the joints, and then there's the actual removal of the entire finger." Paulo clearly took great pride in his work. "Do I saw them off slow and gradual like, snap and rip, or just lop them off fast?"

"I never realized there was so much nuance to the subject." Dardick shook his head at the barbarity of it all. "Oh well, we'd best get started then. The hour's already late."

"Whoa, whoa. No need for any of that. I've got nothing to hide. Ask whatever you want!"

"Who tried to murder me?"

Of course he had to start with a hard question. "I don't know."

Unsatisfied by my answer, Dardick signaled for his bodyguard to get to work. I felt Paulo roughly grab hold of my bound wrists, then he began trying to pry my fingers free of my very desperately squeezing fist.

"Why'd you run from the market?"

"Because I wanted out of Fogo! I'm going to become a wizard and buy my family's freedom." Paulo got my pinky free, and for just a moment, I saw a look of squeamish uncertainty cross the ambassador's face. "I ran because I didn't want to work myself to death on the lava just so your dad could get richer!"

Dardick held up one hand, indicating for Paulo to hold off. "So, your defense is that you're not an assassin, just an oath breaking thief? Splendid."

"I swear I don't know who set off that spell."

From what I'd seen and heard at the gate, the baron's middle son wasn't some hardened combatant like Gaul Haddar. He was a young, gregarious, swaggering storyteller, who came to the Core every month with his noble friends to see the foreign girls and drink too much. He'd probably been content with that routine, until someone ruined it by throwing a curse at him. Though Dardick had been putting on a good show of being the cruel interrogator so far, I suspected torturing confessions out of murderous plotters wasn't something he was used to or comfortable with. Baron Argent was a sadistic, petty man, but his middle son might not be nearly as cruel yet.

I might be able to use that to my advantage.

"Ambassador, please, it's true I broke my contract and ran. I admit to that. I'm sorry. My barge got destroyed. I've seen too many friends killed mining the Red. I just couldn't take it anymore. So when I saw my chance, I was tempted and weak. But I'm no murderer. I swear by all the Saints, I don't know who attacked you in the—"

Paulo snapped my pinky finger anyway.

I yelped. I hate to admit it, as that wasn't a particularly manly sound, but in my defense it *hurt.*

"Why'd you do that?" Dardick looked a little sick after hearing the audible crack of my bone. "He was already spilling his guts!"

"I was just keeping him honest."

Normally I'd be too proud to show weakness in front of a hated nobleman, but since I was really hoping Dardick would lose the stomach for this torture business, I didn't try to hide the fact that having the end of your finger snapped is really fucking painful.

"What did you think I meant by *this*, Paulo?" Dardick made the same stopping motion with his hand again, only exaggerated this time. "Most people would take that to mean pause, not start breaking pieces off him."

"Sorry, Dardick."

"My hell. Just stand over there and try not to hurt anything." Dardick shook his head, exasperated. "Forgive my bodyguards, Mr. Carnavon. They get enthusiastic. What were you saying before that unfortunate miscommunication occurred?"

Through gritted teeth I managed to say, "I was proclaiming my innocence."

"Partial innocence. You're an oath breaking runaway. We've established that. Only right now I've deeper tubes to mine."

It bothered me to hear a nobleman who'd probably never done a day of honest physical labor in his life use cadre slang like he was one of his hard-working subjects, but I wasn't about to bring that up. "Alright."

"Good. Because my father, being understandably upset that someone tried to melt his second—but best looking—son, has dispatched his pet murder wizard to bring my attackers to justice. The deadly Gaul Haddar will be here in a few days. Only, I intend to show everyone that I can handle our family business just fine on my own, and I'll have everything all figured out by the time the wizard gets here."

"I'm happy to help," I lied, because I was about as happy as a man could be with his pinky dangling off sideways and throbbing in time with my pulse, which wasn't very happy at all.

Over the next hour, Dardick grilled me endlessly with questions. Occasionally, Norbert would butt in to clarify something or explain how things worked in the Core City for his cousin. I answered as truthfully and earnestly as I could, because Paulo and Rufino were looking bored and had run out of things to sharpen. At least since this place was inhabited by my fellow Fogo folk, the room was kept at a comfortable temperature, so I was warm for the first time since I'd arrived in this freezing city.

Dardick repeatedly asked me if I knew anything about the different political groups trying to take over, various greedy merchants he'd offended, and even other nobles whose daughters he'd deflowered, but I was ignorant about anyone who might want him dead. A couple of times he asked me the same question, just rephrased a bit, to test if I would answer it differently than before. That must have been some kind of ambassador's trick, but it's hard to trip up an honest man.

During all this, Norbert got my pack and dumped it on the floor to rummage through the contents. "It appears he's also stolen a bargemaster's ceremonial handgun."

"I borrowed that."

"Well, well, well..." Norbert picked something up. "What do we have here?"

"What is it, Norbert?"

He held up the enchanted band I'd taken from one of the pirates who'd destroyed my family's barge. "This bears the timeless mark."

"Does it now?" Dardick's eyes narrowed with anger. "Have we finally caught us a crewman of the infamous *Inferno*?"

Now *that* was insulting. "I took that band off a pirate I killed myself. Look at your family's records. I'm one of the survivors of Barge 519."

Norbert checked Gax's gun. "That's the number engraved here."

"I'm no pirate. I hate the *Inferno* more than you can imagine. They killed some of my family and destroyed my home. I'm going to find the elf who commands that black barge and kill him myself, even if it's the last thing I ever do."

"Such conviction! I almost believe you." Dardick studied me carefully. "Yet, could it be that deadly crew that's seeking my death? Those pirates have terrorized every settlement on the Plane of Fire for years with impunity. They've escaped our best, killed a multitude of miners, and stolen a fortune in Red. You bearing their mark is quite the coincidence, isn't it? I think we might need to adjust a few more fingers to refresh your honesty. Paulo..."

"About time," the bodyguard said as he walked over to me.

Before Paulo could get back to snapping, there was a knock on the door.

"What is it?" Dardick shouted.

The door opened and there was another Argent enforcer standing there, looking sheepish. "Sorry to interrupt, Ambassador, but there's an odd visitor waiting downstairs."

"At this time of night? Tell them to come back during business hours, Tulio. Can't you see we're busy interrogating a pirate assassin right now?"

"I know. I tried to send it away, but it just keeps standing there in the entryway, staring silently through me with its dead black eyes." Tulio shuddered. "This creature must be some kind of mage, because it keeps forcing strange and terrible images into my mind. I think it was offering me rat meat in exchange for the prisoner."

There was only one thing that could be describing. "He does love his ratlets. That's a friend of mine. You guys are going to want to be really polite to him. Squalos don't abide rudeness."

"A squalo? You expect us to believe you're *friends* with a rare and legendarily deadly empire from deep within the Elemental Plane of Water?" Dardick asked. "Nonsense."

I turned toward Tulio. "About six and a half feet tall, thick as a Trog, grey with white spots, and way too many really scary teeth?"

The enforcer nodded. "So many teeth."

I looked back to Dardick. "Yeah. That's Trax Bloodtrail." And as soon as I said the short version of his name, I understood how he'd found me so quickly, for the cut on my scalp had never stopped dripping the entire time the Skerretts had been dragging me here. "He's a very respected monk among his people. I've been serving as his translator here. If you offend him, you'll be offending his whole empire."

Dardick clearly thought I was lying, and he was right, as I had no understanding of squalo politics at all, but there was no denying he had an eerie predator waiting on his doorstep. "An ambassador's work is never done. Norbert, help me downstairs." Dardick grabbed his crutch and grimaced as he got off the stool. "Rufino, go wake up the other enforcers in case this shark monk gets uppity. Paulo, stay here and watch the prisoner. If he tries anything, break his knees."

"Gladly." Paulo looked tough enough to beat me senseless on my best day, let alone with my hands tied behind my back, so they weren't particularly worried about me escaping. Plus, from my limited, on my knees view through the window, it felt like we were several stories up, so what was I going to do? Jump through the glass? That would end well.

It was awkwardly quiet after the others left, so I tried to make conversation with the bodyguard, "You worked for the Argent's long?"

Paulo punched me in the face. So much for conversation.

While I was spitting some blood on the tarp, there was another knock. Not from the door this time, but rather, the window.

Paulo and I both looked that direction and was surprised to see there was a lovely young woman crouched outside.

"Azarin?"

She grinned, waved at me, and then ducked as the glass shattered and the room filled with nightmares.

25

"Merciful Saints save us!" Paulo drew his knife, then screamed as a horde of glowing skull-faced ghosts flew around us. He started swinging wildly at the specters. I threw myself on the ground to keep from getting slashed. When his steel did nothing against the howling terrors, Paulo dropped his blade and ran out the door, crying for help. "The dead realm attacks!"

"Nice illusions, huh?" Azarin shouted to be heard over the wailing ghosts as she climbed through the broken window. She tapped the enchanted bracelet she had around one wrist and the specters vanished. "Neves does great work."

I didn't know who that was, nor what a girl I'd only met once was doing here, but I wasn't about to turn down a rescue. I stood up. "Could you grab that knife?"

She got my meaning, snatched up Paulo's blade, and started sawing at the cords binding my wrists. When she accidentally bumped my broken and dangling finger, I managed not to make any unmanly noises in front of her, though some tears may have involuntarily squirted from my eyes.

"Sorry it took so long to get here. It took a bit, but I finally figured out what your big grey friend was trying to tell me."

The cords snapped and I was free. I grabbed my pack, shoved all my belongings back inside nearly one-handed, and threw it on. "We've got to get out of here." I started toward the door.

"Not that way. There's a bunch of soldiers." She grabbed hold of my sleeve and tugged. "This way."

I followed her to the window and looked down. I'd been right about the elevation. We were four stories up, with nothing but the hard ground of the market directly below. The Fogo embassy was next to a canal, right on the edge of the market disk, and I could see the lights of the Under Slump far below. There was no ladder and nothing to hold onto outside except for a narrow ledge of brick.

"Oh hell no."

Azarin showed me she was wearing a glove. "I've got this. Just hold onto me. My descent spell should get us down safely."

The last time I'd watched her use that spell she'd planted herself into a thorn wall, and I weighed a lot more than she did. "Have you tried it with more than one person?"

"My little sister rode piggyback once, though she's like half your size, and the ground was a lot softer, but she barely even broke her ankle when we landed, and honestly? I think that was entirely her fault for panicking."

That was still a lot better than what the Argents would do to me, and I could hear a bunch of them running back up the stairs. "Let's go."

"Hang on tight."

I wrapped my arms around her and squeezed. Distracted as I was, I must admit that felt nice.

"Not that tight. I need to be able to adjust my aim." I put my arms around her waist and Azarin giggled. "Just like slow dancing!"

And then we jumped out the window.

There was a moment of absolute terror as the ground rushed up to meet us.

She shouted in my ear, "*Descend!*"

My cloak flew up around us. Her hair hit me in the eyes. It was as if the air became thicker. When I looked down, we were falling slower, but were still going way too fast as the stones came up to smack us. Azarin must have realized the same thing, as she adjusted where her palm was pointing and we suddenly lurched to the side.

Rather than falling straight down into the market, we were now moving at a curving angle… directly toward the deep, fast waters of the canal. I desperately shouted over the wind, "I can't swim!"

"That's right, you're from fire!" Azarin tried to adjust our trajectory, but it was too late. We weren't going to make the bank. "Wish you would've reminded me sooner."

We hit with a splash. The water went right over my head. The cold was a shock. We were sinking. I let go of Azarin to not drown her with me and started flailing. My boots and pack dragged me down. I couldn't see. I couldn't hear. Panic took hold of me. Trax made swimming look so easy, but it was *not.*

The water was swift. I bounced off the hard side of the canal and managed to get my head above the surface for a second to gasp for more air. Then I was back under, floundering, getting swept along to a certain watery death.

Something big splashed into the water just ahead of me. A hand grabbed my hood and lifted me above the surface.

"*You are very bad at this.*"

"Trax!"

"*The female is less bad, but not good. She swims like a turtle with two legs bitten off. I have you both.*"

The squalo had me on one side, and I could make out the thrashing form of Azarin on the other as we were swept down the canal. There were lights moving above and men shouting as they searched for us. It was so cold I thought I might die, and if Trax let go, I'd surely drown, but if we crawled out now the Argents would catch us for sure. "Keep going until we're away from them."

"*A fine idea.*" And then Trax was dragging us through the water at what had to be nearly the same speed that Azarin's spell had moved us through the air. He'd dip down, pulling us under for several terrifying seconds at a time, and then pop back up just long enough for us to hurry and breathe, before repeating the process. It was so frightening that it made me wonder if I'd been better off taking my chances with the torture.

On one pop up, I noticed the lights were far behind us, and I was about to say it was probably safe to stop here, but Azarin was screaming something I couldn't understand because of all the splashing and water in my ears. I looked ahead just in time to see the end of the canal, and all the water rushing over the edge into the darkness. Trax was about to swim us over a waterfall.

"Stop! Stop!"

"*Do not worry, Carnavon. Squalo do not* fly."

Somehow, despite all the momentum and the powerful current, Trax simply stopped in place only a few feet from the edge. He lifted his head out of the water, glanced around, and then we veered off to the side, where he shoved first me, and then Azarin, up onto the stones.

The two of us lay there in the dark, breathing hard and shaking, as Trax remained in the water.

"*The surface predators have lost our trail.*" I think if Trax ever laughed at anything, he would have right then. "*They are clumsy and dumb.*"

I was so cold I could barely talk. "Are you guys alright?"

"*Though I did not eat any of them, I am having a splendid time. I have learned much today. I look forward to recording my findings on my thought globe.*"

"That's great. Azarin?"

She had to finish coughing up canal water before she could answer. "I think I'm alive."

We needed to keep moving, to put distance between us and the vengeful Argents, and also to stay warm. I was shaking as I got to my feet. This was somehow even worse than when I'd gotten soaked the first night. The tunnel had been still, while there was a breeze up here, and it sliced through my wet clothing like a knife.

"Come on." I offered my hand to help Azarin. "I don't know where, but away from here."

My fingers were so cold that when Azarin took my hand, I couldn't even feel it until she pulled herself up. "I've got a place we can go, Carnavon. The inn I'm staying at isn't too far from here. It's on a platform just off the market."

The innkeeper would probably take one look at me and Trax and throw us out, but that direction would do for now, so we set out at a brisk pace. Trax hopped effortlessly out of the water and plodded along after us.

"What're you doing here?" I asked Azarin.

"Rescuing you, obviously."

"Thank you." I couldn't believe this near stranger just risked her life for me like that. "But why?"

"You seem like a nice guy and all, but really, it's because I need the money. You owe me now. Big time. I had to pay the Sisters of Saint Olga the last money I had to get a magical healing from all the puncture wounds. Sure, they'll help strangers—to a point—but magical services cost. Your weird fish friend showed me the sack filled with coins he'd give for your return. So, pay up."

I didn't know if it was the cold, pistol whipping, or the near drowning which was making me so slow witted, but either way, it took me a moment to grasp what she was saying. "Pay what now?"

"The reward your big grey guy promised." She jerked her thumb back toward Trax. "His brain pictures are hard to understand, but I got the reward part clear as day."

"*It is not my fault human brains are so squishy.*"

We'd get back to this reward I knew nothing about. "How'd you run into Trax?"

"After getting healed, I was on the low road walking back to the inn, when I ran into our big grey fellow here, on all fours, smelling the ground. He recognized me and put a picture in my head that you'd been carried off by bandits, and then he showed me the reward he'd pay me if I helped get you back."

"He what?" I looked to Trax. "You what?"

"*I was helping.*"

"You don't even understand what money is!"

"*I know surface creatures are motivated to collect these round metal objects. The humans who stole you and froze me did so for these* coins. *When I saw another human I knew, it seemed logical to offer her some of these coins in exchange for assisting me.*"

"We don't have any to give her. We're broke."

"*This is correct. You should probably remedy this.*"

Azarin was only catching half of that conversation, but it was enough. "Dammit all to hell. Did I risk my life just to get ripped off?"

Regardless of my circumstances, I had too much pride for that. "No. There's been a misunderstanding, sure. Trax doesn't really grasp concepts like money, or promises, or a whole bunch of other stuff… but I honor my debts."

"*Isn't it not honoring your debts which caused these humans to be angry at you to begin with?*"

"That's different," I told Trax, before assuring Azarin, "I've got nothing to pay you with right now, but I'll make this right. You have my word."

"Your word won't pay for new clothes, and it sure won't be enough to get me through an academy's door. Now I'm wet and poor and walking in the dark with a ruffian and a fish." Azarin seemed more disappointed than angry as she muttered something else under her breath, too quiet for me to hear.

"*I saw the words form in her mind,*" Trax projected helpfully. "*She said,* Naanwaala, I'm a sucker. I should know better than to ever trust the cute ones... *Is she referring to me? Am I the* cute one?"

I thought extra hard, *Not now, Trax,* before speaking aloud again, "You two saved my life. If the Argents didn't torture me to death tonight, they'd have sent me back through the gate to die in prison. So, you're right. I do owe you, and I will repay you. You helped me. I promise I'll help you."

Azarin sighed. "You'd better. You've got to understand, Carnavon, I can't return to Stormwolk a failure."

I understood how she felt, because the way things were going, the only way I was returning to Fogo was as a prisoner or in a box.

26

Though there was no passage between realms during the night, while the Great Machine rotated toward the next gate, the market still remained busy. The neighborhoods off the market disk were less crowded, but even at this late hour there were people out and about. It was said the Core City never slept, and many of the races which traded here were nocturnal anyway.

Magic was so common here that they had light charms over many of the streets, which was nice for navigating, but made us easy to spot. Trax had lost his blanket and basket, and squalo were rare and noteworthy, so word of his presence would surely get back to the Argents, and they'd come looking. Luckily there was a pond behind the inn Azarin was staying at, and Trax was perfectly happy to take a nap beneath its surface while Azarin and I went inside.

With most of the people staying at the inn asleep in their rooms upstairs, the tavern below only had a few patrons, and they weren't sober enough to notice the two of us standing in the entrance, damp and shivering. I was glad that the fireplace was lit, and went straight to it in a desperate attempt to get warm.

"First time away from home, and I've been nearly drowned so many times I might as well have gone to the Elemental Plane of Water instead." I took off my cloak and set it on the stones in the vain hope it might dry. The rest of the paper cartridges on my belt were feeling rather smooshy, so I doubted any of them survived. Until I could find more ammo, Gax's pistol was basically a decorative club.

"It's not exactly my idea of fun, either," Azarin said. "We do have rivers where I'm from, but only temporarily from the flash floods, so not ideal for swimming."

There'd been no mention of her home in the encyclopedia volumes I'd read. "What's Stormwolk like?"

"High up and treacherous."

"By footing, or culture?"

"Both. My home is one giant rocky peak where the Plane of Earth trespasses into the endless sky. The whole thing's infested with griffons—who're always trying to pluck us humans off the sides to drop us to our doom, because griffons are dicks like that—and it's the home of the giant eagles."

Most of the native wildlife where I was from was on fire. "That sounds majestic."

"They're not really. Giant eagles shit *everywhere*. But Stormwolk's not so bad if you don't mind endless warfare between the clans and getting struck by lightning occasionally. We chase the storms, collect the Clear, then fight over who gets to keep it to sell it in the Core." She peeled off her sopping wet cloak and draped it over a chair.

I couldn't help but notice that Azarin's shirt was clingy and got rather see-through while wet. After a few seconds of staring at the gorgeous girl from the storm realm, I reminded myself I was a gentleman and made sure to watch the fire instead.

"So, who was that me and fish face rescued you from?"

"The Argents," I answered as I adjusted my broken finger back into the right spot, which hurt like a son of a bitch, but miners get used to such discomforts, and I wasn't about to show weakness in front of a girl.

She clearly felt bad for me anyway. "Who are they?"

"Fogo's noble family. Somebody tried to assassinate our baron's son, and they think I'm involved."

"Are you?"

"Of course not." Despite my best efforts to appear invincible, I winced as I used a strip of cloth to tie my broken finger to the next one in line. "Why would I be?"

Azarin shrugged. "Murdering one of your superiors is the most common way to get a promotion in Stormwolk. Our politics are kind of cut throat like that. Taking other clan's important people hostage and holding them for ransom is normal for us."

She was really making me not want to visit the place. "I'm innocent, but they've put a price on my head."

"How much are we talking about?"

"Fifty Obols. Though after tonight I bet it goes up."

"Damn." Azarin whistled. "For a hundred I'd turn you in myself…"

I stared at her, and she looked back at me trying to play it serious, but then she laughed.

"I'm kidding. Relax, Carnavon. My people cut plenty of throats, but I find all that shit tiresome. All that back stabbing and treachery isn't for me. I left because I'm too honest for my own good." Azarin sat on the bricks of the hearth. "I've gone my own way. I love magic. I'm going to make it as a mage."

"Me too." I sat down next to her. The temperature difference was so starkly different from outside that it was making my face tingle. Or that might have just been the proximity to Azarin, who was a very intriguing girl. "The deck's stacked against us though."

"You've tried all the academies already?"

"A bunch of them." I told her about my experience at each of the ones I'd tried, and how Inspector Borg told me us lowly rank ones had little chance at all.

She frowned as she listened to my litany of failures. "After all that, why still do it?"

That was a hard question to answer. "You mentioned your patron Saint after we pulled you out of the thorns. The Saint I follow is Ketekunan."

"Which one is he?"

"The Saint of Persistence. It's a Fogo thing. Ketekunan was one of the first to mine the Red. He refused to give up, no matter the challenge, being a man so stubborn even the Gods noticed and lifted him up as a paragon. My people don't back down easy. Where I'm from, its persevere or perish. This isn't any different. I've got family counting on me. My trying to help them screwed everything up and has only made their situation worse, though. Right now, I'm powerless to fix what I broke, so I need to get power."

Azarin nodded in appreciation of that. "Our circumstances may be different, but I can relate."

"I know I'm just a rank one, but I earned that on my own. I'm no natural talent."

Azarin shifted a little bit closer to me. "You've seen some of my spells. Show me what you can do."

"Well… I've taught myself a few formulae, but they're kinda… destructive." I glanced around the tavern, which looked fairly flammable, and couldn't think of a way to show off for her, tempting as that was. I wasn't about to toss a snail grenade in here, and invoking a curtain of fire would probably set the real curtains on fire, and the screws of chaos would certainly wake up the snoring drunks, summon the proprietor, and get me kicked out of here. "I did make this." I dragged my pack over, rummaged through it and pulled out my copper bowl. "It boils water."

The girl who could fling herself into the sky and then float down like a leaf looked at my sad little bowl. "That's nice."

I put the bowl away. "I promise the other ones are more impressive."

"Sure they are," and she said that convincingly enough I almost believed she meant it. "You know, Carnavon, I've got an idea. If it's a waste of time for rank ones like us to try to get into an academy, the more spells we master, with the more different elements, the higher we'd test."

"Yeah. That's true."

"I know some air spells. You know some fire."

"You proposing a trade? Because wizards don't normally share their secrets."

She leaned in a bit closer, probably to be conspiratorial rather than flirty, but either way, I didn't mind. "You already owe me, hotlander."

I was trying to decide if I should make a move on the exotic air girl when someone bellowed, "Azarin Garzade! Where have you been, cursed girl?"

Azarin quickly scooted away from me. "Oh shit, it's Neves."

"What are you doing out at this ungodly hour?" A hefty dwarven lady, with the volume to match her considerable girth, came stomping down the stairs. Her noisy descent caused some of the drunks to lift their heads and check to see if there was an earthquake going on. Neves wore the same light air realm style clothing as Azarin, but while the others I'd seen today had been tall and thin, Neves was short and as wide as Trax. I'd never seen a dwarven female before, and was glad to see the rumors they grew beards too was false.

"I just got back," Azarin stammered.

"Look at the state of you! What are you doing with this boy?"

"Nothing. We were just talking."

"Sure you were." Neves stomped over to us, oozing suspicion. "*Suuuure.*"

Assuming this had to be Azarin's chaperone, I stood up to be polite as possible. "Hello, ma'am."

Neves stopped before me and scowled hard. "Who're you?"

"Oz Carnavon. It's a pleasure to meet you."

Neves didn't bother to respond to me, looking toward Azarin. "You sneak off as soon as we arrive, and the next thing I know, I find you traipsing about with gutter trash?"

"Hey now." We didn't even have gutters where I was from.

"He's not *trash*, Neves. And I wasn't *traipsing*. I was heroically rescuing a fellow wizard from vile kidnappers. By the way, here's your illusion charm back." Azarin tossed a bracelet to her.

The dwarf caught it. "You little thief."

"Oh, come on. You didn't even know it was gone."

"You're going to be the death of me, girl. If you get in trouble again while I'm supposed to be watching over you, General Mazdak will stick my head on his trophy wall." Neves jerked her considerable chin toward me. "Same fate goes for any boy stupid enough to lay a lustful hand upon the hero of Stormwolk's beloved daughter."

I vaguely remembered Mazdak as being Azarin's father's name when she'd announced herself in the Wynlyn's park. "General?"

Azarin waved that revelation away like it was nothing. "Oh, don't worry. Father only puts the heads of monsters and his very worst enemies on his trophy wall. He's not got the extra space sufficient for frivolous heads. And we're only friends, Neves. Carnavon here saved me after I got stuck in an elven thorn wall. Hence the sorry state of my clothes. Which by the way, do you think I could borrow some money from you to get some new ones in the market tomorrow? I'll pay you back."

The dwarf seemed used to Azarin's rapid changing of subjects. "Where have you been all day?"

"It's a long story." And as she said that, Azarin caught my eye and made an expression that I took to mean she didn't want me to elaborate. "But anyways, I'm back now, and terribly sleepy." She faked a big yawn and stretch, before hopping off the hearth. "I'm going to bed."

"Aye. To bed… by yourself." Neves remained standing there in my way.

"Of course. Perhaps we'll get to continue our conversation about magical education opportunities later, Mr. Carnavon."

"I'd like that. See you later, Ms. Garzade."

As Azarin skipped her way up the stairs, the dwarf remained planted there, watching me guardedly and not saying a thing. She looked about as critical of me as Gax did inspecting a faulty barge.

"I assure you, ma'am, nothing untoward happened. I barely know her."

"That's right, boy, because if you knew her and had half a brain in your head, you'd get scared and run for the mountains, because that girl is a whirlwind of trouble."

27

I don't care where you are, if there's people, there's going to be fights and gambling on them.

Battered, hungry, and cold, I stood in line with the other would-be gladiators, waiting for my chance to win some money or magical element. Apparently, all I had to do was beat the hell out of another low-ranking wizard and not die in the process. It wasn't an ideal plan, but it was something.

The official sanctioned contests between rival academies were held in fancy arenas in the Collegium and upper parts of the city. This was the less legal, less organized battle of the scrubs, held in the Under Slump, far away from the eyes of the City Watch. There were rumors of even baser, crueler blood sports that took place in the ruins of the ancient city beneath, but I wanted no part of that. The Aventines had been built atop the bones of the civilization that existed before the founding of the Core. Supposedly what went on down there in those dark, lawless caverns catered to the tastes of those who came from the more savage kingdoms.

I'd had to leave Trax behind. Squalo were rare enough that if one was seen, Argent agents would be sure to hear. So, I was all by myself.

It was Earthnight, which left me three days before Gaul Haddar arrived to end my life. I'd barely escaped a clown like Dardick. Once a murderous rank eight came after me, I was doomed. I'd spent the whole day searching for an academy again, but that proved just as fruitless as before. Nor had I seen Azarin since last night. She hadn't been there when I'd stopped by her inn. I'd told myself that I needed to find her so I could try to learn some air spells, and not for any other ulterior motives, but even I didn't believe my own lies.

With no other ideas, it was time for desperate measures. I'd heard some talk about these underground fights that were open to rank ones and twos, and paid fairly well, provided you didn't get mangled or killed.

When I reached the end of the line, there was a hideous little green goblin waiting there next to a chalkboard filled with names and odds. This must be the bookie. He looked me over disapprovingly. "You been told the rules. Five percent of the house if you lose. Twenty if you win. You still want to fight?"

"I'm in."

"Name?"

I'd not thought of that. "Do I have to give you one?"

The bookie looked up from writing on his chalkboard and noted I was wearing a mask over my mouth and nose, which I'd been told wasn't out of place when someone respectable didn't want to be recognized in this dishonorable slum. I wasn't respectable, but I didn't want the Skerrets to try and sell me to the Argents again.

"The crowd can't bet on someone if they got no name."

"Sure." I figured my fake laborer name would work just as well for a fighter. "Put down Tom."

The goblin wrote *Put Down Tom* in a bracket. "Type?"

"What do you mean, type?"

The creature stared at me with his big googly goblin eyes like I was an imbecile. "Enchanter, invoker, conjuror, necromancer, or what?"

Being self-taught, I actually had no idea. I'd had my best luck with enchanting objects to use later, though I could successfully invoke on demand most of the time now with my shroud of fire. "Let's go with enchanter."

"Rank?"

"One."

The goblin giggled as he wrote that on the board.

"What's so funny?"

"The thought of humans dying always makes me laugh." The goblin put his hands on his hips, thought it over, then wrote a name in the bracket next to my fake one. *Krachma the Killer. Rank two.* Then he put the opening odds. Twenty to one. They were not in my favor.

"I'm new at this, but that match up seems kind of lop sided."

"You'll be fine," the goblin lied, and it was so brazen, he didn't even care if I believed him or not. "Go down the ramp, get your magic and weapons ready, and they'll call when it's your turn."

Consisting of wooden bleachers that had been erected inside the walls of a burned-out mansion, the arena wasn't much to look at. There were hundreds of raucous people in those seats right now, shouting encouragement or hate at the fighters below. The battle would take place in the pit that had been the house's basement.

I stopped on the ramp to watch the current match up.

One of the fighters was a human, with skin of such a pallor he made me look like a Core dweller, and the other was a dwarf with a gigantic red beard. The human had a sword and was dancing around, wasting far too much energy showing off his fancy foot work, while the dwarf stayed planted behind a tower shield with an axe at the ready. They traded a few blows, but neither were ready to commit. The crowd, being able to see mundane zeros stab at each other at plenty of non-magical gladiatorial events, began to boo them.

"We came to see a mage fight!" shouted a man on the front row. "Do some spells already!"

The human was happy to oblige. He shouted something in a language I didn't understand, and the center of the arena was suddenly engulfed in thick smoke. The spell obscured an area ten feet across so completely, it blotted out the arena's light charms. That was fascinating to me, because I'd never seen a shadow spell from the deadlands before.

No longer able to see his opponent, the dwarf shuffled back, only to have the human jump though the darkness to strike him over the top of his head. The crowd roared.

In a regular fight, that blow would've left brains showing, but mage fight combatants were issued protective charms to keep the events from ending too quickly. When the blade hit, there had been a strange visual distortion over the dwarf's skull. The air was left rippling, and the dwarf staggered away, clearly in pain, but very much not dead.

The shadow smoke dissipated and the human from the Realm of Death lifted his sword, triumphant. The audience loved it.

But the fight wasn't over until their protective charms were used up. The deadlander said something else in his weird language, pointed his sword at the dwarf, and it *shot spiders* at him.

Now that spell—to be honest—was pretty fucking unsettling.

There was still old furniture and broken pillars in the basement, and the dwarf used some of those for cover as black shadow spiders bounced off and went scurrying away. Someone in the audience began to panic and flail as a giant black spider got caught in her hair.

The dwarf ducked behind his metal shield, thumped his axe against the floor, and a bunch of concrete fragments that were scattered about immediately flew up to smack against the deadlander, hard enough to knock him on his ass. The impacts left a mirage shimmering in the air, like watching the heat rise over a fresh lava crust back home.

The crowd was having a great time—except for the one lady who was getting bitten on the scalp by a conjured spider, obviously—and goblins were running up and down the stairs, taking new bets. Now this was a proper show!

"You want to spectate, buy a ticket," snapped the goblin waiting for me at the bottom of the ramp. He was three feet tall, green, and very impatient. "If you're here to fight, now's your chance to kit up, else I'll send you out there with no protective charm, stupid human."

I forced my eyes off the battle and went to my corner goblin. He led me into a little room with various weapons hanging on the wall. The only thing separating us from the battle was a gate of iron bars.

"What do I need to do?"

"Put this on, dummy." He gave me a necklace made from an iron chain. "That should stop two deaths worth of bullet, blade, or magic."

"Should?"

"Nobody's perfect." The goblin shrugged. "The protection's automatic unless you will it off. Yield before the third blow lands, or you'll regret it."

"How will I know when the protections are used up?"

"Trust me, even a stupid dumb idiot human will be able to tell. This charm should stop the wound but makes sure you feel the pain extra good, same as if it had pierced you."

"Is that necessary?" I put the chain around my neck.

"The audience enjoys the obvious suffering, so they bet more. The more they bet, the more you make."

I'd been asking out of magical curiosity, not economic value. "I'll be sure to put on a good show."

"You fight Krachma. You will be lucky to survive. Anything goes out there, but I'll warn you, clumsy oaf, that Carcalla, boss of the Slumps, will make you pay for anyone in the audience you wound on accident. He owns this arena. He does not like when morons kill his customers."

"Got it. Don't kill the audience." So much for using my snail grenade. Its fragmentation was rather unpredictable.

A body slammed violently against the metal gate. It was the deadlander, and the dwarf landed on top of him, slamming axe against neck. The charm stopped *most* of it. But then the screaming and squirting started.

"Damn it!" The goblin seemed very annoyed as he shouted up the ramp, "Get the healer before we have to toss another body in the canal." Then he looked back toward me and grinned, showing his pointy yellow teeth. "You're up."

My hands were shaking. My stomach felt like I was about to chase a Fire Elemental into its lair, only at least there, I would've been warm. I hurried and checked that all my magic was in place. I had my stash of Red, my pocketful of screws, and my last snail grenade, which I couldn't use without risking the wrath of Carcalla, and I'd already made enough enemies here. Then I checked my weapons. I had Gax's gun—though only the single cartridge that had been loaded in it survived being submerged—and my hunting knife.

Several goblins ran down the ramp, opened the gate, and carried the wounded deadlander through. A rotund female goblin wearing the symbol of Saint Olga wrapped a magic rag around his bloody neck, which began to sizzle with the heat of a Red powered spell, as it cauterized the wound. As he screamed and thrashed, the goblin medic screeched, "That'll leave a mark!" and all the other goblins laughed at his pain. At least they seemed to enjoy their job.

The dwarf walked back to the middle of the basement, then raised his axe overhead triumphantly while the spectators cheered. A man wearing the black band of the Latrocinium went into the ring and used some kind of voice magnifying spell to announce the victor.

"Our winner, by what would have been decapitation, Veroy Durrel!" He gave the dwarf another moment to enjoy the adoration, before putting one hand on his shoulder and shoving him toward the exit. There were more fights to hold and money to make. "What a display of mighty earth magic, triumphing over the skeletal hand of the death realm, but get ready, folks, because Master Carcalla has sought out many fearsome combatants for your enjoyment tonight. Our next bout features one of your favorites against a newcomer to our arena."

The crowd began to chant, "*Krachma. Krachma. Krachma.*" Their enthusiasm for my opponent was a bit unnerving.

"Our new challenger, a masked stranger from parts unknown, is…" the announcer looked at the slip of paper in his hand, "Put Down Tom, an enchanter of the first rank!"

Figuring that was my signal, I walked through the gate. The crowd immediately began to boo. A few of them threw garbage at me. I ignored them, because in my head, I was back on the crust, stalking an Elemental. *No distractions.* I recited the Trapper's creed in my head. *Plan. Persist. Survive.* I looked over the terrain, memorizing where the broken desks and beds, chunks of stone, and the partial remains of a curving stairwell were.

"And the gladiator you've been waiting for, invoker of the second rank, winner of five matches so far here in the Slumps, a veteran soldier come all the way from the deep canyon armies of Mooralga on the Elemental Plane of Earth, it is Krachma the Killer!"

The gate opposite me swung open, and everybody in the arena stood up to cheer. As soon as my opponent lumbered in, I understood why the odds were twenty to one. Krachma was a lob, like the academy guard who'd tried to whack me with a spear. He was nearly seven feet tall, and if he was as dense as he looked, probably weighed four hundred pounds. Shirtless, his wrinkly hide was a dull orange, except for where scars had formed like hardened black rock formations, and there were *lots* of those. Krachma didn't so much as acknowledge the adoring crowd, he just turned his big square head my way and stared, nonchalant, as if to say, *It is nothing personal, but I am about to squish you.*

It was a good thing this was a magical fight rather than fists like back home, because I figured I'd need a sledgehammer to make a dent in this fellow. Krachma didn't even have a weapon on him that I could see, other than two great big hands. Despite being unarmed, he didn't seem worried in the least.

"Use your spells, use your weapons, use your might! Fight until one yields or can fight no more." The announcer looked at me, and I nodded that I was ready. Then he looked to Krachma, who seemed bored to be here. "Begin!"

Krachma took one ponderous step my way.

I swiftly drew Gax's gun and shot him.

There was a shower of sparks as his protective charm reacted. The flattened bullet bounced off his chest, and Krachma kept moving toward me, showing no pain. And to think the goblin promised we'd still feel it.

Unless... that reaction *was* him feeling the pain of getting shot... Which wasn't a good sign at all.

Krachma clapped his hands together once. "*Crush.*"

I felt the vibration through my boots as the ground around me trembled. I threw myself backwards, narrowly avoiding two big pieces of concrete floor that were ripped up to smash into pieces right where I'd been standing.

I shoved Gax's gun back into the holster. Even if I'd had more ammo, I doubted Krachma would allow me the time to reload. I really needed more guns! Instead, I pulled out a handful of screws, focused on awaking the Red I'd bonded to the steel, and hurled them at the approaching lob. They were glowing red as they landed at his feet, scattering across the broken ground around him. Then they began to hiss and pop.

Krachma had a very calm, very deep voice as he crossed his arms and declared, "*Impervious*."

Instantly, all of his skin turned stone grey, and he became perfectly still as a statue. He remained that way as the screws of chaos ignited and careened around him. They stabbed and scorched the broken furniture and set some moldy cushions on fire, but rather than sticking and burning Krachma, they bounced off as if he was as solid as the concrete. A few seconds after my Red magic died off, the grey coating turned to dust and fell away. Krachma was once again orange and moving steadily right at me.

I hadn't realized how disproportionately long a lob's arm was until his fist came around and nearly took my head off. I ducked, weaved, and tried to make distance. Krachma followed. I got behind the stairwell just as he punched a wooden step off of it. I grabbed a chair to throw at him and immediately regretted it, because I'd forgotten about my broken finger. Krachma effortlessly smashed the chair out of the air anyway. He kept coming. I ran.

The danger wasn't that he was fast, it was that he was relentless.

I tossed a pinch of Red dust into the air as I retreated. As Krachma blundered right into the cloud, I invoked the Red, and a sudden shroud of fire engulfed his head. It turned out even tough guys could get surprised, and Krachma lurched to the side, bent over, clutching at his eyes.

He surely thought he could take a second to let his vision clear because an opponent with any sense would be trying to keep their distance, so I did the opposite, taking three quick steps his way and kicked him right in the face.

From the crowd's surprised reaction, I don't think they expected a regular sized human to break a lob's big snout.

Krachma slowly rose back to his full height. Then he reached up and cracked his nose loudly back into place.

Blowing bloody snot bubbles, he went at me again, and this time he closed his eyes before walking head first into my next shroud of fire. I rolled over a desk to get away, and his fist snapped the boards in half behind me.

"*Crush.*"

That time, I didn't *quite* make it out of the way as the concrete rose up around me. The pieces of the floor hit like two hands clapping, only with one of my legs still between them. The protective charm activated as the concrete exploded into fragments and dust, but my bones didn't.

Saints have mercy. The goblin hadn't been lying about the enchantment, because it *felt* exactly like my leg had just gotten smashed into paste.

It took a few seconds for that artificial agony to subside, and while it did, I was wrecked to the point of uselessness. I barely got out of the way as Krachma tried to club me again. I fell over some rotting furniture. He simply tossed it out of the way and kept chasing me.

The magically induced pain was *everything* and then it was just gone. Once I was able to think clearly again, I realized Krachma had used my disorientation to maneuver me back into the middle of the basement, where I was surrounded by hundreds of bits of broken concrete, and nowhere to hide.

"*Debris.*" The lob swept one hand wide, and dozens of the smaller chunks on the ground began to shake. When he pointed that hand at me, all the pieces he'd magically gathered flew my way at once, each one moving like it had been thrown by a very strong arm.

It was the same spell the dwarf had used on the deadlander, so it must have been a common one in the earth realm. And I could see why, because it was really fucking effective, and thanks to the last charge on my protective charm, I got to learn what it felt like to be stoned by an angry mob.

I hit the floor, reeling from more impacts than I could count. I'd been hit *everywhere*. If not for the charm, I'd have cracked my skull, lost an eye, and bruised every muscle beyond use. So, I lay there, soaking in that terrible sensation, as Krachma paused to enjoy his victory before his adoring crowd.

This was the most pain I'd ever been in. It hurt so bad, for a second I thought the protection spell had failed and I was actually dying. Except the spell must have worked. I was still conscious, and as far as I could tell, all my blood remained on the inside.

It was over. I'd used up my two protective enchantments. The next hit would be for real. It was give up now or get crippled, or worse. The announcer had even opened the gate to come back out, thinking the fight was over.

I wobbled my way back to my feet. From the surprise on Krachma's ugly mug, he must not have ever met any followers of the Saint of Persistence before. We weren't about to let little things like getting beaten to a pulp stop us.

"Seriously?" the announcer asked me.

"Let's fucking go," I shouted, before I could lose my nerve.

Krachma shrugged, as if to say it was my funeral, then he started toward me one last time.

My opponent was incredibly strong, and his magic was deadly, but he was also methodical, plodding. Having seen how he used his spells, he didn't strike me as the type who could mix it up on the fly. Especially now that he was winning. Why change? Just like taking down powerful Fire Elementals, if you fight them head-to-head, you're probably going to lose. It was always better to outthink them and let their confidence lead them into a trap.

I pulled another handful of screws from my pocket and tossed them at Krachma.

He saw them hit the ground and scatter. *"Impervious."*

Only this time, as Krachma's body turned unmoving as stone, I rushed him. The screws had been a distraction. I hadn't even activated their magic. In the few seconds it took for his spell to dissipate before he could move again, I'd swept around him, jumped up onto his back, wrapped one arm around his neck, and shoved the point of my hunting knife in his ear canal.

"Yield!"

I'll give the big fellow credit. Even with a sharpened blade aimed at his brain, he actually had to think it over and didn't immediately surrender. There was a magical blur around my knife, as his protective charm had already activated to combat the pressure I was applying.

He grudgingly admitted, "Krachma has lost."

I fell off him and backed away, knife at the ready just in case he changed his mind.

The lob turned to me, wiped his bloody nose, then bowed his head in a gesture of respect.

The crowd was quiet, and then they went wild over this upset. There was cheering, booing, and general confusion—I'm sure the handful of gamblers crazy enough to bet on me were the loud happy ones—and then the announcer was between us, declaring Put Down Tom the victor in this shocking upset of fire over earth.

I won't lie. Winning felt good.

I stood there, still surprised I'd survived, until some goblins started dragging me out of the arena so the next fighters could come in.

When I saw my corner goblin in the ready room, he was already prepping his next fighter, but he took the time to snap at me, "Give back my charm, human! No one robs from the minions of Carcalla!"

"I wasn't trying to." I tossed him the depleted chain, disappointed I'd not had a chance to examine it first to try and figure out what elements had been bound to it. Protection would be an incredibly useful spell to know. "Is there any chance you could tell me who enchants these for you? I'd love to buy one of these, preferably without the extra pain added."

"No! Our formula is secret. Go to the market if you want a charm so bad and buy it with your winnings, fool. I lost money betting that big dumb Krachma was going to kill you!"

"Well, you bet like a sucker then, didn't you?" I walked up the ramp without looking back.

At the chalk board, the bookie wasn't very happy as he gave me my winnings. "Krachma was a crowd favorite. Now they will pity him. Pity does not bet high."

I ignored his grumbling. This was more Core money than I'd earned over the last few years of guiding adventurers on the side. I took my winnings half in coin and half in a vial of Clear.

I had spells to learn and ranks to gain.

28

As I walked up from the Under Slump, I felt like someone was following me, but each time I looked back and checked, no one stood out. I had a trapper's instincts. Sometimes we tracked Fire Elementals, and sometimes they tracked us. This felt like that, but was probably just nerves. The fight had left me wrung out. I must have gone from euphoria to paranoia.

It was late Earthnight when I arrived at the inn Azarin was staying at. The proprietor, having found me asleep next to his great room's fireplace really early that morning, had called me a bum and thrown me out. When the old fellow saw me walk in, he picked up a club from beneath the bar and started my way.

"Oh, it's this ass again. I warned you I got no patience for vagrants."

"I'm a paying customer this time." I tossed him a small coin, which thankfully he saw coming, and snatched out of the air.

Rather than trying to club me over the head, he examined it. "One whole Tetar?"

"Is that enough for some food, a room for the night, and a bath?"

He bit the coin to make sure it was real. Satisfied, he said, "Barely. And only if I throw in the bath for free, because the smell of you would chase away my business otherwise."

"Everybody in the Core is just so damned friendly." He didn't seem to catch the sarcasm, but I was happy to not be treated like trash for a minute. "Thank you, kind sir."

After I'd eaten and gotten cleaned up, I snuck some food out to the pond in back. The yard was quiet and deserted. I'd gotten a pail of old scraps from the kitchen, the sort of thing they'd throw to the street dogs, and I set it down next to the edge.

"*Hello, Carnavon. I have remained concealed as you requested.*"

Trax was doing a great job of it too, because other than a bubble occasionally floating to the surface between the lily pads, there was no indication a deadly squalo was hiding in there. If someone decided to go swimming, that would've been quite the surprise.

"I got you some supper. This is the best I could come up with."

A big grey hand reached out of the water, grabbed the pail, and pulled it under.

"*Gizzards? Excellent. That is my favorite part of the avians.*"

"Sorry I had to abandon you, but you stick out like a sore thumb. It was good though. I beat the hell out of a rank two in one of the Under Slump arenas. I wish you could have been there."

There was some thrashing, and then the pail was tossed back onto shore. In his excitement, Trax had bitten a jagged chunk out of the metal. I hoped the cook wouldn't notice when I put it back. "*Do not worry. I have had a fine time meditating and observing the surface dwellers' behavior while remaining unseen. Did you know the innkeeper waits until his neighbor leaves, and then secretly mates with his neighbor's wife?*"

"That's called adultery. It's generally frowned upon."

"*Humans are fascinating.*"

"Yeah, fascinating. Anyways, tomorrow we'll take another shot at the Collegium. I won a bit of money, so in the morning I'll sneak into the market so I can get us outfitted to look more respectable. I really feel like I'm starting to get the hang of this place."

"*The Core City is vast. We have seen but a tiny portion of it, and most of the places we have gone people have tried to kill us.*"

"Figure of speech, Trax. I'm going to go see if I can find Azarin and get her to teach me some air spells."

"*And I will record on my memory sphere how humans think violence for profit is good, but this adultery is bad.*"

"Well, there might be some disagreement, but that's the consensus at least."

I went back inside, and while I waited in the busy common room hoping to spot Azarin, the rush of the fight wore off completely, leaving me exhausted. It was while I was trying not to nod off that I noticed someone sitting on a stool who was using the mirror over the bar to watch me. He was human, of average size, with a black beard, dressed in a long coat and wide-brimmed hat, with nothing particularly noteworthy about him, except something about him seemed familiar. When I spotted him spying on me, he conveniently went back to his drink.

I couldn't remember where I'd seen this man before, but my first panicked thought was that he might have been one of the Skerret family, though that wasn't it. And he clearly wasn't any of the Argents I'd met. Maybe I'd seen him around the Collegium? Regardless, I was now betting that my earlier feeling of being followed after the fight had been correct.

I tried to decide if I should go confront him or not. It might be nothing. It might be something.

"Carnavon!" Azarin bounced up to my table, happy to see me here. The glowering dwarf woman standing behind her was obviously displeased by my presence.

"Oh hey, Azarin." Her arrival brought a smile to my face. Then I nodded politely toward her chaperone. "Mrs. Neves."

"What're you doing here?" Neves asked suspiciously, as if I was about to abscond with her general's daughter.

"I've got a room at this fine establishment temporarily, at least until I find more permanent lodging at a magical academy."

"That's nice," Azarin said. "Isn't that nice, Neves?"

"Yeah… lovely."

I glanced back toward the bar, and though I'd only been distracted for a moment, my watcher was gone. Someone else walked up and took the now empty stool where he'd been sitting. There was no sign of him anywhere in the tavern. The front doors were still swinging shut. He must have moved as soon as I looked away. "I'll be right back."

When I went out the doors and looked around, there was nobody there. The city's light charms illuminated most of the street out front and there were very few people out and about for him to have blended in with. I came back, unsure if my mind was playing tricks on me or not.

"What was that about?"

"Just thought I saw someone I know. Guess I was mistaken." I sat back down.

"You should get some rest, young lady," Neves suggested to her charge.

"Doubtful. I'm too excited. Hey, barkeep! Bring us some beers!" Azarin plopped into one of the chairs. "Today I visited a few academies and got shit to show for it. How about you?"

"I made some progress." I didn't elaborate about my newfound income, as I suspected Azarin would think magical pit fighting was great, but her guardian probably wouldn't.

Neves sighed, held up three fingers to the barkeep, and sat in the chair between us to protect Azarin's virtue.

"You know I'm an adult, Neves. Father doesn't expect you to babysit me the entire time you're in the Core. You promised to get me here safely, and now I'm here. I know you owe him, but I can handle myself."

The dwarf snorted at that and then spoke to me instead, "Lady Azarin told me of your plan to trade her air spells for your fire, Mr. Carnavon."

I'd been unaware that was my idea, but I went along with the premise, "It seems reasonable since we're both independently trying to further our educations. The best way to increase one's ranking is through mastering more spells."

"True, but I warned her against this. There's a reason schools protect their secrets and never share their formula with outsiders."

"Yeah, 'cause they're snoots," Azarin said. "They spent the whole day rejecting me, even though I know if I showed up flashing chests of father's gold, for sure they'd at least talk to me."

"If you could do that, why don't you?" Having always been poor, I was genuinely curious. "Chests of gold aren't really an option for most of us."

Azarin and Neves shared a look that suggested there was something awkward in the answer.

"Well, Carnavon, I no longer have access to my family's fortune, because me and my father had a bit of a disagreement about the best direction for my future. So, I decided to part ways with Stormwolk and make it on my own."

"That's a fine way of saying you're cut off because you sabotaged your own wedding and insulted a rival clan chief in the process by shoving his son—your fiancé—off the back of a giant eagle."

Azarin waved one hand dismissively. "Oh *that*? That was all a big misunderstanding."

"The eagle was five hundred feet up in the air at the time."

"The only thing damaged on Arsace was his pride. He's an insufferable prick, but he had enough protection charms on him he barely even bounced when he hit the mountainside."

Neves frowned at her excuse. "And then young Azarin here got permission to go to the Core City, because she blackmailed our oracle into proclaiming she was destined to become a mage—"

"Blackmail is such an ugly word, Neves! Everybody knows the oracles just make stuff up anyway. I merely helped her interpret her visions the correct way."

"Not that most of our clan was sad to see Azarin go, because we all knew if she remained in Stormwolk, it would probably provoke another war, against the very same clan her arranged marriage was supposed to have sealed a peace treaty with."

Azarin shrugged. "I never had much patience for politics. Oh, beer's here. Thank you."

Mugs were placed in front of us by the serving girl.

"I don't know much about the traditions of the Elemental Plane of Air, but that sounds complicated." It went unsaid, but my biggest takeaway from that story was to avoid riding on a giant eagle with Azarin if she was ever cross with me.

"It's not complicated at all, Mr. Carnavon. This is what she does. I've known Azarin since she was a toddler, and she was just as reckless and headstrong back then."

"I shall take that as a compliment," Azarin said.

"You shouldn't!" Neves snapped back. "That attitude is what got you one step from being exiled. I needed to come to the Core anyway because I've got clan business in another realm, but I promised your father I'd look after you until the Great Machine aligned with my gate. The Core City is a wicked place, filled with criminals, perverts, cultists, and assorted scum eager to take advantage of a naïve girl from the realms."

"I'm not naïve, Neves."

"So you claim, as you go about doing risky and stupid things, but my honor demands I do my best to protect you."

Neves was genuinely concerned, so I did my best to placate her, "We're just going to share our knowledge of spell craft. We're both self-taught, so that's not stealing formula from any other school. No academy is going to get offended and come looking for retribution because a couple of rank ones traded enough spells to get themselves to rank two."

"Do you have any idea how many fools have blown themselves up toying with magic they don't understand, Mr. Carnavon?" the dwarf asked.

"I've got a pretty good idea. I've got some impressive scars on my chest to prove it."

Azarin perked up at that. "Ooh, can I see?" She reached across the table for the buttons of my shirt, but Neves reflexively slapped her hand away. Azarin really wasn't helping her case.

"I'll not return to Stormwolk and tell General Mazdak that I allowed his daughter to consort with a low-class ruffian hotlander so she could curse herself to death playing with amateur fire magic."

"Then if I die poorly, make up something better. Tell father a dragon attacked the city and I went out heroically battling it or something. He would *love* that." Then, surprisingly, Azarin went serious for once. "You've been like an aunt to me, Neves. My whole life you've been there, but you're leaving tomorrow, and then I'm on my own no matter what. As much as you may want me to, I can't go back home, and I can't live by the old ways in a new land. Deep down you know I'm right. Learning magic is all I've ever wanted to do, so I'm not going to let anyone stop me, even if their intent is pure and they're trying to do it out of love."

"You're on a fool's errand."

"That's what us fools do. You might as well forgive me for doing what you know I'm going to do anyway and get it over with."

Neves scowled, having no good response to that. Finally, she picked up her mug, chugged the entire thing in what I assumed to be proper dwarven fashion, and thumped it back down. Dwarf women might not have beards, but they could certainly drink as good as their men. "Alright then." Neves stood up and tossed a few coins on the table. "I'll check on you when I come back through the gate in a few months on my way home. If you've met a bad fate by then, back in Stormwolk I'll say death by dragon it was."

Azarin stood up and engulfed her in a hug. "Thank you."

They walked to the stairs and I tried to give them their privacy as they said their good byes and good lucks. A few minutes later, Neves left, Azarin surreptitiously wiped her eyes, composed herself, then returned and sat next to me.

"Let's get to learning some magic."

29

I hit the ground face first and ate dirt.

Azarin shouted encouragement from where she sat atop the inn's roof. "That looked like it hurt a lot less than your last landing!"

I lay there on the cool grass for a while. Grass didn't grow on Fogo, and when our ground was soft, that meant it was molten. Learning a falling air spell back home would've been fatal. Here, when I screwed up, it was only painful and embarrassing.

The top of Trax's big grey head was sticking out of the pond so he could watch me repeatedly throw myself off a roof. "*This is why squalo do not try to fly, Carnavon. Swimming is much safer.*"

"Well, I didn't cut a deal with a water wizard, now did I? Nope. I found crazy air girl."

"What was that?" Azarin asked.

"Nothing." I groaned as I got off the ground and dusted myself off. "Just annoyed at being so damned bad at this."

After spending most of the night trying to bind Clear to one of my work gloves under Azarin's direction, I'd only gotten a couple hours of sleep, and then I'd spent the whole morning being humbled.

"You'll get the hang of it."

"Maybe."

It was an immutable law of magic that every mage had an affinity for one of the seven elements, usually corresponding to the realm of their heritage, and a corresponding deficiency in one of the others. We could sense the element we were attuned to more easily, while the one we were deficient in we were nearly blind to. Fire came naturally to me. Maybe with air magic I was doomed to failure?

I immediately dismissed those defeatist thoughts. Azarin, despite her flighty nature, had actually been really good at walking me through how her spells worked step by step, so my attempt at enchanting something with Clear achieved at least a little success after only ten or so attempts. Which was remarkably fast having never worked with the air element before, and this being the first time I'd managed to stick a spell to something other than metal.

"Don't beat yourself up, Carnavon."

"I'm fine. Face planting into the ground is what's beating me up, Azarin."

"Ground tends to do that. The hard part's getting the spell to stick right, and yours are certainly flawed, but it's working a little, otherwise you'd be hitting *a lot* harder. Your technique on the other hand... well, to be diplomatic, it's like seeing a baby griffon with two broken wings fall out of its nest... Which, by the way, is hilarious, because griffons are such assholes. Just follow carefully how I do this again. With the enchanted hand, imagine you're pushing back against gravity. This spell can't negate it, but you can resist it enough to slow yourself down. Aim your feet at where you want to go and then maintain your balance. *Descend.*"

She jumped off the roof.

Even though she came down at about the same speed I had, her trip was more of a graceful floating action than my flailing plummet. With cape and hair whipping around her, it was visually impressive too. Her shoes met the grass gently, and she walked right out of the fall. "See? Easy."

"Too bad you didn't nail it like that in front of the elves."

"I blame that performance on the different air pressure here. I had to get a feel for it. Now I'm good. Enough lollygagging. Come on, back up we go."

I'd wanted to enchant my left glove because I was righthanded and figured it might be useful to be able to take the high ground with a weapon at the ready. But my left hand was home to an obnoxiously throbbing broken finger, so the last thing I wanted to do was move it any more than I had to, so I'd enchanted the right instead.

I raised my right hand. "I've got this."

"If *descend* is a push, *ascend* is a pull. Eyes on your destination, focus your mind on the Clear. Imagine the strands of air in front of you entwining until they're solid as a rope, grab hold tight..." She closed her fist. "And *ascend.*"

Azarin went straight up into the air, parallel with the outer wall of the inn, and she even did a little spin for me at the top before stepping back onto the roof. "It's that simple. Come on."

Just like I did with my Red stuck to metal, I thought hard about the Clear I'd bound to the leather, until it was as if I could feel the magic curling around my fingers like a living thing. Then I imagined that thread of air until it became solid enough to take hold of. Though it was invisible, I could feel it wrap around my wrist, solid as any of the ropes on my home barge.

I took a deep breath then exhaled. *Fuck it.*

"*Ascend.*"

The invisible rope snapped tight, and if I'd not been ready for that it would've popped my arm out of the socket. I was jerked violently into the air so hard I forgot Azarin's advice to keep my eyes on the destination, which caused me to start spinning. Unlike her elegant twirl, mine wasn't near as graceful, and I ended up banging my leg against the wall, went too far up before I let go, and fell on the shingles on my hands and knees.

Azarin snagged my sleeve so I wouldn't topple over the edge. "That was much better."

I knelt there dizzy and a little nauseous until the inn stopped rotating. "What happens if I forget to let go of the invisible rope?"

"Huh... Good question. I never tested the upper limit. I suppose you'd just keep going straight up until the spell burns out... Then with nothing left to power a descent..." Azarin giggled at the thought, then made a *splat* noise by blowing air past her tongue.

I made a mental note. *Don't forget to let go.*

"On the bright side, your grasp of the Clear is still so weak that the enchantment is bound to burn out long before you get that high. But it'll get stronger with practice."

The inn was only two stories tall, but from up here we had a pretty good view of the market below and the sun rising over the Collegium above. As fun as smashing myself into the dirt over and over had been, that view was a good reminder that I had other things to do.

Today was Liveday. Which meant I had three days to find a home and get claimed by a faction powerful enough to thwart Gaul Haddar.

"I've got to call it for now, Azarin. I need to buy some things in the market before taking another shot at the academies."

"That's unfortunate. You can brag to them you know six spells now, even if two of them but very poorly, while I've not managed even the smallest act of magical arson yet. You're either a remarkably fast learner, or fire is my weakness."

I'd shared the last of my Red dust with her, and she'd used most of it up without even being able to make a strip of copper get slightly warmer. "Naw, it's because you're a better teacher than I am. How I do magic, it's hard to articulate."

"Articulate?" She gave me a very nice smile. "For a guy who says he grew up on a working man's barge, you sure do like to use big words."

"I just mean that I've never had to explain the things I've figured out about magic on my own to anyone else before. I'll get it though. Once we come up with some more Red for you, we'll try again."

"So, you're not just going to steal my spells and skip out?"

I knew she was kidding, but I still feigned great offense at that and acted as if I'd been stabbed in the heart. "My honor is wounded."

"Neves warned me about you clever hotlanders and your tricks."

"No tricks. If no academy wants us, we'll teach ourselves until we're too good to be ignored. Besides, in the meantime, I enjoy your company."

"Yeah, it's been fun." When Azarin realized I was staring at her intently, she blushed. "Back to work then. See you tonight." And she promptly rolled off the roof before I could make the attempt to kiss her.

Thwarted, I watched her land softly in the grass. As she walked away, she shouted, "I'm off to the Collegium then. We'll practice more tonight. Try not to get arrested in the meantime, Carnavon."

I waved goodbye, then sat atop the roof wondering why it was so much easier to understand magic than what a woman wanted.

"*I told you the best way to impress a female is to kill a whale for her.*"

"I know, Trax. I'll keep on the lookout for any stray whales wandering the city's canals." I peered over the edge, checked to be certain I could still feel an enchantment bound to the leather glove—which meant the Clear I'd bound to it hadn't run out yet—and I worked up my nerve to try one more time.

Extending my hand toward the ground, I imagined using it to hold up my weight. This enchantment didn't need a verbal component to activate, but Azarin claimed saying it out loud helped her focus. "*Descend.*"

And then I went over the edge.

Even at half speed, falling is frightening. This time, I concentrated on landing feet first rather than face. I reached half my goal, in that my boots touched down, but I was leaning too far forward, and my momentum caused me to fall on my shoulder and roll through the grass until I flopped to a stop next to the pond.

"*It is good she was not here to see that, or you would have to kill for her two whales to make up for the shame.*"

30

I'd gone back to the market and found it even busier than the day I'd arrived. Today, the Nexus was aligned with the Elemental Plane of Life. That was the most important day of the week for trade because its magical element was arguably the most valuable. The Green was what kept millions in even the harshest of the thousand kingdoms from starving. It could heal injuries, prevent or cure disease, and even make crops grow in places as inhospitable as Fort Silver.

I knew even less about life magic than I did air, but I was glad for the crowds it brought to the market. The bustle enabled me to get in, find and buy the things I needed, and get out without being noticed by any Argents. When I spotted a member of the City Watch with a reddened face and a missing eyebrow, I kept my head down and went the opposite direction.

With my winnings from the arena, I bought a box of ammunition for Gax's pistol to replace the rounds I'd used or ruined. The gunmonger even had ammunition made of brass rather than paper, but those were too expensive. Then I bought a new coat and cloak which didn't look like ratty Under Slump hand me downs, as well as some other respectable clothing, and even something special for Trax. I had enough money left over to buy a small pouch of Red dust, and I made sure to get that on a row that wasn't home to any Argent merchants. The merchant even threw in a few small iron snail shells to close the deal, because to everyone else in the Core, those were just decorations.

Like the other six, the life gate was held aloft by two giant statues, except both of them were so covered in flowering vines, I couldn't tell what manner of creatures they were supposed to represent. Even though I was a man on a mission, the parade of strange and colorful creatures here was so interesting, I stopped and marveled at the spectacle for a while. There were gigantic beasts of burden, some big as a house, with baskets on their back for people to ride in. There were races I'd never even seen mention of in the encyclopedia. It was said there were more kingdoms in the Realm of Life than on any other plane, and from just what I saw in the course of a few minutes, that must be true.

On Firedays, the market gradually heated up, and from what I'd seen, that made the Core folk short tempered and cranky. Liveday was rather festive in comparison. Through this gate came a fragrant breeze. On the other side was a realm supposedly of endless jungles and forests, and a multitude of kingdoms, both thriving and lost. Someday, I would like to go there and see it for myself.

Tomorrow, the Great Machine would turn toward the Realm of Death, and everything I'd ever heard or read about that place made it sound dark, mysterious, and unsettling. The day after, Eternaday, the market would be at its quietest, as the gate was forever barred to protect the Core from the greatest evil which had ever been.

Then it was back to Fireday, one full rotation of the Great Machine since my arrival… When Gaul Haddar would cross through to find and execute me.

That was a good reminder for me to quit my gawking and get back to my mission.

"A scholar of the Elemental Plane of Water, you say?" the rank four looked Trax over suspiciously. I'd replaced the squalo's dirty blanket with some shiny curtains I'd gotten a good deal on in the market, which I thought made for much more convincing monk robes on his wide form. "From which kingdom do you hail?"

"Master Bloodtrail comes from the mighty Squalo Empire."

"Squalo are rare in the Core. It is said very few of their kind are civilized enough to move among society without bloodshed."

Since the mage sounded impressed by their fearsome reputation, I decided to run with that angle, "This is true, which is why surely a wizard as powerful as your instructor would be interested in the rare opportunity to speak with such a fearsome being." I thought extra hard to make sure Trax would pick up my next unspoken message. *Uncover your head and show him your teeth.*

"*You warned me not to frighten the land mammals.*"

Trust me. And when Trax didn't immediately comply, I bumped him with my elbow. *Try to look majestic and intimidating.*

"*If I am set on fire again it is your fault.*" Trax pulled back the curtain sections that served as hood and scarf, and stared at the wizard with his tiny unblinking black eyes. Then he gradually displayed his many terrifying rows of teeth. I'd tried to explain the concept of *smiling* to Trax earlier, and he'd clearly been practicing, but the expression wasn't comforting when it came from a creature equipped with a mouthful of razors.

The mage gasped and took a step back. "Saints protect us. It really is one of the beasts of the deep."

"*Hello.*"

The mage winced as Trax's letters punched him in the brain. "What was that?"

"Squalo communicate mind to mind using a picture language, which is difficult for most humans to understand. That's why Master Bloodtrail has employed me to be his interpreter." And since both of us were actually presentable, clean, and groomed for once, he didn't immediately assume I was a lying scammer or desperate beggar. I put my fingers to my temple and feigned concentrating. "Master Bloodtrail says he would be honored to speak with your instructor."

"*That is not what I said.*"

"Please, wait here, frightful lord of the depths. I will check if he's here." The mage bowed to Trax, before retreating back into the mansion and closing the door behind him.

So far so good. I'd been listening to the talk around the Collegium, and the Korrigan Academy was small, but known for its specialization in water magic. Surely their teacher had to be interested in the realm they got their magical element from. I'd decided to play it smart and lead with Trax's exotic nature. Once we got in, I'd subtly drop the fact that I, speaker to squalos, knew six whole spells—which was only a slight exaggeration—and was in need of a home.

The academy had a big statue of gentle Saint Olga out front, which suggested someone as quarrelsome as me probably wouldn't fit in here, but I was desperate. While the two of us waited on the porch, Trax sent to me, "*Squalo mages do not have to go through this strange process to find a teacher. Squalo have our own school of magic. Unlike the Core, our admission process is sensible.*"

"If this doesn't work out, do you think I could get in there?"

"*To enter you must swim to the bottom of the deepest trench in the empire, then face your competitors in unarmed ritual combat, defeat them, and devour their flesh.*"

"So probably not."

"*Probably not,*" Trax agreed.

The Korrigan Academy was situated on a very bustling street. There were hundreds of mundane and magical carriages passing by. The Collegium sidewalks were crowded with hundreds of people from many different kingdoms going about their business. And as I looked over all that chaos, I couldn't shake the feeling that somebody was watching us.

Part of being a good trapper was recognizing that sometimes when you were tracking an Elemental, an Elemental was tracking you. A noisy street in the big city was a very different place than a lava rock mountain, but the sensation of something stalking me was the same. I'd had it last night on the way back from the fight, again in the market this morning, and now here.

"I think we're being followed."

Trax perked up. "*Who pursues us? I will demonstrate I am not prey.*"

"Be on the lookout for this guy." Squalo mental language remained odd, but I tried really hard to remember the face of the stranger who'd disappeared from the tavern and put that image at the front of my mind.

Trax got the picture. "*I do not know this human.*"

"Neither do I, but if you see him, let me know."

Trax slowly turned his big wedge of a head, taking in the street from one end to the other. Then he turned back to me and put his curtain hood back up. "*The suspicious human is to our east, seventy-two paces away. Behind six other humans and a gnome, leaning on a post at the establishment with the white and red sign, using the reflection in the window to observe us.*"

I casually turned my head that direction briefly, and sure enough, it looked like it was the same man, and he just happened to be waiting in line at a nearby apothecary shop. "That's impressive, Trax."

"*Only squalo who are good at spotting danger live to adulthood. The rest of us get eaten young.*"

I didn't ask if that was by ocean predators or other squalo. Truthfully, I was afraid of the answer. I risked another look. Our pursuer didn't have the complexion of someone from Fogo, so I doubted he was an Argent retainer, but they could have hired an outsider. If they'd suspected I was part of the plot to kill Dardick, they must doubly believe it now after I'd escaped them, and though I'd seen no more notices posted, there was probably still a price on my head. Or it was possible Inspector Borg hadn't believed my story and put one of his watchmen on me, waiting to see if I tried to make contact with the would-be assassins. As a relative nobody in the Core, who else would bother going through the effort to tail me? I was too poor to rob.

It was strange having somebody eavesdrop on your thoughts, but it did save time. "*If he is from your nobles, I should eat him, but if he is from the City Watch, I should not. Correct?*"

"How about we see what we can learn first and take it from there?" But when I looked back again, the man was gone. "Where'd he go?"

Trax scanned the street as he had before. "*Most curious. This human must possess the camouflage skills of an octopus, for I see no sign of him.*"

I didn't know what an octopus was, and I really didn't like the picture of the extra limbed squishy animal Trax put into my brain explaining it. "I'm betting he's got some enchantments to make him stealthy, and the second he suspects we're onto him, he bolts. Stay alert."

"*I am always alert.*"

The academy door opened again, revealing a little old lady wearing a blue gown, and leaning on a staff topped with some ocean animal's curling shell. "I'll be damned. He was right. It is a squalo in the flesh."

After so many failed attempts to speak with somebody actually important, this was probably the head wizard herself. I'd best not screw this up. "Hello, ma'am. I am—"

"Shush, kid." She was looking at Trax intently. "I made my bones adventuring on the Plane of Water. I don't need a translator to know the deep speech."

And for the next two minutes, I stood there awkwardly as the rank ten and Trax stared at each, saying nothing. At one point she laughed, as if Trax had just told her a funny joke.

"Well, that was amusing, but I must return to my duties. Good day."

I was so close. "Ma'am, if I could have just a moment of your time—"

"Oh, your friend already made the pitch for you, lad. Self-taught rank one, and he even showed me images of you using your spells, but it looks to me like you're an aspiring combat enchanter with an affinity for fire and the contentious temperament to match. You should be honored that a squalo of his peculiar sect would vouch for any land walker, but I mostly teach how to sustain and purify. I'm afraid my gentle academy is not where you belong."

"I can learn."

"No. You really couldn't. I forsook violence long ago, yet before that, I knew it well enough that I can see a great capacity for it in you. That's not by itself a bad thing. It is at times a very necessary thing, but it is not our way here."

"Did Trax tell you the part where I've got two days to get claimed by a faction, before I get hauled off to prison or executed?"

"Basically." The powerful wizard gave me a grandmotherly smile. "Good luck with that, sonny." And then she closed the door in my face.

"*She was pleasant,*" Trax projected. "*It was nice to find a human who is fluent in squalo.*"

I was so frustrated that I was tempted to kick her bronze statue of Saint Olga, but that would have been sure to invite all sorts of terrible curses and bad luck down on my head, and I had plenty enough already.

31

After a fruitless Liveday, Trax and I left by the low road to head back to the inn. Despite the majesty of floating palaces overhead being painted gold by the setting sun, I was in a foul mood. Dressing respectable had gotten me close enough to actually talk to a few real wizards, but clothes alone weren't enough to disguise who I was, and to these stuck-up pricks, I was a low-class laborer from a bad realm with a terrible reputation, and less magical talent than their lowliest servants.

"*You could become one of those lowly servants,*" Trax projected helpfully. "*It would be easier than getting into an academy.*"

"I didn't fake my death and stick a century of extra labor on my family just to end up scrubbing some rich wizard's floors for the rest of my life."

"*It would get you inside, and you could work as you continue improving your magic on your own.*"

I wasn't so proud that I'd not thought about that, but being some mere employee wouldn't be good enough to stave off the Argent's having an actual contract claiming my life. "They'd still drag me off."

"*Your time is short. Perhaps it is time to do as Inspector Borg suggested and escape.*"

As furious as the idea of quitting made me, Trax wasn't wrong. Tomorrow morning, the Nexus would be aligned with the death gate, and I didn't particularly want to flee to a place I'd only heard bad things about. However, there were kingdoms that bordered the Core, and I doubted even the mighty Gaul Haddar would bother searching very long for someone as unimportant as me.

"Screw that. I'm not giving up. Whatever happens, happens. I'll deal with it."

"*I do not wish to see you be violently murdered or imprisoned for the remainder of your life, but I will not attempt to dissuade you from your stubborn path. Observing your many setbacks has been valuable for my learning about the cruel nature of the surface world.*"

"I'm always happy to help."

Trax continued plodding along. "*By the way, we are being followed again.*"

I was smart enough not to look back. "The same guy?"

"*Correct. Only he is not alone this time. It appears he is better at making friends than you are.*"

That made me look, and sure enough, there were about a dozen men behind us, and they were walking fast to catch up. Several wore the same style of striped shirt.

"Shit. It's that one academy. Frunza something. I bet it's that ass who tried to pick a fight." They'd backed down that time because there had been four of them and two of us, and they'd not wanted to try anything in the Collegium with watchmen nearby. Now they'd tripled in number, and we were on a bridge with few witnesses. We were about to catch a beating.

We could make a run for the Slump. That would be the smart thing to do, but I was tired of running away. I'd been running all week and look where it had gotten me. I stopped in the middle of the road and waited.

"*Do you not wish to flee?*"

"Naw. You should go though. No need for you to get hurt on my account."

"*Weak and fearful creatures can only hunt in packs. Our realms have that in common. I shall stay to make it an even fight.*"

Twelve against two didn't sound very even to me, but maybe squalo weren't good at math. "Thanks, Trax. You're a good friend."

When they saw we'd stopped to wait for them, our pursuers hesitated. They'd certainly not expected that. There was some heated discussion among their ranks, before they started our way again. The few other travelers along this road must have sensed there was trouble brewing and were quick to walk away. In a city with gang fights below and rival mage schools clashing above, the locals were clearly fairly used to this sort of thing.

This part of the elevated roadway was about twenty yards wide. There was a waist high wall at each side, and beyond that was a rather nasty drop toward the Slumps. This was likely to end with us taking the fast way down.

"*Do you think the City Watch would be upset if I ate some of them?*"

"I'm not sure." I opened my coat so I could access Gax's gun faster, then I started checking on all my enchanted items. "Probably."

"*If I maul the toughest of them, that should establish dominance.*"

"Well, I suppose teeth or bullet, they're dead just the same." I put on my gloves. I didn't expect to use the hastily enchanted one to descend, but based on experience, it hurt my hand a lot less to punch someone in the jaw while wearing these. "Let's see how they want to play this before you start digesting anybody."

Sure enough, the one in the lead was the Frunza Tarlev kid I'd clashed with before.

"Well look who it is," he said, as if this meeting was innocent happenstance, and he'd not gathered an entire gang to wail on us. "The trash tried to clean itself up."

"Charlu, right?"

"Right."

"So you finally found the balls to take me up on that challenge, but you must have missed the part where mage fights are supposed to be one on one."

"I didn't miss a thing. Challenges are between equals. Getting rid of the likes of you is more like scrapping dogshit off my shoe."

"That probably sounded tougher when you practiced saying it in the mirror, but what kind of dumb ass needs a dozen friends to scrape shit?" I gestured at his mob. "You're a fucking moron, Charlu."

His little gang was half other Frunza students, and half tough guys who looked like they actually worked for a living who'd probably been recruited from a tavern to help. The mages all had at least one visible charm or wand on them, and the zeros were armed with the kind of cheap improvised weapons—like sticks, chains, boards—that could get tossed over the edge if the watch showed up and no tears would be shed at the loss.

And standing a bit back from the rest of them was the man I'd spotted following me. This was the best look I'd gotten of him so far. He was probably thirty years older than the rest of us, thickly bearded, and wearing a big hat and long black coat, which when he opened, revealed a brace of gold capped pistols holstered beneath.

Rather than draw those weapons to end me, he pulled a cigar from a pocket on his vest, stuck it in his mouth, and lit the end with fire that sprang from a finger of a Red enchanted glove.

I ignored the posturing mages and nervous thugs and addressed the confident stranger instead, "Who are you?"

"Don't mind me," he said as he went over and found a comfy place to lean on the wall. "I'm just here to see the show."

"That's Mr. Adderlane," Charlu proclaimed, like that should mean something to me.

The senior man sighed. "Don't go spreading my name about, stupid."

"Sorry. He showed us your bounty poster, Ozwald Carnavon of Fogo…" And when I didn't deny my identity, Charlu smirked. "Two hundred Obols for us to split it is then."

"I'm up to *two hundred* now?" With the Argent's being so notoriously cheap, Dardick hadn't been lying when he'd said he wanted to solve his attempted murder before Haddar could to impress his father. "Two hundred is real money!"

"Two hundred, alive," Charlu corrected. "Only a hundred dead, which would be a shame, but I wouldn't lose sleep over it."

"No wonder you were able to hire some help." I addressed the thugs, "I don't know what this idiot told you, but you boys really don't want to get involved."

Most of their eyes were nervously on Trax, who was still hidden beneath his curtain robes, but who was also obviously very large and not easily identified as one of the common races of the Core.

Smile for them, Trax.

Trax let his robe fall on the ground, looked around the crowd, and *smiled.* The hirelings and younger mages all took one step back, because there were so *many* teeth.

"What the hell is that?"

"That ain't no hump back ogre like you said."

"That there's a fucking squalo!"

With all those serrated murder teeth and generally intimidating dead-eyed carnivorous demeanor, I'd forgotten Trax also carried a blade, until he reached around behind his back and drew the wickedly curvy short sword, formed out of that strange material he'd called coral.

"*Hello.*"

One of the mages and one of the thugs stumbled a bit when they got hit in the mind with Trax's word picture greeting. That last one dropped his club and ran away, which made him the smartest one here.

"Come back here!" Charlu shouted after him, but that order did no good. He turned back to the rest of them and forced a smile. "That much more reward money for the rest of us to split then."

I was angry enough to fight all of them but also had enough sense to not want to die. I made one last plea to the remainder, "Listen, I'm a roughneck too. I get times are lean and money's tight. Saints know I've earned some dishonest coins handing out beatings myself, but this pampered ass has dragged you boys into a fight you do *not* want to have."

"It ain't nothing personal," one of them said. "Man's got to make a living."

"Take a good look at this one." I jerked my thumb toward Trax. "You think you're living after he bites you? Walk away and there's no hard feelings."

Two of them, who were probably brothers by how similar they looked, exchanged a glance, and then they broke off and started walking quickly toward the Slump.

"Where do you think you're going?"

The elder brother gave Charlu what was probably a vulgar hand gesture in whatever realm he came from. "You didn't say nothin' about fighting some face-eating water monster!"

"Fine. Run away, cowards." Charlu was exasperated, but he still had all his mages and some muscle. The other students were here because of pride or loyalty to their dumb leader, and the remaining toughs must have been really hungry.

The stranger, Adderlane, helpfully shouted, "You'd best get down to business, Mr. Charlu. It seems the more you let this hotlander talk the greater the attrition to your forces."

"Alright," Charlu snapped as he worked up his courage. He reached for the wand stuck in his belt. "Let's do this."

I sent Trax a thought.

Establish dominance.

32

There's fast, and then there's squalo fast.

Trax covered the distance between us and Charlu in an instant. The young mage barely had time to raise his wand before Trax's jaws locked around his arm. Then it was like a terrier shaking a rat. And everybody stood there, stunned, for several terrible horrifying seconds as Charlu got flung about, screaming, with blood flying everywhere.

Then they reacted. The nearest mage aimed his wand at Trax and began screaming some magical focus word, except I shot him in the head first.

There are some advantages to being the one who gives the signal to start. While they'd been staring at Trax savaging their leader, I'd been tossing handfuls of screws and drawing my gun.

The young mage must have been wearing a protection charm, because there was a flash of light as my bullet bounced off his forehead, but the impact was still enough to send him stumbling.

As the thugs stepped through the grey gun smoke, the screws of chaos rolling between their feet ignited, screeching and bouncing about. A few red-hot screws stuck to flesh, instantly burning through skin, and setting clothing on fire. A man roared and clutched at his side. Another began jumping around on one leg, desperately trying to pluck a burning screw from his knee. I stepped in and smashed him squarely in the nose with the butt of Gax's pistol.

Trax hurled the screaming Charlu into another wizard so hard it set off his protective charm in a shimmer of light, only this projectile was probably a hundred and eighty pounds of blood-squirting wizard, so it didn't do either of them much good and both went down in a heap.

A chain was whipped at Trax's head. He ducked it easy, and his coral sword sliced a chunk out of that man's leg. He followed that up by sweeping the feet from beneath a wizard and slamming his palm into another man's chest hard enough to break ribs.

When Trax first told me he was a monk, I'd thought he meant the scholarly type, not the martial kind, but I'd been so very wrong. Trax was a beast. I'd describe his fighting style as *relentless*. But then my squalo friend was knocked backward as if he'd been struck by an invisible hammer.

Thinking Trax was the bigger threat, three of the mages went after him, calling up spells. Before I could help him, another student mage swept his wand toward me. "*Burn*!"

An arc of flame leapt from the enchanted wood. The heat rolled over me, singing my hair, then it was gone, and I was unharmed. Really, *really* angry, but unharmed. Before that kid could grasp the magnitude of his mistake, I caught him by the neck, squeezed so he couldn't escape, and slammed the steel barrel of Gax's pistol against his face four times. His protective charm spared him from the first two. The last one sent a gob of blood and his front teeth flying.

"Never use an elemental curse on someone from that same realm," Adderlane shouted helpfully from his spot on the wall. "Of course he's going to have natural resistance to fire. Did your instructors teach you nothing?"

The three mages who were trying to kill Trax must have heeded their instructors' lessons, because beams of fire, daggers of air, and claws of shadow formed to attack my friend from the Plane of Water. We were all too close to risk a snail grenade, so I threw a cloud of Red their way and ignited it in the air, hoping the flash would throw off their aim. I got tackled from behind by one of Charlu's hired goons before I could see how that worked.

Landing on my face, he started punching me in the back of the head. I lost hold of my gun but managed to buck him off enough to roll over. I caught another fist in the eye for the trouble. Sadly for him, brawling is the main thing Fogo folk do for fun. Catching his wrist, I pulled it hard to the side so he fell forward off-balance. Then I grabbed hold of his collar, drove my knuckles into his throat, and began choking him mercilessly with his own shirt. Five seconds of that was enough to convince him he was on his way to sleepy town, so he quit trying to hit me and switched to trying to get away instead. Which was fine by me, and I let him go, because I had wizards to fight.

Still lying on the ground, I retrieved Gax's gun, broke it open, plucked out the smoking paper shell, and reloaded. While I watched, Trax dodged around a swirling pillar of fire, ducked a knife made of hardened air, and slashed his coral blade through the talons of shadow. The mage who'd cast that spell staggered back as Trax gut punched him with one big grey fist, then there were sparks as the sharpened coral struck protective charm.

That protective enchantment was immediately overwhelmed as I shot that mage in the ass.

I'd been aiming for his spine, but I'd had the sunset in my eyes so couldn't find my sights. Either way, the Frunza student cursed and fell over, so that would do.

Not having signed up for this, the hirelings broke and ran—or hopped—away. And as soon as the student mages realized how many of them were wounded and they'd lost all their help, they fled too. Trax crouched calmly next to the wall as a student haphazardly tossed one last fire spell his way, but he was so panicked, the fire bolt missed Trax by a mile and sailed uselessly out into the night before dissipating into sparks. The people of the Slump below probably thought someone was setting off fireworks.

Adderlane began to clap, slow and sardonically. "Good show. Well done. Another fine reminder why I shouldn't recruit morons."

I plucked another paper cartridge off my belt and reloaded, but by the time I looked back toward where Adderlane had been, he was already gone, vanished as swiftly as he had from the street earlier. I could still smell his cigar smoke in the air.

Charlu and the second mage I'd shot had been abandoned by their friends, and both were lying there, crying.

"Quit your whining," I snapped. "You started this."

"You shot me in the ass!"

That looked painful as all get out, but the wound looked shallow, with the bullet going through one cheek and out the other rather than tearing through his guts and pelvis, so he'd probably be fine. "Just put pressure on it."

Charlu on the other hand was a mess. He lay there, using one hand to hold together the mangled remains of his other arm. As a Red miner, I'd seen a lot of horrible injuries, accidental and on purpose both, but seeing Charlu's bones sticking out and the tendons moving around them was enough to make even me nauseous. Squalo teeth are *sharp*.

Charlu's face had gone white and there was a spreading red puddle beneath him. "I don't want to die."

"*We are victorious. Should I eat them now?*"

Tempting as it was to tell Trax to enjoy his well-earned supper, I was trying to stay on the City Watch's good side. "Do either of you have any healing magic?"

"No," the one said, and all Charlu could do was stare wide-eyed and scared and shake his head in the negative.

"Give me your belt." The other mage complied, and I looped it around Charlu's arm, pulling it tight as I could. It was still leaking rapidly though, so I picked up one of the cudgels dropped by a thug, shoved that through the leather, and twisted the shit out of it until it was *really* tight. That shut off the blood faucet, but must have hurt a lot because Charlu passed out.

"Alright, hold onto that nice and tight until someone comes to help you. If you let go, your friend's going to bleed to death. Got it?" I waited for him to nod in understanding and place his hand on the stick. "Good. Now I'm taking all your charms, coins, and elements."

"You're robbing us?"

"Don't act all offended. You were stupid, so now you have to pay the stupid tax."

I took everything the two had on them as fast as I could, and shoved things into my pockets without examining them; we needed to be long gone before the watchmen arrived. I didn't even consider this thievery. It was more like the spoils of war. I tossed one of the two protective bracelets to Trax, who nonchalantly caught it. "Put that on. It should help next time someone tries to shoot or stab you."

"*Being your associate, that is a likely occurrence.*"

"Let's get out of here." We left the wounded students on the bridge and hurried downhill. "We'll divide up our loot later. I know Charlu had a wand too, but I didn't see it."

"*I think I might have swallowed it along with his thumb.*"

"You can keep that one then."

33

"What happened to your face?" Azarin asked when she joined me for spell craft practice just before sunrise the next morning.

There was no way I could have hidden my black eye. "We had a little run in with some Frunza Tarlev students on the road last night. No big deal."

"Is that so?" Then she grimaced, rubbed the side of her head, and looked toward the pond, where Trax was submerged and recovering. "Why did Trax just proudly send me a brain picture of him biting someone's arm off?"

Azarin was getting a lot better at understanding squalo thought language. "His arm didn't come *all* the way off. Just mostly. We were outnumbered but whooped them. They got fired up by someone named Adderlane. Heard of him?"

"No. Why'd they attack you though?"

"They were trying to collect the Argent's reward on me." I shrugged like that was no big deal.

"Fifty Obols is a lot of money, but not worth having your arm torn off. Especially for somebody fortunate enough to already be in an academy… Which one was it again? Because if he dies and they've got an opening…"

"Frunza Tarlev." I couldn't even blame her for trying to get in there, because if the tables were turned, I'd surely do the same. "And my bounty got raised to two hundred Obols now."

Azarin whistled. "That's getting up there." She glanced around the inn's back yard—it seemed fitting that Deathday morn was quiet and foggy—but we were alone so she could speak freely. "You're crazy to stick around with that kind of price on your head. That's enough that even in the respectable parts of the city, even the polite folk would try to collect. Everywhere else?" She made a throat slitting motion. "We're on the edge of the Slump, for Naanwalla's sake. The government in this sinking district is whoever's the toughest gangster. And you're hanging around with the one creature who manages to stick out in a city with a hundred races populating it."

Trax took that as a compliment. "*Yes. I am notable.*"

"Seriously, you need to get out of here while you still can, Carnavon."

I'd already had this argument with myself and lost, I wasn't about to have it with her too, so I changed the subject, "Are you ready to practice? Because I found some more elements to experiment with."

"Found?"

"Well, some Frunza students helpfully donated to our cause. Check this out." I dropped my pack on the grass and opened it up to show her. "I picked up a few different charms we can try to figure out the formula on them to recreate their enchantments. Then I got some Red dust, a vial of Blue, and a little snuff box with a pinch of Green left in it. I took a wand off one, but I don't really know what it does. Trax digested the other."

"*Sorry.*"

"Hold your eagles." Azarin was intent on stomping on my enthusiasm. "It's one thing for us to teach each other spells we came up with on our own, but if we start reverse engineering other schools' formulas, that's stealing. Those are close guarded secrets for a reason. That's the sort of transgression wizards go to war over."

In my treasure fueled excitement, I hadn't thought of that. "Only if they find out."

She looked at me incredulously. "Are you *trying* to collect more enemies? Don't you have enough already?"

"Fair point…" She was probably right. If copying other wizard's creation didn't get me killed, it would at minimum get me labeled a thief, which wouldn't help earn a spot in an academy. "I guess we'll stick with what we were already doing."

"Good. Because making bad rash decisions is my thing. If I'm urging caution, you know the idea is extra dumb. How about you show me how to burn stuff already."

I'd been so distracted experimenting with the various Frunza charms, and Azarin had been trying to enchant some steel screws with Red, that it was Trax—meditating in the pond—who warned us that someone was approaching.

I immediately moved one hand to the pistol holstered on my belt, and thought back hard, *Is it Adderlane?*

"*One is human, but does not smell like cigars, so it is not him. The other is a lob.*"

Azarin and I were sitting on the grass, which still astounded me that there could be such a soft and inviting thing as *lawn*. She noted my sudden alertness. "What?"

"We've got some visitors."

I would have preferred someplace more private to practice spell craft, but if we used one of our rooms, Azarin was likely to set the enclosed space on fire, and I couldn't very well practice ascending indoors. We'd picked this spot behind the inn because it was off the main path, though there were still regular people out doing their business. It was most likely some locals curious what we were up to back here, but I was paranoid. I thought to Trax that he should stay hidden, just in case we needed a squalo surprise.

There was barely a ripple as his head and back fin sank beneath the surface. "*I shall lurk in ambush.*"

The idea of Trax lurking was somehow even more intimidating than him just standing there. "You do that."

Two figures walked around the side of the inn. One was a gigantic, hulking lob, who I recognized. It wasn't easy to forget a face as ugly as the one belonging to Krachma the Killer. He still had white bandages shoved up his nostrils from where I'd broken his nose the other night.

I sprang to my feet, ready to fight, thinking Krachma must have come to take his revenge for my embarrassing him in the arena.

"Easy there. We're friendly," the human next to Krachma exclaimed. "Hold your fire, hotlander."

White skinned and black eyed, it took me a moment to realize where I'd seen this man from the Realm of Death before. "I know you. You were in the fight before mine. You lost against that dwarf."

"Only because Veroy cheated." He pulled his collar away from his neck, revealing a bright red scar that was the mark of a recent magical healing. "I think he bribed my ring goblin to give me a faulty protective charm, or he had a little extra something special on his axe, if you know what I mean."

Though he had long white hair like a grandfather, he was probably a little younger than I was. I'd heard everybody who came from the haunted realm tended to look corpselike. Despite his declaration of friendliness, the deadlander was wearing a sword and some daggers. Krachma was carrying a spiked mace, and from what I'd seen the other night, a weapon wasn't necessary for him to mess someone up.

Azarin was glancing nervously between me and the two dangerous-looking strangers. "Are these friends of yours, Carnavon?"

"Forgive my rudeness, my lady." The deadlander gave her a sweeping bow. "We know of Put Down Tom here because we are brothers of the arena, fellow gladiator mages who've fought for honor, pride, and coin, providing entertainment to the good people of the Slumps."

"Tom?" she asked.

"It's a long story."

"I take it Carnavon's the real name then. A pleasure to meet you. I am Rade Tartaros. My taciturn friend here is Krachma."

"Krachma the Killer," I added.

Krachma frowned.

Rade smiled at the lob's obvious displeasure. "The bookie goblin added that last part for dramatic effect. The crowd loves titles like that. Unlike my people, Krachma's people aren't inclined toward the ostentatious. I wanted them to call me *Rade Tartaros, the sword of the underworld*, but they said I needed a better record first. I'm currently at three wins and zero losses in this arena."

"Three and one," Krachma corrected.

"I already told you Veroy cheated, so I'm not counting that one."

They weren't here for revenge, and if they'd come to earn the Argent's reward, they wouldn't be wasting time talking first. "What do you want? Are you more friends of Adderlane?"

"The only Adderlane I've heard of is some high-ranking wizard out of the Collegium. Don't think we've ever met. Do you mind if I sit?" Rade didn't wait for my answer and sat down across from Azarin. "I'm ashamed to admit that I'm in a bit of a predicament. I had to pay for a magical healing because a certain cheating dwarf trying to chop my head off, and magical healing enchantments are *very* expensive."

"Tell me about it," Azarin agreed. "The price for healing a hundred puncture wounds is downright staggering."

"I imagine. Anyway, the arena goblins stopped me from bleeding out at the scene, but then it was either linger in misery for months while trying not to get gangrene until my wound healed naturally, *or* make a sufficient donation to the nuns of Saint Olga to get a full rapid healing. Unfortunately, the only thing I had of sufficient value to pay the sisters was the last of my precious magical element that I brought with me from home. So alas, now I am bereft of magic, and a gladiator without magic in this town is basically useless. I'd go to the market and buy enough to get me through a few more bouts, but in a sad turn of events, I bet every coin I had that I'd beat Veroy… which I would have, if the dwarf hadn't cheated."

I'd never spoken to anyone from the Plane of Death before, but I'd been expecting something grimmer. For someone from the haunted realm, Rade was remarkably upbeat, and I kept expecting him to sell me something. "This involves me how?"

"I was just getting to that. Fortunately for me, today the Great Machine is aligned with my home kingdom, and there just happens to be a very accessible source of Dread Thanatos—the element the Core folk colloquially refer to as Black—just inside the gate. I simply need a little help gathering it. Specifically, I need someone who knows a bit of fire magic. Your pay is you get to keep whatever element you carry out. The trip would be a short one. Not more than two or three hours on the other side. If we left now, we'd be back in time for lunch."

That sounded far too easy. The reason magical elements were so incredibly valuable was the scarcity and the danger of collecting them. I couldn't imagine Black would be that much easier to obtain than Red.

Azarin must have been thinking the same thing. "You know, where I'm from, we'd get these dumb adventurers coming through our gate thinking they could cut us middlemen out and just collect some Clear for themselves. I mean, how hard could it be, chasing Air Elementals through lightning storms, right? Turns out, it's really hard, and they mostly die horribly. On the bright side, when they die, we do get to keep their stuff, the ones whose corpses we find at least."

Rade had a smile more fitting for a merchant trying to move product than a sword mage. "The lovely air maiden brings up a logical point. I didn't say it wouldn't be dangerous, but it is a manageable amount of danger. I can explain the details as we walk to the market. And before you express your next understandable concern, if this source of Black is so easy to harvest, why doesn't everyone? They don't know about this place because it's a Tartaros family secret. I'd do it myself, but unfortunately, entry requires fire magic, which sadly is my area of deficiency. With no money to hire a trained wizard to help me, I was adrift until Krachma here suggested we seek out the fire enchanter who just defeated him in the arena."

"You burned Krachma good," the lob explained.

That I had, but that still didn't answer all my questions. "How'd you find me?"

"Krachma again. Lobgoblins all have this peculiar ability, where he can sense the direction of the last thing to wound him, through the ground or something. I don't get it myself. But you hurt him, so I guess the earth points at you, until something else wrongs him instead."

Krachma nodded at me, like what Rade was saying was true, though it made no sense to me at all. "It is called *grudge*."

"Yeah, lob grudge. That's it. So what'll it be, Carnavon? If you've got no stomach for a bit of easy adventure and vast reward, I've got to hurry and find another fire mage. I can't afford to wait another month for the next gate."

It would be nice to have another element to experiment with, but my time was too short to go galivanting around other realms. "Unfortunately, I've got my own problems right now."

"Maybe I can help. You do me a favor, I do you a favor. I know you work cheap because you wouldn't be fighting in the Slumps arenas otherwise."

"Carnavon's only got two days to learn enough new spells to earn his second rank in a last desperate effort to get into an academy before he gets sent to prison forever," Azarin explained. "The poor guy's got a lot on his mind."

"That's it?" Rade laughed. "Why didn't you say so? If it's spells you need, I've taught myself a bit of shadow magic. A few hours from now you'll be rich with Black, and in payment for your service, I will teach you the formula for one of mine. What do you say?"

"Perfect. I'm in," Azarin said. "Let's do this."

"Wait. Hold on." This had to be one of those rash decisions she'd been warning me about. "Don't listen to her. She doesn't know Red magic yet."

"I know what you've shown me, and I've been practicing all morning. Watch." She extended one red stained finger and shouted, "Fire!" There was a burst about as big as a match being struck and then nothing. "It's not much, but come on, Carnavon. Your four spells, my three, we pick up a shadow one. That's eight spells from three elements, we'd be shoe ins for an academy."

Rade grimaced at her volunteering. "I'm sorry, my lady, but this expedition might be a *little* more dangerous than I've described so far. The magical fire is to ward off the angry spirits in the tomb."

"Oh, I figured it was something like that. It's the realm of the dead after all!" Azarin exclaimed with great eagerness. "I've never been to the ghost lands before. What undead monstrosities do we have to destroy? Never mind, you can tell me on the way. I'll go get my gear from my room."

Azarin wasn't my responsibility, but I couldn't hardly let her run off with some untrustworthy gladiators to fight ghosts without me. "Alright. I'll do it."

Trax lifted his head out of the pond. "*I am excited for this learning opportunity.*"

"What's that?" Rade asked nervously as he slowly moved his hand toward the hilt of his sword.

"That's my squalo. He's going to come along and make sure everybody stays honest."

34

Getting Trax through the market unnoticed by Argents was easier than I'd expected. Just as all the merchants and customers had complained about the excess heat coming through the gate on Fireday, every Deathday, the market filled with a cold fog, so gloomy and thick I could barely see a few feet in front of me.

This was the least busy I'd seen the market so far, in that there were only thousands here instead of tens of thousands. The visitors from the Elemental Plane of Death were a grim and colorless lot. Rade might be the only one from his realm who actually smiled. The chill was almost unbearable, but at least today bundling up and trying to stay warm didn't seem so out of place.

I flinched the first time I saw a ghostly apparition floating down an aisle.

"Visitors from my home realm get a bad reputation here. Everybody loves the Elemental Plane of Life." Rade put on a mocking falsetto voice. "*It's so vibrant. It's so pleasant and nice.* Bah. There's got to be a balance in all things. None of us could survive in the pure parts of any of the planes, which is why all our kingdoms are built on the edges where the planes collide and mix. We've got to have ground to stand on, and air to breathe, water and heat, and life, obviously, yet everybody gets squeamish about death."

The ghost was translucent, the market stalls visible behind it, *through* it. The fleshy bits glowed with a sickly hue, and most of the body was cloaked in billowing robes made of living shadows, so it was hard to tell its true shape. As unnerved as I was by the sight, the experienced merchants weren't bothered in the least as they haggled with the dead.

"It's truly unfair," Azarin agreed, even as she walked the long way around the spectral customer.

When I passed by, the mere presence of the thing made all the hairs on my arms stand up. It was difficult to tell since I was already so damned cold, but the nearness of the undead seemed to suck even more of the warmth out of me. For the first time in my life, I saw my own breath come out as steam, and it was so alarming that for a moment, I thought the ghost cast a spell and that was my soul being ripped out my mouth.

"As the Saints have taught, there's a heaven and a hell for everyone's eternal reward or punishment. My realm is simply the passageway to get to either of those, and some spirits are too stubborn to move on, or they get stuck. I don't really understand how it works. But we get used to them." Rade politely tipped his wide brimmed black hat toward the ghost and said something in an oddly disconcerting language.

The ghost gave him a slight nod of acknowledgement before returning to its wares.

"Powerful wizards are especially notorious for refusing to move on after they die. Their purposes are usually beyond mortal understanding, and their spirits linger, doing various things. Which isn't troublesome for the most part, unless they're particularly evil, or go insane. Then we get all the weird monsters, mutations, and cursed beings that are drawn to that sort of arcane energy, which leads to my realm earning such a sordid reputation, but really, it's not entirely unpleasant once you get used to it."

In the shadow of the Great Machine, the death gate was held aloft by two gargantuan skeletal statues, though they too were obscured by the clinging fog. There was a lot of traffic going into the gate, but very little coming out. Of all the realms, the dead produced the least, which made a sort of morbid sense.

The five of us reached the bottom of the ramp. "Most of our living settlers are there to harvest the Black, because it's the best element for staving off death or causing it, but we've got other industries same as everyone else. This week the Nexus is aligned with the gate at Acheron, which is one of the more... lively settlements. Just follow my lead and do as I say, and I'll take us straight to our destination. It's not far at all."

This would only be the second time I'd traveled between realms, so I was nervous, but tried to only show steely resolve on my face. Azarin was downright gleeful to see another plane of existence. Trax only had one expression, and the last thought he'd sent me was *fascinating.* Unlike Trax, Krachma could actually talk, though he hadn't bothered to the entire trip. Lobs didn't strike me as brilliant conversationalists.

An elderly man in a very fancy uniform was seated on a padded stool next to the gate, observing the merchants pass by. I'd been told the Core Warden was a mostly ceremonial position, but it was always held by a high-ranking mage, which meant this man possessed a lot of power, both political and magical.

The Warden saw us and shook his head. "More adventurers, eh? Looking to strike it rich?"

"Good morning, Warden," Rade said politely. "We've got a bit of business to attend to in Acheron."

"From the quality of the charms you bear, what are you, rank ones and twos? I'd advise picking some other realm's ruins to loot for treasure. The traders I've talked to today have all said the same thing. The dead are extra restless in Acheron right now."

"Thank you for your concern, kind sir, but we're merely on a brief visit to pay respects to my family's ancestral tomb."

"I wasn't warning you, deadlander. You clearly know what you're walking into. I was warning the others who don't look like black eyed, corpse color fiends, not wearing all black as if they're going to a funeral."

Rade grinned. "My people dress like we're in mourning because every day is someone's funeral, Warden."

The old man chuckled at that, then he looked over the rest of us. "And you lot trusting a deadlander? Heh. Good luck, and keep track of the time, as I don't think any of you want to miss the turning of the Great Machine and have to spend a month among the hungry dead."

He said that, but it was still tempting for me, because ghosts might be easier to escape than Gaul Haddar. "Thank you for the warning, Warden," I said politely as we passed.

I could sense the powerful magic coming off the gate, but just like before there was no real sensation to moving between worlds. The first time I'd crossed realms I'd been overwhelmed by the brightness of an unobscured sun and the sudden chill. This trip lacked that because both sides were grey and cold today. But when I looked up on the other side, the mountainous Great Machine was gone, and there was nothing above us but a sky full of dark clouds.

Before us was a castle that made the Argent's hold in Fort Silver look like a shack in comparison. The walls were over a hundred feet tall, and its towers were crooked, twisting spires which clawed at the sky. The castle extended as far as the fog allowed us to see, and I could only tell it kept going because of the shadowed shapes and the flickering green beacons atop the walls. Beneath the castle was an old, decaying settlement, made of three-story buildings of stone, brick, and wood. Bisecting that town was a wide sluggish river, the waters of which appeared far too grey.

When I turned back, the foggy market was there, but when I looked up and to the side, I realized that just as the Fogo gate had been magically created, the Acheron one must have been as well. While ours was made out of a violent lava plume twisted into shape and then frozen in place, this gate was made of bones. Millions and millions of bleached white bones, of various sizes, and from more species than I could imagine, all perfectly knitted together into a gigantic arc.

Azarin looked back too. "Well… that's something."

"Welcome to the land of the dead," Rade said proudly. "One of my ancestors built that."

"*By killing all the things in it?*" Trax asked me. I just shrugged, as Rade hadn't elaborated and it might be impolite to ask.

Our path toward the town was lit by braziers that burned with an unnatural green fire. The merchants' wagons around us were moving slowly, as if the beasts of burden pulling them really didn't want to be here either. The trees were haggard, bare of leaves, and flocks of large black birds sat on the branches, studying us.

"Dour," Krachma muttered. "Gloom."

"You get used to it. Come on, right this way." Rade led us down the path toward the river.

There were guards posted near the gate. They were also dressed all in black, and a few even wore full suits of archaic armor. It wasn't until I got closer that I realized the suits were actually empty, and even though the helmets turned, tracking us, only shadow lurked inside.

"Don't make eye contact with those," Rade warned. "They don't care for that."

At the riverside, there was a dock. "Wait here." Rade went up to where a gaunt man was sitting near a tied-up boat and spoke with him. They reached some kind of deal, shook on it, and he returned. "I got us a ride to the tomb city. It's faster than walking."

I'd never ridden in a watercraft before. I found the slow, rocking motion unsettling. As the gaunt man silently pushed us along with a long wooden pole, Rade continued to proudly tell us about his homeland.

"The civilization that built the tombs was already dead for a thousand years before the legendary Nyx Tartaros arrived here from the Core, built this gate, and attached it to the Nexus. The first settlers explored the ruins, banished most of the monsters, claimed what was useful, and each branch of the founding families have retained a plot there ever since. We're going straight to the one that belongs to my family."

"You're a descendent of the founders?" the boatman asked suspiciously.

"Of course," Rade said indignantly. "I'm a direct descendent of Tartaros herself."

"I ain't seen you around Acheron." The boatman shared Rade's complexion and solid black eyes, so was also obviously a local.

"That's because I've been away in the Core making my fortune and learning powerful magic."

"Sure you have..." The boatman went back to poling.

Rade scowled, then continued being our enthusiastic travel guide, "Premium element comes direct from Elementals, but Death Elementals are extremely dangerous. However, the Black also tends to naturally collect in tombs, graveyards, battlefields, anywhere there's lots of corpses and lingering ghosts, that sort of thing, and it has been a while since this plot has been touched. Black deposits attract wraiths and sometimes even ghouls, but that's where our Red mage comes in. Undead hate magical fire."

My nobles had issued various charms to help our cadres successfully mine the Red. "Why doesn't your family just buy some fire enchantments?"

"That's a good question, Lord Tartaros," the boatman said. "Why didn't your family give you some fire wands?"

Rade ignored him. "They do hand out enchantments for official business, but this is more of an unofficial, unplanned visit. Hardly worth bothering my relatives at the castle over it. They're big on pomp and circumstance and would probably want to throw a banquet in my honor or something, and who has time for that? This way we'll be in and out before they know it and never need to trouble them."

Azarin and I shared a nervous glance at that. Even Trax, who struggled to grasp the most basic of human interactions—hell, he'd barely learned the concept of pants—thought at me, "*I do not wish to be rude, but I believe this human might not be entirely truthful in his descriptions."*

I thought back to Trax, *He's lying his ass off, but we're already here, and I really could use another element to experiment with.*

"Regardless of my family affairs, if there's wraiths inside, throw some magic fire on them. If there's ghouls, same thing, but since they've got bodies, we can shoot or stab them. Ghouls have soft heads. Krachma could club ten of them by himself, easily."

Krachma patted the spiked end of his mace like it was a beloved pet.

Azarin drew a small, double barrel pistol from her cloak, and broke it open. Satisfied it was loaded, she snapped it shut, then saw that I was looking at her. "What? Neves gave it to me."

I didn't want to say aloud that her being armed somehow made her even more attractive. "I'm just glad to see you're serious about protecting yourself."

"Of course I brought a gun. I already admitted my one Red spell still needs a bit of work."

"A bit?"

"Says the man who seemingly enjoys the taste of dirt the way he dives head first off of roofs."

The rest of our river journey was spent in nervous silence. The fog made everything feel padded and distant. Strange animals bubbled beneath the water. Trax asked if he could jump in and see what they tasted like, but I told him that was probably a bad idea.

The ruins appeared through the fog.

They were a low crumbled mess now, overgrown with trees and covered in moss, but it was obvious these buildings had been vast once. It was hard to imagine something that had already been ancient when the Core was young.

Rade directed the boatman where to land. The old fellow seemed to be enjoying our discomfort. Strangely enough, having guided many bold but ignorant adventurers to various ruins across Fogo myself, I understood exactly how he felt. There was nothing quite like watching outsiders thinking they were clever enough to thwart the dangers of the realm you called home. Half the time, I'd guided the fools to their destinations, only to leave alone when none of them came out alive.

Now, I guess it was my turn to play the fool.

35

The door to the tomb was sunken into the side of a low hill, or more likely from how old this place was, the hill had grown up over it. Coming from a land that was constantly, violently changing, the idea that people could stay on the same patch of solid ground for thousands of years amazed me.

The great stone door in the hillside was magically sealed, but regardless of Rade's overall truthfulness, he did at least know the secret words to unlock the spell binding it shut. He whispered a phrase to the stone so the rest of us couldn't hear, and then the door slowly moved aside with a sick grinding noise.

Even standing outside the entrance, I could already smell the stink of decay coming from below. Which made no sense, for a place that was supposedly unused for such a long time. "What's that smell?"

"Oh that?" Rade sniffed. "Unfortunately for us that's most likely the smell of ghouls. Some of them probably burrowed their way in since the last time anyone in my family came here to check on this place. No worries." He drew his sword with a flourish. "We'll make quick work of those beasts."

It looked like it would be pitch-black in the tomb. Krachma had brought some torches, rags to wrap them in, and oil. I took my crawler's light charm out of my pack, activated it, and set it floating slightly ahead of me. My light source was brighter and more reliable, but his could also be used to ward off ghouls or hit them over the head if all else failed.

"This is rather exciting," Azarin said. "Gimme a torch."

"Everyone ready?" Rade asked. We all nodded, except for Trax, who was doing his usual stare silently into the distance thing, but Rade took that as a yes. "Alright. Follow me then."

Inside were stairs leading downward. Except for our footsteps, the place was dead quiet. For whatever reason, I'd expected a tomb to be a cramped space, but the ancient race who built this place must have been rather large, because the steps were wide enough for even Krachma's big feet to fit comfortably, and the ceiling was so high he never once had to duck.

The farther down we went, the walls got slicker and wetter. There were patches of moss, mottled grey and green, and small puddles in the low spots. Spiderwebs hung down, and when we brushed them out of the way they clung, sticky, to our hands and faces.

Rade had the lead with torch and sword and thankfully wasn't talking for once. Krachma followed him. I was behind Krachma with a handful of Red at the ready. Azarin was after me with torch held high and pistol down low. And Trax wandered around behind us, poking randomly at the moss patches, splashing in puddles, and occasionally plucking spiders off the wall to eat.

"*Do not eat the furry brown ones. They are mildly venomous and make my mouth tingle.*"

"Thanks for the heads up, Trax."

"What did he say?" Azarin asked nervously.

"Don't eat the furry brown spiders. They're bad for you."

"Huh… I wasn't tempted to, but that's still good to know, I guess.

The stairs went down for what seemed like far too long, until we reached a second massive door, this one made of rotting wood. It was so heavy, it took Rade and Krachma both to push it open.

On the other side was a room big enough that our lights couldn't illuminate the far end. There were bones *everywhere*. The bones were stacked along every wall and in chest high piles in the middle. The ceiling was twenty feet tall, and all the way to the top were alcoves dug into the walls, each filled with what were obviously human bones. A thousand skulls stared at us.

I didn't know what I'd been expecting, but it hadn't been rough piles like this. In Fogo, we cremated our dead. This just seemed… disrespectful.

Rade must have caught my disgusted expression. "Anywhere we put our dead, the Black collects, and where the Black collects, monsters are drawn to it. So our cemeteries near civilization are kept well protected. When those get too full, we dig up the old graves and move all the old bones down into the ruins. There's hundreds of plots like this, and miles and miles of tunnels between them, and they're all about this full. Afterall, it's been forty-five hundred years since Nyx Tartaros built our gate."

Azarin whistled. "That's a lot of dead people." Then she walked over and knelt next to one of the bone piles. She pointed at something growing on the floor. "Is this what I think it is?"

At first, I thought it was some kind of oily moss, but Rade took one look and told her, "Yes. Don't touch it. That's the Black… It generates naturally in places like this ossuary. Be careful. You really don't want to get it on your skin." Then he noted there were several patches like that, and even more growing on some of the bones. "By the ghost of Nyx! That is *a lot*! We've struck it rich!"

"Really?" Azarin asked. "How rich?"

"Just from what's beneath our lights right now, this is easily a thousand Obols in the market!"

I couldn't believe it. That was a life changing amount. I exchanged a look with Azarin, because surely she was thinking the same thing I was. That kind of money could buy our way into an academy. She started to laugh. Rade's excitement was so contagious that even Krachma smiled.

Rade was grinning like a happy fool, when his grin abruptly died as some terrible realization set in, replacing his good mood with a sudden terrible unease. "It's *too much.* Quick, scrape some up and let's get out of here."

"What's wrong?"

"Black grows naturally in this realm, but this is a surprising amount for how little time has passed. I was here only a couple of years ago, and even though it hadn't been disturbed for a decade, I still barely gathered enough to fill a thimble. When this much spontaneously generates it's only because there's a dark influence."

Azarin looked around at the thousands of skeletons. "Worse than *this*?"

"Much worse! These belong to people who move into the afterlife willingly. Others tend to linger." Rade stopped as something farther inside the tomb emitted an animalistic growl. "Like that…"

The thing that shambled into the light might have been human once, but it was hard to tell now, since its yellow flesh was so bloated and puffy. The flesh around its jaws had rotted off, revealing blackened, decaying teeth. Its eyes were milky, but the way it was looking hungrily at us, it wasn't blind. It stopped ten yards away, teetering on legs far too thin for its round, bulging, body. It was naked, but so corroded and falling apart that I couldn't have told you if it started out as a man or woman.

"That's no ghoul," Rade muttered as he took a step back.

"What the fuck is it?" I snapped.

Then something moved *inside* the creature's belly, as if climbing its ribs like a ladder, and once at the top, it began to push against the flesh at the base of its neck, bulging like a bubble.

"Sometimes little Death Elementals will inhabit a corpse and wear it around like a suit of armor made of flesh."

The yellow skin stretched until it violently split open. Ooze splattered the floor a foot in front of the corpse. Through the new gaping wound, we could all see something shiny and black moving inside. Then two glowing points of light appeared, and then disappeared briefly, as the Death Elemental blinked.

"That explains why there's so much element here." Rade kept his voice calm, even though he obviously was not. "Everybody move back up the stairs… real slow."

I'd killed Fire Elementals before, but only with a team of experienced trappers, a lot of careful planning and preparation, and a bit of luck. Retreat sounded like a splendid idea.

As we started backing away, the monster contorted its body, stretching one hand toward the open door behind us. The door began to rattle on its own, before slamming shut with incredible force.

"*I'll get it.*" Trax grabbed hold of the door handle and pulled with all his squalo might. The massive door didn't budge, even when Trax put one foot on the wall for extra leverage. He tugged so hard he ripped the handle off. "*That is not good.*"

Satisfied we were confined, the Elemental lurched toward us.

"Chop the door down!" Rade shouted.

That man had clearly never worked as a manual laborer, because I took one look at how big the door was, how fast the Elemental was approaching, did the math, and knew that wasn't going to work out in our favor. "There's no time."

Krachma needed no urging to fight, because he stepped forward, threw his torch aside, and clapped his big orange hands together. "*Crush.*"

Cracks formed in the floor around the Elemental's nasty feet, but the tomb must have been far more solid than the crumbling basement we'd fought in, because only small bits of it flew up to strike the monster. It didn't even seem to notice.

I had Red, but needed to get a whole lot closer to hit the monster with a sustained shroud of fire. Drawing Gax's pistol, I aligned the front sight on the rotting corpse and pulled the trigger. The roar was terrible in the enclosed space. There was a puff of yellow dust as the bullet struck its chest and a spray of gore as it flew out its back, but the monster kept lumbering toward us. I immediately pulled the lever to break open the action and begin the reloading process.

Azarin shot at it as well. Her little double barrel wasn't nearly as deafening as my gun, but it was still loud enough to make us all flinch. She managed to miss it twice. I looked at her, incredulously.

"I've not used one of these before," she shouted in apology as she ran behind Trax to reload.

"*I will fight this creature, but if we are victorious, I do* not *wish to eat it afterward.*"

"Well that's a first!" I shouted back at Trax as I pulled out the smoking paper cartridge and shoved in a fresh round. I slammed the pistol's action shut just in time to see that Rade was running straight for the Elemental. He was a braggart and most likely a liar, but he certainly wasn't a coward. I knew nothing at all about sword fighting, but his strike looked clean as the edge of his sword sliced through half of the monster host's neck.

The rotting head began flopping about wildly from side to side, eyes bulging, teeth snapping.

Rade smoothly stepped back as the monster stumbled. "Begone from here foul denizen of—"

It extended one hand, and an invisible force punched Rade back ten feet into one of the bone piles. He disappeared in the dust as the bones collapsed around him.

I cocked the hammer, aimed, and fired again. That bullet took a chunk out of its sternum and the little beast ducked in its rotten flesh window. Which told me that just like Fire Elementals, tough as they may be, they were still vulnerable to physical attacks. "Target the thing riding in its chest!"

Trax leapt past me to land in front of the monster and slash it across the chest with the coral sword. It tried the same magical force trick it used on Rade, only Trax was too fast for that, and as the squalo dived out of the way, the wall of bones behind him were pulverized into dust.

Swinging from the hip, Krachma smashed the flopping head with his mace so hard it was ripped from the body entirely. The rotting skull flew across the room, splattered against a wall, then rolled across the floor, teeth still chomping.

However impressively fatal that blow would've been against a living opponent, it didn't do a thing to the Death Elemental controlling the puppet. The corpse backhanded Krachma, and despite being twice its size, our lob went flying off into the darkness.

I rushed the beast with a fistful of Red. I'd been hired because magical fire was good against the common monsters of this realm. All I could do was hope it worked on its Elementals too. Two glowing green eyes fixed on me from the hole in its chest, as one of its palms extended to magically bash me as it had Rade. I concentrated on the Red, awakening the fire inside, but I wasn't going to make it in time.

"*Jolt!*" Azarin shouted.

Something bright flashed past me to hit the monster. Whatever she'd thrown stuck to its putrid belly, crackling with energy, like miniature lightning.

So that was the third spell Azarin knew!

As the monster twitched uncontrollably, the concussive force spell meant for me was directed into the ground instead. The top half inch of stone got crushed into gravel. Azarin's electrical spell only flickered for a few seconds, but while it did, the monster's puppet was unable to do anything other than twitch uselessly as its muscles spasmed.

The electrical jolt was so bright it left a blue image lingering on my eyes, but as soon as her spell died off, the monster shook itself back into fighting shape.

Right before I engulfed it in flames.

This was by far the most Red I'd ever used up at once. Normally, a shroud of fire would be a dusting, or at most a pinch. In my haste and fear, I'd scooped up a handful from my bag, and as the Red cloud spread, I activated it all.

FOOOOM!

The concussion sent me sliding across the floor on my back. When I sat up, the corpse was completely engulfed in flames. For a moment, it was so gloriously hot that it was like I was back home.

Then I remembered I wasn't wearing the protective leather armor of a Fogo miner anymore, just regular Core dweller's clothing, so I had to roll in the dust until I put the fire on my chest out.

The corpse was burning so hot that the fat deposits left on it ignited. Through that oil fire, I heard the most ungodly shriek imaginable, which told me that, yes, Death Elementals are in fact vulnerable to magical fire.

Trax rushed back to stab it some more, but he had to stop because the fire was too hot for him to get that close. Luckily, the creature couldn't cast any other spells while it burned. All it could do was thrash about, crashing haphazardly into the piles, scattering bones. I reloaded my pistol, thinking I might get lucky and put a bullet into the Elemental itself before it got refocused on us.

When Krachma came staggering back into the light, looking a lot worse for wear, Azarin yelled at him, "Hey, big guy! Now'd be a great time for you to bust down this door!"

She was right, because that fire was going to run out of fuel fast, and then we would be in deep trouble.

While the lob began wrestling with the door, I looked for my shot, except the burning meat sack was moving too erratically. I popped a shot into its torso with no idea if I actually hit the Elemental inside or not. Its agonized wails were nearly as loud as my gunshot. Then I ran to where Rade had disappeared and desperately began throwing bones out of the way. I tossed aside a ribcage and found him there, conscious, but dazed. I grabbed him by the sleeve and pulled him free.

"Let's go!"

The blessed heat was tapering off. The fire was going out. When I looked back toward the corpse, all that was left was ashen destruction. It was still moving, if slowly, its flesh burned to a crisp and big chunks falling off the bone.

Trax swept in, chopped one of its arms off, then spun, and sliced both its legs out from under it.

The blackened body hit the ground in a cloud of hot ash.

"*It is defeated,*" Trax sent triumphantly.

We all stilled. Krachma even stopped hammering the door with his mace to look. The tomb was quiet as the mangled, headless, mostly limbless torso lay there still... for a moment... and then it sprouted spider legs made of pure shadow from out of its back.

"*Never mind. I was mistaken,*" Trax thought as he retreated.

The eight new legs found the ground, the smoking body lifted, and the thing scurried up the nearest wall with unsettling swiftness. Gravity meant nothing to it as the torso moved across the ceiling above us.

"It's been freed." Rade was obviously shaken to the core. "It's going to want one of us to inhabit as its new home."

"And I thought I came from a shitty realm," I shouted while half dragging, half carrying Rade to the door. "Get us out of here, Krachma!"

Krachma had smashed enough of a hole in the edge of the wood that he was able to shove the steel shaft of his mace through to use as a pry bar. The lob was incredibly strong, but the Elemental had bound the door so hard that even he couldn't move it. Then Trax jumped in, and the two of them pulling together cracked it open enough for us to slip through.

"Go!"

I went through last. I make no claims as to being a hero. It just worked out that way.

The shadow spider thing dropped from the ceiling, flipped over on the way down to land on its legs, and scuttled toward the door just as I went through. The others were already running up the stairs, so in an attempt to buy us some time, I grabbed some more Red from my pocket—not nearly as exorbitant an amount this time—and bathed the entire door in flames.

The wood caught, and the monster stopped on the other side.

I'd not known Elementals could talk, but its whispered voice had the consistency of the tomb's spider webs, "*We will meet again, fire mage.*"

"No, we won't. I'm not coming back here!"

"*All mortals pass through this realm eventually. I will be waiting.*"

36

I didn't stop running until I was out of the tomb and could look back to make sure nothing was chasing me. Thank the Saints, it appeared the monster stopped at the burning door. So I paused there between the trees, trying desperately to catch my breath. This forest was a grim place, but I felt a whole lot better back here in the fog and mirk than I had down in the darkness of the tomb.

"Ahem."

I glanced back to see that my companions were there, only they all had their hands up and open in a position of surrender, because there were a whole bunch of pale skinned, black-eyed men pointing guns and wands our direction. The enforcers were all mounted on horseback, and though I didn't know much about horses, these seemed large and scary looking, probably bred for war.

"*These humans arrived just as we reached the surface, and they rudely threatened to shoot us,*" Trax explained to me. "*I do not know why I have raised my hands, but the others have, so I copied them.*"

The man who'd gotten my attention was the only one not holding a weapon, though he was riding on a horse that was so big it could have stomped Krachma. With an enchanted silver amulet around his neck and clothing that was far nicer than that of his men, surely this was some local official, and likely a noble.

"Is this the entirety of your merry band?"

Rade answered, "Yes, Lord Brugan, it's just the four of us."

There'd been five, but as I glanced around the clearing, I saw Trax, Krachma, and Rade, but no sign of Azarin, though I was certain she had been the first up the stairs.

"What should I do with you?" the noble asked, seemingly annoyed. "Trespassing is a serious business, Prescott."

I was very confused. "Who's Prescott?"

Lord Brugan gestured toward Rade. "That one, of course. Braden Prescott, notorious scoundrel, liar, and thief, who I thought Acheron had finally been rid of years ago."

I was still coming off the rush of surviving a Death Elemental. In comparison to that, ignoring a bunch of weapons and spells aimed at me was easy. "Hold up. He told us his family name was Tartaros."

The nobleman snorted at that. "Of course he did."

"Me being Baron Tartaros' unclaimed bastard son doesn't make my lineage any less righteous."

"Yes, it does, Braden. That's literally how claims to the throne work. We've been over this a hundred times before you got banished." The noble sighed. "This fucking guy, I swear."

"I've missed you too, cousin." Rade turned to me and spread his hands apologetically. "Don't mind my more legitimate relative. Prescott was my mother's family name."

"His mother was a village whore. The only evidence there's ever been for his so-called noble lineage is her deluded claims."

Rade smiled despite the insult. "Well, that and the striking family resemblance. Don't you think Brugan and I could pass for brothers, Carnavon?"

Everyone from this foggy land of decay looked like a walking corpse to me. "If I may speak, your lordship?" Brugan nodded for me to continue. "Regardless of how me, the lob, and the squalo were led here under false pretenses… there's a Death Elemental down there right below us, and it is not happy."

"They seldom are… But we should be safe for now. They'll not come outside during such a bright day."

It saddened me that this was what they considered a bright day here, because this was dismal, even by Fogo standards, and they didn't even have volcanos to blame for it. "I apologize for any trespass we may have inadvertently committed, but that was not our intent. We thought we were aiding the rightful landowner."

"Of course. Your accent… Are you a hotlander?"

"Yes, sir. I'm from Fogo."

"Ah, then you know well the pettiness of the Argents and all their tricks to keep their people in endless servitude. We don't play those kinds of games here. Let it never be said that the Tartaros family delights in unnecessary cruelty as many of our noble peers do. You will not be punished for being misled, but we also cannot allow thieves to profit." He turned to one of the enforcers. "Search them. Confiscate any Black they may have collected."

A few of the men approached to pat us down. Krachma shoved one into the dirt. There was a series of metallic clicks as rifles were cocked and aimed at the lob.

"Krachma is no thief."

From the looks on the enforcers' faces, they wouldn't hesitate to gun the threatening lob down.

"Easy there, big fellow." I tried to use a calming voice. "I don't think they mean any insult. You can't be a thief if you thought something was free for the taking." I looked to Lord Brugan. "Isn't that right, sir?"

Luckily, the real Tartaros wasn't lying about his family not wanting to be unnecessarily cruel, because he quickly offered the proud gladiator a way out. "This is true. There is only one dishonest snake here, and it isn't you, earth realmer."

Krachma grunted, annoyed, but he let the enforcers search him. I got a rough pat down as well, and grimaced when the man hit my broken finger. These deadlanders must have been fairly honorable though, because even as they found my valuable enchantments and my bag of Red, they didn't take the opportunity to rob me.

I felt bad for the poor fellow who was hesitating to check Trax though, as the squalo stood there, *smiling.*

Don't hurt him, I sent, before saying aloud, "I give you my word the toothy fellow won't bite. Despite his fearsome appearance, he's really rather civilized."

"*I shall bear this rudeness in stoic compliance.*" When the enforcer was done checking him, Trax told me, "*That tickled.*"

"They've got no Black upon them, sir."

"Not even that one?" Brugan pointed at Rade. "Check him again just to be sure."

"I'm telling you, cousin, there's a wealth of element down there for the taking, but we had nary the time to collect a bit before the Death Elemental attacked us. Now that you're aware, you can send in the castle's wizards and harvest to your heart's content." The enforcers who searched him the second time weren't nearly as gentle or respectful to Rade as they'd been to us outsiders, and the slightest failure to cooperate ended up with him getting a hard punch to the ribs.

"Warlock Murran, go and reseal the tomb. We'll need to put a new password on the door later." One of the men with wands dismounted and headed for the tomb. "I really don't know how this scum learned a family password."

Even with Rade bent over and clutching his ribs, he still couldn't manage to shut up when it was good for him, "It came to me in a dream, a gift from our common ancestor, Nyx. You know, Brugan, you should at least pay us a finder's fee for discovering all that element down there."

"I should have you flogged for trespass and then leave you for the ghouls. The only reason we threw you out instead of executing you to begin with is my father took pity on an imaginative child being led astray by the hysterical ramblings of a dying prostitute. You're lucky I'm the one who rode by here and saw the tomb was open, since I hate you slightly less than my brothers do." The nobleman nudged his horse, and the giant steed began clomping away. "Leave now, and I won't inform them you came back."

"Brugan and I grew up together," Rade told me. "He was always the kind hearted one… Thank you, Brugan."

"Be gone before the gate closes, Braden, or I will change my mind."

I remained glaring at Rade as the Tartaros wizard finished sealing the door. When he was done, he mounted up, and all the enforcers rode after their leader. I waited a bit longer to make sure they were all out of sight before approaching Rade.

He stood up, rubbing his bruised ribs. "Good show, Carnavon, setting that monster ablaze like that. Rather impressive work with the Red, my fri—"

I punched Rade in the mouth.

He landed on his ass, surprised, and sat there, waiting to see if there were any more fists coming, but when I just stood there, seething but in control, he wiped his bloody lip with the back of his hand and admitted, "I suppose I had that one coming."

"Damned right. You're lucky I don't set you on fire. We almost got killed for nothing."

"I wouldn't say *nothing*, Carnavon." Azarin's voice came from high up in one of the moss shrouded trees above.

And that was when I understood why she'd been missing.

Azarin parted the hanging plants and looked down at us. "Wow. That was a close one. I thought for sure they were going to shoot all of you, which would've been tragic. *Descend.*"

She floated down and landed between me and Rade, who eagerly asked her, "I saw you grabbing bones on the way out—what did you get?"

Azarin pulled off her travelling pack to triumphantly show us her haul. "I suppose if they'd shot you guys, I'd get to keep this for myself rather than having to split the proceeds five ways. Oh well."

Inside the bag was a human skull, half covered in pulsing Black.

37

The Tower of Primopolus had been the tallest building ever constructed in any of the realms. Erected by incredibly powerful magic, it had been even taller than the Great Machine, and lofty bridges once spanned between the tower's various levels and the districts floating around it. Thousands of residents had lived in its multitude of rooms, and no matter how high up their homes, they were carried quickly there by lifts powered by air magic. It had been home to the laboratories of some of the most prestigious wizards in the Core. According to the *Encyclopedia Ettymus*, the tower was one of the greatest magical wonders to have ever existed.

The day it toppled over must have *really* sucked.

The five of us stood in front of the broken section of tower which lay sideways through the outer edge of the Under Slump. It was a testament to the toughness of the building's magical construction that this section was still mostly in one piece, even though it hit the ground hard enough to smash through an entire neighborhood and embed half of itself into the rock beneath.

"The old timers told me that when the tower toppled, it went over just like a tree getting chopped down near the base," Rade explained. "The stumpy part still stands beneath the Palentine, nearly a mile away, though it's only ten stories tall now and jagged at the top. It smashed everything in a line from there to here, and the very top hit above and took a chunk out of the Slump, though they didn't call it that back then."

The tower had been incredibly tall. Thankfully, it hadn't been that wide, as everything caught directly beneath it had gotten pulverized on that fateful day fifty years ago. From what I'd seen along our walk from the market, the places where the construction magic failed and the tower exploded into manageable size bits, the rubble was cleared away and the people had built new buildings. The places where the tower sections still remained in one piece, they had been forced to rebuild around them. This part was still in one piece, but nobody was going to invest in the condemned Under Slump, as it was slowly being crushed from above. Why rebuild somewhere that was inevitably doomed?

But as I'd seen during my time here, just because a district was forsaken and lived in perpetual fear of getting smooshed didn't mean that people wouldn't keep moving in anyway. The Core was the most populated place in all the realms, and the poor had to congregate somewhere.

Oddly enough, this tower section was the only place I'd come across in either of the Slumps that looked abandoned. When I remarked on that, Rade just smirked and replied, "That's because everybody thinks it's haunted."

"Why would they think that?"

"Because it is. You think you can squish thousands of innocent people with an enchanted tower because of a mad wizard's hubris and *not* accumulate a bunch of angry ghosts in the ruins? This place is lousy with vengeful spirits. But I'm used to those, so I get to stay here for free. Come on."

Rade and Krachma kept walking, but me and Azarin shared an uneasy look. Trax didn't really know what was going on, but since I stopped, so did he. Rade turned back to us, exasperated. "You still don't trust me, Carnavon? I've already apologized for not explaining the complex nature of my relationship with the Tartaros, but in my defense, it is a long and sordid tale of family drama, and we were on a tight schedule."

"Whatever you say, Rade Prescott."

He sighed. "That's my name by law, but not by right. Whatever name they put on the books, I remain a man of my word. I promised that in exchange for your helping me, I'd teach you a spell. The only ones I know are too disruptive to do around the polite company of the inn you're staying at. Whereas here at my humble abode, you could summon a dragon and nobody would notice."

Azarin laughed at that, but nobody else got what she found so funny. "I take it none of you guys have ever seen a real dragon then?

Because they're pretty hard to miss, what with all the mayhem and carnage and whatnot."

"You get what I mean. Do you want to learn some shadow magic or not? Because if not, let's divide up the Black and go our separate ways."

Though I suspected Rade was a buffoon with delusions of grandeur—I think he truly believed his own story about being nobility—he didn't strike me as the type to lead us into an ambush, double cross, or robbery. Krachma, quietly belligerent as he was, actually struck me as an honest sort. This probably wasn't a trap. On the other hand, I'd made enemies in the Under Slump. Although, the tower section was on the opposite end of the district from the Skerret's lair, so it was doubtful I'd run into them.

I looked to Azarin for her opinion. She shrugged. "It would be nice to have a place I could practice tossing some fire with reckless abandon."

"That's the opposite of how you should play with fire, Azarin, but alright... Lead the way, Rade."

"That's the spirit, Carnavon. Which reminds me though, if you see any actual spirits, just remain polite."

Several hours of practice later, I'd only just begun to sort of grasp how the death element worked. Red, I understood instinctively. Clear, not so much, but I could at least think of it as heavy air and that was enough to sort of manipulate it with my mind. Black, however, was complicated, because it wasn't just condensed death. It was more like the absence of life, and not just life either, but also light and energy in general. Of the seven magical elements, it was the ingredient used in a formula whenever a wizard needed to extinguish, diminish, or undo something. It was the end.

It was also rather frightening to work with, because you did not want to accidentally get pure distilled death on you. I didn't know exactly what it would do, but Rade assured us that even one drop was corrosive and rather painful.

Rade had tested as a natural rank two, but knew no spells that required more than one element. Which frankly was fine by me, because learning Black by itself was complicated enough. Even as proud and stubborn as I was, I recognized I wasn't ready to combine elements yet. Though I was very excited about the possibilities, like combining fire and death, or fire and air. Depending on the amounts of each element and how the effects could vary by what material I bound them too, there were so many combinations, it felt like I could accomplish anything.

Oh, who was I kidding? I'd spent most of my day trying to figure out how to darken a small area, while ranks tens were out there combining all seven elements together to grow cities anchored in the sky. I had a very long way to go.

I threw the clay sphere at the ground as hard as I could. "*Obscura!*"

It shattered on impact and rapidly disintegrated as the Black inside was released. Smoke billowed outward and then I was blind.

"Well done, Carnavon," Rade shouted.

It was dark as standing in a volcanic plume, except I could breathe just fine. It wasn't pitch-black, as I could still barely make out my hands when I held them in front of my face. I'd previously set my light charm floating ten feet above at full strength, and it was nothing but a dim yellow circle through the magical effect. The effect this spell created wasn't dark as the Tartaros tomb, but it was close.

I could hear Azarin counting steadily, "Four… five… six…" The magical darkness began to dissipate. "Seven." And by the time she said, "Eight," it was gone entirely, and I could see normally again. "Wow. Nearly eight seconds that time. Not too bad."

"How big was the area?"

Azarin had been observing from the far end of our oddly shaped practice area. "The black circle was about twelve or fifteen feet wide I'd guess, but it was fuzzy and see-through around the edges. In the middle though, I couldn't see you at all."

That brought a grin to my face, because that was by far the best one I'd pulled off so far.

"*Obscura* is a very handy spell if you ever need to make a hasty exit," Rade said.

He was sitting above, on what had once been the edge of a doorway. He lowered his voice and spoke like a guardsman, "*Oi, what're you about there, cut purse?*" Rade's voice went back to normal. "*Obscura!* And by the time that copper can see again, I'm gone… Not that I'd ever engage in such low behavior, mind you."

I was standing on a concave floor that had once been the exterior wall. One issue with living in a fallen tower, was the rooms were sideways, so the interior of this place was rather disorienting, but our host insisted it wasn't so bad once one got used to it. "I could think of a few uses for this beyond petty thievery."

"My thievery is never petty, Carnavon, but if a cheating dwarf is ever trying to chop your neck with an axe, drop one on the ground, and it'll buy you some time to maneuver. It's a very simple enchantment, really, but as your connection to the element improves with rank, you should be able to change the duration, density, or area affected. I imagine a rank fifteen could black out an entire city for a month if he was so inclined."

"I love it." Azarin couldn't keep the glee out of her voice, because if anything, she'd taken to this one far faster than me, producing an even thicker darkness which lasted longer and covered more of the room. It was funny how different spells clicked into place better for different people, or maybe she was just more attuned to shadow magic than I was. "This has been very educational. I must admit, you really are a man of your word, Mr. Tartaros."

Rade tipped his hat in acknowledgment of her choosing to use that name rather than his given one. "It was my pleasure to share a bit of knowledge with some fellow seekers. Nyx knows I've had not a bit of luck going through official channels."

I took a seat on the oddly shaped floor. "So you've tried your hand at getting into an academy?"

"That I have, though I've not had a bit of success. Though I know if my lineage was actually recognized, they'd be fighting for the honor of training a direct descendant of one of the twenty-eight wizards who originally created the Nexus. Instead, I'm reduced to fighting in a poor man's arena, trying to get famous in the hope that some instructor hears of my abilities and comes to watch, and is impressed. So far, all I've done is enrich seedy goblins."

Rade was naturally born with talent an entire rank ahead of me and Azarin, so that didn't bode well for our chances.

"What's his story?" Azarin asked, gesturing toward where Krachma had gone to sleep, as the lob apparently had no interest in our lessons.

"I don't rightly know. Krachma's a bit of a cipher. He doesn't really talk much. From all the scars and a few things he's mentioned, he used to be some kind of soldier. His kind turn to rock when they die, and from all the bits of him that are already stone, he's halfway there. When I saw him sleeping in the streets, even though he'd just won a match, I felt pity for the big fellow and told him I had a place to stay that was warm, dry, and only moderately cursed with ghosts. He's been here ever since."

I had to disagree with Rade's assessment of warm, because the fallen tower was just as cold as everything else in this city, but having seen his land of mist and moss, these sideways rooms of bare stone walls were probably very comfortable in comparison. As for ghosts, I'd only seen a few strange movements out of the corner of my eye, and though that potential presence probably added to the chill in the air, if there were apparitions here, they'd been considerate enough to not interrupt our practice.

"You know," Azarin mused, "Carnavon and I have worked out an arrangement to help each other get into a magical academy. You see, he owes me, big time."

I couldn't even curse Trax for making promises I couldn't keep because he didn't know any better. And he was currently outside in the canal anyway. "What are you doing, Azarin?"

"Potentially expanding our catalog of spells…"

I trusted Rade not one bit. "You sure that's a good idea?"

"No, but anyways, as I was saying, Carnavon here has agreed to share his fire spells with me in exchange for my air spells. With you being a rank two, you surely know at least…"

Rade help up three fingers. "I inherited the natural inclination but have lacked the time and opportunity to study."

"So you know three spells, as do I, and he's got four. Together that would get us *ten*. Which even though they're all low level and brewed at home, one must admit that ten's an impressive catalog of spells to choose from. Then there's him." She nodded toward where Krachma was snoring. "If he's amenable, that would introduce earth magic into the mix. And what about fish face?"

"Trax isn't a wizard. He's a monk."

"He's from the Realm of Water, so I got my hopes up." Azarin plowed ahead anyway, "That's half the elements there, more really, since it isn't like there's hardly any time mages around anymore. If we were to all work together and compile our knowledge, there's no telling what we could accomplish. And how many more are there like us, talented, with a bit of knowledge, but no other place to go?"

"Are you proposing we form our own magical academy?" Rade sounded intrigued.

"Sorta, maybe, I suppose."

"You do realize there's a high and mighty council of wizards hovering high above us in the opulent Pallentine, who administer such things, right? They frown upon upstarts like us toying with too much magic on our own. Supposedly, it's to keep fools and imitators from accidentally cursing their precious city."

Azarin shrugged. "I assumed there had to be something like that."

"There is. Only everyone knows the real reason they put such a limit on who can learn magic is because they don't want competition. That's why only rank tens get to start academies, and the only way to reach that mighty rank is the Nexus Council appoints you to it, unless you defeat and replace a rank ten in a magical contest they were dumb enough to agree to." Rade made a big show of glancing around the vast and mostly empty space. "I don't see any rank tens here to claim us."

Tomorrow was the quiet day, the end of the week, and once the Great Machine rotated past the barred gate of time, would bring Fireday, and the arrival of my persecutor. Teaming up with a potentially delusional liar might not be the wisest thing to do, but I was running low on options.

"If being an illegal academy would attract the wrath of the Council, then let us be something else," I said. "We'll be an unofficial study group. We've got some elements. We've got a few formula. We've got a bit of space to work." I didn't add that what I didn't have was time, but I was motivated to learn fast. "If the authorities find out and tell us to knock it off, we stop. But what are the odds of that in the forsaken Under Slump? In the meantime, we try to learn as many spells from each other as we can in order to gain another rank."

Rade chuckled. "I never said I was against the idea, just that it's probably illegal. I'm not exactly adverse to illegality, provided it's for a good cause. Having a bit of fire or air magic would help me put on a much more impressive show in the arena to draw a better audience."

"What's the worst that could happen?" Azarin asked innocently.

I could get sent to prison anyway, or we might accidentally blow ourselves to pieces, but there was no reason for me to say that aloud and ruin everyone's good mood, so instead I said, "Everyone wins."

"If I return to Acheron at a high enough rank, my family will have no choice but to admit who I really am, and finally give me the respect I deserve…" Rade pondered on that for a long moment, then shouted, "Hey, Krachma. Wake up!"

The lob opened one eye. "What?"

"I think we just formed an illicit underground magical academy. You're our instructor of earth magic now."

Krachma snorted at that, rolled over, and went back to sleep.

38

We'd spent most of the night trading spells and training. Even Krachma grudgingly joined in, though he was a terrible teacher because he could barely speak the trade tongue, and none of us knew the lob language. This led to Azarin nearly electrocuting the poor fellow with her jolt spell, as he'd forgotten the right words to surrender.

Despite discovering that scorched lob smelled horrible, it was a surprisingly productive night.

But the sunrise brought with it my last chance to find a real home. Fleeing was no longer an option. It was find an academy today or hide out in a broken tower in the Under Slump learning magic the slow, dangerous, and probably illegal way, while I hoped Gaul Haddar passed me by.

I decided to go to the Collegium by myself. Trax was observing humanity from the safety of the canals. Azarin was off trying her luck at the various academies that had already turned me away. There'd be no tricks today. I'd present myself honestly, humbly, and hope for the best.

I'd been putting one particular academy off for last.

The park around the Wynlyn's giant tree was covered in fallen leaves of gold and red. As I walked toward their wall of thorns, I said a prayer to Saint Persistence because my own determination could only carry me so far.

There were two guards posted at the living gate, and they didn't sneer outright as I approached. Thanks to my winnings in the arena, I wore a decent cloak and appeared halfway respectable. It wasn't until I got close enough that they could see my black eye and bandaged hand that they assumed I was some kind of ruffian and adjusted their stances accordingly.

"State your business here."

"I'm Ozwald Carnavon of Fogo, come to speak to one of your wizards about gaining admittance to this academy. I know your customs, but I bring no gifts. I do, however, have this..." I held up the pirate band so they could see the writing on it. "Which I think your employers will find of interest, as it concerns the criminal actions of one of their former students."

The guards were human hirelings, but they worked for elves, so they knew an elven enchantment when they saw it. "What did this former student allegedly do?"

"He's murdered a lot of innocent people across the Elemental Plane of Fire."

Of the great many aspirants who tried to talk their way through this gate, that must have been a first, as they didn't immediately send me away. While one watched me, the other walked back to the wall of thorns and began whispering to it. Unsurprisingly, the wall whispered back.

The guard nodded toward me. "Wait here. Mistress Magnorin wishes to speak with you."

"Who's that?"

"One of our senior instructors."

We stood there in an uncomfortable silence for several minutes, until the vines of the gate retracted and slithered aside. Standing on the other side was a tall, eerily striking woman who I recognized instantly, because this was the one I'd spoken with my first day in the market.

She didn't seem the least bit surprised to see me, or maybe elf faces were just naturally set that way, slightly askance, as if asking themselves why one of us short timers was bothering them?

"When the guard said a hotlander aspirant showed him a protective band bearing Elven script, I suspected it would be you. Have you come seeking a reward, Ozwald Carnavon of Fogo?"

I was confused. "A reward for what?"

"Risking your safety to aid me while I was trapped beneath that broken air cart, of course."

Honestly, I'd not even thought about that. I'd simply done what needed doing in the moment. I wouldn't have reacted any differently if it had been a crawler stuck in a tunnel with a gurgler approaching. "That wasn't my intent in coming here, but if there's a reward to be had, I'd take it in the form of you giving my application for admittance your honest consideration."

"You fancy yourself a mage then?"

"I do."

"Then I shall grant you this reward." She turned into the academy. "Walk with me."

After a week of constant rejection, I was nearly too surprised to follow, but I rapidly rectified that. The guards stepped aside to let me pass through, and the thorn vines moved, twisting together into a solid mass behind me.

Magnorin led me toward the base of the gigantic tree. "What rank do you test at, Mr. Carnavon?"

Lying would do me no good here. "Of the first. Though I know seven basic spells now—to one degree or another."

"An impressive number from someone with such lowly test results."

"I'm confident in four enough to demonstrate them on demand."

"That is not necessary." The path we were on took us between many smaller buildings, which appeared to have been grown organically from the ground. Through the windows built into each of those hollowed out roots, I could see young mages studying. "And of how many elements are these spells of yours?"

"Three. Mostly fire, but recently a bit of air, and a small amount of death."

"An odd progression."

"Purely based on availability. I wasn't born with any magical talent, but I am persistent. When given the opportunity, I learn whatever I can."

The base of the tree was nearly as big as the Argent's keep, and from all the structures and doors built into it, had to be nearly as hollow. It was hard to imagine that something so large could actually be alive. This clearly was, as the endless rain of golden leaves demonstrated. There had to be hundreds living inside, and from what I could see, the overwhelming majority were elves.

"Have a seat, Mr. Carnavon."

I was about to ask where, but with a casual gesture of her hand, two wooden chairs sprouted from the ground. They were made of elaborately intertwined roots, and despite their origin, didn't appear to have a speck of dirt on them.

We both sat down at the edge of what had to be some manner of practice field. There were about twenty children present, being directed by a single teacher, and every last one of them had pointed ears. I knew elves had unnaturally long life spans, but if those kids were human they would've been about ten or twelve. What that meant in elf terms, I had no idea.

"Thank you for taking the time to speak with me."

"That was a particularly nasty curse someone loosed. Your intervention kept me from having to burn up another valuable protective charm. Your actions saved me from some inconvenience."

Despite her nonchalance, I wasn't sure if she was being entirely truthful about that, because at the time, she'd certainly seemed stuck and genuinely terrified of those caustic tendrils reaching her, but I wasn't about to push my luck by saying so. "I was happy to help."

"Before we continue, I must address this band you've already shown me, with the maker's mark upon it. How did you obtain it?"

"Four years ago, a gang of pirates, led by an elf, attacked and destroyed the Red mining barge I grew up on."

"You had family aboard."

I nodded.

"Did they survive this pirate attack?"

"Some did. Some didn't."

"I am terribly sorry to hear that."

I really didn't feel like elaborating. That wasn't a story I wanted to share with this stranger, and though I desperately needed a place, I wanted no one's pity. "But I can say the same for the pirates we fought. Every one of their bodies we found afterward wore enchantments bearing that same word."

"*Aarhobad*," she said wistfully. "The Elemental Plane of Time was the original home to the elven people. Today is the quiet day, our constant reminder of what was stolen from us. It seems appropriate that this is when you'd show up here, seeking your revenge."

I didn't deny that, because I'd love nothing more than to kill me some pirates. "I recognize my limits. I'm seeking education first. Our nobles have already sent a powerful wizard searching for this particular pirate, but he's eluded capture for years. I'm under no illusion I can succeed where the legendary Gaul Haddar has failed."

She nodded at that name. "I know of Gaul Haddar. If this pirate has the power to avoid someone so deadly for so long, then you would have no chance against him at all."

"Give me time. I'll learn."

"Of course you would." And though she was trying to be polite, it still came off as patronizing.

There was a sudden *crack* from the practice field. One of the children had thrown a bolt of lightning at another, so big and bright it made Azarin's little shock spell look like the static pops from moving a rough blanket. Even from this far away, the energy released made the hair on my neck stand up. I thought for sure the other child must have been killed, but when my vision cleared, he'd turned the lightning aside. Instead of blasting him into burning chunks of meat, the crackling energy had been directed into the ground, and the only thing harmed was the blackened grass.

Until that chunk of burning grass rose atop a pillar of earth, higher and higher into a ten-foot-tall wave of dirt and gravel heading straight for the lightning hurler at an incredible speed. Just before that kid was about to be crushed, he activated some manner of protective spell, so the avalanche crashed harmlessly past him.

And the battles kept going, with the children taking turns attacking each other with spells that were far beyond my meager capabilities.

"This is our basic defensive training," Magnorin explained.

The teacher moved between them, shouting commands, and occasionally using a wand to tamp down some magical effect before it got out of control enough to kill somebody. The display was incredibly impressive.

"Basic?"

"Those are our lowest ranking students, Mr. Carnavon. They are relatively new here. Do you really expect to contend against one of our graduates?"

"I already have once."

"Then you were very lucky."

A child flew into the air and hit his enemy with a fireball that made what I'd done to the Death Elemental look like a pathetic ember.

So *that* was my competition for a spot? "Give me time. I'll catch up."

Magnorin's laugh actually counded genuine. "I was warned hotlanders are determined. I have honored your request for a fair interview, but I must be honest, Wynlyn produces the finest wizards in the Core. I would not fill your head with impossible dreams. Perhaps one of the lesser academies might consider you, but truthfully, there is no place for a rank one here. We constantly turn away natural born threes and even fours. We start them while they are young, when magic is understood more easily. Our students who are your age have already been training for years. You will never surpass them. I do not tell you this to be cruel."

"The world's a cruel place," I muttered.

"I wish it were not so, but cruelty is an inevitable outcome in a system that is dying a slow death."

That was so unexpected, it took me a moment to respond. "What's dying? The Core?"

"Is it not obvious? Especially today? Have you not yet witnessed the decay of this once magnificent place for yourself?"

I'd been here a week, and half of that had been spent sleeping in ratlet infested tunnels or a ditch. Despite that, the water was drinkable, the food astoundingly good, I'd seen very little disease, and nothing was on fire that wasn't supposed to be. "No offense, but compared to where I'm from, it seems like you've got it pretty nice here."

"Compared to many of the realms, we still do. But the long, slow death of the Core began five hundred years ago."

"You mean when the time gate was blocked?"

"Of course. It saddens me how little the common people grasp this, but it is not my place to fill them with dread." Magnorin sighed, as if she'd said too much to someone too dim to understand, but she must have been too much the teacher to not give a lesson when the opportunity presented itself. "The barring was the beginning of the end. The Nexus and the Core were created and maintained using all seven elements, the last of which effects time. The others can do great things, but only one of the elements can make magic endure indefinitely. The last element is Permanence. Deprived of it, even the mightiest spells eventually begin to wear out, break down, and collapse."

I'd never thought about that before. Then again, I'd never even seen the rare element of time. "Is that why the Slump is slumping?"

She nodded. "That is one example of many you will find here. I must remember that human lives are so short, they cannot grasp how much things have changed from before. However, this entropic process will only accelerate as time goes on and more of the old magic dies. We once bent reality to our whims, but reality always pushes back. We have been cut off from the last element since the greatest evil to ever exist took over the Realm of Time. What little Permanence remains is scarce and so valuable it must be controlled by the Nexus Council, to be meted out only when it is absolutely essential."

"You mean, like the Great Machine?" My mind struggled to grasp the ramifications. "Without a gate, Fogo would starve to death in a few months."

"Indeed. It would be an abrupt ending for many kingdoms who cannot survive on their own for long. Followed by a stunted base survival for the remainder, for even in those lands blessed with resources, once cut off, they would only have one form of magic. Five thousand years of civilization will have been wiped away."

This was a lot to take in. "How long do we have?"

"No one knows. It has already been many human lifetimes since the end began. Your grandchildren may live to old age, or the Great Machine could grind to a halt tomorrow. Decline is slow, until it is not."

"Can't the greatest wizards do something? They built all this to begin with."

"Sadly, Mr. Carnavon, we are a shadow of what we once were. None of us are worthy of our founders. Only the most ancient of elves were old enough to remember the accomplishments of before, and those have aged and perished since being cut off from our home.

Even if we had the knowledge, we lack enough of the final element to recreate the Nexus."

That was horrifying. "Why're you telling me all this?"

The elf mulled that over. "Considering your application—when you never had a chance to begin with—seemed an insufficient reward for the service you have done for me. So instead, I have given you rare knowledge to do with it as you will."

It turned out that nigh immortal ethereal beauties could still be profoundly annoying. "The world's going to end, and we can't do anything about it. Well, thanks for that, I guess."

"I was not finished. I have explained the deeper crisis to you so that you may better understand the nature of that maker's mark you hold. I cannot identify your pirate by name because this academy has thousands of graduates spread across the realms, but I can tell you what using that mark signifies to us. For one of us to invoke the true name of our lost home, it suggests that he is a cultist of Tempus Metum, a banished and forbidden sect, whose ultimate goal is to reopen the time gate."

I'd never heard of that group before. "That's madness. Unlocking that gate would let the things that destroyed your realm loose into the Core. Everyone would die."

"It would doubtlessly slaughter every living thing in this city, and then use the Nexus to spread into every other realm. Yet some would prefer a swift demise to our managed decline. They would risk the future of every life in every kingdom in the vain hope that by allowing the evil in, the evil might reward them for it. The cult have forgotten the nature of our fall. They believe the invader is something that can be reasoned with. This makes them very dangerous in their delusions, because it cannot. It can only destroy."

The way she was speaking made me wonder… "Were you there? Did you see it?"

Magnorin nodded, but clearly she felt like talking about the fall of Aarhobad as much as I did the burning of Barge 519. "The Council and the City Watch have scoured the Tempus cult from the Core long ago, and every noble has banned them from their lands. I do not know where they hide now. Do with this knowledge what you will, Mr. Carnavon. I can help you no more."

39

Outside the wall of thorns, I found someone waiting for me, and this wasn't a friendly meeting.

"Ah, Mr. Carnavon. A pleasure to see you again."

"Mr. Adderlane." Even as I nodded politely at the man who'd tried to have me and Trax murdered the other night, I was positioning my hands to grab pistol and magic.

"Calm yourself, lad." He put on a big fake smile which did not reach his eyes. "If I intended you harm, it wouldn't be here. Simply look around you and take comfort from the sheer number of respectable witnesses."

We were standing at the edge of the Wynlyn's park, out of earshot of their guards. The Collegium was busy as usual, with hundreds going about their business all around us. Illusionists and lesser magicians were plying their trade in the hopes of entertaining someone enough they'd drop some coins in the cups at their feet. If we started slinging spells and lead, a lot of people would surely notice and the watch would come running.

"There's no need for any rambunctiousness. As you can see, I'm all by myself. I've brought no associates with me, and you've got no killer shark man with you. Let us converse like gentlemen."

Adderlane wore a long coat. It was open, and the butts of two pistols were visible at his waist. He wasn't a physically intimidating man, but there was something about his confident manner that suggested he was very dangerous.

"A friend of mine told me he knew of an Adderlane who was a high-ranking mage in the Collegium. Is that you?"

"More than likely. My family's been in the Core for many generations, and I've got some less accomplished cousins, but I'm the only rank ten in the city with this surname that I know of."

Oh fuck.

"A ten, you say?" If he was telling the truth and wanted me dead, there wasn't a damned thing I could do about it. A ten could squish me like a bug.

"You heard correctly. So, do you want to sit on that bench there and have a polite conversation like proper civilized types, or should I just obliterate you and get it over with?"

"What about all those witnesses you just mentioned?"

He shrugged. "I'm a man of status. When the watchmen arrive I'll just tell them you foolishly tried to rob me, and I had no choice but to melt you. Turning to banditry is a tragic, though not uncommon, fate for refugees from the poorer realms here. It would be a brief investigation, since your remains would consist of nothing more than a stain on the sidewalk."

If he was what he claimed to be, the watch would surely take him at his word. I relented and sat on the bench. He sat next to me.

"See? That's much better. So let's clear the air, Mr. Carnavon." He tapped a golden ring on one finger to activate an enchantment. "No one will be able to eavesdrop on us now."

"Why have you been following me?"

"Curiosity. You came to my attention because you were in the wrong place at the wrong time. I wanted to be sure you were what you appeared to be. You convinced Inspector Borg that you're a nobody, but Dardick Argent seems to think you matter. I had to see which group was right. Hence, the little test the other night with me siccing those Frunza Tarlev morons on you."

"Did I pass?"

"With flying colors, though not in the way you're hoping. I thought you might secretly be a mage of some skill, dispatched by forces unknown to meddle in my plans. But I came to the conclusion that you are in fact just some determined peasant from a dogshit realm, who just happened to be nearby in the market when I tried to kill Dardick Argent, *but*, the Argents thinking you're one of their enemies makes you useful to me."

So this was the wizard who'd set off the caustic curse. I wanted no part of that plot. "To hell with the Argents." I held up my still bandaged hand. "Good luck to you in your murdering, sir. I'll be on my way."

"Let me show you something first." Adderlane reached into his breast pocket and took out a green gem. At first I thought something was encased inside of it, then realized it was a moving picture. The clarity of the image was finer than anything from the street illusionists. I could see a blonde woman, hands chained above her, imprisoned in a brick room.

"What's this?"

"This viewing gem is set to peer into a basement a few blocks from here."

When the woman angrily lifted her head to shout something, I saw it was Azarin.

"Move your hand away from that gun slowly, Carnavon, or neither of you will survive the day."

I'd not even realized I'd reached for Gax's pistol. Reluctantly, I did as I was told.

"She is safe for now and will remain so as long as you do as I tell you."

A dark seething anger came over me, and it took everything in my power to not do something stupid. "How do I know that's real?"

"Well, I had to turn the sound off because all her roaring of threats and obscenities at my henchmen who are guarding her would surely overcome my eavesdropping charm and upset everyone in this park. But there's this." He held out a white leather glove, which I recognized because it was the enchanted one Azarin used to teach me her *ascend* spell. "When I saw your girlfriend was in the Collegium, knocking on academy doors, I thought to myself, what a fine opportunity."

Azarin was in grave danger, and it was entirely my fault. "You hurt her, I'll kill you."

Adderlane chuckled. "You could try. Far greater wizards than you have made similar threats."

"What do you want from me?"

"You're going to take a walk to the market. Overcome with the profound guilt of being an oath breaker, you're going to turn yourself over to the Argents and confess all your crimes in person. I'm going to give you something to take with you."

This madman had unleashed an acid curse capable of dissolving bone and stone onto a market full of innocent bystanders. "What vile curse are you sending me with?"

"Don't worry. It's nothing as haphazard as last time. Having seen what protection spells Dardick has available, I was able to tailor something a little more specific for just him. You'll only need to get close. Which, from what I've heard, since he's fixated on solving his own assassination attempt, he'll surely confront you himself. You *might* even escape in the confusion, though that's not my problem. As soon as you deliver this curse to your ambassador, I'll let her go."

"You think I'm stupid? What's to keep you from killing Azarin the moment I leave here?"

He spread his hands apologetically. "What choice do you have?"

"I could go to the City Watch."

"Except I shall have eyes upon you the entire time. If you linger to talk to anyone along the way, I order my men to slit the air girl's throat, just like that." He snapped his fingers. "After her body is fed to the ratlets, leaving no evidence behind, who will the inspectors believe? Runaway scum from a realm known best for its ill-tempered criminality, or a respected mage?"

"If you're so respected, why are you even doing this? If you're really a rank ten, you could start your own academy and get fat and wealthy off the gifts of desperate nobles and rich parents to instruct their kids."

Adderlane seemed genuinely amused at my suggestion. "Such a myopic view of a wizard's life. From your spot down in the mud, you probably think reaching master rank takes care of all your problems, but it's a great big world out there, with a whole lot of shit needing to be shoveled. We all answer to someone. There's hundreds of rank tens in this city, and some of us have a higher purpose than coddling snot nosed brats."

"What's the great purpose to killing Dardick Argent then?"

"I don't ask my clients why they need anything in particular done. *I don't care.* All I need to know is somebody important is paying me a lifetime's supply of high-quality Red to make sure Fogo's ambassador dies. All you need to know is that if you don't do as I've commanded, that pretty girl's death will be on your head."

He wanted me shaken, so I tried not to give him the satisfaction. "I just met her. I barely know her."

Adderlane mimicked my voice, "*She means nothing to me.*" He had a cruel laugh and crazy eyes. "Lies. I've studied you long enough to know what manner of man you are, Carnavon. Loyalty and idealism are rare traits in this city nowadays, but I do love when I come across them in others because you honorable types are the easiest to manage. Do as I say, and I'll let her go. Don't, and she dies. It is that simple."

"I don't trust you'll keep your word."

"Of course not. Why should you? I'd offer to cast a geas on myself—that's a spell that binds one to a particular vow—but you've got no reason to believe I'd be honest about that either. So I guess you're trapped."

"I guess I am." If bitter anger could kill, Adderlane would have spontaneously combusted right there on the bench. "What do I need to do?"

"Take this." He handed me the green gem that contained Azarin's image. "When the curse ignites, I will use this to show you that I've kept my word and set her free."

"A bit late by then, ain't it?"

"True, but you can go to your fate knowing you did the right thing. I hear that matters for men like you. Trading the life of a brutal noble for a kind maiden should seem like justice. I'll even allow the sound so you can say your goodbyes and confirm it's truly her and not some mere illusion. I'm considerate like that."

Adderlane was a fucking lunatic. There was no correlation between moral fiber and magical ability, so it shouldn't have been galling to me that someone so awful could obtain so much power, but it still pissed me off anyway. "And the murder weapon?"

"It's already in your hand."

I looked at the green gem. "You son of a bitch."

"By about rank six or seven you start figuring out how to apply multiple enchantments to one object. You've got until sundown to deliver that, or I'll kill her anyway, so you'd best walk fast. Don't worry. The curse won't activate until its within ten feet of Dardick Argent."

"Then that's a problem. They'll search me when they take me captive."

"But it isn't *my* problem. The girl goes free when the curse goes off. The curse goes off when it gets close to Dardick. Figure it out, Mr. Carnavon."

40

With grim determination, I made my way toward the market.

I won't lie and claim to be motivated by heroism or anything so noble. I gave serious consideration to pitching the gem over the side of the low road and making a run for it. I'd only known Azarin for a few days. I liked her, but I really didn't want to die for her… Except I was no coward, and the idea of abandoning anyone to manipulative scum like Adderlane made me angry at myself for even thinking about that option, however briefly.

But I sure as hell didn't want to serve as a mad wizard's assassin either, especially if it was a suicide mission. Which, despite Adderlane's assurances that his curse would be aimed solely at Dardick, there was no chance he'd reveal his crimes to me and then allow me to live. He must have thought I was some kind of gullible bumpkin to even suggest it. This was meant to be a one-way trip.

I saw blue-coated watchmen along the path, but if I paused to speak with any of them, Adderlane would surely know. I suspected he was following me now, or he had other conspirators doing so. Rank tens probably knew hundreds of spells. He surely had some magical method of making sure I didn't rat him out. If the gem I carried could transmit sound and images, it could probably watch and listen to me as well.

Adderlane was evil, but I figured it was a clever kind of evil. He'd use me as a scapegoat and I'd take the blame for both attacks. I'd be dead. Dardick would be dead. Baron Argent would be so furious at the loss of a son that he'd likely punish my entire family so much my third cousins would get extra centuries of labor stuck on their contracts. And Azarin would certainly be dead too, because there was no way Adderlane would risk having her disrupt his carefully constructed narrative of an angry Fogo runaway assassinating a noble. Inspector Borg would probably get reprimanded for letting me off the hook for the first attack, and nobody would doubt I was the real killer.

Taking the gem from my pocket, Azarin's image was still visible inside. She remained shackled, looked extremely angry, and kept pulling against her chains. Either this really was her, or it was a very convincing illusion. I'd feel extra stupid dying for no reason if that was the case. I put the gem away and kept walking.

My dad used to tell me that desperation makes a man dumb and can get him killed, or it can focus his mind and keep him alive. His advice kept me safe in the lava tubes, and it still applied on the streets of the Core City. I had to be smart. I needed a plan.

I couldn't let Adderlane see me talking to anyone, but one of my only friends in the Core didn't talk anyway.

The problem was finding Trax so I could get close enough to send my thoughts to him. He was off swimming the canals, stealthily observing people go about their daily chores so he could record it on his crystal globe. Hopefully Trax would live up to his full name once more.

It was so cold, I walked with my hands in my pockets anyway, which enabled me to surreptitiously open my pocket knife and slice open the end of my thumb. Which stung, but I made sure I didn't let any pain show on my face. When I reached an intersection of bridges, I paused, acting like I was lost. Hopefully, Adderlane wouldn't find that too suspicious since I'd only been here a week. It was easy for a newcomer to get turned around in a place so huge and confusing.

Only, I had a great sense of direction, I just needed time to bleed. And I stood on the metal grating long enough to be sure several drops made it into the canal below. When I could delay no longer, I picked the road to the market and started off again. It wasn't the most direct route, but I took the path around the outer edge of the market so I could stay close to the water.

Today was Eternaday, or as it was now called, the quiet day, the one time the Nexus was closed. Yet the market remained noisy, and there were probably more people here right now than in all of Fogo put together.

The Great Machine was slowly turning past the time gate. The statues which held this one aloft were made of jade. If I were to guess based on the graceful proportions of the limbs, they were carved in the semblance of elves, but they were both missing their heads, so I couldn't tell. This gate was blocked by an enchanted steel wall, so it looked more like the statues were holding a door closed than lifting an arch up.

Five hundred years ago, the most terrifying force ever known had come through that gate and attempted to conquer the Core. Only a miracle stopped it from destroying us all, and a great many new Saints had been named that day. Except from what Mistress Magnorin claimed, perhaps everything really had ended on that fateful day, and most of us just hadn't caught up yet.

Past the time gate was fire, and at the outer edge of the market's disk from there was the Argent's embassy. I was going as slow as I could without looking too suspicious, because I didn't know how far away my trusty squalo was, assuming he'd smelled my blood in the water at all.

Come on, Trax. Swim fast, buddy.

I stopped for a moment as if collecting myself. Adderlane couldn't find that too odd. I was marching straight to certain death after all. That takes a bit of composure.

"*You really should stop injuring yourself, Carnavon. Where I am from, all of this bleeding would attract predators.*"

Thank the Saints, he was here! I risked a glance toward the water, and thankfully, Trax remained unseen.

I thought as hard as I could, *Stop where you are. Don't break the surface.*

"*What is wrong? Your head is filled with many images. Why do you so fervently wish to set the human called Adderlane on fire right now?*"

Listen carefully, Trax. Azarin is being held captive somewhere in the Collegium. Adderlane is forcing me to assassinate Dardick Argent or he'll kill her. You've got to hurry and free her. Then I recalled the image of her in chains and sent that as well.

Some bubbles rose to the surface. Trax's *voice* never gave away much emotion, but I could tell he was greatly perturbed. "*I am offended. People shall be eaten for this. However, there is no trail for me to track the female. How can I find her?"*

"Shit..." I slipped and muttered that aloud, but if he caught it, Adderlane would probably assume I was working up my courage to face the Argents. I'd not thought of how to find her, and oblivious Trax would stick out blundering about the Collegium smelling everyone's basements... And then I had it.

Go get Rade and Krachma. The lob can find her.

"*How?*"

The last spell we'd all worked on before turning in for the night had been Azarin's jolt spell, and she'd ended up accidentally giving Krachma a nasty burn. If my breaking his nose enabled him to find me across the whole city, surely that would be the same, and Azarin had been the last to wrong him.

Lob grudge. It's worth a shot.

"*I understand. What about you?*"

The sun was getting lower in the sky. Azarin's time was running out.

Don't worry about me, Trax. I'll do what I've got to do.

41

As I walked toward the embassy, I put on every charm in my possession. Even the ones I'd taken from the Frunza students that I didn't know what they did, in the hopes that if they were protective, they might activate automatically if needed. I unwrapped the gauze holding my broken finger in place so I could put on my gloves—which was profoundly fucking painful—in case I needed to *ascend* or *descend.* Only the right one was enchanted, but wearing one glove would look too suspicious. I had some Red and some Black, my gun, a bit of spare ammo, snail shells, screws, and my knives. Adderlane told me to figure it out. I hadn't yet, but all I knew was that I wasn't going to let the Argent's murder me quietly.

A block away from the Fogo embassy, I stopped and waited. Adderlane had given me until the sun went down. Let him think I was a hesitating coward. I was going to use up every minute I could in the hopes Trax might somehow save the day.

When I checked the gem, it still displayed the tiny image of Azarin, though she'd finally exhausted herself and quit struggling. She was just hanging there, despondent, which made me even angrier. Her giving up wasn't the only thing that changed though, because for the first time, there was someone else in the picture. Though the man in the basement was wearing a mask that covered his face, from his considerable height it clearly wasn't Adderlane. Somehow the masked man must have known I was watching right then, because he held up his thumb and made a slitting motion across his throat.

The message was clear.

I couldn't hear them, but maybe they could hear me, so I spoke into the gem to Adderlane's servant, "I'm doing it, but as soon as I'm inside their walls I expect to see you let her go, or I'm going to tell them who sent me."

That must have worked, because the masked man nodded, and Azarin looked up, suddenly hopeful at hearing my voice. She shouted something that was probably a warning, but Adderlane's man backhanded her across the face for it.

If I'd known a spell that would have allowed me to shoot him through the viewing gem, his brains would've decorated the bricks for that. "Leave her alone. I'm going in."

I dropped the gem into my breast pocket and took one last look around the crowded market. The fact it was someone else standing by to execute Azarin in the Collegium told me that Adderlane was probably nearby spying on me. I saw no sign of him, but I'd heard there were spells to change your face or even turn you invisible, which would surely be child's play to a rank ten. It disgusted me that someone could achieve such power yet use it so cravenly. The Argents sucked, but if you're going to kill somebody, at least have the decency to do it honestly, face to face. Don't coerce some poor fool into taking the fall for you.

The sun was beginning to set behind the Great Machine. My time was up. Gathering my courage, I said a silent prayer to Saint Persistence, and headed straight for the gate of the Argent's courtyard.

There were two enforcers stationed there. For just a moment, it felt like I was about to apply to another magical academy. Sad part was, this was the only place sure to take me in.

"I need to talk to Ambassador Dardick Argent."

They looked up, bored, until one of them realized who I was. "It's Carnavon."

Before he could grab the rifle leaning against the wall next to him, I spread my hands wide to show them I had no weapons at the ready. "Easy, boys. There's lots of Core folk standing behind me who don't want to catch a stray bullet. This is a Fogo affair. We should probably conduct it inside in private."

"Sounds reasonable to me." The older of the two guards calmly picked up his rifle, keeping it pointed toward the ground. Then he told his friend, "I'll keep an eye on him. Alert everybody. See what Norbert wants to do."

The other guard rushed inside while I stood there, really wanting to say aloud that this wasn't my doing, but Adderlane would surely hear and Azarin would die. "I'd like to keep this peaceful if I could."

"That's not my decision, now is it?" This enforcer struck me as a grizzled old coot, probably glad to be serving out the end of his contract in the comfort of the Core instead of out on the crust. "I come from Barge 231. I met your dad long ago. He struck me as a good fellow."

"That he was," I agreed.

"Myles Carnavon would die of shame knowing one of his sons has fallen in with pirates." He spit some tobacco juice in front of my boots. "Imagine working for the same scum who burned your own family's barge. Disgusting."

I'd come here to be killed, not insulted. "That's trogshit. I'm not with that crew. I hate their guts."

"That's not what the ambassador thinks."

"Well, Dardick's an idiot, so—"

The gate creaked opened and several more enforcers came out, all of them with weapons in hand, trying to be discreet in front of the outsiders. It appeared I was right, and the Argents didn't want the City Watch meddling in their business. The enforcers spread out around me until I was surrounded.

"Let's take this inside, Mr. Carnavon," the old guard suggested. "After you."

I followed some of them in, and there were more behind me. It was well known Argent enforcers were recruited from the toughest cadremen in Fogo and usually had the patience of Fire Elementals. The second I made a move, I'd get shot, stabbed, and bludgeoned.

The last time I'd come through here, it had been with a bag over my head, so I'd not seen anything. The embassy's courtyard was fifty yards across, and the walls were constructed of the same black lava rock as their castle back home. Large braziers burned all along the ramparts, surely powered by Fogo Red, which kept the place comfortably warm for us, and probably made it crushingly hot to any visitors. Core residents surely wilted as they walked through here, which the Argents likely enjoyed, as it would remind anyone they were negotiating with how much tougher we were than them.

"Where's Norbert?" the old guard asked.

"He went to fetch, Dardick," another answered. "There he is."

Dardick Argent was coming down the stairs, hobbling angrily on his crutches. There was no sign of his corpulent cousin, Norbert. When the nobleman saw me he grinned in delight. "I can't believe you came back here, Carnavon, you dumb son of a bitch!"

I risked a glance down at the gem. Azarin was still chained. Adderlane had told me she'd go free when the spell went off, but he was surely lying. I almost expected it to blow up in my face right now and take the whole embassy with it, except nothing was happening yet.

Once the iron gate was closed behind us and locked, the elder guard said, "Search him and bind him."

"Wait!" I shouted, and I did it with enough force that the enforcers actually paused.

Something was moving upon the gem. The masked man must have been informed I'd entered the embassy, because he'd drawn his knife, and was heading straight for Azarin with cruel intent. Adderlane must be a sadistic bastard, because now that I was trapped in here with his target, he was going to murder her right before my eyes anyway.

The masked man grabbed hold of her hair and pulled, exposing her neck, and—

Trax appeared from out of nowhere and ripped off his head.

Even though the image was tiny, it was unmistakably my squalo gnawing away on that masked skull. The headless body flopped over. There was no sound, but I could imagine the sick crunching of Trax's chewing. Then Trax swallowed, looked right at the viewing gem with his cold black eyes, and waved at me.

A whole lot happened all at once.

Dardick had hobbled almost in range of what Adderlane specified for his proper murdering.

The guards moved to subdue me before their boss got here.

The gem in my pocket audibly *cracked.*

Knowing that something truly horrible was about to happen, I reached up and desperately shouted, "*Ascend!*"

As the heavy air curled around my arm and yanked me violently into the sky, enforcers collided where I'd been standing, tackling each other instead of me. Twenty vertical feet zipped past in the blink of an eye. I looked toward the rampart along the top of the wall, and by some miracle actually managed to let go of the spell in time to land atop it.

The old man was the fastest with his rifle, and that bullet slammed into my stomach. The lead projectile flattened against the Frunza shield, but it still felt like the world's worst gut punch on the other side. As I stumbled back, a few others fired. I didn't know how fast the Frunza enchantment recharged, but thankfully the others missed.

The bullets weren't what I was most scared of, because the gem in my pocket was *moving*. I yanked it out just as little caustic tentacles began to sprout. The viewing spell was gone, and now I could see the other enchantment Adderlane had placed on the gem was to make it into a cage. Inside was some kind of tiny thrashing monster.

It was growing rapidly.

I threw the monster seedling gem into the nearest brazier.

Even in the very brief time it sailed through the air, the gem prison crumbled and the creature had tripled in size. It looked a lot like the thing Trax had shown me that he'd called an octopus, only this one appeared to be made entirely out of acid and malice.

It landed in the roaring flames and began to screech and thrash, even as it continued to grow.

The fire wasn't strong enough to stop it.

I could have run and left the stupid greedy Argents to face whatever the hell this thing was. Only, I'd brought this curse upon them, and I was no assassin.

I had to turn up the heat.

"What's he doing?" Dardick demanded as I ran toward the brazier and the shrieking acid octopus stuck inside, before he came to the entirely wrong conclusion about my motives. "He's summoning a monster. Shoot him!"

I had to dive against the wall as the wooden rampart all around me got blasted into splinters. "I'm trying to save you idiots!" None of them could hear me over their gunfire.

Drawing my bag of Red, I crawled the rest of the way to the brazier. The flaming octopus was now big enough its many arms were flopping over the sides, and if I'd not dunked it into a magical fire, it would probably be killing people already. I had to roll aside as a tentacle whipped the wooden beams. The fire scorched it black, then the residue left by the monster began to bubble, hiss, and steam its way through the floor.

I winced as a bullet punched through and grazed my arm. The Frunza protective charm hadn't recharged yet, so I stayed as low as I could, with tentacles thrashing above and enforcers launching lead below, until I was so close to the brazier that my old crawler charm activated to keep my clothing from combusting.

The monster, now big as me, was rising from the brazier. If its gooey acid flesh hadn't been getting charred away this entire time it would probably have been ten feet tall by now. I don't know how many eyeballs Trax's home octopuses had, but this one had *a lot*, and at least six of them were looking balefully right at me.

I threw the *entire* pouch of Red at it.

As the elemental dust spread in a sparkling cloud over the monster, I invoked it to ignite as I got up and ran for my life.

This was by far the biggest shroud of flame I'd ever attempted. The word *shroud* didn't do this one justice. It was more of a pillar of fire that engulfed the octopus as the rest of my hard-won arena earnings were consumed in a fiery blast that shattered the wooden rampart, melted the brazier, blasted apart some of the stone wall, and dropped that whole burning mess into the Argent's courtyard.

Adderlane's summoned creature exploded on impact, and the enforcers had to run to get away from the spreading cloud of noxious gas left by its demise. For a moment, I felt a supreme sense of triumph, because I, a lowly rank one nobody, just single handedly thwarted the curse of a rank ten master. That nice feeling of triumph was quickly replaced by the awful feeling of getting nailed in the ribs as one of the Argents shot me.

The Frunza charm had recharged enough to keep the bullet from piercing my body, but the impact of it flattening against the shield still sent me reeling backward to topple over the wall.

The market rushed up to meet me. I didn't even have time to shout *descend*. All I could do was extend my glove toward the ground and imagine pushing back. My body slowed quite a bit before impact, but I still hit *really hard* and went rolling away.

Cobblestones are far more unforgiving than soft grass.

I lay there, hurting, as my fire spread to the roof of the embassy. Merchants were shouting and pointing. A lady rushed to my side to see if I was alright. Blue coats moved through the throng. With Azarin freed, and the Argents on the other side of the wall, this was my chance to tell them who the real assassin was.

"Watchmen, what's all this noise about?" someone shouted. In my dizziness, it took me a moment to recognize that was Adderlane's voice. And then I saw him, walking imperiously through the crowd like he owned the place. "What's going on here?"

Surprisingly, the watchman Adderlane was addressing *saluted* when he saw the wizard approaching. "It appears there's been another attack against the Argents, Chief Inspector."

Chief Inspector?

“So our mysterious killer has struck again. Run and tell them to close all the market exits,” Adderlane commanded. “No one enters or leaves except for the fire crews.”

With so many people in the way, he’d not seen me lying there yet. Needing to get out before this place got locked down, I smacked the helpful merchant’s hands aside and drew a clay ball from beneath my cloak to dash against the ground.

“*Obscura.*”

They’d assume the smoke came from the embassy fire. Once everyone nearby was blinded, I got up and limped away.

42

Fireday morning, I woke up in the sideways ruins of a haunted tower with a lot of bruises and a bad headache.

I'd made it out of the market before the watch had gotten the bridges locked down, and then limped to the Under Slump. Adderlane had known what inn I'd been staying at, so that was compromised. With nowhere else to go, I'd gone straight to Rade's place. Nobody was home, so I'd found a corner and wrapped myself in my cloak to try and stay warm through the night. Other than the occasional ghostly noises, the broken tower section had been quiet.

That was no longer the case.

"There you are! Hey, guys, Carnavon's here."

I opened my eyes to see Azarin standing over me, looking tired and roughed up, but very much alive. I leapt up and grabbed her by the shoulders. "Are you alright?"

Despite the purple and yellow swelling on her cheek she managed to give me a big bright smile. "Yeah, thanks to fish face, the rock guy, and the moody one." She nodded toward where the rest of our odd band was making their way into this section, having to crouch to get through the sideways door. "And you, apparently. On that note…"

Azarin slapped me across the face.

"That's for getting me involved in your nonsense and kidnapped!"

I rubbed my stinging cheek. "That's not entirely undeserved."

Then she quickly leaned in and kissed me on the lips. Which was far nicer, but so unexpected that it took me a moment to realize it'd happened at all. "And that's for sending Trax to eat the men who were detaining me while you marched to your certain doom on my behalf."

I was still puzzling over that kiss, but had to ask, "How many people did he eat?"

"It got a little confusing on the way out of the house, and it's not like he ate all of them, just took big bites out of them at least…" Azarin shuddered at the memory. "At least two or three I'd guess."

I looked toward Trax.

"*Three were partially devoured, and only because they tried to stop us from rescuing the female. I corrected them for this terrible rudeness.*"

"Good job, Trax." Then I nodded toward stoic Krachma. "Your grudge must have led you to her."

He grunted in the affirmative. "Krachma tore a man's arm off last night. You owe Krachma for this."

"No doubt. It's appreciated, big fellow."

Rade came over and roughly put his hand on my shoulder, which sadly was the one I'd bashed against the market's cobblestones. "It was a triumphant expedition, my friend, but you've got some serious explaining to do. The blue coats are up in arms. The watch won't come down here with us Under Slump dregs, but if the gang lord, Carcalla, hears that I'm harboring a wanted man, his Latrocinium might snatch you up to give to the law, just to avoid the hassle."

We spent the next little while catching each other up on what happened, and that included me telling them the entire sordid story of skipping out on my family's contract. Rade had a bit of food stashed, which we ate while we talked. Since all the tower's furniture had been looted decades ago, we sat on the floor which had once been a wall, eating our meager fare. For once, Trax actually wasn't hungry, and I really didn't care to dwell on the ghastly reason why.

Trax had found Krachma and Rade as I'd asked, but their mission almost fell apart entirely because of how poorly either of them understand squalo picture language. It was only the image of Azarin chained that made them realize what was going on, and Krachma—who I was starting to believe was far smarter than he looked—used his innate ability to track her to a humble home on the outskirts of the Collegium. The thugs Adderlane had left guarding her hadn't fared very well against two amateur gladiators and a squalo, and they'd managed to escape without the authorities noticing.

As I told my side of the story, Rade grew increasingly flustered. "So if I'm getting this right, your enemy isn't just a mighty rank ten wizard—who could surely destroy us all in the blink of an eye—he's also a Chief Inspector of the City Watch?"

"It's looking that way."

Rade laughed. "We're rightly fucked then!"

"I don't think he's doing any of this on behalf of the city though. Talking to the man, he's on his own. Being one of the city's guardians provides cover for his crimes, but honestly, I think he's got a few screws loose."

"I hear that's not too uncommon among advanced wizards," Azarin pointed out. "Slow descents into madness, I mean. That's something that big council of mages who rule this city are supposed to be on the lookout for."

"Instead they gave Adderlane a job, so apparently they're shit at it… He said somebody is paying him to kill the ambassador. I just ended up being handy to blame the whole thing on."

"Corrupt or not, I'm accessory to murdering some of his men now," Rade said. "By helping you, we might have dug our own graves."

He was right, and that galled me to no end. It seemed no matter what I tried to do, I kept harming family and friends. "I'm sorry you got dragged into this. I'm going to make it right."

"How?" Azarin asked. "No offense, and I know you've tried so hard even your patron Saint must approve, but you've not got a lot of success to show for the effort."

"I don't think the watch is corrupt, only Adderlane. Inspector Borg struck me as an honest man. I just need to find him, tell him the truth, and let him do his job."

"You think it's going to be that easy?" Rade asked incredulously.

"Probably not, but you got any better ideas, deadlander?" When he said nothing, I looked around the rest of the group. Krachma just scowled. Azarin shrugged.

Trax stared, unblinking. "*I do not know. I do not understand any of this land business.*"

Rade grimaced at the noisy pictures forming in his head. "What did the squalo just say?"

"He said my plan is brilliant and nothing could possibly go wrong."

"There's one other problem, Carnavon," Azarin pointed out. "It's Fireday."

"Shit…" I'd been distracted enough to temporarily forget my impending demise. "Gaul Haddar arrives today. Hell, the sun's already up. He's probably already here." I could easily picture him angrily pacing on the other side until the instant the gate opened enough for him to squeeze through. "With what happened at the embassy last night, there won't be any convincing him I'm not to blame."

Trax's head tilted slightly. "*Someone approaches.*"

From the way I sprang up and drew my pistol, the others didn't even need to ask what it was Trax had said that time. "What's your nose tell you?"

"*There are five of them. Four of various mammal species, and one lizard.*"

It might be the watch, more of Adderlane's allies, the local criminals looking to collect a reward, or it could be something entirely innocent. We all started preparing weapons and enchantments.

There was a shout from the lower end of the tower. "Hello? Is anyone home?"

"I'll greet them and see what they want." Rade began clambering up one of the sideways balconies. "Back me up."

Because of the tower's curious construction and lopsided position, moving through this place was a chore, but we all found spots where we could peer through doorways or holes toward where the intruders were arriving, and still have stonework for cover.

They walked into the big area we'd used for spell practice, illuminated by a single floating light charm and a bit of early morning sun that snuck through the windows. It was a motley bunch. There was a tall lacertian, a dwarf, a gnome, and a pair of humans. Their garments were poor. They had a few obvious weapons between them, but none looked like experienced combatants. The lizard man was the only one who looked like he'd be capable in a fight, and that was only by virtue of size and teeth.

Rade stepped out on a ledge high above, drew his sword, and roared, "Who intrudes upon the Fallen Tower of Primopolus, the home of house Tartaros in exile?"

The strangers stopped and looked up at him, confused. The dwarf asked, "Who?"

"Never mind. What do you want?"

Apparently, the gnome had been appointed their spokesman, as he stepped in front of the others and politely addressed Rade, "We have come here seeking the new wizard school."

"The what?"

"Apologies, my lord. The unofficial magical academy of the Under Slump. There is a rumor that a group of mages have gathered here to train and practice their spell craft without interruption by the authorities. Is this not so?"

Rade looked down toward where the rest of us were lurking in ambush. "You guys know what's going on here?"

One of the humans pleaded, "We're begging you to hear us out. No academy will take us. We've got nowhere else to learn."

"I think I know what this is," Azarin whispered to me. "Sorry. I might have mentioned our secret arrangement to a few other seekers around the Collegium before I got nabbed."

"It's hardly a secret if you go telling everyone about it," I said.

"I was only making conversation."

Since they obviously weren't here to fight us, Rade sheathed his sword. "I'm terribly sorry, everyone, but there's been a misunderstanding."

"Please, sir," the lacertian's voice was a hiss, "each of us knows at least a spell or two and has some element to share. We wish to learn and grow stronger."

The gnome spoke again, "And though we do not possess coin sufficient for the Collegium, we do have some money if that will help pay our instructors."

"Hold on." That had certainly gotten Rade's attention. "You're paying for what now?"

Their timing was terrible, but this presented an amazing opportunity. If what the lizard man was saying was true, that could easily double the number of spells we had available to learn. Knowing twenty different spells would easily get us to the second—maybe even third—rank!

Azarin was clearly thinking the same thing I was and nodded eagerly at me. So I holstered my pistol and walked around the corner so the newcomers could see me.

"It sounds like everyone here knows the pain of being excluded in the Collegium." I walked right up to the gnome and extended my hand in friendship. "Welcome to our academy."

Before their gnomish spokesman could shake my hand, Gaul Haddar appeared in a flash of light, grabbed me by the throat, and dragged me into another dimension.

43

For a second, we passed through a land of confusing colors and shifting images, before reentering the real world.

Haddar slammed me violently against a wall.

It all happened so fast, I didn't know what was going on or where we'd wound up. The sun was in my eyes. Our appearance must have been rather sudden, because people were screaming or shouting in surprise. A dog began to bark.

I couldn't breathe. The way Haddar effortlessly held me a foot off the ground with one extended arm, he must have had a spell that granted him incredible strength.

"Hello, oath breaker."

He lifted me from the wall and hurled me to the ground. I hit something made out of flimsy wood and wire, which broke and crumpled around me. Birds were squawking. Feathers were flying.

"You thought you could attempt to spill the blood of the noble family I am sworn to protect, and still escape my wrath?"

Haddar got a fistful of my cloak and yanked me out of the chicken coop. He slung me around and sent me spinning into another wall. I broke more wood with my back, and these boards were a lot more solid than the last. I hit the dirt on the other side and raised a cloud of dust.

As the furious wizard approached, I recognized the area. We were just outside of the fallen tower section in the impoverished Under Slump. We'd not travelled far.

"Wait. That's not—"

He kicked me in stomach hard enough to send me sliding back between some shacks. I tried to speak, to protest my innocence, to name the real enemy, but all that came out of me was a pathetic wheezing noise. And it was in that very painful moment that I realized Gaul Haddar was about to beat me to death, right here, in front of all these people. Sure, he had magic sufficient to kill me instantly, but he seemed like the sort to appreciate doing a thorough, hands-on execution.

I struggled to my knees and lifted both hands, signaling for him to pause.

But Gaul Haddar had not crossed a giant swath of the Elemental Plane of Fire in a week to *pause*.

When he swung for my head, I dropped and rolled out of the way. That only annoyed him even more, and he kept after me.

The gasping noise I made then was supposed to be *obscura*, but the important thing was I still managed to focus on the Black embedded in the clay ball to release the spell. When it hit the ground, a cloud of blinding smoke hissed out. I used that distraction to keep crawling.

"There will be no escape for you, oath breaker." And then Gaul Haddar clapped his hands together.

A powerful wind gust rushed through the Under Slump, hard enough to tear the roofs off of some of the flimsier shacks, and all my obscuring smoke was blown away in an instant, leaving me there in the open like an idiot.

Then Trax hit him like an avalanche.

My squalo came up behind Haddar, incredibly fast, and was just on him, striking over and over, with coral sword, fist, and the flashing snap of razor teeth.

But Haddar had come ready for a fight.

The air rippled around him as multiple shield spells activated, turning aside all Trax's attacks. Then Trax's pointy snout flattened as he gnashed his jaws against an invisible barrier. One of Haddar's rings glowed with a yellow light, and when the wizard stepped back and Trax tried to follow, the squalo remained stuck in place.

Trax looked down to find that the ground had grown up around his big grey feet. He struggled, proving there was no give to the trap.

Haddar was striding toward me when a chunk of road cracked apart before him, and the pieces rose between us. I heard Krachma's booming voice coming from the tower, "*Debris*." When the spell was launched, all the rocks flew straight for Haddar, only to explode into fragments and dust against his shields.

Haddar just shook his head, mildly annoyed at the interruption. "Are these your fellow plotters, oath breaker?"

"Back off, fiend." Rade was crossing the street, sword at the ready.

Azarin was right behind Rade, and she threw something at Haddar. "*Jolt!*"

The experienced mage waved one hand dismissively, and Azarin's spell reversed course in midair, to fly back and stick Rade in the chest. Our deadlander dropped and flopped about as it shocked him.

Azarin looked down at Rade twitching at her feet, and said, "Well… shit."

Our low-level spells had done nothing to Haddar, but they'd bought me enough time to get up and catch my breath.

"It's Adderlane you want."

Haddar paused his rampage long enough to frown at me. "Don't waste my time with games."

"Adderlane's the real killer. That's who tried to murder Dardick. He set me up."

Haddar glanced around the Under Slump. A great many locals were watching the show from a safe distance. Azarin's jolt had worn off, so Rade was slowly picking himself back up. Trax remained stuck, and was using his sword to chip away at the hardened earth around his feet. Krachma wasn't a fast runner, but had finally caught up with the others, and surprisingly enough, the five newcomers were right behind him, preparing their meager weapons and spells. When Haddar saw so many foes, he actually smiled a bit, as if amused he got to battle an entire gang.

And to think people said us Fogo folk were hot headed and always looking for a fight. Haddar wasn't even from the realm he served, but he possessed the disposition to match us. He'd gladly kill every well-meaning soul here and then congratulate himself for a job well done afterward.

"Everybody, calm down! He's a rank eight." My warning made all the new guys shuffle back nervously… except the lacertian, who menacingly licked a dagger with his forked tongue. Maybe lizard folk were nuts, or maybe they couldn't count, and he didn't realize eight was greater than one. "You don't want to fight this mage."

"They really don't," Haddar stated flatly. "Though I don't mind the challenge."

"Stay your hand, Haddar, please. They've got nothing to do with this. I'll tell you everything I know. Adderlane's who you're after, not me."

Haddar walked up to me and got in my face, unworried. "Do you speak of Linus Adderlane?"

"I don't know his first name. I think he's a Chief Inspector for the City Watch."

"That's the one." The wizard stared right through me with eyes that were colder than Trax's, and I wasn't even sure if squalos were warm-blooded. "That's a bold accusation to make against a respected man. What part did you play in this plot?"

"Nothing to begin with. I skipped out on my contract the same day is all. It was afterwards he tried to use me to get a curse close to Dardick, and he forced me to do that because otherwise he was going to murder her if I didn't." I nodded toward Azarin. "And the instant I knew my friends here had freed her, I threw that curse in a fire."

"That sounds like utter horseshit," Haddar snarled, but then he lifted one hand to show me a golden amulet he'd been palming.

Carved on it was the symbol of Sarda, Saint of Truth, and it was currently glowing a bright blue. "Except you believe it."

He'd been using a spell to weigh the truth of my words the entire time, and I'd not even known it. "Yeah, I'm a runner, but I'm no assassin."

"Damn it…" Haddar grew angry, likely for having come all this way for a petty criminal instead of the true villain. He stuffed the amulet back into his vest, then put two fingers to his lips and whistled. A moment later, one of the magical carriages came rolling around the corner. The Under Slump observers had to hurry and get out of its way to keep from getting run over.

While I was distracted by the strange vehicle, Haddar tossed a length of cord at me. "*Bind.*" It hit me in the arm and rapidly crawled down to wrap itself around one hand, launch itself across to loop around the other wrist, and then pulled itself tight. In an instant, my hands were tied with a knot strong enough to moor a barge.

"You're coming with me." Haddar roughly shoved me toward the waiting carriage. "Let's go."

"Hold on now," Azarin protested. "You just heard Carnavon's innocent. You're not taking him anywhere."

"Regardless of any extenuating events, his ancestors signed a contract. Contracts must be honored."

"That's not a contract, that's a suicide pact!"

"It's alright," I assured Azarin. She was a fighter, but there was no need for anyone else to get hurt on my behalf. I'd done my best. Nobody who mattered wanted me, so there was no claim on my life greater than the Argent's. It was over. I'd failed.

"*I would bite him, but I am currently stuck,*" Trax sent. "*What would you have me do?*"

I thought back, *You've done enough for me by being a loyal friend. Goodbye, Trax.*

My friends watched, angry and bitter, as I climbed into the waiting carriage. The driver was a simple golem made of wood sitting up top, though there were no animals for him to whip. Haddar got in, sat across from me, and commanded the unliving driver, "Return us to the market."

Powered by spells beyond my understanding, the wheels began to turn. The benches were cushioned, as befitted the clients who could afford to travel in such a marvelous device, so I sat there in relative comfort as I was hauled off to prison.

44

The magical carriage was smooth and quiet, so we rode in silence as the Under Slump shrank in the distance.

Grim, merciless Haddar was studying me. "I remember you. Years ago, you blew yourself up on a barge, while foolishly trying to teach yourself magic. It appears you did not learn your lesson."

I gave him a sullen nod. "We met once before that too, when you'd first arrived in Fogo. It was out on the wastes. I was just a boy and Elementals had just killed the rest of my crawler crew."

"I do not recall that."

"Why would you? You defeated a giant with ease. That's just another regular day to a mighty wizard." Now that the rush had worn off, the aches, pains, and corresponding bitterness had set in. "But to me, that was the day I decided I'd do whatever I needed to do in order to become a mage, powerful as you."

Haddar scoffed. "Are you attempting to blame me for your silly ambitions? It was not I who convinced you to fake your death or lie to your nobles."

"Naw," I muttered. "That was all me."

He said nothing for a long time as the carriage maneuvered its way up the road between the slower wagons. It moved about as quickly as a fast man could jog, only this thing would never get tired. Out the windows rolled the sprawling majesty of the Core, from its decaying underbelly to its heavenly castles above, and I soaked it up while I could. Debtor's prison surely wouldn't have this nice of a view.

"I did not choose to be a wizard. I was born possessing great talent, among a people where such gifts are rare. I tested as a rank three, so was an asset to my tribe. The choice was made for me. My people are warriors. Thus, I was sent to an academy that studied magic suitable for war. War is all I have ever known… Until my people defeated the last of our enemies. And now they have no war left for me to fight."

I'd not been expecting the infamous Gaul Haddar to share his life story. He must have felt sorry for me or something. "So then you got sent to serve some dodgy nobles on the ass end of the realms instead. I bet that's been rewarding."

He snorted.

"How'd you find me anyway?"

"You kept some of the protective charms the Argents issued you. I made one of those for them."

I'd not even thought of that. If I'd known Haddar could find his own enchantments, I would've sold that band in the market, preferably to a merchant who'd have carried it off to a different realm. "The trapper's protection one? That's the newest."

"Correct."

I still had it on me, as well as my weapons and the rest of my charms, which I could try to use even with my hands bound. Then again, Haddar didn't seem the least bit worried about me escaping. My ability to hurt someone of his rank was negligible, and we both knew it.

"You accuse a powerful man of a terrible crime. Before I send you back through the gate, tell me everything you know about Adderlane."

So I did. I told Haddar the whole story. Every single detail I could think of about that bag of feces, because regardless of what happened to me, Adderlane deserved to die. And Gaul Haddar seemed like the kind of wizard who'd see to it that got done.

At one point, he stopped me, "Adderlane mentioned he'd be paid in Red?"

"Yeah, assuming he wasn't lying, but I don't think so. A lifetime's worth of high-quality Red."

"Interesting… Continue."

There wasn't much left after that. I told him of how once I'd known Azarin was safe, I'd done my best to thwart the curse before escaping Dardick a second time. If Haddar could weigh the truth of my words, then I'd still be condemned as a runaway, but let it be known that I'd done my best to avoid shedding any innocent blood… Not that an Argent could ever really qualify as innocent.

When I finished my tale, Haddar looked genuinely curious. "That gaggle of low-ranking fools who came out to fight me… You honestly believed you could form your own magical academy from the dregs of the Under Slump?"

"Something like that."

"That was more of a gang than an academy." He laughed at me, and Gaul Haddar's laugh wasn't a kind one. "The innocence of ignorance never fails to amuse. The Nexus Council would never allow a band of outcasts to organize their own school. It is one thing for the greatest among us to allow weak individuals to play at being mages. They will tolerate that. Most on their own might gain one or two ranks over his entire life, not nearly enough to endanger the system or threaten the balance of power. It is another thing entirely to allow a group of would-be mages to pool their knowledge."

"We can't be the first to have thought of this."

"Of course not. But order has not been maintained for over four thousand years by the Council taking chances. They are very careful who is promoted to sufficient rank to take on students of their own. They prefer flatterers and sycophants—men like Linus Adderlane—to someone who speaks bold but uncomfortable truths. That is why I will never be promoted to master, even as a deceitful serpent like him is granted access to powerful magic. They'd rather exile an honest man than risk him upsetting their traditions of corruption."

When he spoke about the Core's politics, Haddar sounded about as bitter as I felt. "Yeah, it sucks living under unfair rules made up by some aloof pricks, doesn't it?"

He scowled, not caring for the parallels in our situations. "I have said too much."

"The only rank ten who didn't tell me to shove off is the homicidal maniac who's trying to kill me, so we all got tired of waiting around for someone to claim us leftovers. If nobody wants to teach us, we figured we'd teach ourselves. I imagine they'll carry on without me just fine."

"Until the Council finds out and steps on them."

I stared out the window as the Under Slump was lost in the shadows of the sinking district above. "Yeah… I guess that's not my problem anymore. So what're you going to do about Adderlane?"

"He holds a position of authority in this city. It would be difficult to accuse him directly based only upon the testimony of an oath breaking liar. I will have to tread carefully, but I will see to it he pays for his crimes."

Now it was my turn to give him a sour laugh.

"Why do you scoff, Carnavon? I have said a thing will be done, then it shall be done. Do you doubt the word of Gaul Haddar?"

"How's it going, finding those pirate cultists who burned my family's barge? You catch them yet?"

A look of anger crossed his face. Apparently, the mighty war wizard didn't like being reminded of that continuing failure. "That one has proven to be a wily opponent."

"Oh, but you're going to go take on this other rank ten, no problem, right?"

"The elf who murdered your people is *far* more capable than that. I have studied his craft and killed many of his servants across the elemental plane. I can say with certainty that if he followed the same Code as the rest of us, he'd be at least a fifteen or higher. Easily equivalent in might to some of the high masters of the Council."

I was taken aback. "How's that possible? There aren't very many masters, ranks ten to twenty, in all the realms. How can he be that powerful, but nobody knows his name?"

"This mystery is why your people have not yet had your vengeance, and why I remain trapped serving your noble family until my vow is fulfilled."

So not only was I going to prison, the man responsible for killing my parents turned out to be an untouchable super wizard. My dreams of getting retribution never stood a chance to begin with. Today was certainly filling up with disappointments.

"I've got one last request, Mr. Haddar… When you send me back through the gate, can you at least let the Argents know my family had nothing to do with any of this? They're good, hard-working folks. I came here on my own. They shouldn't be punished because of my ambition."

Haddar thought that over, then nodded. "Your request is an honorable one. Among my people, one warrior's misdeeds should not stain an entire family. I do not know if the baron will care—he is not a forgiving man—but I will make sure their innocence is known."

"Thanks."

The view out the window grew darker as we rode down into a tunnel. Only I didn't recall there being a tunnel along this part of the road.

Before I could say anything, our magical carriage drove off a cliff.

45

The carriage dropped, spinning through the dark. We hit something hard. Glass shattered. Boards splintered and snapped. I fell against the roof, then was slammed against the wall. Up and down kept switching directions as we tumbled end over end. The darkness was temporarily interrupted by a flash of fire as the spell which powered the wheels burst.

The carriage flipped several more times before sliding to a stop.

I lay there, blinded, and breathing hard. The Frunza protection spell had activated, probably saving my life from the many impacts. Our landing raised so much dust that my air charm came on to keep me from coughing myself to death. I didn't think any bones had broken, and I didn't feel any blood leaking out, but I was so dizzy I couldn't tell for sure.

A light charm winked to life and floated from Haddar's hand to the center of the compartment, revealing that the walls and floor of the carriage had been crumbled, and all the windows smashed. The end of a cracked axel was sticking through the cushions, having barely missed my head by only a few inches. I tried to grab that to pull myself upright, but forgot my hands were still tied, and had to struggle my way into a sitting position instead.

Gaul Haddar was crouched across from me, and despite what we'd just gone through, he was unreasonably calm. Of course, from the flickers around him, he was wearing so many wards and protections that riding a spinning box down what felt like a mine shaft probably hadn't even hurt.

"It appears someone does not want us reaching the market."

"What happened?"

"A stone shaping spell was placed on the road ahead of us." Haddar glanced up through one of the broken windows, and though it was pitch-black outside, pronounced, "The hole was quickly closed back above us the instant we passed through… Very clever."

"Where are we?"

"Some abandoned part of the ancient under city, I suspect. A place where there will be no witnesses to our murders and the ratlets will consume the evidence of our corpses." Haddar held up one hand, indicating the need for silence. I listened, but my ears were ringing too badly to catch much beyond the fact one of our wheels was still turning. "We're not alone."

There was a shout from somewhere out in the darkness, "Are you still alive in there, Gaul?"

I knew that voice. "Adderlane."

Haddar nodded at me, before shouting back, "You know I don't die easily, Linus."

"You two know each other?" I whispered.

"While I was in the academy, we fought in the arena."

"Which one of you won?"

"He did."

"*Shit.*"

Then Haddar raised his voice again, "You know I hate this city. Why did you have to try and assassinate one of my noblemen?"

"It's nothing personal. Dardick Argent, foppish whoremongering drunkard that he is, is still rather astute when it comes to monitoring the Red trade. His attention to detail has been making life complicated for my client."

"I assume your client is Norbert Argent."

I looked to Haddar, confused. "The fat cousin?"

"Who else has something to gain, and can pay the killer with endless Red?" Haddar asked.

Adderlane was quiet for a considerable amount of time. "You always were an astute one, Gaul. You would've made a good inspector."

"I lack the patience… So a nobleman steals from his family, hires you to kill his rival before he is discovered, and now you must silence me before I spread word of your treachery. An inspector violating the Code of the Core is a rare and terrible thing. The Council will make a cruel example of you."

"We can't have that now, can we? I'm disinclined against having a public trial and messy execution. That's why when I heard you'd found Mr. Carnavon, and that he was slandering my good name across the Under Slump, I arranged this hasty ambush."

Haddar was still listening carefully and must have had some spell that helped him to do so better, because next he said, "It sounds like you have brought some friends."

"I wouldn't call them friends, Gaul. More like associates, temporarily united in common cause. Norbert is selling Red to the Cult of Tempus. Luckily for me, the Cult had a hideout not too far beneath your route, and they really don't care for the fact you're trying to cut off their supply of smuggled element. They graciously lent me some of their disciples to make sure you don't get away. And here they are now…"

Outside the carriage, several more light charms ignited simultaneously. We were completely surrounded. With all that new illumination, I could see that our carriage had landed in the rubble of an ancient, crumbling building. We were in some kind of massive, subterranean lair, filled with ruins that—at least the parts that weren't covered in moss and mushrooms—weren't too different in style from those in the Under Slump, just older and long abandoned.

Crouching among that crumbling stonework were a whole bunch of… people? Except that wasn't the right word for these things, which looked to have been born from a variety of different kingdoms, and had long since degenerated into terrible, mutated, forms. They were wearing ragged black robes that partially hid their bodies, but each of them were lumpy and misshapen somehow. From beneath their cowls, they stared at our crashed carriage with gigantic, unblinking yellow eyes, set deep in pallid, sweaty faces. And in their greasy, wet hands, they clutched a variety of weapons, like guns, knives, and a couple of them even had wands.

There were at least ten, and that was only the ones I could spot beneath the lights. There were probably more lurking in the shadows.

I stuck out my bound wrists toward Haddar. "Cut me loose."

"You would try to escape."

"To where? Don't insult me. You've lived among my people long enough to know we don't shy away from fights."

Proud as Haddar was, even he wasn't about to turn down help in this situation. "*Unbind.*" The knots unfurled. "Be aware Adderlane is a capable enchanter. He prefers to deliver spells by element bound bullets. His affinity is air, and his deficiency is death magic."

"I wouldn't have guessed that by how much he seems to enjoy murder." I yanked the cord the rest of the way off and desperately tried to rub some feeling back into my tingling hands. "How about I leave the rank ten to you and I concentrate on these cult weirdos?"

"That would be wise."

I did a rapid pat down to make sure I had all my gear in place before the disciples of Tempus attacked. I had my gun and knives, a few different protective charms, my ascent glove, and a pocketful of enchanted screws. Though I still had my share of Tartaros tomb Black, I was out of obscura bombs and didn't have time to make more. I'd used up the last of my Red protecting Dardick, but I had enchanted a couple of the snail shells I'd picked up in the market before that and had those on me. I pulled one of them out.

Haddar scowled when he saw my snail grenade. "Isn't that how you nearly killed yourself the last time we spoke?"

"Hell yeah it is." I tried really hard not to sound scared. "Let's go."

Adderlane walked out onto a ledge above the carriage, holding a pistol in each hand. One gun was glowing an icy blue and the other a fiery orange. "So Gaul… Do you fancy a rematch?"

46

The top of the carriage exploded.

Adderlane's bullet must have been enchanted with a Red spell that made my snail grenades look like children's toys. We would have died horribly, except Haddar threw up some kind of protective spell. I could only tell the protection was dome shaped by the way all the sparks and flaming bits rolled down around us as the carriage disintegrated. I could still feel the intensity of the heat through the shield, blistering as a gurgler.

"My spell will hold for one more. Run after his next shot."

The second bullet hit Haddar's invisible dome and stuck in it, still spinning from the rifling. It went from Fogo hot to a cold beyond my understanding in the blink of an eye. I'd never seen real ice crystals before, but I was pretty sure they weren't supposed to expand that rapidly, because within seconds, there was a crystalline sheet an inch thick overhead. It made an ominous, creaking noise as it grew.

Haddar drew a curved sword, and slashed upward, shattering the ice dome. "Move."

I leapt up through the sparkling bits and sprinted toward cover. The entire underground world was briefly illuminated as Haddar hurled a bolt of lightning so potent, it chewed through the rock beneath Adderlane's feet.

I was an ant stuck in a battle between giants.

Luckily, that flash revealed a few of the Tempus disciples hiding behind the fallen pillar I was running toward. If it hadn't been for that, I would've leapt over as planned and gone right into their waiting knives. I veered to the side, concentrated on unleashing the Red infused iron shell in my hand, and tossed it over the pillar.

It exploded right as I dove behind another stone block.

Cultists screamed when they got ripped by shrapnel. The others began gibbering and screeching at this offense. Light charms bounced wildly as more of them ran my way. Guns barked and bullets buzzed past me.

While I crawled for better cover, I saw that Adderlane had holstered his first two pistols and drawn two more. One of those was giving off a sick green light, and the other a bright yellow. He pointed them down at Haddar, but instead of one target, there were now ten Haddars moving in different directions.

"Illusions won't save you, Gaul."

The yellow pistol fired a beam of scalding light that tore through the fake Haddars. Five of them came apart and drifted away like smoke on the wind. Then the green pistol discharged. At first I thought Adderlane had simply missed, with the way his bullet struck a rock in the middle of a clearing. Only a moment later, a terrible buzzing noise came from that spot, as a cloud of stinging insects erupted forth. They flew after the other illusions, causing them to flicker and dissipate. The real Haddar was revealed as he engulfed himself in a swirling cloud of protective fire to block the swarm. The insects popped when they touched it.

I didn't grasp how incredibly deadly Adderlane's summoned swarm was until a bunch of the insects landed on a cultist who'd strayed too close, and they immediately started tearing him to pieces. Blood was getting flung everywhere as he thrashed. When he cried out in agony, the bugs flew into his mouth and went to stinging.

That convinced me to run the opposite direction.

The titanic wizard fight was lost behind me as I stumbled blindly through the ruins. If I used my light charm, it would lead the cultists right to me. So I crashed and tripped, feeling my way along walls, making my way forward using the brief flashes of magical battle to guide me. Despite their big yellow eyes, the mutants chasing me must not have been able to see down here very well either, enabling me to track them by their light charms. There were far too many. They were right behind me. I was going to die here, and nobody would ever know.

That's when I stopped there in the dark and collected myself. *Fuck this.* I was done running.

I was a trapper by trade. I *wanted* them chasing me.

The next lightning flash showed me there was a wide balcony fifteen feet above. I tossed a handful of screws across the floor, then lifted one hand.

Ascending was a whole lot harder in the dark, but I managed to fly up and catch the ledge without smashing my head into it. I clambered over, then nearly slipped back down because of how squishy and wet the moss was. There was a roar of magical fire as Haddar ignited the upper levels, followed by a series of crashes as Adderlane tore stone blocks from the walls to hurl down at him. All the noise they were making provided cover so the cultists probably didn't hear me clawing my way up. Atop the balcony, I drew Gax's pistol and waited.

A moment later, the first of the light charms blundered into the area below me. My pursuers were snuffling about, shouting in some strange language. There was a tiny one in the lead—it had maybe been a gnome once before whatever foul magic these things practiced had corrupted it—and it was bowed over, smelling the ground like it was following my scent. That weird little creature must have had a nose like Trax.

I waited until there were several of the cultists in my trap before igniting the screws of chaos. They made a whistling noise as they heated up, but since they were scattered all around their feet, they didn't know which way to run. Then I leaned over the edge and shot their sniffer right through the top of its hood.

As the screws performed their painful burning dance, I pulled back and reloaded. Then I popped back out, picked the biggest target—this one may have been a monstrous orc once—and nailed him. My bullet must have caught him square in the heart, because he flopped over, dead in an instant.

Some of the cultists spotted me and pointed upward, screeching. Bullets smacked into the stone beneath. Then one of the magic users let rip with a wand. I couldn't see it, but a terrible stink of rot and corrosion filled my nostrils. I didn't know what manner of death magic that was, but I didn't want to get it on me!

I ducked through a hole on the back side of the balcony. "*Descend!*"

It was hard to judge a fall in the dark, but thankfully, Haddar or Adderlane set off some big flashy spell right before I would've planted my face into a flight of stairs. Instead, I hit on my hands and knees. I cursed as I jammed my broken finger, then scrambled up to the next level. Which I could see a bit better now, but that was only because the cultists were sending their floating light charms ahead so they could track me better.

There was a plinth at the top of the stairs which must have had a large statue on top of it once, but the only thing left were the feet and everything above the ankle had been snapped off. I paused there to reload Gax's pistol. Between the loud bangs of Adderlane's enchanted guns and Haddar's noisy counter spells, I could still hear the cultists shouting, they were that close. Their guttural degenerate language was nothing like the trade tongue, so I didn't know what they were saying, but they sounded *really angry*.

I risked a peek back and saw a bunch of them running up the stairs I'd just climbed, so I threw my last snail grenade their way. As it went bouncing down the stairs, some realized what was happening and vaulted over the sides. One of their mages swept his wand my way, and a silver beam blew one of the remaining statue feet into glowing bits. That spell kept slicing its way through the plinth, seeking my flesh, until the grenade went off. The beam abruptly died as hot iron snail chunks cut the mage's legs out from under him. He went rolling wetly down the steps past a few of his dying brethren.

"That's how we do it in the fire realm, you boggle eyed sluts!"

The cultists at the base of the stairs were taking cover. Though I was out of snail grenades, I picked up a loose rock and chucked it at them. When it landed in their midst they squealed and scrambled away from it. That was my opportunity to reposition.

I made it around the corner before crashing into another mutant. He reacted first and slashed me across the throat. Stumbling back, I fired from the hip.

My neck stung, but I wasn't squirting blood. Thankfully, my stolen Frunza charm had recharged and blunted the blow, otherwise his knife would've split the artery. The poor cultist must not have been wealthy enough to afford a fancy academy charm like that, because my bullet passed right through his guts to splatter the wall behind him. He fell over, moaning, so I jumped over his body and kept going. With no time to reload, I shoved Gax's pistol back in the holster.

Haddar and Adderlane had been moving too. Now they were battling it out a few levels above. I caught glimpses of them as I ran. Even scared to death and being chased by angry freaks, a mage fight of this magnitude was an incredible thing to see. They were using enchantments to bound with incredible speed across the ruins, leaping up and down whole floors effortlessly, and ducking bullets and wand blasts that were powerful enough to pulverize the cave walls.

Like me, Adderlane was an enchanter, which meant his spells were coming from various pre-empowered items, like the bullets he kept launching Haddar's way. Haddar was shaking out to be a combo of enchanter and invoker, as he switched between wands and devices on offense, but also threw up spells of pure elemental energy to protect himself, seemingly at will. I didn't know what it took to reach such advanced ranks, but even though Adderlane was two ahead of Haddar, the Argent's wizard was holding his own.

Until Adderlane blasted Haddar backward through an entire gigantic building, which just went to show how little I still knew about magic!

Haddar crashed through the bricks, plummeting all the day down to my level, to land in an empty fountain. He hit hard enough to crack the tiles. I thought for sure Haddar died right then, but he must have had some spell working before impact because he staggered back to his feet, and didn't have any bones sticking out.

I stopped there in the open, with several stupid light globes following along to make me a big easy target, and realized I really didn't want to be anywhere between these two, but too late now!

Haddar shook one angry fist at his opponent. "Is that the best you've got, scum?"

Adderlane appeared in one of the windows above, calmly breaking open one of his handguns. "I'm just knocking the rust off, old chap."

It was then that I realized the various color lights Adderlane's weapons gave off came not from the gun itself, but from the cartridge he loaded in them. The Chief Inspector was wearing several pouches across his vest, and he plucked a red glowing cartridge from one. With practiced hand, he shoved it into the breach and snapped the gun shut with a flip of his wrist.

Haddar held out a wand and shouted something in his language. A great spectral fist—big around as a barrel—appeared floating in the air. Rather than striking at Adderlane—who wore all manner of defenses—it slammed into the structure beneath him. Rocks cracked. Dust flew. Adderlane stumbled and dropped his gun.

These rotten foundations were no match for such magical might. As several stories of ancient structure began crashing down, both wizards cast spells to save themselves. Adderlane's skin turned to iron as he rode the avalanche down. I could only tell Haddar had thrown up another shield dome because of the way the falling stones crashed over and around it.

It was an incredible sight to behold, except I was in the path of all that falling shit.

Stones rolled past. Pillars shattered. Some of the cultists pursuing me got pulverized into bloody chunks. I was gonna die.

"*Ascend!*"

I didn't even have a target, I just didn't want to be here. As I was yanked upward, a boulder crashed through the floor I'd been standing on. The entire level fell apart and collapsed into the darkness. The disciples of Tempus fell screaming to their doom.

Unfortunately, their light charms died with them.

The chasm was plunged back into pitch-blackness. Still rapidly ascending, I panicked because I didn't know how high up the ceiling was right here. Was I about to bash open my head or impale myself on something? Except the ground below was still rumbling as more of the ruins collapsed. There was no stop and wait option. It was fly or fall.

I cut the spell and dropped. "*Descend.*" I could only point my hand vaguely downward to slow myself and hope for the best. Even falling at half speed, all I could do was pray that I wasn't going to float myself into a pile of jagged death or some bottomless pit. I couldn't reach my own light in my bag. It was terrifying.

Below me appeared a line of flames. It was a sword. That had to be Haddar! Desperate, I aimed for that, but I'd already drifted too far to the side and wouldn't make it all the way. I could barely see the ground in the flickering firelight, but the part I was about to smack into looked relatively flat.

It was flat. Though I still twisted my ankle, fell on my side with enough force to crack a rib, and slammed my head against a rock hard enough to knock myself stupid.

47

I lay there dazed and bleeding into my eyes from a cut on my head, as the two powerful wizards extricated themselves from the rubble. I could see Haddar by the flaming sword he was using to cut his way through the debris. Then there came a golden glow from where Adderlane had fallen. He tripled in size, and the giant simply shoved boulders out of the way. Once he stepped free, he immediately returned to normal size and dusted off his coat.

"It's a good thing we took our duel down here. This would've made quite a mess back in civilization."

"You hide your shame and crimes, and then pretend it was for the common good." Haddar slashed the last leaning pillar out of the way. A ton of marble fell with a crash. "If you cared about the Core or its people, you would never have broken your oath."

"The Core's on its death bed and the people are too oblivious to catch on. They're still stacking towers made of gold on a foundation of rot. The watch has become nothing more than glorified rat catchers. The Council only cares about staying in power. I'm just getting mine, while the getting's good."

"By aiding doomsday cultists, who'd throw open the last gate to kill us all?" Haddar sneered as he climbed atop the rubble.

"They make some good theological points too, though they might be insane." Adderlane shrugged. "Regardless, they and their allies are rather generous with the bribes, so by the time Tempus puts this place out of its misery, I'll be retired to some quiet corner of the realms living out the rest of my life in abundant luxury. By the way, Gaul, you're bleeding to death."

Now that he was free, it was obvious that Haddar was in bad shape. From the gaping hole across his abdomen, that man needed a healing, and fast.

Even mortally wounded, Haddar sneered at the pain. "Then I will die with courage as I have lived. Unlike you, Linus, who has always been an opportunistic fool."

"Maybe… But I've been a fool who's better at magic than you." Adderlane tossed a handful of silver coins at the other wizard. "Catch."

Haddar reacted, slashing one from the air, but the others landed all around him. Once the coins stopped rolling, from each one rose a ghostly figure—similar to the specter I'd seen in the market on Deathday—but these were ragged, haggard things, skeletal beneath suits of rotting armor. Their bodies were translucent and gave off an eerie light. Their swords were crumbling to rust, but even an amateur like me knew those weren't meant to wound with sharpness, but with death magic.

Haddar was completely surrounded.

"Death magic isn't my strong point, but this spell in particular practically casts itself. Some of these old Ashen Harran soldiers might even be ancestors of yours, Gaul."

"Enslaving the souls of the dead warriors… is there no low you won't sink to?"

"I haven't found it yet," Adderlane replied. "Slay the wizard."

The specters attacked as one. Haddar's Red sword flashed hot enough to cut ghosts, but there were too many. He moved with inhuman speed, trying to pass between them, to get at his real enemy, but the death blades kept on striking. Each time Haddar slashed through a specter, another took its place.

As that terrible sword fight unfolded only a few yards away, I noticed a red glow partially buried in the broken stones just ahead of me. I crawled toward it, reached into the crack, and found the butt of a pistol. I pulled out the heavy, ornate thing—it was the gun Adderlane dropped, already loaded with a bullet enchanted with some incredibly deadly spell.

I had an idea.

Haddar grimaced as he got stabbed in the back. When he lurched forward, another death blade slashed him over the shoulder. Another pierced his arm. No blood flew, and the swords left no visible wounds, but each hit drained more life from him. Haddar fell. The specters crowded around to finish him.

"Hold." Adderlane held up one hand and his slaves obediently froze in place, with their swords aimed at all of Haddar's vital organs.

Haddar rolled over onto his back. Shaking, suffering from invisible wounds, he struggled to sit upright, and barely managed even that.

"I am defeated."

"Took you long enough realize it. However, this being a proper mage duel, the killing blow should be mine to dispense rather than some ghosts." Adderlane reached for one of the holsters on his vest, only to find that one was empty.

"Looking for this?" I asked.

Adderlane turned to see me standing there, only ten feet away, with his glowing pistol in my quivering, bloody hand, aimed straight at his face.

"Well, I've got plenty of spare guns, but the thought of finishing off someone who works for Fogo with what's basically a miniature volcano amused me." One of his light charms activated above us, and Adderlane actually laughed when he saw the sorry state I was in. "How the fuck is a worm like you even still alive?"

"Just stubborn I guess."

"Then take your best shot, Mr. Carnavon." Adderlane spread his arms wide, to make himself a bigger target. "It won't work though. The enchantment I've got on that round is a potent one, far beyond your meager capabilities. The odds are shit that a lowly rank one has the focus needed to activate it before you pull that trigger. You'll merely send a mundane bullet my way, while I'm wearing so many protective spells, even if you hit me dead in the eye, I wouldn't even blink."

"That's probably true." Gun still pointed his way, I limped closer. "But what do I have to lose?"

"Shoot him," Haddar encouraged me from between the ghosts who were poised to execute him. "It is better to die defiant."

"Defiant?" I stopped there and shouted back at Haddar, "My defiance is what got me into this mess. It was why you were hauling me off to prison! I just wanted to be a wizard. That's it. But oh no, I get dragged into everyone else's trogshit. So fuck you, Gaul. And fuck the Argents you serve, working my people to death for generations for nothing!"

"The nerve of this guy," Adderlane said.

"And fuck you too, Adderlane. You threatened me. You threatened my friends. I ought to blow your head off."

"You could certainly try."

"Except you're the only rank ten I know..." Then I surprised Adderlane by spinning the gun around, so I was holding it by the barrel. I extended the grip toward him. "Need an apprentice?"

Adderlane looked at the offered gun, then at me, incredulous, until the absurdity of the offer sunk in and he began to chuckle. "You treacherous rat... I respect that."

"Oath breaking bastard!" Haddar bellowed.

"I just want to be a real wizard, whatever that takes. Teach me magic and I'll work for you."

"You know, I'm amenable to the idea of taking on apprentices... The Adderlane Academy. I like that. It's got a nice ring to it." The mad wizard slowly outtook the gun from me.

I let go and stepped back. For a moment, I thought he might just shoot me anyway, out of spite, but in his own lunatic way, Adderlane must have been a man of his word. "I'll deal with you in a minute." Then he turned the gun on Haddar. "Where were we?"

"I was cursing both you cowards to hell." Haddar spit a gob of blood on the stones. "Do it."

Adderlane thumbed back the hammer. "With pleasure."

In the seconds between taking the gun and pulling the trigger, Adderlane didn't notice some of the Tartaros Black I'd filled the barrel with was beginning to drip out. While he'd been watching the ghost fight, I'd poured the entire vial of the deadly elemental sludge into it.

The hammer fell. The powder ignited. The Red spell activated, turning lead into molten doom. But rather than speeding down an open barrel, that lava bullet collided with a blockage made of pure distilled death...

And exploded.

The blast knocked me on my ass.

I hadn't known what would happen, but it turned out the high velocity combination of death and fire is really bad for the poor sucker holding that experiment. And even worse for Adderlane, the explosion was contained *inside* his protective shields.

The pistol barrel burst wide open in the shape of a star. Pieces of the gun and Adderlane's hand went flying. Rade had warned us not to get any Black on our skin, and I saw why now, as everything it splattered immediately began to decay. It was like a corpse rotting away, only dramatically sped up. The mangled limb turned grey and necrotic before my very eyes. As the blasted remains of his hand disintegrated, the death magic kept creeping its way up Adderlane's arm.

And *then* the Red spell ignited.

The flesh that wasn't rotting away burst into flames. That spread to his clothing, and Core folk cared about style and comfort, not fire resistance. Wool burned and silk melted and stuck to skin.

Adderlane stumbled backward, probably too shocked and disoriented to activate another spell... Which was when Haddar somehow found the strength to leap up, cover the distance, and ram his fiery sword through Adderlane's sternum.

The two mighty wizards stood there, face to face. Then Haddar gave the sword a violent twist and ripped it out the side.

Adderlane collapsed in a heap and slowly burned.

When their master died, the ghosts shrank back into their coins. Thankfully, Adderlane's light charm remained hovering above. The only sound in the cavern was Haddar's ragged breathing and the crackling of fire. The air was choked with dust and spreading smoke. Burning flesh and hair is a horrible smell, but being from Fogo, I was used to it.

"You owe me a vial of Black."

Haddar turned to face me, disbelieving. "You tricked him."

"Well yeah. He was crazy. Who'd want to study magic under the tutelage of a murdering lunatic?"

"You'd be surprised." Haddar took a few halting steps before falling on his face.

I knelt by the mage's side. He gasped in pain when I rolled him onto his back. There was blood everywhere. The wound on his stomach was even worse than I'd first thought, with a laceration so deep, I could see his guts. It was amazing he'd been able to get up at all.

Haddar struggled to draw something from a pouch on his belt, and failed because his fingers must have gone numb and clumsy from blood loss.

"Help me... There's a healing potion."

"Hang on." I got the pouch open, found a silver flask inside, took it out, and began unscrewing the cap.

And in that moment, a very evil thought came upon me.

One of my tormenters was burning to ash. The other was rapidly bleeding out. Both were in a long-forgotten cavern with no witnesses. All I'd have to do was withhold this potion for a few more seconds, and my biggest problem would be no more. What was I supposed to do? Heal the mage who'd been taking me to prison so he could finish the job? It wouldn't even be murder. Adderlane had struck the killing blow. I was just a lowly rank one bystander to their mighty duel.

As I withheld the potion, Haddar's fading eyes met mine, and he must have realized my temptation, but there wasn't a damned thing he could do to influence my decision. To his credit, the dying wizard didn't try to bargain or beg. He was far too honor bound for such low behavior.

And frankly, so was I.

"Fuck, I'm an idiot."

I gave Haddar the potion.

After he drank all of it, he still lay there for such a long time, breathing so shallowly, that I thought I might have the best of both worlds, in that I'd tried to do the right thing, *and* he'd die anyway!

Alas, the bleeding stopped, and the gigantic wound knitted itself closed. Once it was mostly sealed, Haddar slowly got up, wincing against the many lingering pains.

"Are you going to live?"

"You ask that as if it is a bad thing, Carnavon."

I shrugged.

"I'll still require the services of the nuns of Saint Olga the Merciful to repair everything, but that should do enough to get us out of here."

"Great. Speaking of Saint Mercy… I could've let you die just now. And before that, I could've let Adderlane kill you. After all that, you can't still hand me off to the Argents."

The deadly wizard didn't answer. He went over to the silver coins which contained the ghosts of dead warriors and began gathering them up. "Such a vile curse, to trap someone and force them to serve against their will."

"Yeah, that sounds awful."

"I do not appreciate your sarcasm." Haddar pocketed the coins. "Freeing these will be a small thing to me, but a great kindness to them… Come on. There's a long climb ahead of us."

48

Hours later, I was sitting in a room at a City Watch station on the market disk. I wasn't in chains, but the watchmen had confiscated all my weapons and magic. A surgeon had washed and stitched up my cuts, and before locking me in here, a kindly guard even left me a ham sandwich and a bottle of watered-down wine.

I sat at the lone table in that room, bruised and sore, eating, drinking, and sulking. I'll say this for the Core, even their basest rations they gave to suspected murderers awaiting interrogation was profoundly tastier than the old dry stuff we lived off of back in Fogo.

A key turned in the lock, the heavy door swung open, and Inspector Borg entered. "You can remain seated, Mr. Carnavon. There's no need to rise on my account."

That was good, because moving that much made my cracked rib ache, so I'd not intended to anyway. "Evening, Inspector."

He pulled up a chair and sat down across from me. "You've certainly had a busy first week in the Core, haven't you, boy?"

"It's had its ups and downs, sir."

"So I've heard." He adjusted his ponderous mustache, then launched into his questioning, "We have already recorded the testimony of the war wizard, Gaul Haddar. As to the matter of Chief Inspector Adderlane…"

I got ready for the worst, because him being villainous or not, I'd still helped kill a rank ten master mage, who was in the employ of the mighty Council of even higher-ranking mages. "I hope Haddar explained what he was doing to you already."

"He did. He told us that the Chief Inspector was being bribed by one Argent nobleman to murder another, so that the first's illegally selling Red to a banned sect could continue unabated. Do you concur with this testimony?"

"Yes, sir. That sounds accurate to me."

"And then the Chief Inspector attempted to kill you and Haddar to conceal his actions, so you acted in self-defense."

"That's correct."

"Good, good." Borg leaned back in his chair and clasped his hands before him. "I have only one last question to clarify matters, and this is a very important question, because you were the only observer who is still alive. And in this particular matter, the Council requires that there be a corroborating witness. You were there at the beginning of their fight, and in full possession of all your faculties?"

"Uh… yeah." I had no idea where this was going. "I was."

"Excellent." Borg shouted toward the door, "We are ready, Councilman."

The door opened and a short stranger waddled in. He was of that strange race of frog creatures, but while the others of that species I'd seen had been dressed in rags, this one was dressed in fine robes, decorated with so much enchanted jewelry that his outfit was probably worth more than all the barges docked in Fort Silver.

The frog wizard said nothing. He just stood there, neck puffing in and out as he breathed, studying me with his two bulbous eyes that seemed way too far apart on his bumpy head. In one of his webbed hands he held a staff, which practically hummed with built up magical power, and in his other dangled a medallion on a chain, similar in design to the one Haddar had used earlier to test the truth of my words.

"So, Ozwald Carnavon of Fogo, for the official record, did Linus Adderlane of the tenth rank challenge Gaul Haddar of the eighth to an official duel?"

What an odd question. "He did. I guess the two of them had dueled before a long time ago. Adderlane asked if Haddar wanted a rematch."

"And Haddar accepted?"

"Well, Adderlane started shooting, but Haddar put a shield around us then threw a lightning bolt back at him."

Borg looked toward the frog wizard. "Invoking the Code, followed immediately by an attack, more than satisfies the terms, your excellence. As Haddar claimed, that makes it a proper duel."

The frog wizard checked the medallion, which shined with a blue light.

"So be it." Then he emitted a long croaking noise, which sounded disappointed, before shuffling out of the room. While the door was open, I noticed there were two more bipedal frog things outside waiting for him. Both of those were huge, easily seven feet tall, and dressed in intricate steel armor.

After the door closed, I asked, "Who was that?"

"That was the illustrious Councilman Hoach."

"Like, from *the* Council."

"Yes. The same wizards who rule the Core, control the Nexus, and maintain the Great Machine. He's rank *sixteen.* If you'd tried to lie to him he would've had you skinned alive. I don't think he's happy about how this turned out, that's for sure, except the Code of the Core is clear on what must be done. But speaking of you getting flayed," Borg went from cordial to deadly threatening in the blink of an eye, "it would be in your best interests to not go spreading any ugly rumors about high-ranking watchmen taking bribes to murder nobles. Got it?"

"I think so."

"Don't think. Know that it's a pity poor Linus Adderlane died in the line of duty while battling some cultists down in the abandoned ruins."

I was fresh off the barge, but the politics of this city weren't that different than home. Families were only as good as their reputation. "It was a tragic loss of a great hero, sir."

Borg nodded, then went back to smiling. "Good. You're a smart lad, Carnavon. If you keep out of trouble from now on you might have a bright future in this city."

I'd not known I was going to have a future at all. "Does that mean I can stay?"

"I don't know. Since last we spoke, does any faction of note put greater claim on you than your nobles?"

"Unfortunately, no. I tried, but as you warned me, it's tough out there."

"The Core's a glorious place, but it's a cruel one. Then I'm afraid as far as the watch is concerned, that decision is up to the Argents and their representatives here." Borg stood up. "However, Haddar—ruthless bastard that he is—may be inclined toward leniency once he hears that your testimony has sealed his promotion in rank. He's off dealing with your corrupt nobleman. You're free to go."

I got that last part but remained there, confused. "My testimony did what?"

"You confirmed that Adderlane challenged Haddar to a mage duel. There's only two ways to get the tenth rank and achieve the status of master wizard. Most of the time it's through the Council promoting you because you somehow serve the needs of the Core, or your home kingdom gives them a big enough gift, but the other, older tradition remains, though it isn't as popular nowadays since it requires defeating an existing rank ten in a duel to the death and claiming their place."

I couldn't believe it. "Wait. So Haddar's a master mage now? He said that would never happen."

"Normally he'd be right. As men of authority, the higher rank always holds the ability to turn down lesser challengers as unworthy, so this kind of replacement rarely happens. Only, Adderlane was a pompous son of a bitch, with the ego to challenge a mad dog killer. Plus, Haddar skipped an entire rank!" Borg—who seemed to have a lot of issues with authority for a lawman—laughed at the absurdity of the situation. "There's going to be a lot of really offended mages over someone like him getting ahead of them."

"But…" I stopped myself before saying aloud that I'd been the one to defeat Adderlane. Haddar had been dead meat before I'd intervened. Except, I was a lowly rank one nobody, and I'd not won by magical might, but by deceiving a wizard too prideful to realize a nobody could still pose a threat.

"What is it? Something else you want on the record?"

"It's nothing… I can go?"

"I said that already. Get out of here, Carnavon." Borg held the door open for me. "And good luck with your nobles."

49

I walked directly to the Argent's embassy.

I'd thought about making a break for it, but once he was done with Norbert, Haddar would surely come collect me as well. It was better to get this over with, and I hoped being the one to deliver the good news might put a thumb on the scale in my favor.

The sun was nearly down. The gate to the Elemental Plane of Fire only had a small fraction left. The heat of my home realm still lingered in the market, making the Core folk sweaty and miserable, but I loved it. Despite having every part of me hurt from my exceedingly violent week, it was nice to be close to warm for once.

The watch had given back all my belongings, but I was really hoping to not have to use any of them here. Since I limped along with determined purpose, and my cloak was so filthy and stained with undercity dirt and dried blood, that even in the extremely crowded market everyone gave me plenty of space.

The embassy still smelled like smoke from the other night. Part of the roof had been burned off, and the beams beneath stuck out like the ribs of a decaying carcass. Surprisingly, there were no guards posted at the Argent's gate, but when I got close, I could hear people yelling on the other side. From the sound of things, Haddar must have revealed Norbert's complicity. That explained the lack of sentries. No Fogo folk were going to miss the chance to see a nobleman catch a beating.

So I knocked. And when nobody answered, I started pounding with my fist. And kept pounding until someone approached on the other side, saying, "Oh what nonsense is it going to be now? Hold your trogs!"

The door opened, and it was the old cadre man, who immediately reached for his slung rifle when he saw it was me.

Really not being in the mood to fuck about, I shoved Gax's pistol in his face first.

He slowly moved his hand away from his weapon. "Not this again."

"I keep trying to do things polite. It isn't my fault nobody else around here ever does. I need to talk to Gaul Haddar right now."

"The wizard's a bit occupied."

"Beating the stuffing out of Norbert Argent?"

He nodded. "Aye. How'd you know?"

"Long story." I gestured with my gun. "Lead the way."

We entered the courtyard and made it all of twenty feet before somebody else spotted us, and then there was a lot of shouting as weapons were swung my way. Apparently, my last visit had made quite the impression.

I hid behind the old guard, who was kind of skinny, but hopefully, if anybody got really exuberant, his body would at least slow the bullets down.

"I've had a really long day after a really shitty week! Don't make me wreck this place again. Somebody fetch Gaul Haddar."

"Do as he says," my hostage yelled at his comrades, before warning me, "That wizard's gonna rip your head off."

"Naw. He's going to be happy I'm here. You'll see."

A minute later, Gaul Haddar arrived, and contrary to my claims, he was *not* happy to see me. "What are you doing here, Carnavon?" He was dragging Norbert Argent down the stairs by one foot. The hefty man's hands were tied, and he cried out each time his head banged off another step. "What's all this foolishness? Everyone, lower your weapons."

The enforcers grudgingly did as their wizard commanded. I removed the muzzle of my gun from the base of the enforcer's neck and put it away. "Sorry about that, old timer."

Haddar dropped Norbert at the base of the stairs, and it looked like that poor bastard had gotten absolutely worked over. His face was a mess of purple and yellow bruises. I figured that had been Haddar's doing, because he was an angry sort, only Dardick came out next, wiping his bloody knuckles on a white rag. He stopped when he saw me in his damaged courtyard. "It's this prick again?"

"I come in peace with news for Gaul Haddar."

"Last time you came in peace, you nearly burned down the embassy and a tentacle monster tried to kill me!"

"That was a misunderstanding."

"A misunderstanding? A bloody *misunderstanding*?"

"*Enough!*" Haddar roared, and though he wasn't the nobility here, Dardick shut his mouth. "I must get this scum back to the Realm of Fire before the gate closes. Walk with me, Carnavon."

"So it's less effort for you to shove me through the gate so I can spend the rest of my life behind bars? I don't think so."

"Shut up and walk. You too, traitor." Haddar hauled Norbert up by the ear. The fat man whimpered, getting to his feet before Haddar ripped any appendages off. The wizard was thoroughly disgusted. "I refuse to spend another week in this nest of poisonous snakes they call a city."

The old enforcer grudgingly opened the gate so we could leave.

"I'm coming too," Dardick said. "I want to see the look on my dear cousin's face as he crosses the Nexus. Paulo, Rufino, with me."

Two of the enforcers followed their noble. I recognized the one who'd snapped my pinky. He kept one hand resting on his pistol just in case I was dumb enough to try anything. As if I'd be so dumb to do so with murderous Haddar right there.

We set out for the gate at a brisk walk. Haddar had not been lying about his disdain for the Core, because he kept hold of Norbert's ear, and whenever the prisoner slowed even a little, Haddar didn't hesitate to give it a good yank. It was a struggle to keep up on my swollen ankle. Dardick and his bodyguards followed. It said a lot about the chaotic nature of the market that our odd group didn't stand out that much.

"What is this news you bring me, Carnavon?"

"A Councilman came to take my testimony. I told them it was an official duel. You're going to get promoted to rank ten."

Haddar stopped so suddenly, Norbert nearly lost his ear. "Do not lie to me."

"I'm not. Congratulations, Master Haddar."

The wizard gave me a suspicious scowl. "That is all you told them?"

"That's it. I was just a helpless bystander as you defeated him all by yourself."

He glared at me for a long time, but must have accepted I wasn't pulling his leg. Ever so slowly, a cruel smile formed on his scarred-up face. "This must infuriate the Council… Good."

"They're making *you* a master wizard?" Norbert asked incredulously.

"Silence." Haddar began dragging him along again. "This changes nothing for you, cur. The baron will surely leave you staked out on the wastes to slow roast for your greed."

Norbert launched into one last desperate pitch, "But upon achieving such a rank, you'd no longer have to answer to my baron! Everyone knows you hate Fogo. Leave it behind and go do whatever you want. A master wizard is entitled to a life of ease. They'll send some other, lower wizard to replace you in your futile search for pirates."

"I have made a vow to catch your foul allies. Do not insult me."

"My friends would reward you for looking the other way and—"

Haddar slugged Norbert in the face so hard I heard teeth break and bones crunch. His corpulent form dropped, floppy as a sack of grain. The people of the market looked our way, saw who'd done the hitting, and wisely went back to their business.

Dardick was profoundly disappointed. "I was hoping to hear him wail and beg for mercy as the gate closed. I'm deprived of that satisfaction if he's in a coma, Haddar."

"Then go home, Ambassador. I have no patience to listen to lies, but alas… He is too fat to carry, and time is short." Haddar glanced around, saw a merchant with a small air cart, and held up a coin. "You there. I must rent your cart."

Once Dardick's bodyguards hoisted the limp Norbert atop the cart, we resumed walking.

"With my backstabbing cousin in dream land, I'll just have to be content listening to the pleas of this runaway instead," Dardick mused. "This ought to be good."

"I'm staying here, Argent, as a free man, with my contract done and clear. And my family isn't on the hook for anything I've done either. Isn't that right, *Master* Haddar?"

Dardick laughed at my mad boast. Haddar said nothing. Not only had I saved his life, I'd helped him get the promotion he'd thought impossible. If it came out that a lowly rank one tricked his opponent into blowing his own hand off, that would probably be considered cheating, or at least cast some doubts on the whole thing. Haddar had a strong code of honor, but I figured it was a pragmatic one.

"Carnavon may stay," Haddar pronounced.

"Wait a minute," the noble protested. "You're freeing the likes of him? After all he's done? He brought a curse to my door. Over my dead body!"

Haddar looked back and frowned, as if tempted by the thought of Dardick becoming a dead body. "Despite that event, he has done a service to me. Your family has tens of thousands of laborers. The loss of one means nothing to you."

"Nonsense. Rewarding disobedience invites more disobedience."

"Do not play at being as callous as your father, second son. You are not nearly as suited for it as he or his chosen heir."

Dardick was clearly furious at the sleight, and though technically Haddar had been pledged to work for his family, the wizard was a dangerous man to trifle with. I could tell the young nobleman was stewing over what to do as we walked the rest of the way to the gate. I'd offended the Argents in general, but by escaping him twice, I'd offended this one personally.

By the time we reached the gate, Dardick had plenty of time to work up his courage for a confrontation. We stopped atop the ramp, with only a few feet of the Elemental Plane of Fire left visible on the other side. As much as I was enjoying the heat billowing through, and I genuinely missed the honest harshness of my homeland compared to the deceitful coldness of the Core, I'd rather die than return as a defeated prisoner.

"Send Carnavon to Fogo, Haddar. That's a command. I'm the ambassador for the family you've made a vow to serve. And with Norbert done, I'll be in charge of all my family's business on this side of the gate. I've spoken. The rules are the rules."

I'd done Haddar a great favor, but this was someone who'd rather die than go back on his word. He'd still grudgingly take me back for sentencing, only because that's what his honor demanded. Sure, he'd hate it the whole time, but that would be a small comfort to me as I rotted away in some dungeon.

Except I had another idea, and it was so ludicrous, it might just work.

"The rules are the rules, Ambassador. And the Code of the Core—which all trading kingdoms must abide by—says that if one of the factions here claims one of the realm's subjects to serve the city's needs, you've got to honor that. Those factions include magical academies."

"You expect me to believe someone took you in? We have to gift wagons full of Red to an academy to get them to take our most talented people. Which academy claims your broke ass?"

I jerked my thumb toward Haddar. "His."

The wizard looked up from roughly dumping Norbert from the air cart into the other realm. "Mine?"

"That's right. Rank tens can take on apprentices and form their own academy in the Core. I'd be your first student, and I know where there's a bunch more, eager to learn."

Haddar clearly wasn't amused by this. "Why would I form an academy? I despise this corrupt place and its dishonest system. I have no desire to remain here. I am not a teacher. I am a killer of evil men. I have made a solemn vow to destroy a gang of pirates, not teach the brats of wealthy merchants how to grow flowers. Until the enemies of Fogo are dead, I cannot rest, nor distract myself with frivolity."

"Good. I want those pirates dead more than you do. Except I don't think the master in charge actually has to be here. Just put your name on it. Command me to get things running while you're gone, and I'll have it all ready for you once your mission's complete and you return triumphant with that elf's head stuck on a pike."

Haddar crossed his arms and thought about my offer as the gate narrowed behind him. He needed to decide fast.

"You can't seriously be considering this," Dardick said. "You're a pariah here, Haddar. You got sent to us because you've offended everyone else. Someone like you taking on students would piss off half the high-ranking wizards in the Core."

Which turned out to be exactly the wrong thing to say to Gaul Haddar. As he pondered Dardick's words, a mean smile gradually spread across his face. "Excellent… Then let it be done. Make it official. This one works for me now, Ambassador. His family shall be treated accordingly."

Dardick gritted his teeth, then slowly, grudgingly, accepted the fact that Haddar left him no other way out. "Very well. I'll inform the Council of your intent to form a school."

"You are a wise statesman, second son. It is good to see that your family's interests will be well represented in the Core." Haddar gave Dardick a coldly polite nod. "Farewell for now."

"I hope in the meantime your apprentice doesn't screw this up." Dardick turned and walked away. "Come on, boys."

I grinned at *apprentice*. I liked the sound of that.

The gate was almost closed. Norbert lay on the black rock on the other side, groaning pathetically. Haddar took stock of how much time he had left, then grabbed me by the arm with a grip of iron. "I do not know when I will be able to return. Understand that when I do, if I find that you have brought dishonor to my name, I will kill you."

"Duly noted, sir."

"We are out of time." Haddar let go of me and had to turn sideways to fit through the last sliver of gate. "Do not make me regret this, Carnavon."

The sun set. The Realm of Fire vanished.

And I had a new home.

50

It was really late by the time I reached the sordid outskirts of the Under Slump.

Of course, Trax smelled me a long way off and rushed out to greet me on the road.

"*Hello, Carnavon. Your still being alive makes me happy.*"

The only locals who were out this time of night were up to no good and had surely been eyeing me, injured, limping, and all by myself for potential victimization. When Trax appeared in all his fearsome carnivorous glory, those shadows wisely decided they'd have better luck robbing elsewhere and slunk away.

"It's good to see you too, Trax. How are things?"

He sent me several rapid mind pictures to catch me up. Azarin—reasoning that Haddar would take me back through the fire gate before it closed—had hatched a scheme to sneak into the market to try and snatch me back before we could cross, and somehow, she'd gotten the others to go along with it. Except the watchmen had grown suspicious of them loitering there and sent them on their way with a warning.

Having known them for such a brief time, I was moved that they'd take such a risk on my behalf. Camaraderie grows fast when you're in it together and it seems the whole world is stacked against you.

Of course, Trax understood very little about what he was showing me and was just along for the ride when it came to the affairs of us confusing land creatures, but that was what I gathered from his pictures at least.

"*I do not know what happened, but I was prepared to eat many people.*"

"That's appreciated, my friend." I'd have patted him on the shoulder, but didn't want to risk cutting my hand on his abrasive skin.

Azarin, Rade, and Krachma were waiting at the fallen tower. She rushed out and engulfed me in a ferocious hug, which despite my many injuries, I still rather enjoyed. Rade started peppering me with questions about what happened, and when Krachma saw it was just me again, and we weren't under attack, he went back to bed.

"It was a hell of a fight, and I'll gladly tell you all about it, but first, I've got a big announcement to make." I whipped open my cloak and took out the official notice Dardick had grudgingly scribbled for me. "Behold!"

"What is it?" Azarin asked.

"The solution to all our problems and the key to our bright future as wizards." I'd been told the Code required I post this for the public, but I wasn't really sure how to go about that. So I took the paper over to a board that had been laid across one of the tower's windows to serve as Rade's front door and I stuck it there with my knife.

Rade sent up a light charm so he could read it aloud, "Wizard of the provisional tenth rank, Gaul Haddar of Ashen Harran, announces the formation of his magical academy, yet to be named, at a location in the Core City as yet to be determined. This declaration has been witnessed by Lord Dardick Argent, 3rd Fireday of the Tenth Month, 4581 AN." He read it again silently. "I don't get it."

"That's us. *We're* the magical academy."

He stared at me, baffled. "You mean our scam? Because the gnome with all the money left after you got taken away—"

"No, it's not a scam. We're legitimate. Don't worry. The students will come back, and there will be more where those came from. According to the Code of the Core, we're an actual magical academy now. As apprentices, we can learn all we want."

Azarin scratched her head. "So our teacher is that frightening follow who beat us all this morning?"

"Yeah, but he's not actually going to be here. I think he's just doing this to spite some high-ranking wizards he doesn't like… and if I make him look bad he's going to kill me."

She looked at me like I was daft. "Then who's going to train us?"

"We don't actually have anyone for that yet. It's just us, same as before." I'd been thinking through all the ramifications of my hasty arrangement while I'd walked here, and it was quite the list. We were a handful of nobodies, with little knowledge, and fewer resources, but we had a piece of paper that said we got to play the wizards' game and that would have to be enough. "We're official now, but we don't have instructors, or money to live off of, or hardly any magical element to practice with, or frankly, much of anything at all."

"What do we have?"

"We've got a chance… Welcome to the Academy of Outcasts."

The Story Will Continue In
Academy of Outcasts
Book 2

SIGNUP FOR LARRY'S NEWSLETTER

https://monsterhunternation.com/signup-for-the-newsletter/

We won't sell your info or spam you with too many posts. This is almost exclusively for book related things!